THE MESSENGER BOY

Oh, it is hard to work for God,
To rise and take his part
Upon the battlefield of Earth,
And sometimes not lose heart.

He hides himself so wondrously
As though there were no God
He is at least seen when all the power's
Of ill are most abroad.

Ah, God is other than we think,
His ways are far above,
Far beyond reasons height, and
Only by childlike love.

Workmen of love, O lose not heart
But learn what God is like.
And in the darkest battlefield
Thou shalt know where to strike.

Then learn to scorn the praise of men
And learn to lose with God,
For Jesus won the world through shame
And beckons thee his road.

For right is right, as God is God,
And right the day must win.
To doubt would be disloyalty,
To falter were to sin.

TO BE YOUNG

Ireland

December 1905

Rossbridge, a small village 5 miles south west of the town of Tralee, County Kerry, Ireland.

"Aibi, Aibi" whispered Malacay as he walked slowly towards Donnell's wood. He and Aibrean always met here, it was the only safe place they knew. The wind was drowning his whisper as it blew through the valley towards the small village of Rossbridge about half a mile away. He raised his voice now confident that nobody, apart from he and Aibrean, would be out on this horrid winters night.

With no moon in the sky, he was now struggling to see. As he got to the edge of the wood, he shouted.

"Aibi, come on now, don't mess me about I haven't long, Aibi.... Please Aibi".

He stopped at the edge and looked hard into the wood under the entrance by the large chestnut tree, its branches swaying heavily as the wind grew stronger. He couldn't see a thing, it was too dark.

"Okay, have it your way but I have to go, my Daddy will kill me if I'm not back by nine".

As Malacay turned to walk back down the track towards home, she came at him, screaming out of the dark, hitting him full on, causing them both to fall on the wet muddy ground rolling over and over, each trying to get the upper hand.

"Jesus Aibbi you scared the living shit out of me, why do you do that", Said a breathless Malacay.

Aibbi couldn't breath either, she was laughing too much, her smiling eyes looked down upon the boy of her dreams. Mally was her life, she loved him and he her, or so they thought. She was 16, 'what did she know about love at such a tender age' her mother constantly told her. She also told her that Mally was but a boy at just one year older. Aibbi now straddled him pinning him down with her knees, her beautiful strawberry red hair now gently tickling his face.

"Your mad, bloody mad you are, I really don't know what you will do next" Malacay whispered.

"You love it Mally, you know you do. You would moan that I'm boring If I didn't" said Aibrean as she slowly released her grip on him.

He slowly kissed her tenderly on her cheek and brushed her hair behind her ear.

"I cant stop long Aibbi, my Daddy is mad as it is that I'm out at this hour, he thinks I'm over at 'Shylows' helping with the calf's".

Shylows was the farm 3 miles out of the village to the West and was run and owned Mally's uncle Michael, his dad's brother. The farm was one of only two within 18 square miles not owned by the Milburn family. The Milburn's had wanted to buy Shylows, as they had already done so to all the other local farms, but Michael had refused to sell it to them. They had offered him not a quarter of what it was actually worth but he wouldn't have sold it to them anyway. Michael had seen the true Milburn way on many occasion. At cattle auctions they would intimidate other farmers into not bidding for cattle they wanted, and if they were selling themselves, then they had been known to threaten the auctioneer if they didn't get the price they had wanted, often refusing to sell the cattle and taking it back home.

The Milburn's lived at Manor Farm which stood remote and alone, 3 miles to the south of Tralee and a mile and a half to the north of Rossbridge. Its position was on top of cliff hill, imposing itself on the village further down below in the valley.

Manor house was a truly impressive building, it had been the country estate of the Connolly family since 1710 and had remained in the family until the Milburn's had purchased it nearly 50 years ago. Built of large stone blocks and three storey's high, the frontage of the main building had large bay windows to either side of the huge front door. It looked down upon Rossbridge to the South and also towards Donnell's wood which stood about half a mile to the right, west of the village. It had several large out buildings and barns which held the feed for the cattle and sheep.

The Milburn's now owned most of the land and farms around Rossbridge. They were a ruthless family and you stood out of line at your peril, farmers were two a penny and you were soon replaced with someone who wouldn't complain. They rented the land out to local farmers charging extortionate rates.

But in this Ireland, beggars couldn't be choosers. you got what you could and you survived. It was a dog eat dog world now, to survive was all that mattered. Family against family, brother against brother and father against son.

Since the famine, Ireland, this beautiful wonderful happy go lucky country, was at war within itself. The protestants were trying to take over the North and were winning, the Catholics hated the Protestants, and vice versa. It was a country on the brink of civil war and nobody knew what was going to happen next.

And there on this wet muddy ground lay the biggest problem of all, side by side, arm in arm, staring into this dark starlit sky. Aibbi the beautiful, red headed, full of life young girl, the daughter of Daibheid and step daughter of Riley Gillain, was a Catholic, and Mally, the strong dark handsome young boy with jet black hair and dark brown eyes, son of Samuel Lord, was a Protestant.

They always knew that it would be a problem, but as time moved on and as they got older, it was becoming very clear to them both, If they stayed where they were, they didn't stand a chance. The two religions didn't like each other let alone love each other. To them it was a silly argument between two sets of people, they were in love and didn't care about religion. But, it was slowly becoming very clear to them that this relationship, this love they had, could not, and would not, be accepted by some people and they both knew who those people were.

The Milburn family were well known for not liking Protestants. The ones that worked the farms for them were virtually slaves. They both knew that when the word got out of their feelings for each other, it wouldn't be popular.

They lay there in each others arms on the muddy ground neither wanting to move or say anything but eventually, it was Mally who spoke first.

"Aibbi what are we going to do, we cant keep meeting like this. I'm going to tell my Daddy about us and if they don't like it so be it, but they are not ruling me", Said Mally.

"No, no, no, Mally you can't, if you do, that will be it for us. You must not say a word to anybody, no one, absolutely no one, do you understand" said Aibbi.

"But your'e Ma knows about us" said Mally,

"My Ma, my Ma", Aibbi was angry now.

"My mother will say nothing to nobody Mally because she knows that if she did, then I would run away with you",

"Then perhaps thats what we should do", whispered Mally "Run away, just you and me, go up to the North, I can get some work on a farm somewhere, we would be okay",

"Oh yes" said Aibbi "And where do you think we are we going to live" said Aibbi somewhat sarcastically.

"it's okay Aibbi, I've got some cousins up there, they will look after us till we get sorted",

"Really Mally and who are you going to say that I am, Oh this is Aibbi and she's 16 years old, Oh and by the way, she's a Catholic. Really Mally sometimes you live in a total dream".

"Okay then, what do think we should do",

"We wait, we wait until we are old enough to manage on our own and then we wont have to worry about what people think, it will be up to us and it wont have anything to do with anybody else, and I've told you before, we go to Dublin, nobody would take any notice of us there".

They lay there both wishing that it was going to be that simple, but both secretly knowing that life, especially their life, was never going to be that.

This was a dream that was slowly turning into a nightmare.

....

"Where is that girl out at this time of night" said Daibheid.

"Relax woman" said Riley "She will be with Mally somewhere".

She interrupted him.

" I don't care who she's with Riley, it's what she's doing, thats what I'm worried about",

"Daibbi, she's barely 16 years old, she's not going to be up to anything, give her a break, you'll drive her away if you keep on at her" Said Riley.

"I'm telling you, if people round here get to know whats going on, they'll be done for they will. Them Milburn's will sort that, you know what they do, they drive them away or they disappear, and nobody sees them ever again, they wont stand for them having any sort of relationship. They are evil men and they do evil things".

Riley knew what she meant, he had known Cain Milburn since he was at school. Cain was a year older than him and he was always the school bully, picking on the weak and the quiet ones.

It was Cain's treatment of animals that Riley had detested most though. Even at the age of 8 it had started. Cain would take great pride in the killing of any animal and would tell many stories in the playground about the latest cat he had killed or the horse that he had beaten. On one occasion he had bought a chicken into school. He let some of the girls stroke it and play with it, until he got bored. He then took it from them and in front of them all, he broke its neck. He then laughed at all the traumatised young girls, running away, screaming at what he'd just done. Yes, he was an evil man, but as was all his family, it ran in their blood.

His father Edmond was old now, in his late 70's, but it was well known that not so long ago he had killed a man beating him to death with a shovel because he'd dared to stand up to him and question him. Riley knew of all the family. Cain had two Brother's, the eldest Henry, was 2 years his senior, but he had seen him only once and that was over 12 years ago. He remembered that he was a big man, built like his father, at well over 6' tall and very muscular with thick wavy black hair. They, the Milburn's, would speak of him occasionally but Riley himself, was never allowed to be involved in the conversation. From what he had heard though, he knew that Henry had moved away sometime ago, where and why, he didn't know, but he knew well enough not to ask any questions.

Cain, being the second eldest, had now taken on the mantle of his father and was in charge of all the farms and land for miles around but his father still made the rules.

The youngest son was Glendon, to the Milburn's he was known as 'Boy'. Riley had always thought that there was something different about him. At times he would appear a very kind child, he was a year younger than Riley, they had gone to the same school and had grown up together in the village. Riley wouldn't describe him as a friend, nobody had a Milburn as a friend, but they would socialise occasionally. When they had been around five or six years old, Riley had pulled a drowning

Glendon from the River Lee when some of the boys from his school had gone to swim there one hot summer's day.

He had slipped down a 30' long grassy bank and hit a tree half way down, the coming together had broke his knee cap, something that he never really recovered from and had walked with a limp forever after. On their return to the village, Glendon's mother, Aubrey, had already heard of what had happened and far from thanking Riley for saving her sons life she had screamed a torrent of abuse at him and the other boys for letting her son get into difficulty, and had told them to never come near them again.

Aubrey had died shortly after Glendon's eighth birthday. She had been the real driving force of the family. She ruled the roost with an iron fist, sometimes literally. She would beat all the boys badly if they stepped over the line. She was the decision maker for all of them, including her husband Edmond, what she decided was final, no arguments. Subsequently the boys lacked having any kind of mind of their own, all the decisions made by their mother for them meant that they were themselves incapable of making one.

Her death had hit Glendon the hardest and he became very withdrawn for a number of years. It also caused him to developed a very bad stutter which had got better over time, but when he was nervous or agitated it would return. As he got older and was required to earn his living, he seemed to struggle with the usual Milburn way of dominance and bullying. He tried to do it but you knew his heart wasn't really in it. He was Cain's gofer and would travel around the farm's issuing orders from Cain, trying to be authoritative but not really ever carrying it off.

Riley and Daibbi Gillian, the G sounded as in 'God' not like the girls name of 'Gillian', lived at Rose cottage, a tiny little farm house that belonged to the Manor farm estate. It was situated on the edge of the estate between Manor farm itself and Rossbridge. When you looked at it, it was as if a child had drawn it with its two windows upstairs and two windows downstair separated by the front door in the middle. Beautiful climbing roses of all colours covered the front and curled they're way around all of the windows. On a hot sunny day the wonderful fragrance from them would drift through the open windows and into the house.

At the rear it had a courtyard about 40 yards square and a small barn beyond that, in which Riley kept a handful of cows and a horse, known affectionately to them as 'the Bear'. Bear was a stunning 16'3 grey Irish sports horse with the heart of a lion but was a truly gentle giant. He had been owned by the Milburn's, but Riley was persuaded by Daibbi to buy him as she couldn't bare to see him take anymore beatings from Cain. Riley rode him virtually everyday to travel to work at Manor farm and would ride him whilst rounding up sheep or getting the cattle in for milking.

To the left of the rear courtyard was a rusty metal fence and gate, through which was a hedge lined path that led around to the front of the house. Beyond the courtyard to the right hand corner was a wooden gate that led to their 10 acres of land, About 400 yards beyond that to the West, and further down into the valley bottom, lay Donnell's wood.

Riley had worked for the Milburn's since he had left school at 14. He had left with little prospects other than following in his Grandfathers and Fathers footsteps to work on the farms. His father had died very young, not long after he was born and he had been raised by his mother with the help of his Grandparents at Rose cottage. Riley now 33 and almost 18 years on, was still there. He didn't really have a choice, well his choice was, stay where he was or take the family across the sea to England to find work there. The prospect's in England were reasonably good as regards to work but Daibbi had refused to go. She loved her little part of Ireland and the thought of going to England with its big industrial cities filled her with dread.

Riley had met Daibbi at a village dance in Elmthorpe which

was about 3 miles south from Rossbridge. He had liked her from the first moment they had met. He loved her beautiful green eyes and her happy smile. He immediately knew though that he would have his hands full, she had a spirit and would kill people dead with one line if she didn't like them. He would know when that was as well and would whisper in her ear "The eyes don't lie Daibbi, the eyes don't lie". Her eyes could tell a story on their own, no words were ever needed.

Daibbi had been married at 17, had had Aibrean just nine months later and then her husband had left her for another women not two years later. Her life had been in turmoil ever since until she had met Riley two years after. Eventually after much pleading and begging from Riley she and Aibbi moved in with him at Rose cottage. She loved the cottage, it was a blissful place, it was small but they didn't need a big house, Riley's mother and grandparents had long since passed away so it was plenty big enough for the three of them.

Daibbi had turned it into a homely place, with little things she had made out of scrap that most people would or had thrown out. Little plant pots made out of an old teapot and saucepans, an old potato weighing machine now had beautiful trailing flowers completely covering it. She would walk along the lanes in the village and salvage little, or sometimes, big things that people had thrown out. She would return home carrying and sometimes dragging "her little finds" behind her, "and what would you be doing with that" Riley would jokingly ask, "wait and see" she would say and sure enough a week or so later there it would be, a little garden table made out of some scrap iron and planks of wood.

The squeaking sound of the rusty metal gate that opened onto the courtyard alerted them both that it was Aibbi returning. Daibbi had asked Riley to oil the gate numerous times but he had said it was ok as it was as it warned them that somebody was around the back of the house.

Aibbi burst into the back door and into the small kitchen. Daibbi started on her immediately.

"Where have you been my girl until this time of night, up to no good I'm sure, you shouldn't be out on your own after dark there's bad things out there Aibbi"

"Oh god Mother, stop being so dramatic, this is Rossbridge not Tralee or Dublin for gods sake".

She had never been to either but had heard her Mum and Riley speak of them both.

"It doesn't matter where you are Aibbi, there are bad people wherever you are, and would you please stop using the lord's name in vain",

"Oh he's going to cast me down again I suppose, like he didn't the last time and the time before that. I've not been on my own anyway, I was with Mally, there are you happy now".

"No, I'm not happy, not happy at all" said Daibbi "Your both but kids, I want you back before dark from now on and there's no buts, thats it, before dark or you'll be grounded again for a week".

The last time Daibbi had grounded her, Aibbi had secretly climbed out of her bedroom window every evening to see Mally.

Riley had seen her returning one evening, climbing back in the window off the shed roof and Aibbi had looked at him with that cheeky grin and put her finger to her mouth to tell him to keep quiet about it.

Riley and Aibbi had a special bond. He had raised her as his own since she was only three years old. She had always called him Riley, he was happy with that, but they both knew that he was a big father figure to her. He was strict with her but she and Daibbi always joked that she had him wrapped around her little finger. She had a great respect for him though and she knew that if she ever needed him, he was always there and would never let her down.

Aibbi looked at her mother and shook her head but didn't answer back she knew that her mother wasn't going to give in but give it a few days and she would have forgotten about it.

"I'm going to bed to have some sweet dreams" she smiled at them both and started upstairs.

"And I'm going to bed to have some nightmares" said Daibbi.

※ ※ ※

THE WARNING

February 1906

It was cold, very cold. The snow had been heavy and it wasn't going to go away anytime soon. Rose cottage's roof seemed to bend under the strain of the thick snow upon it. Smoke bellowed out from its single chimney and drifted slowly off towards the East from the westerly wind. When the wind blew in from the West and across the Atlantic it usually meant bad weather in the winter. Nothing was in its way until it hit Ireland. "It was Englands windbreak" people used to say.

The smell of a recently split log from an ash tree and now burning on the open fire filled the cottage with a wonderful aroma.

"I have to go to Manor farm" said Riley.

"What in this weather, are you serious, what do you have to go there for that cant wait a day or two" said Daibbi looking out of the kitchen window at the snow covered courtyard.

"Cain wants to see me, Glendon came by last night and said that he wants to see me this morning" said Riley,

"about what",

"I don't know Daibbi, but you know what he's like if he doesn't get his way. I will be back as soon as I can, I promise".

Daibbi knew only too well what Cain was like. If he didn't get his way he would quite often go into a rage beyond belief. She had never told Riley but Cain had, on a few occasions, tried to force himself upon her when he had visited Rose cottage and she had been alone. He seemed to visit a lot when Riley wasn't there and she had wondered if it wasn't just a coincidence. He would make suggestions to her and once, when she had refused, he had grabbed her by her thick blonde hair and whispered in her ear "You know you want it, stop pretending you don't, just give in you know you'll enjoy it having a real man for a change". Daibbi could look after herself despite being at least a foot shorter than him at 5'2", but she had needed to resort to biting his hand on one occasion to make him let go of her. When he didn't get his way with her he would storm off in a rage telling her that he was going to 'throw them out' of Rose cottage and sack Riley from his job. Up to now he never had as he knew that Riley's knowledge of animals and farming were far too good to lose.

"Okay she said but don't stay out too long in this, make sure your back well before dark".

Riley walked into the barn and saddled Bear who stood patiently eating hay from the rack. Riley looked at him and said "Yes Bear, we are going out" Bear seemed to look at him as if to say, you might be but I'm quite happy here thank you.

A few minutes later they set off for the short ride of just under two miles, a ride that normally took them about twenty-five minutes. It took them nearly an hour. Bear, who was a very fit horse was breathing heavily on their arrival and seemed very happy as Riley stabled him in the barn's behind the Manor House itself. The weather had now worsened and the snow was now falling very heavily. They had struggled through a number of three to four foot high snow drifts on the way and Riley didn't want to be out too long or they wouldn't be getting back home tonight. The Milburn's were not renowned for their hospitality and the thought of sleeping in the stable next to Bear, however much he loved him, was not very appealing.

He walked to the kitchen door at the rear of the house and could smell the distinctive aroma of a freshly baked apple pie. Mrs Harrigan, the Miburn's house keeper was clearly wasted on them. She had been employed by Edmond shortly after his wife's death and had been there for nearly 22 years. She was a fantastic cook and had a soft spot for Riley and Daibbi and often gave them food which she had cooked for them without the Milburn's knowledge. They were her only bit of normality that she had and they would talk whenever they could but never if there was a Milburn around.

As Riley walked towards the door he saw her looking at him out of the kitchen window. He smiled at her but the usual smile that would always return was not there, she had a very worried look on her face and he knew immediately this was not going to be a pleasant visit.

He opened the door and she quickly walked towards him and gave him a hug and softly whispered to him "Speak to me afterwards if you can, Please Riley, promise me that".

"I will Ellen, don't worry, whats all this about" said Riley softly, but she never got chance to answer as a very pale and worried looking Cain came through the door from the hallway.

"Inside now" said Cain and turned back from where he had come.

Riley started to follow and Ellen held him by the arm and whispered "stay calm Riley, please I beg you" her look on her face was filled with worry and fear, he had never seen her like this before, no matter what the Milburn's had thrown at her in the past, she had always shrugged it off with her 'don't you worry about me, I can handle them Milburn's don't you worry yourself' attitude. This though was different, very different.

Riley followed Cain through the hallway and towards a doorway on the opposite side. The smell of cigar smoke drifted out of the open door. He knew it meant only one thing. He walked slowly into the room and there sat Edmond Milburn in his red Chesterfield chair. Riley had never been allowed access into the study since he had started working here almost eighteen years ago.

Edmond was a big man. Even for his age of 78 he was still a big man. He was still over 6', he had shrunk slightly in his old age from his 6'4" but he was still impressive and intimidating. His hair was still thick, wavy and black and he could quite easily have passed for somebody 15 years younger.

His downfall was cigars. He smoked at least 15 to 20 of them a day and his cough was now a deep throaty one that would take at least 30 to 40 seconds to get over once he had started and which would leave him breathless for minutes on end.

He blew out a thick mouthful of blue grey smoke as he looked at Riley with his dark brown almost black sunken eyes and said to him in his deep gruff voice,

"Sit down".

Riley looked at him looking at him in the eye and still trying to understand what this was all about, he said "It's alright Sir, I can stand".

Edmond's voice didn't change as he slowly pressed the red hot end of the cigar onto his desk putting it out in another cloud of smoke.

"I said sit down".

Riley walked forward towards the chair that was in front of the desk and faced Edmond on the other side, about 5' away. He sat down and was aware that Cain had now walked behind him and was stood about 2' from his right shoulder.

"Whats this about Mr Milburn, I was told Cain wanted to speak to me".

"Soon enough Riley, I think you'll find that I still ask the questions around here", said Edmond as he lit another thick cigar.

He waited for what seemed like minute's before he spoke again.

"How is that beautiful wife of yours Riley, I hope she's well",

"She is Sir yes, she's very well thank you",

"Good Daibbi is a fine woman, a good woman, you're very lucky to have her you know Riley, is that not true Cain".

Cain went to answer but Edmond interrupted him.

"Does she know you're here",

"Yes sir she does, I told her that Cain wanted to see me",

"Well let's keep it at that then, she doesn't need to know about this, do you understand what I'm saying Riley",

"Well no Sir no not really, I don't really know what this is all about",

Edmond interrupted him "Your about to find out Riley, soon enough Riley soon enough........ What I'm saying to you is this, that lovely wife of yours doesn't need to know about the conversation that you and I are about have, do you understand, have I made myself clear",

"Yes Sir you have" said Riley.

"Good, ...now shut the fuck up and listen" he blew a cloud of thick smoke towards Riley and stared at him for almost half a minute.

"You see Riley, we have a problem, well should I say, you have a problem, because we" and he waved his arm around as to mean the Milburn's, "are very unhappy about the situation".

Riley sat and fidgeted uncomfortably on his chair, not afraid, but not happy at all because he hadn't a clue about what Edmond was talking about.

"The situation as it is, cannot continue as I'm sure you will agree, but it's what we, or more importantly, you, can do about it. So I thought it best that we could all sit down, as in me, you and Cain here".

Cain opened his mouth as if to speak again, but was immediately cut dead by Edmond again with a wave of his hand to silence him.

"and we need to try and come to some agreement as to how we can, shall I say, resolve the issue".

Riley looked at him thinking hard about what this could possibly be about but he was at a total loss and he decided that it was time that he should ask.

"I'm very sorry Sir, but I really have no idea what you are talking about and as to why I am here today, I'm very sorry, but that's the truth. If I can help I will, but until you tell me what this is all about, I'm at a loss as to how I can help you",

Edmond stared at him.

"Oh Riley, I can assure you that you will be able to help us, and………… indeed, you will help us, I've no doubt about that".

He again paused just staring at Riley,

"because if you don't help us then that lovely wife of yours won't be looking so lovely, do I make myself clear",

Riley looked at him in the eye "Are you threatening me Mr Miburn",

"Now your'e getting it Riley, Yes I am fucking threatening you, and mark my words, I don't make idle threats as well you know. So here's what you and that whore of a daughter, or should I say, step fucking daughter of your's are going to do".

He slowly got to his feet and walked around his desk and walked to stand directly in front of Riley. So close that he could smell the stale smell of smoke on Edmonds breath.

"It has been bought to my attention by my son Cain here, that your whore of a daughter Aibbi, has been seeing that thick fucking Prodi bastard son of Samuel Lord, Malacay, and,

I might add, not only just being with him, but, my son has actually witnessed this horrid scene, the Prodi bastard having his evil way with her in Donnell's wood. But this is the thing Riley that repulses me most, she was really enjoying it and was begging him for more, I mean for fucks sake, begging a fucking Prodi to fuck her, what in hell's name was she thinking of".

Riley sprang to his feet and stood face to face with Edmond, trembling with anger, he struggled to hold himself back from hitting the old man that stood before him.

He then sensed Cain behind him and Edmond looked at Cain over his shoulder and shook his head....

Edmond spoke softly "Sit down Riley",

Riley stood and stared at him breathing hard.

"Sit..... down"

Riley slowly sat back in his seat.

"Your'e lucky Riley, your'e lucky because I actually like you. I like your spirit and I like the way that you react, it shows that you have some balls lad. But, I am going to tell you what is going to happen next regarding this unfortunate situation, And happen it will, because Riley, you won't have any fucking choice".

What 'Had' actually occurred wasn't the same as how Cain had earlier described it to his father.

Not the same at all.

The previous day in the late afternoon, Cain had been out in the snow looking for poachers with one of his farm workers, Danny. Danny was known locally as Parrot. He had been known as that for years after he was nicknamed it by one of the other farm workers because he had a habit of repeating the last few words of each sentence each time he spoke. He had worked for the Milburn's for the last 8 years and Cain knew that he would do anything he asked of him without asking 'why or what for' and he also knew that he could trust him to remain silent if anything should occur that other people shouldn't know about.

He was also a very good shot with his long single barrelled shot gun.

Poachers had been causing havoc on several of the Milburn's farms and Edmond had told Cain to sort it out and send a message to the would be poachers, that if they steal wildlife from their stock then they do so at their peril.

Cain and Parrot had been approaching Donnell's wood where it was believed that poachers had been recently operating and were skirting around the southern edge of it when Parrot softly whistled to Cain to signal to him that he had found something. Cain quietly walked over to where Parrot stood and both of them looked down to the soft snow beneath their feet. There on the ground were two sets of foot prints, one set was clearly bigger than the other, which obviously meant that there was at least two people and they were going further into the wood.

Cain looked at Parrot and smiled, they were fresh prints no doubt about it. Parrot looked back at Cain and whispered softly.

"I think we might have some of them poachers, I say some of them poachers Sir".

Cain nodded back at him and with now gentle quiet steps they raised their shotguns and slowly started to follow the two sets of footprints further and deeper into the wood.

As they continued walking they could see that the footprints were clearly walking side by side and showed no sign of separating. They quietly moved on still deeper into the wood, the snow was not as deep now as the thickness of the overhanging trees was providing some shelter, but now they were also making it a little darker.

Then they heard it, the distinctive sound of a young girl's

laugh coming from not too far ahead of them.

They both stopped walking and Parrot, already feeling excited and coiled like a spring ,went to shout out but was stopped abruptly by Cain placing a finger to his mouth. Cain started slowly walking on towards the direction from where the laughter was coming from with Parrot following on just behind him, their breath, showing a shiny haze into the air, was the only thing giving them away.

It had stopped snowing now and the dying sun had come out low on the horizon, splicing through the tree's and making the snow almost blinding.

Like the snow, the laughter had also stopped.

It was a different noise now.

Panting.

Heavy panting.

Cain now moved even slower through the snow, his feet softly crunching as the snow compacted beneath him. He stopped. Stone dead. There before him, in a small clearing not 30 yards in front of him, lay a girl on her back, her legs splayed apart and a man, or more like a boy with dark hair, laying on top of her with his trousers pulled half down.

He knew who they were almost immediately.

"Well, well, what have we here, if it's not young Mr Lord, for I'd recognise that backside anywhere", Sneered Cain.

Mally scrambled trying to get to his feet as Aibbi tried desperately to get her unbuttoned clothes pulled around her to hide her nudity.

"And if it's not young Aibbi too...... well what be you two doing out here then, I wonder" snarled Cain, his face now turning into a smirk.

"We were just laying in the snow Mr Milburn we were just going to go back home" stammered Mally.

Cain looked at Mally and then slowly turned towards Aibbi his eyes giving him away as he focused on Aibbi's bare breast's.

"Oh I know exactly what you were doing Mally" said Cain.

Cain continued to stare at Aibbi and slowly looked her up and down.

"And what have you got to say for yourself little Miss Aibbi".

Aibbi hated Cain, she always had. She had hated him since she had caught him trying to kiss her mother in her kitchen years ago and she had never forgotten it. Her mother had told her not to whisper a word to Riley about it because she knew what trouble that would bring upon them. Aibbi had done what she had asked but that hate for Cain had festered and had burned inside her from that day on.

She looked at him with a look that her mother would have been proud of, a look of utter distain, and then she spoke well beyond her sixteen years as she quietly unleashed six years of hate,

"I'll tell you what I've got to say Mr Cain Milburn. I think your'e a fucking horrible perverted man, sneaking up on us like that and frightening us. You should be ashamed of yourself".

and then it was Parrot's turn as she turned to him.

"And what the fuck are you looking at Parrot, have you never seen a woman before".

Cain threw his head back and laughed, a full belly laugh, he had always liked Aibbi, she had a spirit like he had never seen in a girl before. She wasn't afraid of anything or anybody. He'd seen it get her into trouble in the past but he'd liked it. A rebel, he always had time for a rebel, he had an almost jealous admiration of her, the way that she didn't seem to care for authority or the hierarchy. If she didn't respect you, you wouldn't get any. You earned your respect with Aibbi, it was never just given.

He stopped and stood staring at them both, and then he spoke.

"There's no denying where you come from is there Aibbi. You

have that mother of yours tongue thats for sure. But let me tell you this Aibbi Gillian, You are not a woman, you are just a stupid little girl".

Aibbi went to interrupt him but Cain pressed a finger to his lips to silence her.

"And as for frightening you, well, I haven't even fucking started yet".

He slowly walked over towards Aibbi who was now standing up, but had still not managed to fully dress herself.

He was now just an arms length from her as he said softly .

"Do you know that we have poachers in these woods, and do you know that Parrot and I are out here trying to catch these Poachers, and, if and when we do, do you know what we are entitled to do to them Miss Aibbi".

He looked down at his gun in his right hand and then carried on.

"Thats right, we can shoot them, now, have you been poaching in these woods I ask myself".

He looked at them both, into their eyes, fear in one set, utter hatred in the other.

He carried on.

"Do you know that poaching is a very serious offence. Well let me tell you this, we Milburn's consider it a very, very serious offence and we take it very personal if anybody try's to steal from us. and we also know that people that poach, they hide their game on their person".

As he said it, Cain grabbed Aibbi loose dress and ripped it open exposing her breast's and waste.

Aibbi screamed and tried to grab her clothes to cover herself just as Mally flew at Cain knocking him sideways and causing him to stumble "Run Aibbi, run now" Mally shouted, as he tried to aim a kick at Cain but missed.

Aibbi coming to her senses sprinted past the flaying arm of

Parrot who was now trying also to grab hold of Mally. She ran, she ran as fast as her legs could take her dodging the trees and bushes. She carried on running until her lungs were burning but she daren't stop. She carried on running praying that Mally had managed to get away and was close behind her. She had been running for what seemed like 2 or 3 minutes and there, about 60 yards in front of her, She could see the edge of the wood. As she burst out through the trees and into the fields, she heard it and froze.

A gun shot.

Then, a few moments later, another.

She knew exactly where it was coming from but it wasn't aimed at her it was too far away. It was back from where she had come from.

She was torn.

Go back for Mally or save her own skin. She looked In front of her at the fields full of snow and nothing else. No trees, no hedges, no shelter, no cover. Nothing, for a good half mile at least. She slowly walked back to the edge of the wood.

'Surely they wouldn't shoot at Mally would they. They hadn't done anything'.

She crouched there, staying as low as she could at the edge of the wood, scared out of her mind and trying to decide what to do.

Run or go back.............

A split second later the decision was made for her.

Another gun shot, followed immediately by the splintering of wood above her head.

She ran.

Turning right and now running in the field with the wood just to her right hand side, trying to give herself cover from he would be attacker by using the wood itself.

Her problem was that she was now running in the opposite

direction from the safety of her home, but she couldn't go that way as it meant running across the open field which was now covered in a foot of snow.

The sun had now gone down beyond the horizon and soon it would be dark. If she could escape and get to hide somewhere for a while and then make her way back home in the dark she would be safe. She knew the land around here like the back of her hand and there were numerous ways she could go.

She had always felt that when she walked home in the dark, from wherever she was, it was like her body or brain just knew the way. She would walk as if in a trance and arrive back at home without even having to think about it. But right now there was one big problem.

The snow.

Every step she took was like drawing an arrow on the ground pointing the way for her would be hunters to follow. The stream, she thought, head for the stream. She carried on running keeping the wood to her right hand side, another 50 yards or so and she knew there was a small opening back into the tree's where it then met a small track that led towards the stream and some rocks.

But then there was another gun shot.

Further away this time but back in towards the centre of the wood.

'Had Mally managed to get away or had they shot him again'.

She got to the opening and turned to her right back and stepped back into the wood. She turned left on the track then ran down the slope towards the stream and the rocks. A thick envelope of trees swayed above her giving her some cover for the moment at least.

And then she heard him.

Shouting.

There was an almost panic in the voice.

It was Cain's voice. She was absolutely certain of it.

It had come from the same direction as where the last shot had come from further into the wood. It was distant and echoey but it was definitely him.

"Parrot, Parrot, leave it, come back to me………now Parrot, do you hear me, come back here right now……."

'Parrot, he must be the one behind her' she thought.

She quietly stepped into the stream. It was about a foot deep and was absolutely freezing. She knew she wouldn't be able to stay in it for long she was already struggling to feel her feet.

She walked slowly down the stream which was getting deeper now and was nearly up to her waste. She knew that in about it 40 yards or so it went around to the right and there it widened and became much deeper. She also remembered that it had a rocky overhang on the right hand side and there, she hoped she would be able to hide in amongst the rocks. It was getting dark now and she was getting very, very, cold. She rounded the corner and she slowly waded over to the rocks and pulled herself out of the water. Her legs were now almost completely numb and she shivered from head to toe, shaking almost uncontrollably. She climbed about 5 or 6 foot or so above the now fast flowing stream and backed into the rocks. To her right she knew that there was a small opening that went back on itself.

She and Mally had often sat in there watching the stream flow by down below them, they had even seen ducks paddling along totally unaware of their existence just above their feathered heads.

Now she could hear something in the water.

She slowly felt around her, not daring to take her eyes off the stream below.

She found a loose rock about the size of a large potato. She gripped it in her right hand.

Another splash.

And there he was.

Parrot, stood below her not more than 2 feet away.

He had blood on his face.

Did he sense her or could he hear her beating heart. Either way it mattered not.

It then all happened very quickly.

He turned towards her and their eyes met and a smile spread across Parrot's face.

It didn't last.

Aibbi jumped down from above him, smashing the rock into his face as hard and as fast as she could.

He went straight down.

Aibbi landed on top of him. She plunged her hands under the water hoping to find the shot gun. She couldn't.

But she found another rock.

She pulled it out of the water, two hands this time, it was bigger with large jagged edges on it. She rammed it into his face, then again and again.

Blood flowed from him into the river and as the current grabbed hold of him, he slowly floated towards the overhanging rocks on the right hand side. As he slipped under the overhang, his body got caught and rapped in the trunk's and roots of the overhanging trees, into a place where he never would be found.

Aibbi climbed down and waded across the stream and then climbed onto the bank on the opposite side to the rocks.

It was dark now, very dark.

She knew she was still in danger but the dark was her friend now. But the cold wasn't. She knew that if she didn't get some warmth soon, she could die out here in the woods.

She was at least a mile from home but it seemed like it was a thousand. She slowly walked towards the edge of the wood and then she could turn right and go over the small hill to give her some cover and then turn left back towards home and safety.

Almost two hours later, she climbed quietly up the drain pipe and onto the shed roof and then slipped through the window and into her bedroom.

Back in the wood Cain was deciding what to do next.

It had all gone horribly wrong.

They had caught Mally, but he'd managed to get away from their grasp and had started to run in the opposite direction from Aibbi. Cain had raised his shotgun and he had deliberately fired a warning shot just above his head, hoping that Mally would stop. Parrot, seeing his boss shoot, also raised his gun and fired.

Parrot didn't miss. He never did.

The shot hit Mally in the lower back.

He had dropped instantly.

Cain stared, temporarily stunned by what had just happened. As if he was weighing up their options, he turned to Parrot and very calmly said "Get her, go and get her and be quick".

Parrot ran in the direction that he had last seen her.

Cain had walked over to where Mally lay, face down and clawing at the snow beneath him. To his left hand side the snow had turned a deep red as blood flowed from the whole in his back.

He was dying, Cain knew that.

If he didn't get him some help he would be dead within minutes.

Time seemed to stand still as he stood there contemplating what to do.

He needn't have bothered.

He heard the shot. It had come from the edge of the wood.

'Parrot didn't miss, he never did'.

'Jesus' he thought 'this it turning to rat shit' he turned back towards the boy laying on the ground. "I'm sorry lad but now I have no choice". He reloaded and then raised his gun and blasted him through the back of his head.

He dragged the body into the undergrowth of some bushes and brushed the snow over it. He would come back tomorrow to hide it properly in the daylight. He had shouted Parrot but had no reply, he would see him when he got back home.........

"So Riley, here's whats going to happen" said Edmond.

Edmond then went on to tell Riley that he must put a stop to the sordid goings on. He didn't care how, but stop it will. If it didn't stop Riley and Daibbi would be thrown out of Rose Cottage and he wouldn't be held responsible for what may happen to his daughter or her 'Prodi lover Mally'.

"Cain here will be overseeing it and if he's not happy with the situation then he will report to me. I'm glad that we've sorted this out Riley, its been playing on my mind all day".

He then waved his hand to tell him the meeting was over and it was time to leave.

Riley followed Cain out into the hall and Cain closed the study door behind them.

Riley looked at him and quietly he said,

"Cain, what the hell was that all about".

Cain looked at him, worry written across his face.

"Don't worry Riley I've got it sorted, you just keep your side of the bargain and keep Aibbi away from that Prodi and I will look after my father. Just tell Aibbi that I need to speak to her tomorrow. Have you seen her today",

"No I haven't, and I can't say that I'm looking forward to it either, but that apparently is my problem isn't it", he stared at

Cain.

Cain nodded to him and turned towards the front door, he seemed to have other things on his mind.

On the ride back Riley was lost in thought.

He rode back in a daze thinking about what had just happened. He had met Ellen back in the kitchen and she had told him that she had seen Cain come back the previous day with blood on his clothes. She hadn't thought too much about it until she had heard him talking to his father in the yard the following morning about him seeing Aibbi and Mally in Donnell's wood the day before and that Parrot had gone mad at what they had seen and he had had to restrain Parrot from attacking them both. He had told his father that he had sacked Parrot on the spot and told him not too come back to Manor farm. She had said that Edmond was fuming because he had thought Parrot was a good worker and he should have been told about what had happened and he would have dealt with it. She told Riley to ride home and make sure that Aibbi was safe and to keep her close to home for the time being.

As he rode into the yard almost an hour later he realised that he couldn't even remember any of the journey and that the Bear had in fact rode him safely home.

Cain wasn't happy either.

Parrot had abandoned him.

He had shot the boy and done a runner. Probably shot the girl as well.

What a mess. He needed to know if Aibbi was still alive and quick. He doubted that she was but If she was alive, he needed to silence her before the trouble started. He'd been looking for her all day but to no avail. He'd find her, he felt sure of that, she wouldn't stray far, not on her own. And after all, she was, on her own, that was for sure.

* * *

THE LEAVING

Aibbi hadn't slept.

She had turned the events of the previous evening over and over in her head throughout the night. She couldn't understand why it had accelerated as it had. Where was Mally, was he injured, had he managed to escape, had they captured him and were they now holding him prisoner somewhere up at manor farm.

Over and over it went through her head. But it always came back to the same conclusion. He was dead, they had shot him and he was dead.

They had shot at her and only just missed and then Parrot had tracked her and she had had no doubt in her mind that he would have killed her had she not hit him with the rock.

She knew that she was in trouble. When she had hit Parrot the second time she had looked in his eyes as he stared at her but they hadn't moved. They were wide open and he was looking straight at her and straight at the rock but he didn't flinch. He didn't flinch because he hadn't seen it coming, because he was already dead. She was sure of it.

And then who was going to believe a sixteen year old girl against the word of a man, and a Milburn man at that. She had no chance. She had to go and she had to go now.

She packed some clothes as much as she dare in a small suitcase and lay on the bed, what was she going to tell her Mother and Riley.

She knew that she couldn't tell them anything. If she told

them then they wouldn't just let her go, that was for sure.

She decided to leave a note.

She crept out onto the stairs and heard Riley and her mum talking and could just about make out that Riley had been summoned to Manor farm. It had made her mind up. She needed to get away as soon as possible.

She had watched as Riley and Bear rode out of the yard and a tear slowly ran down her cheek as they slowly disappeared into the snowy gloom. A few moment later she heard the backdoor go and saw her mother cross the yard and walk into the barn to tend to the cattle.

She crept downstairs with her bag having left a note at the side of her bed. Out the front door and she quickly walked towards Rossbridge. Little did she know then that she wouldn't return for almost three years.

It was evening when Riley walked in through the kitchen door. A nice warm smell of a freshly cooked stew wafted out to meet him. Not that he had much of an appetite.

Daibbi had heard him in the yard and walked into the kitchen to greet him. She knew straight the way that the meeting hadn't gone well. It was all over his face. Daibbi was first speak.

"You look like a ghost Riley, what on earth has happened up there".

Totally ignoring what Edmond had said about not telling her, he relayed the whole sordid details. He had never hidden anything from Daibbi and he was definitely not going to start now.

When Riley had finished telling her he could see the shock and worry in her eyes.

"My god Riley, what are we to do",

"Well we need to sit down and speak to Aibbi first to find out exactly has happened and then we can take it from there",

"Your not saying that we just do as them Milburn's say are you,

I'm not letting them rule me or any of my family. I'd sooner see them in hell first",

"Daibbi, Daibbi, I'm not saying anything of the kind, all I'm saying is we need to speak to her to find out what actually happened. I know Cain Milburn and he was clearly not happy about something, I just have a feeling that what I have heard today is not the entirely the truth. Now have you seen Aibbi today',

"No I haven't seen her all day, in fact Iv'e not seen her since yesterday".

They both looked at each other thinking the same thought. They walked quickly to the stairs and both ran up them towards Aibbi's bedroom.

It was Daibbi that found it.

"Oh no, oh god no, please no", she said,

Riley turned to see Daibbi holding a piece of paper "What is Daibbi, what does it say".

She handed him the small piece of paper and just managed to whisper the words "She's gone, she's gone Riley, she's run away".

Riley held the note and read slowly to himself,

'My dear Mother and Riley,

I have had to write this as I couldn't bring myself to tell you both personally, and if I had done then you wouldn't have let me go.

I have done something really bad, I know that, but I beg you to please forgive me.

I will understand if you can't but I will always love you both with all my aching heart.

I have to get away from here for a time but I hope that one day, I will be able to return and explain fully what happened.

Mum, I thank you with all my heart for being you. Your kindness and loving way I will treasure for the rest of my life. I hope that one day I can return and you can be proud of me once again.

My dear Riley, thank you for being my dad, because to me, thats what you have always been and always will be. Please look after my Mother, she will need you now I know.

Please don't come looking for me, this is something that I have to do.

I will see you again I promise.

All my love

For ever

Aibbi x x

They both slowly sat down on Aibbi's bed and Riley put his arm around Daibbi as they sat in silence, tears flowing from their eyes.

It wasn't long before the word got about the village.

The rumour was that Aibbi and Mally had run away together because they were worried that they were going to be told they couldn't see each other anymore.

Mally's father Sam Lord had visited Rose Cottage the next day and they had talked through what little they knew and where they may have gone but they all realised that they really didn't know anything. He had taken a little solace in the fact that Aibbi had left them a letter but you could hear the sadness in his voice when he said that Mally hadn't left one. He had put it down to him being a boy and "boys didn't do that sort of thing did they". You could tell though that it had cut him in half and he was worried sick with the not knowing were his beloved son was.

They both agreed that it was futile to try and find them but Sam had said that he would write to his relatives in the North telling them to contact him if they turned up or heard of their whereabouts. In return Riley and Daibbi said they would contact all of their relatives in the South to do the same. They all knew however that the likelihood of them going to relatives for them to be then returned home was highly unlikely. They tried to appease themselves with the knowledge that no news was good news.

The next day, with Daibbi's blessing, Riley went back to work.

The snow had gone but it had now turned to wind lashing rain.

Within an hour Cain had tracked him down at Mellor farm. Riley had been repairing some fencing when Cain arrived on his horse and cart.

"Riley lets go into the barn" he shouted trying to get himself heard above the wind and rain.

They walked into the barn both dripping wet and stood with steam coming from them like two thoroughbreds after an 8 furlong sprint.

"What do you know then Riley",

"I know that you have created a right fucking mess Cain, thats what I know",

"Riley why is it always somebody else's fault. They knew what they were doing and they both knew that it was wrong",

"They are kids Cain, they are 16 and 17 years old, it didn't need to be like this",

"They didn't look like kids to me Riley, not at all, they were",

Riley interrupted him and lowered his voice and said sternly,

"what is it you want Cain, I'm busy".

Cain looked at him but knew not to antagonise him any further,

"I was just wondering if Aibbi was ok and if I could speak to her that was all".

Riley looked at him shaking his head "you mean you don't know".

Cain didn't know, he'd been too busy the previous day disposing of Mally's body by tying him to some bricks and throwing him in the River Lee.

Cain shook his head as if to confirm Riley's question.

"They have run away".

Cain looked at him with a face of disbelief.

"Ran away, what do you mean, both of them, where too, can't you go and get her back",

"I would do just that if I knew where they had gone Cain, but I don't, nobody knows. Sam Lord has no idea either. The only thing we know for sure is they are not coming back, not for a long time anyway. Aibbi said just that, in the letter she left to me and her mother".

Cain stood there trying to comprehend what Riley had just said.

A note, she'd left a note.

Parrot had missed.

She was alive.

Slowly coming to his senses, Cain looked at Riley with a puzzled look.

"So you think that she and Mally have run away together then",

"Well, she wouldn't go without him would she. Thats what all this is about. The pair of them being together is it not".

Cain stood there in a daze until he eventually answered him.

"Yes Riley, yes I suppose it is".

Cain walked out of the barn and got back on his cart. His head was running through the different scenarios. This wasn't brilliant, but it wasn't as bad as it could have been.

She was alive, not good, but she had run away, which was good, and more importantly, they thought that she had run away with Mally, which was excellent. There would be no questions asked as to where Mally had gone which meant he was in the clear, for the time being, anyway. That was until Aibbi decided, that she wanted to come back.

That was for the future, he could put some feelers out with his contacts to try and locate her. In the meantime Mally's body would be rotting away with the fishes.

The coming months were hard for Daibbi, Riley also, but he could go to work and forget about it for a time. Daibbi didn't like him working for the Milburn's because she blamed them for Aibbi and Mally running away but she knew that Riley had to work. And unless they moved away, they had no choice, Riley had to carry on where he was.

The post at Rossbridge was bad to say the least, but when she did see the postman her heart rate would increase rapidly hoping that she had at last received some form of communication from Aibbi. The utter deflation when she didn't was becoming increasingly hard to take to the point where now she would feel utter sadness at just seeing the postman before he had even arrived.

She had become very withdrawn and would very rarely speak of her anymore as it bought it all back and the sadness inside was beginning to eat her away.

And so they plodded along in their own little world both secretly praying everyday that she would write or send a message somehow to say that she and Mally were okay.

✽ ✽ ✽

GOODBYE AGAIN

October 1908

Daibbi lay in bed wide awake it was barely light but she couldn't sleep.

Riley lay next to her sound asleep. She felt like waking him but she knew that he would need to be up in half an hour or so to go to work so she left him, just softly stroking the back of his head.

But then she heard it. The gate. The squeaky gate onto the rear of the yard. Somebody had opened it. And then she heard it again. It was shutting this time.

"Riley wake up, wake up, there's somebody come through the gate".

Riley struggled to wake but he slowly came to his senses.

"The gate Riley, somebody has just come through the gate".

Riley got out of bed and pulled on his trousers before making his way down the stairs still pulling on his boots. 'Never fight in bare feet' his Grandad had always told him.

Daibbi followed behind him holding a wooden cosh that was always at the side of the bed.

They reached the door at the bottom of the stairs and Riley slowly pushed it open into the kitchen.

And there she was. Sat at the kitchen table.

A frail thin pale skinned young woman with greasy light brown unwashed hair.

Daibbi looked at the women's thin gaunt face and saw straight away the beautiful smiling eyes looking back at her.

"Oh my god. ….Aibbi, its Aibbi" she leapt across the kitchen as Aibbi got to her unsteady feet. "Hello mother, I've come home if thats okay".

Daibbi couldn't speak, she just held her in her arms shaking with happiness tears streaming down her face.

And then she saw him.

He was hiding behind Aibbi.

Aibbi looked at both of them and smiled as she said.

"And this is Connor, your Grandson, say hello to your Nanna

and Grandad Connor".

Daibbi and Riley stood opened mouthed as Connor smiled at them both "Hello" he said in a quiet but confident voice.

Aibbi then sat down and the three of them sat and talked for what seemed like hours. Mainly talking about Connor and what a good boy he was.

Eventually though, Daibbi needed to ask the question she had been wanting to ask for nearly 3 years.

"Aibbi why did you run away, we could have sorted this out, you know we could, and why didn't you write. Just one letter would have eased my worry",

"Im sorry mum but I couldn't, it wasn't safe for me to do it and it's still not safe now. Iv'e bought Connor here to hopefully see his Dad and leave him with him for a while".

Daibbi looked at her not quite believing what she had just said.

"You mean Mally just up and left you, left you with a child".

Now It was Aibbi's turn to look confused.

"He never left me Mum. Iv'e not seen or heard from Mally since the day before I left. I had to get away and I hoped that Mally would come and find me. We had talked about running away before so he knew where I would be going. But I heard nothing, and after a few months, I knew he wasn't coming but then I realised I was carrying his baby, but I can't cope anymore Mum, I need help. I need Connor to go to his Dad for a while until I get better. Look at me mum just look at me, I need to go and sort myself out",

"I know, I know" said Daibbi looking at the pale faced young girl. "but we can look after you both, we can get you better, It will just take time."

She interrupted her mother.

"Mum you don't understand I can't stay here, it's not safe and I'm still in trouble".

Daibbi looked at her, she barely recognised her it was so pitiful.

Riley broke the silence.

"Aibbi, we thought you had run away with Mally".

Aibbi looked at him and softly smiled back at him.

" No Riley I went on my own, I didn't know where Mally was, I haven't seen him since that day in the woods. He doesn't even know that I was carrying his child".

Daibbi looked stunned.

"You mean you have been on your own with this child since then, my god Aibbi how have you managed to survive".

"Iv'e managed Mum don't worry, I don't know how some days, but I have. He's a fine boy Mum, he's got your eyes and your spirit thats for sure. He has his Dad's patience though, definitely not mine" she smiled again, it was lovely to see her still smiling.

And then she asked the question which she didn't want to ask, but she knew she had to, the answer would decide her fate, as to whether she would stay or go.

"And how is Mally, have you seen anything of him".

Riley and Daibbi looked at each other not knowing what to say, eventually it was Riley that spoke.

"No Aibbi we haven't seen him. We haven't seen him since the day's before you left and neither has anybody else, including his father. He's disappeared".

Aibbi knew in her head that that was what the answer was going to be, but she needed to hear it for definite. He was dead there was no doubt about it in her mind now. If he had been alive he would have come looking for her.

And so her fate was decided.

She said nothing of Mally being dead but she knew now that she would leave again in the morning only this time she would say goodbye properly.

Daibbi ran her a bath and she washed her hair for her while they talked about Connor and what Aibbi's hopes were for him. They both knew what would happen in the morning but neither mentioned it. They just wanted to enjoy this fleeting moment together like it was a beautiful dream that neither of them wanted to end. But soon they both knew that they would wake up from their beautiful dream and try as they might they wouldn't be able to get back to sleep to carry on with this magical wonderful moment.

They woke in the morning and sat at the table having breakfast, quietly, as Connor was still asleep upstairs. Aibbi, Although still painfully thin, her hair now shone a beautiful light red, her skin had now more freshness and colour to it, but most of all, a heavy burden had been clearly lifted from her shoulders.

She looked and sounded more like the old Aibbi, fiery, more confident, her free spirit had returned and she spoke positively of her life ahead. It had been agreed in the early hours that she would leave Connor with them for the foreseeable future to enable her to get her life back on track. She would return to where she had run away too, Dublin.

Dublin was no place for a girl of 16 and on her own, let alone having a two year old with her. But now at 18 she was more confident, more sure of her future. She would cope. She would miss her son badly, she knew that, but for her sake and more importantly Connor's sake, he needed to stay here with his Nanna and Riley.

She had promised to write regularly and asked for them, when they could, to send photographs of Connor and report on his progress to her. She would try and return whenever she could, providing it was safe to do so.

They didn't ask why she felt unsafe, or why she couldn't stay, they knew that Aibbi wouldn't tell them anyway. They trusted her judgement and promised that should that all change she could return at anytime she wished.

In the meantime they would take care of her beautiful little boy.

They gave her some money, what little they had, and they told her that they would send her some more when she was settled again and had an address to where they could send it.

Aibbi said her sad goodbyes to her sleeping son, promising him she would return and see him soon.

She hoped with all her splintering heart that she would.

As she was about to leave, Daibbi held her in her arms and kissed her on her forehead and then placed in her palm, a small gold ring with a small deep red stone in it.

"This was your Grandma's ring, she gave it to me just before she passed away, take it and if you are in trouble then sell it, she would understand Aibbi don't worry".

Aibbi looked down at the tiny gold ring in her frail hand and then placed it on her ring finger "thank you Mum its lovely but I could never sell it, and if I can promise you nothing else, I will promise you that".

With that she smiled at them both and slipped out the kitchen door, she didn't turn around, she didn't want them to see the tears streaming down her face.

Riley and Daibbi heard the gate squeak and then she was gone, for how long they didn't know, but then, neither did Aibbi.

As the months passed they didn't hide the truth from Connor, or anybody else for that matter. They told people that asked, that Aibbi had gone away again and had left her son with them. They didn't tell anybody where or why she had gone, they didn't need to know.

Apart from the Lord's that is.

That was different matter entirely.

The following week Riley visited the farm belonging to Samuel Lord. He had been dreading it for days. He knew that Sam had taken his son's disappearance very badly, blaming himself for him leaving. Riley knew that Sam had travelled a lot of miles trying to find him and was asking if anybody had seen or heard of him. All his questions had been met with a 'no'. It was if he had just disappeared off the face of the earth.

As Riley rode up the lane towards the Lord's farm house he saw Sam in the field up ahead. Sam saw him almost at the same time and waved his hand in acknowledgement towards him. As Riley rode over to him, Sam could see that Riley looked pained and worried. As Riley got off the Bear, Sam looked at him and said.

"you look like you have seen a ghost Riley, whats the matter, is Daibbi okay",

"Yes Sam she's fine, but I need to speak to you".

Sam looked inquisitively at him trying to fathom out what was wrong.

And then it hit him…….

"Its Mally isn't it, you have heard something haven't you, where is he, is he okay".

'Too many question's with no answers to give' thought Riley

"No Sam, it's not Mally, it's Aibbi, she came home".

Riley went on to tell Sam all about Aibbi's return and that she had had a baby who was now two and his name was Connor. He also told him that Aibbi hadn't seen Mally since the day before she had run away and that she hadn't heard from Mally either.

"Mally wasn't with her, I don't understand, they ran away together" said Sam.

After a pause he continued "They were inseparable, Aibbi wouldn't run away without him, and he definitely wouldn't go anywhere without her".

He stood there shaking his head trying to make some sense of it all but he couldn't, it just didn't make any sense at all.

For about a minute, the two of them stood in silence until Sam broke it.

"And you say that she has a baby now, my god, where has she been Riley, and where's the father did he not come back with Aibbi".

Riley looked at Sam, looked him in the eye as he said,

"No Sam, the father didn't come back with her, she came on her own with Connor, that's the boy's name."

Riley put his hand on Sam's shoulder.

"Sam, Mally is Connor's father, and you Sam, you are Connor's Grandfather".

Sam reeled back in shock, his legs buckled beneath him and his head was now swirling. He couldn't believe what he was hearing 'he had a grandson who was two years old, but yet, he still didn't know where his own son was'.

"My god Riley are you sure, I mean is this true, Can I see him Riley, can I come and see Connor and Aibbi".

"Of course you can Sam he's your Grandson, but I'm afraid you won't be able to see Aibbi because she has gone away again, she has left Connor with us",

"She's gone again, ... where has she gone, has she gone back to Mally",

"No Sam, I told you she hasn't seen Mally since she went the first time",

"Yes, yes of course, I'm sorry Riley this is such a shock,.... Do you believe her Riley, do you believe that she doesn't know where my Mally is".

Riley looked at the broken man in front of him and felt utterly useless.

"Yes Sam, I do believe her, she thought that when she came back she would be able to see Mally. She thought that Mally was still here in Rossbridge. Thats why she came back, she wanted to let Connor see his father".

"Oh god Riley. if she doesn't know where my Mally is, then who does".

They both stood in silence again.

Riley looked at him, if only there was something he could do. But he knew there was nothing.

"Sam, I think you should go and tell your wife about Connor and then bring her over to Rose cottage to see her Grandson, he's a fine young boy, I'm sure you will be very proud of him",

"Yes,……..yes I will, I will go and tell her now. Will it be okay if we call over tomorrow before we go to church",

"Yes Sam, of course it will, that would be fine, I will see you tomorrow then, goodbye Sam, see you tomorrow".

The next morning a very emotional Grandfather and Grandmother Lord were introduced to their wonderful, full of energy, happy Grandson.

They agreed between them all that they could visit whenever they wished and if Aibbi should return could they please come and see her to talk to her about Mally and what had happened. Riley and Daibbi said that they would let them know if and when Aibbi returned. But they both knew that that could be a very long wait for all of them.

As the months moved on, Riley and Daibbi tried to fill Connor's day with as much activity as they could, hoping to take his mind from other things. They needn't have worried. Connor was quite happy with the situation. His mother had told him that she would be back for him one day and he was happy with that. His day was so full of new and wonderful things that he didn't have time to sit and worry about when and where he would next see his mother. In the day his Nanna, Daibbi, would take him wherever she went and if she was at home he would help her bake cakes and prepare the dinner. In the evenings, once Riley had returned from the farm's, Connor would follow Riley about like his shadow copying whatever he did. If he was mending farm machinery then Connor would be the other side fixing it as well. He loved 'fixing things' and was soon calling himself 'the fixer'.

His favourite time though was with the animals. Connor adored them. He loved being with them, touching them, caring for them, and learning all about them. There was a strange bond that Connor seemed to have with animals. They seemed to like him too. Since the day he arrived he was his happiest when he was with the horse and the cattle.

Riley would talk to him about them all the time, he would say, 'I prefer animals to people, you can trust an animal but you can't trust people, and he told him that if he looked after an animal, whatever it was, then that animal would look after him. It was something that Connor would never forget.

As the months slowly turned into years Daibbi and Riley seemed like a mother and father to him. They explained to him that they were his grandparents and they were looking after him because his mummy and daddy couldn't be here. He accepted it completely, he was very happy with his life in the country.

Aibbi wrote letters to him which they would read to him as Connor couldn't read or write. They sent her photograph's of him when they could and kept her informed as to how he was getting on at school.

They in turn, told him stories about his parents and about what they were like, and Riley would always say to him that his mother would be very proud of him. She had asked them to make sure that he always knew right from wrong and that he should always do the right thing, not the wrong one.

As he grew older Daibbi could see that he was like his mother in many ways, not just in looks, yes he had his mothers lovely green oval shaped eyes, her strawberry blonde hair, which was wavy thick like his fathers, but he definitely had his mothers spirit. If he wanted to do it, whatever it was, then he was going to do it. It produced many a battle of wills between him and his Nana though never with his Grandad Riley. He knew that if he pushed his Nana hard enough he usually got his way, but with Riley, that was a different story, he knew it was pointless, if Riley said no, then that was what it meant, no meant no.

And so the little boy born of a Protestant father and a Catholic mother, began to learn his way in this oh so complicated world.

But he was just a little boy, he didn't care.

8th May 1915

It was mid afternoon when Riley walked into the kitchen of Rose cottage and although it was a Saturday it was still a surprise to Daibbi that he should be home so early. Connor had heard him come in to the yard and had come racing down the stairs to greet him.

"Riley can we go fishing, I want to catch some fish so Nana can cook them for dinner" said a very excitable Connor.

"He's been on about going fishing all day Riley" said Daibbi "he's been learning about it at school, I've said that you would take him when you get time",

"Thanks" smiled Riley raising his eyebrows sarcastically. Daibbi knew that Riley hated fishing. He had told her several times that since he was a boy, he'd found it very boring and tedious, his father had taken him when he was around Connor's age and he had absolutely hated it, he couldn't see what the attraction was at all.

She looked at Riley her head bent slightly to the side.

"Sorry, but its no good me taking him, I wouldn't have a clue what I was supposed to do",

"And neither would I Daibbi, neither would I".

Daibbi smiled at him. She knew he would take him.

"What are you doing home so early anyway, it's only just gone three".

The smile had gone now from his face and he looked a little serious and concerned over something. Daibbi left him for a few moments, he'd tell her when he wanted to, there was no point in pushing him, it didn't work. Eventually he spoke.

"There has been a terrible tragedy Daibbi", He said.

And so he and Daibbi sat and talked about the events of what had happened the previous day.

"They are talking about it all over the village. The Germans have sunk a large Liner bound for Liverpool from America. Its called the Lusitania and there have been hundreds of Men, Women and children drowned just off the South coast near to Kinsale" Said Riley.

Daibbi knew that this awful tragedy would be the catalyst for Riley. He had been fighting against the pull of his heart to sign up and go and join the war in France. They had talked about it for hours over the last few months but his head had kept telling him no, and to stay here with Daibbi and Connor. She knew now though, just by looking at him, that his mind was made up and that he wanted to go. She couldn't stop him, and she knew deep in her heart she had to let him.

She looked at him sadly and placed her arms around him with her head on his chest.

Daibbi spoke softly now hoping that Connor wouldn't hear.

"I know what you have to do Riley. I won't stop you, if it's something you feel that you have to do then go and do it. We can manage, it will soon be over anyway, they keep saying that it should be done by Christmas, and Christmas won't be long will it".

And so....

Within the next two months Riley had been sent to France to fight with the 16th Irish Division.

It wasn't going to be done by Christmas.

1st September 1915

Daibbi sat in her kitchen lost in her thoughts. Her mind was busy, which wasn't unusual as she was generally busy thinking about what to do next. But this was different, she couldn't get the worries out of her head. She worried about Aibbi, she worried about Riley and she worried about how she was going to manage running the farm on her own. She hadn't heard from Aibbi for over six months now. She had been sending letters every 3 or 4 months telling them that she was okay and had got herself a job working in a knitwear factory. She would always ask how Connor was getting on. But she had now heard nothing and now with Riley having gone to France to fight for the British army she felt totally alone.

He'd been gone for only a couple of month's but to Daibbi it already felt like a lifetime. She hadn't heard anything from him either and whilst that didn't surprise her, she craved just some sort of security. She knew that to receive a letter from him would be nothing short of a miracle ,not only getting it sent from France but to actually receive it at a remote Irish country farm would be just that, a miracle. She began to again dread seeing the postman and it felt like the nightmare returning to haunt her all over again. And now there was another problem, The farm, she was struggling to cope on her own and the money or lack of it was now a concern. She was still getting a wage as such from the Milburn's but it had been reduced and was a lot less than what Riley was earning before he had left. At least she had Connor, She thought, which seemed to wake her from her from her daydream and so she slowly got up from the kitchen table and went to find him to let him know his dinner was ready.

She shouted upstairs but had no reply so she went out into the yard and shouted again.

"Connor, Connor, would you come here child and eat your dinner, if you don't come here and eat it then it will be for the chickens".

Daibbi listened for Connor's response but none was forthcoming, she knew that this was nothing unusual as he was normally off doing something that generally he shouldn't be doing. He was now a wonderful little boy of 9 years old and was for most of the time a pleasure to be around. He had his mothers spirit though that what for sure. If he didn't want to do whatever it was his Nana was asking of him it was a battle of wills before it would be done, and, usually, it would be done.

She stepped out the door into the yard, it was dusk and the remnants of the sun's heat still warmed her face as she walked into the farm courtyard. It had been a scorching day and the heat from the brick walls could still be felt warming the forty foot square yard between her and the barn. Aggie woke from her light sleep as she lay on the warm cobbles, after her hard day chasing rabbits.

Aggie and Connor were rarely far apart these days since Riley had left for the war. It had been Riley's instruction that he, Connor, was to now be in charge of Aggie and Connor had relished in the responsibility. Truth be known though, that nobody, even Riley, actually owned Aggie. She was as loyal a dog you could ever find but nobody would ever own her, she was a free spirit and would wander the land in search of a rabbit or even better, a hare to bring back home, sometimes having to drag it due to its size. She had been known to return home alone when going out hunting with Riley, from as far as seven or eight miles away usually getting back before anybody else, and be curled up in front of the fire and opening one eye to anybody entering as if to wink at them to say 'Hello, yes I'm back, what took you so long'.

"Where is that boy Aggie, and don't you be covering for him so you can have his dinner" Said Daibbi, who was now losing her patience, she was a kind and loving women but patience was definitely not one of her strongest virtues.

It was then that she saw the shadows in the barn. The sun had set behind it and between the vertical wooden slats that ran from the floor to the roof, she could see the silhouetted shadows of two people, one very small and the other, very large and broad. Panic hit her immediately, that was Connor in there but who was he with. She ran across the yard and Aggie got up and followed her sensing something wasn't quite right.

Daibbi burst into the barn, her eyes darting about to locate who it actually was in there.

She froze.

They both stood there with their backs to her. Connor was looking down at a calf that had been born three days previously and there at his side was Cain Milburn.

Cain having heard the barn door open, slowly turned to see who it was that had entered. He acted surprised but he knew full well who it was going to be.

"Hello Daibbi, Connor here is just showing me the new member of your family. He looks like he's going to be a fine bull doesn't he" Said Cain.

Daibbi moved over to Connor quickly grabbing his hand, her protective instinct kicking in almost immediately.

She looked sharply at Cain and the eyes had already said it but she said it anyway.

"It's his dinner time and I would appreciate it if you would come and see me first before you even think about taking him off anywhere",

"For your information Daibbi, he was already in here, I've not taken him anywhere, I was just passing by and I thought I'd stop by to see how the pregnant lady's we're doing, I didn't know that you had had a new arrival until Connor here told me about it",

"Well, you know now don't you, and if there's nothing else

Connor is going in for his dinner".

She took Connors arm and began to walk towards the barn door.

"Well, it's funny you should say that Daibbi, but yes there is something else, I have a proposition for you, let's go inside and discuss it while you have your dinner and if you have some spare I wouldn't say no, not to your wonderful cooking Daibbi" Said Cain smiling and winking at Connor.

Daibbi looked at him deciding what to do. She really wanted to tell him to go, but she knew that wouldn't do her any good. She gently nodded her approval and the three of them went inside.

Cain sat and had some dinner and listened as Connor told him all about how he had helped his Nana as the calf was born and how he wanted to be a vet when he grew older.

Daibbi sat and smiled at him as he went on in great detail about his role in the birth of his knew best friend who he had named 'Billy the bull'.

"You won't be a vet at all unless you start doing your school work and learn how to read and write" said Daibbi.

"I can read Nana" said Connor looking up at Cain and rolling his eyes in disgust.

"No you can't Connor, you just guess, you need to start sitting down and learning how to read properly. All your school friends can do it, and if you don't start knuckling down and trying to learn you will be left behind".

"Oh stop worrying Nana I will learn it one day, there's no rush you know".

"Its a boy thing Daibbi" said Cain "I couldn't read properly until I was about six or seven, I was too busy doing other things, I had no time for reading",

"That may be so Cain, but he can't read or right a single word, it's like he's got a mental block. Riley and I have sat for hours with him, trying to teach him to read but whatever we do nothing seems to work. He just doesn't get it".

Daibbi looked at him and shook her head, she couldn't help but smile at him, this carefree happy smiling little boy without a care in the world, smiling his absent mother's smile for her.

She turned and looked at Cain "So Cain, what is this proposition that you have".

Cain sat and explained that since his father had taken ill just over a year ago, he was struggling for time to get all his jobs done and Riley leaving to go and fight in the war and having never really replaced Parrot, it left him short of time. He really needed to spend more time with his father in the afternoons. Ellen was taking care of him but if he could lessen her load by helping her in the mornings and a little in the afternoon it would give her a break. He couldn't rely on Glendon to do anything he was useless and unreliable.

Edmond had had a massive stroke and hadn't been expected to survive it but he had. But now he was virtually bed ridden and couldn't do anything for himself.

"What I also need Daibbi is some help in the mornings with the milk round which would let me get back home earlier to tend to my father. So I was wondering if Connor here could come to work with me and help me deliver in the town and perhaps when he's a bit older he could even take over the round from me once he'd learnt the ropes".

She looked at Cain not sure what to say. "He's barely 9 years old Cain and he has school to go to, and as I've just said he is struggling with his work now, let alone having time off to go delivering milk".

'But thats the good thing about it Daibbi, he'd be done by 9 o'clock, he could go straight to school when we'd finished, I could just drop him off at school on the way back".

Connor had sat there listening to the conversation intently.

His eyes getting wider and wider, as he heard at what Cain's plan was to be.

Connor had sat long enough and couldn't restrain himself any longer.

"Oh Nana please let me do it, please, I promise that I will go to school everyday and do my best to learn my spelling and stuff, please Nana, please".

Cain looked at Connor and smiled at him, he liked Connor, he reminded him so much of his mother Aibbi. He was a nice kid.

"Well Daibbi, Connor here is fine with it so what do you think, if it helps your decision, it will mean that the wages will be made up to just about what you were earning before Riley went away, I think thats only fair, don't you".

Daibbi looked at him in disbelief.

"Well".

She eventually replied.

"I suppose that we could give it a try".

Connor jumped up and started running around the kitchen shouting "Yes, yes, yes, yes I'm going to be the milkman".

Daibbi and Cain stood and laughed at him until Daibbi stopped and said to Cain.

"You give me your word that he won't come to any harm and that you will make sure that when he's finished, he goes to school everyday and he has to be there by 9:30 and no later".

"He'll be delivering milk Daibbi, don't worry and I promise he will not miss one day at school. Both you, and Connor, will be doing me a great favour".

He stopped and looked at Daibbi and she was sure his eyes looked to water a little.

"You see Daibbi,…… my father hasn't long in this world, and it would just be nice to spend a little more time with him, so if you can do this for me, I would appreciate it greatly".

They agreed to let Connor start the following Monday.

Connor had taken some waking, but there he was, stood outside the front door of Rose cottage as Cain pulled up on his horse and milk cart. It was just after 5am.

They turned around and slowly made their way northwards towards the town of Tralee, the back of the cart, full of bottled milk and churns. Connor had his lunch packed into his bag and was dressed ready to go straight to school once they had returned.

It was a nice clear morning and there was a thick frost on the ground and it wasn't long before Connor was beginning to shiver.

"You cold lad" said Cain

" I'm okay", said Connor trying to be brave,

" Then why are you shivering then. I tell you what, you can do what I had to do when I was your age, get out and run behind the cart, that'll warm you up".

Connor looked at him trying to see if he meant it or not.

"Go on, out you get".

He pushed him off the cart and Connor began to jog behind him.

After no more than five minutes Connor was back on, now sweating and his body warmed through.

" Its works lad doesn't it", said a laughing Cain.

As they travelled along through the stunning green hills of south west Ireland, Connor was enjoying himself tremendously. 'It was like going on an adventure' he thought, his mind full of fantastic ideas of what might happen.

It took them nearly 40 minutes to make the journey to the edge of the town. As they approached the first dwellings Cain drew the cart to a stop and looked at the child, full of anticipation, sat next to him.

"So now Connor, this is where your work begins. Take two of those full bottles there and take them to that door over there and if there are any empty bottles then you bring those back, got it",

"Got it" replied Connor.

He jumped off the cart and did as he was asked, walking not running, as Cain had told him 'never run with bottles in your hand unless you have too', they were soon on there way again, now going further into the town.

As the early morning moved on, Cain was already happy to let Connor deliver the milk on one side of the street, while he also would deliver to the house's on the opposite side. Occasionally, Cain would ask him to swap sides, and go on the other side of the street.

The horse, Duke, would slowly follow them down the street, dragging the cart behind him. Every now and then, Connor would see Cain return with a small piece of paper in his hand which he would place under his seat where Connor had also seen a large piece of wood that to him, looked exactly like his Nana's rolling pin.

As they entered the town square, Connor sat in utter amazement as to the noise and vastness of it all. He had never seen anything quite like this. He had been in Dublin with his mother of course, but he couldn't remember that.

The square was about 120 yards wide and just a little longer. It rose uphill from South to North, with the Southwest corner dropping down rapidly towards the River Lee.

The hustle and bustle of the market in the centre had already started and it was only 7am. The three storey buildings that surrounded the square on all four sides seemed to tower up above him.

There were just three roads out of the square, one to the North, one to the South, which they had come in from, and one on the Northwest corner, with the East side having no road, just buildings which included shops, a public house called the Reindeer, a clothing store and two hardware stores. The three other sides were all very similar, with houses dotted here and there in between stores and shops.

With a population of around 16,000 people, the square serviced the needs of the town of Tralee quiet adequately, there was no need to go further afield. The two other public houses within the square were Mulligans, which was on the South side and The StoneBridge, which was just above the South west corner. The rear of The StoneBridge backed onto the River Lee and had an old stone bridge which crossed the Lee from behind its back yard and led to a small community of houses on the West side that was separated from the rest of the town by the river. The people that lived on that side of the river were known as 'The Bogmen' as the area was renowned for flooding during harsh winters.

It was also where almost all of the protestant families of Tralee lived.

As Connor looked around, flocks of pigeons swooped down around them, at times almost brushing his hair as they passed him. The noise was tremendous with people shouting and hollering their prices of the goods they were selling, but it was the smell of the place that amazed him the most. The smell of fresh fruit and vegetables, the smell of the smoke that billowed from the chimneys and the wonderful smell of freshly cooked meat from one or two of the stalls.

Cain looked and smiled at the opened mouthed child sat at his side. "Busy place this lad isn't it" he said.

Connor just nodded in reply, still trying, but failing to take it all in.

"Okay Connor, grab a basket and come with me".

They left Duke and the cart and both walked together around the square delivering bottles to various houses. They returned to the cart once their basket's were empty to replenish their stock and off they would go again.

As Connor walked at the side of Cain he was introduced to men that said hello as they passed their stalls or met them in the street. Cain could see that Connor was a bit bewildered by it all, to a little boy of 9, it all seemed so vast and chaotic with people running or walking everywhere and bumping into him as if he wasn't even there.

As they returned to the cart Cain said.

"Okay Connor, now listen because this is important, we have got to go through to the back streets now. I will show you which houses we go too and which streets to use, but remember that there will be some of them that you mustn't go down, and I mean, mustn't, understand, they are not safe for a young lad like you on your own and I've promised your mother that I will keep you safe".

Connor looked at him and nodded but didn't seemed to phased by what he had just said.

With full baskets of milk they walked towards the western side of the square, passing the Stonebridge public house and the bridge itself, on their left, and then travelling North before stopping 40 yards further on, at a five foot gap between two 3 storey houses. The gap was in fact a cobbled alleyway that led off the edge of the square at right angles and then it could be seen twisting and turning heading West and deeper into the backstreets on the West side of the town, with the Bogmen estate further on beyond the river.

Cain stopped in the gap and turned and looked back into the square as if looking for somebody. He looked down at the blonde haired little boy stood next to him, his young eyes looking back at Cain and still looking like he was on great big adventure with his new friend.

"Now then Connor, this here, this alleyway is called The Wind" Cain then pointed to the alleyway that led to the back of the Stonebridge pub and the bogmen estate beyond "the one down there is 'The Walk' and that one on this side further up there is 'The Wall', but this gap here, right here, leading into the Wind, to you and me, we will call it 'The Point'.

He looked at Connor and nodded as if to extenuate the serious of what he was saying.

"This boy, 'The Point' is a very, very, important spot".

Cain paused and pointed into 'The Wind' and beyond as he said,

"If you ever get into trouble in there, you make your way back to here, 'The Point', as quick as you can, once you get to here, don't worry, you will be safe, do you understand".

Connor looked at him with totally innocent eyes and said.

"Yes Mr Milburn I will, but why would I get into trouble, I've not done anything wrong have I".

Cain looked at him and laughed.

"No Connor ,you haven't, but there are some people that live around here that are not very nice and they don't like strangers wandering about, most of them are Bogmen but you will soon recognise them after a while, don't you worry about that".

"Bogmen" said Connor, now twisting his head and trying to look further into the alleyway "they don't sound very nice".

Again Cain laughed and said.

"well Connor your right, they aren't very nice, but don't you get worrying about them now, your with me so you will be ok, now come on let's get moving or you'll be late for school".

They walked into the alleyway and as Connor looked up, it looked like the buildings were trying to fall down on top of him, he stopped and just stood almost in a daze before he realised he was being left behind as he ran on trying to keep right behind Cain who was walking quickly through the cobbled walkway. There were houses on both sides, their front doors facing each other at times barely 4 to 5 foot apart. String hung from upstairs windows and was tied to the window of the building opposite with most of them having washing hanging from them which was blowing in the strong breeze that was whistling down the gap like it was a vast cavern between two huge rock faces. Every 40 or 50 yards or so, an alleyway would cross going left to right, each with more houses on them, with more string and more washing. The town was in fact a huge maze about half a mile across consisting of small twisting narrow alleyways that carried on all around the square, only stopping briefly where the roads dissected them and then starting again on the other side repeating itself in a full three hundred and sixty degree circle.

The Square itself was firstly fed by the three roads and then also from ten alleyways which consisted of three to the West side, The Balla (wall) at the top, The Gaoth (Wind) in the middle and The Siul (Walk) to the South end and next to the Stonebridge pub. On the North side from West to East were two more Alleyways, The Nadur (Nature) and The Naofa (Holy). On this East side from North to South were three more, The Eorna (Barley), The Eala (Swan) and The Easpag (Bishop) and finally on the South side from East to West were The Sagart (Priest) and The Saighead (Arrow). Each one led out from the square where it met two alleyways that circled the square in a full 360 degree circle, the inner one, Clog Istigh (Inner Clock) and outer one, Clog Seachtrach (outer clock). All of them had their own story to tell. Over the hundreds of years that they had been here, there had been many parties, celebrations, meetings, weddings, processions, fights, robberies and many murders. All of them had had several name changes in their chequered past, and the ones to the East, which led to the protestant side of the town, had been recently changed from their English names to their Gaelic equivalent. Each and everyone one of them could be a lively and wonderful place, full of life and frivolity, but on any a new dawn, they could be a horrible place to be, full of hatred and death. And at this point in its varied history, it was much more of the latter that now prevailed.

They carried on delivery their milk travelling too and fro from their milk cart and stopping occasionally for Cain to place the small bits of paper he had taken from some more doorsteps, again placing them under his seat.

By now it was gone 8 o'clock and Cain didn't want Connor to be late for school after his first day at work.

As they walked back to the cart Connor walked as fast as he could but occasionally breaking into a jog in order to keep up with Cain. As he got level with him again he said "Two hundred and twelve".

Cain not really realising what he had just said turned to Connor.

"What you saying lad",

"Two hundred and twelve", repeated Connor

"Two hundred and twelve what",

"Two hundred and twelve bottles, …..Iv'e delivered two hundred and twelve bottles today".

Cain looked at him in amazement

"How on earth do you know that",

"I have been counting from when I started this morning, it's a lot isn't it".

Cain looked at him trying to work it out for himself but he knew that he was probably about right, he didn't really need to do the math.

"Thats very good Connor, you see, its going to help you with your maths at school, you working for me".

They got on the cart and made their way slowly back towards Rossbridge. They arrived at the school with time to spare and Connor waved a cheery goodbye before running inside.

Cain watched him go. 'I like that kid' he thought. There was something about him that he liked a lot. He was going to be very useful, very useful indeed.

※ ※ ※

THE 'POINT'

Over the next few weeks Connor continued to work with Cain on the milk round. It was working well. Even at his young age Cain could tell that Connor was going to be a good worker. He seemed to thrive on it and if you gave him praise, he worked even harder. He was like a sponge, whatever you said to him, he took it all in and seemed to remember everything he was told. He already seemed to know his way about the back streets but was always very wary when they went anywhere near to the stone bridge which crossed the River Lee towards the Bogmen estate.

Cain was amazed at how quickly Connor had learnt his way around the streets of Tralee. He already somehow, seemed to know every little lane and alleyway and every little shortcut available, of which, there were many.

It was like he had drawn a map in his head and could memorise it at will.

Cain had even tried to test him on a few occasions sending him off with milk to houses that were difficult to get straight too, but within minutes Connor would return empty handed and ready to go again.

He was beginning to wonder if Connor was just putting the milk down anywhere and returning empty handed, so he decided to follow him. He again picked him a difficult house to find and, as usual, Connor was off and gone into the alleyways beyond 'the Point'. Even though Cain knew the way he struggled to keep up with the young boy. Sure enough a few minutes and several twists and turns later, Connor delivered the milk to the required doorstep and was now making his way back to the cart.

As he walked up to it, Cain was sat on its wooden bench and was grinning broadly at him.

"Whats up Mr Milburn",

"Nothing Connor, nothing at all",

"Why are you smiling then", said Connor "and why did you follow me".

Cain laughed loudly shaking his head in disbelief,

"and how do you know that I followed you, young lad",

"Because I saw you, I saw you twice, once on the way and once on the way back, I thought that I must have forgotten something",

" No lad, you didn't forget anything at all".

Cain looked at him still smiling but he was smiling at him for a different reason now.

He knew now that this boy was a gift from God. He would need a little tuition here and there but he knew that the boy had a gift. He didn't know how he did it. He couldn't even read for gods sake, but he could do it and that was all that mattered.

The Messenger boy was here.

✽ ✽ ✽

A LETTER OR TWO

October 1915

It was the 3rd October when Daibbi finally heard from Riley. It had actually been sent from somewhere in France, somewhere that she had never heard of, on the 15th September 1915, but that didn't matter. She sat down in her kitchen and opened the envelope, excited that she had at last got some news, but a little apprehensive as to what that news would be. She unfolded the two sheets of writing paper which had Riley's writing on all four sides and began to read,

' My dear Daibbi and Connor,
Firstly, let me apologise for the lack of letter's sent from myself since I left. It has been very difficult to get my hands on any writing material such as pencils and paper and the like since I arrived at Aldershot(crossed out) in Britain.
But now that I have a new posting, (more on that later)
I can get access to them more frequently. We have spent some time there training and last week I arrived in France at a place

called Etaples(crossed out)

and I have done very little since.

The whole place is full of soldiers with little or no idea with what they are supposed to be doing.

I have been assigned to the 16th Irish Division and a few of my new friends have come from the town of Killarney. I have had to fill out forms with what skills I have and I felt a little embarrassed with the little that I could put down, however they seemed quite pleased that I could ride a horse. I say this because they are sending me tomorrow (apparently) to a stabling yard where I am to help with the horses, presumably I will be a glorified groom for an officer of some kind. I have been told, unofficially, by the sergeant who has given me my new job, that he doesn't think that we will be in Etaples (crossed out) for long, and that soon we will be moving to nearer to the western front.

Wherever that may be?. I'm sorry my love that I can't give you more exciting news but it all seems a little boring at the moment.

Anyway thats enough from me, I hope that you and Connor are well and that he is still enjoying his school. How is the farm going and my trusty steed, the Bear. Oh how I wish he was out here with me. They say that if you want to write back you Just put my name on the front, start it with 30739 Private, that's my army number.

They might cross some bits out but don't worry if they do, its just to stop the Bosch spying on us. Have you heard from Aibbi recently. I've heard from one of the boys from Dublin That there has been some trouble brewing in the city and it seems to be getting worse. Still I'm sure Aibbi will be ok, we both know she can look after herself don't we !!

Anyway thats all from me my love for now. Give Connor a big hug and kisses from me. But save the biggest for yourself.

Let's hope I will be home soon.

All my love always

Riley x x x

Daibbi read it again, in fact she read it four more times before she slowly folded it and placed back into its envelope.

She sat and quietly cried a little, missing him so badly. He seemed so far away, but he seemed unconcerned as to any danger he might be in. And if he was going to looking after horses, then he should surely be safe.

She comforted herself with that thought.

Two days later she received a second letter, this time from Aibbi.

Hello My Dear Mother,

I hope that you and Riley are well.

How is my boy doing is he behaving himself.

How is he getting on at school?.

I write to let you know that I have started working at the Gaiety Theatre here in Dublin. I am helping in the costume department and the man in charge, Mr Clancy, has asked me if I would be interested in a small part in the next production!!

I think he was probably joking but you never know, you always said Mother that one day 'my name would be up in lights'.

I'm sorry I've not been in touch for a while but you know what I'm like.

Give my boy some kisses for me and I promise that I will try and visit very soon.

Love, as always,
Aibbi X X X

Daibbi held it close to her chest. Perhaps it was all going to be okay. Soon they might be both back home and they could all be a family again. She so hoped so.

❋ ❋ ❋

THE LIGHT WALK

It was time to learn some new tricks. Cain had been thinking long and hard at how he could teach Connor what he wanted him to do without scaring him and making him not want do it.

He decided that he would try and make a game of it.

The messages were not the problem. They, as far as Connor would be concerned would be about milk and money. Nothing else.

It was avoiding detection that was Cain's, or more to the point, Connor's problem.

If he, Connor, was caught with a note then they would soon know who was responsible for it.

They, being the police. The police were now using some underhand tactics in trying to wheedle out who were behind some of the attacks on Protestants and their properties. The attacks had been increasing over the last few months and the violence used by the perpetuators has started to escalate. One man had come close to death following a beating in one of the alleyways behind the Stonebridge pub. It had been reported that it was just some drunks fighting amongst themselves but those that were in 'the know' knew differently. The man had been left blind by the attack and the word on the street was there would be reprisals in store. Week by week more beatings and damage was done by both sides. One attack caused another attack and so on and so on.

The police had now started putting officers out patrolling in plain clothes in a hope that they could find out who the organisers were. They had tried to recruit informants from both sides but the slightest suspicion that you were one, led to some horrendous assaults taking place.

Cain had told Connor on the way to Tralee that they were going to play a game during their round. He told him that once Connor had gone beyond 'The Point' and he was on his way to deliver his milk to a house, he was going to follow him and, once Connor had spotted Cain following him, Connor had got to try and get away, but, 'there was no running allowed'. If Connor saw Cain behind him, he should keep walking until he went around a corner and then hide somewhere out of Cain's view. But he must remember that once he was happy that he had got away then he had to continue on to where he was supposed to be delivering too.

Connor thought it was brilliant. "This is going to be great" said Connor.

Connor looked at Cain with excitement all over his face and said "Once you catch me, then is it my turn to try and catch you",

"No" said Cain "I'm rubbish at hiding so I'm going to try and follow you all the round",

"Okay" said Connor, "brilliant, this is going to be brilliant".

They arrived at Tralee Square and Cain jumped off the cart.

"Ok then lad, off you go".

Connor walked quickly with his bottles in his small basket trying as hard as he could to quell the urge in his head to run.

He walked through 'the Point' and turned to look to see if Cain was behind him. Cain, was already not happy with what he was doing and waved him back towards him. Connor turned and walked back, non plussed as to what he had already done wrong.

Cain said sternly this time, "Connor listen. When you get to 'the Point' never, and I mean never, look round behind you, do you understand, when you walk through it you keep looking straight ahead ,okay".

Connor nodded his agreement but couldn't resist asking the question.

"why",

"Never mind why, Connor, I will tell you why one day when you're old enough, but you're not old enough yet, now off you go, let's try it again".

And so, off they set. Walking through the alleyways, the house's towering above them, the occasional person coming in the opposite direction and causing Connor to hang the basket in front of himself so he could get by. As Connor walked ahead he occasionally looked around but he saw nothing. After several alleyways Connor hadn't seen Cain once and was beginning to wonder if Cain was actually following him or, in fact, he was playing a joke on him and was still sat in the cart. He stopped around a corner and waited, about 10 seconds later Cain walked around the corner and almost walked into him.

"Now whats the matter, why have you stopped" said Cain,

"I haven't seen you, I thought you weren't really following me", said Connor the disappointment clearly in his voice.

"Don't you worry about me Connor lad, I'm following you, I'm just clipping you thats all",

"Clipping me, whats that",

"It means that I'm just seeing a bit of you when you go around the corner and then I lose sight of you for a bit, but then I just catch site of you again when you go around the next corner. So when you walk along the straight bit and you turn around, you won't see me because I'm still around the corner, it's called 'clipping'",

"Oh I see, so when I walk along a straight bit, I won't see you and you can't see me",

"Yes thats right",

"But how do you know where I've gone then",

"Because lad, I know these alleyways like the back of my hand and I know when there's another alleyway coming up. So I will close up to you when I know its coming",

"Why is it like the back of your hand".

"Connor, do you want to play this game or not, we haven't got time to mess about".

They set off again and Cain could see immediately that Connor had already worked it out.

As he approached a right turn into another alleyway, there it was, the slightest turn of the head to see if Cain was coming around the corner.

That young brain had already worked it out. 'Unbelievable' he thought.

They continued on the twisting and turning streets and alleyways, same result every time. The slightest glance back, still a little too much but they could work on that.

As they walked on, Cain walked around the corner, ...he'd gone, Connor had completely vanished.........

He walked on a few more steps.

"Morning Mr Milburn", came Connor's voice from behind him.

Cain swung around his mouth open wide "where".

"I was in there", laughed Connor pointing to a gate that led to one of the house's rear yard.

"This is a great game this isn't it", giggled Connor again and set off again happily on his merry way.

Cain stood watching him go as he thought ' Yes Connor, it is a game, for now anyway, but soon, it might not be just as much fun'.

As the week went on they continued to play 'the game' and every day Connor continued to improve and they had ironed out the looking back problem. Cain couldn't see him looking behind him hardly at all now. It was time to step it up a level.

"Okay Connor" said Cain, "today we are going to do some other things, I'm still going to follow you but I'm going to show you some new stuff".

Connor nodded his approval, smiling as usual and full of anticipation.

"Okay Connor, this is what we are going to do today, you lad, you are now going to follow me. Do as I did and time it right and try and stay just away from view as best you can. You won't get it straight the way, this takes a lot of practice and I'm sure I will see you for the first few times, but don't worry, it will come. The more you do it the better you will get".

They both grabbed their bottles and Cain set off at the front.

As Cain went around each corner he would glance back every now and then, seeing Connor on a few occasions, but not too many, 'not bad for his first attempt' he thought.

But as he walked along a straight part of an alleyway he stopped. And waited.

A few moments later Connor came around the corner and looked at Cain in the eye and turned straight around and started walking back to where he had come from.

"No" shouted Cain "come back here".

Connor turned and slowly started walking back to the waiting Cain, the disappointment written all over his face.

"Two things wrong with that" said Cain "do you know what

they were".

"Yes" said Connor " I came around the corner too fast and caught you up".

"Well, yes you did but that will happen, you can't help it if I just stop, but what you did was look me straight in the eye. Never ever look at me in the eye, if they get your eyes they've got you, do you understand, always look at the bottom of their back then if they turn around, your not looking at their head, and if they have stopped, then just walk straight past till your out of their view and then find somewhere, like the other day when you went behind the gate, or a shop that you can go into, and let them walk past, then you can come out behind them again and carry on, okay lets have another go".

He looked at Connor and there was clearly something on the young lad's mind.

"What is it Connor, what's the problem now'.

"Who are 'they',

"Eh" said Cain.

"You said 'they will have you', well, who are 'they'",

"The person that you are following" said Cain,

"But why will I be following them" said Connor looking even more puzzled,

"Don't you worry about that now, now let's give it one last go, times getting on and we need to get you to school".

They carried on for another half hour or so. Again Connor continued to improve even walking in a few gateways when Cain stopped. There was no more eye contact, not once. But the best thing that was happening was how natural Connor was. He would walk by him without the slightest of glance's or any nervousness at all. It was all still a big game.

The weeks past and Connor's improvement continued in leaps and bounds. He had even learnt, when being followed, how to stop and look into the windows of shops to look at the reflection to see where Cain was or if in fact he was following him. Cain had only once found fault when Connor had stopped and looked in the tailors window at the mens suites and Cain had asked him what he needed a suit for.

"Try to pick your windows Connor, you looking in there, it wasn't natural, always try to make it as natural as you can, look in the sweet shops and the toy shop round the corner but not the bloody tailor's".

❋ ❋ ❋

THE DARK WALK

24th December 1915

The winter had now well and truly settled in to South West Ireland. The wind was blowing in from the West and the wind break for England was really taking a battering. The cobbled streets shone shiny and wet from the last storm clouds that had not long passed over Tralee. It was only just after half past five in the evening but it was already dark and the street lighting, of which there wasn't much, lay patches of light here and there. The back streets were in total darkness apart from an odd lamp positioned on a few random corners. Heavy puddles still lay in the street and the drains were struggling to cope with the deluge it had just deposited.

Cain had decided that it was time to see how Connor coped with the dark. He knew that there would be times that he would need the boy to run him some errands or, as now seemed more likely, to follow somebody for him. Cain had now seen the true potential of his new foot soldier and his uses were becoming endless, after all, who would suspect a boy of nine years old.

Connor was now constantly telling Cain how he knew his way around the town like 'the back of his hand', something that he was now very proud of.

Well now he was going to find out if he really did.

The streets of Tralee were very different streets in the evening hours of darkness to the quiet daylight of the mornings.

Daibbi had been little concerned when Cain had told her that he needed Connor to help him with collecting the bottles on some evenings. He told her they needed to be collected as too many of them were being stolen and used for weapons and missiles since the latest outbreaks of violence. Eventually, she said he could go, but with the condition that he wasn't out after 8pm as that was his bed time. She had been struggling to get him up on some mornings as it was but she knew that he loved 'his job' as he called it and couldn't wait to help in anyway he could. 'One day Nana, I will be able to do it all on my own' he was always telling her.

As Cain stopped the cart in the town square the noise and din was still there but it was a different noise to the normal sounds that Connor heard in the early morning, which was the sound of market stall holders shouting in their singing tones. This was a much angrier place now. Fuelled by the beer and liquor that flowed from the pumps and taps within the three public houses that looked onto the square from three sides. The Stonebridge was the drinking house of mostly protestant men, although on several occasions recently, some of the catholic males that normally drank in the Reindeer, had crossed the square to try and claim the Stonebridge as their own. A full pitched battle had ensued which spilled out onto the square itself, with both sides suffering some injuries, two or three of them quite serious ones. A very uneasy peace had returned but you could feel the tension and anger bubbling just under the surface, ready to erupt at any given moment.

As Connor got off the cart, two drunken males fell out of the entrance to the Stonebridge grappling with each other in a playful game which was clearly in danger of turning into something more violent. And it was still before six o'clock in the evening. It could only get worse as the evening went on.

And it would.

As Cain and Connor walked towards the two men, in order to get to 'the Point', the men's 'game' was halted as both of their attention was turned towards the two of them, or more to the point, towards Cain. They knew who he was and by the look on their faces, they weren't very pleased to see him.

Connor could see it, it was that obvious, even to a nine year old. Connor instinctively dropped behind Cain and used him to shield him from the two men. Cain had sensed Connor's movement and without taking his gaze away from the two men, reached back with his left hand and grabbed the boy pulling him even nearer into his back for protection.

As they got almost level to them, the bigger one of the two cleared his throat and spat a mouthful of slime and snot towards Cain. Cain stopped dead, causing Connor to walk straight into the back of him as the mouthful dropped at Cain's feet, some of it splashing onto his boots.

Cain said nothing but stood staring at them both.

A quiet and stillness seemed to descend onto the square, as if the entire population of Tralee was about to witness the biggest boxing bout in Ireland's history, as they waited with bated breath for the first bell to sound.

But there was no bell. Cain knew very well when to pick his fights, and this was not one of them.

He looked at the man who had just spat phlegm towards him. He knew who he was. He'd seen him before, goading one of his farm workers a few weeks prior. He also knew his name.

He said in a quiet calm voice " Mr Bennett, this is your lucky day, its lucky because the boy here doesn't like violence. Now if you don't mind we will be on our way as we have work to do".

For a moment or two there was a uneasy standoff as the men decided what their next move would be. It was the other man that moved first, standing to the side to let them pass. Cain still held Connor behind him as he walked by.

As they got about 10 feet past them, Cain whispered to Connor, "turn around boy and look at them" Connor turned and did as he was asked and saw the two men follow them with their eyes, but nothing more.,

"it's okay Mr Milburn", said Connor "their not following us".

"Oh I'm not worried about that" said Cain "I knew they wouldn't follow us, I just wanted you to remember their faces, thats all".

Connor had done that already. He didn't know he had. But in his subconscious mind, Connor had memorised everything about them, their height, their build, their faces, their hair, their voices, even their smell. It was a gift that he had been given, and up to now, he didn't even know that he had it. But he was learning and he was learning fast. His senses were beginning to develop way beyond that of a normal person, let alone that of a 9 year old boy. His brain could store information from anywhere or anything within a millisecond and when he needed that information again, days, months or even years later it would appear immediately as if it had only happened yesterday. It was true, he did indeed have a gift, a wonderful unmeasurable, unseen to the naked eye gift, which, over the coming days, months, years and decades, would be used by both the good and bad.

"Ok boy, time to work" Cain said clapping his hands. The little incident that had just occurred was now of irrelevance, for the time being anyway.

"Now Connor, when we get behind 'the Point' you need to have your wits about you, all the time".

As soon as he had said it, he knew what was coming.

"What are my wits" asked Connor,

" I mean Connor, you need to be careful, and not only watch what you are doing, but you also need to watch what everybody else is doing too. There are some very nasty people out here tonight and a lot of them are up to no good. Just remember, don't look at anybody in the eye and before you say 'what does that mean', I mean don't look at anybody's face and do exactly what I have told and you won't get into any trouble".

Connor gave a rather nervous nod but he wasn't looking at Cain, he was looking at the mess and mayhem that was starting to build all around them as the square became alive with the buzz of people talking, shouting, arguing and laughing and all of it, at the same time.

"Come on let's go, I will follow you first then we will swap over", said Cain.

Connor slipped into the alleyway beyond 'the Point', empty basket in hand.

Before Connor had gone more than 30 yards he could barely see his hand in front of his face. It was pitch black. As he moved on, occasional bits of light seeped through the closed curtains of peoples windows but it wasn't much. 'How on earth was he going to see if anybody was behind him' thought Connor.

He needn't have worried. One of his senses was already kicking in and coming to his rescue.

Sound.

Beyond the square, in the back alleys surrounding it and especially at this time of night, they were virtually like a ghost town. You could hear a pin drop.

Without him knowing it, his sense of sound had gone into overdrive. As Cain followed him completely out of view, Connor could hear him. To his ears, it was if Cain were wearing wooden clogs, loud and clonking ,wooden clogs. His ears and brain were working together to block out all other sound there was and to concentrate on what was relevant.

Footsteps.

Nothing else. Just footsteps.

Without Connor knowing, his brain had also worked out that it was definitely a man's footsteps, not a woman's, the steps were too heavy and the stride were too long. It wasn't quick, but it was staying at the same distance from him, so it was a man. If it was a woman she would be walking quicker and with shorter steps.

Without thinking about it, without trying or having to work anything out, his natural instinct's had done it all for him. His brain was informing him that he was being followed by a heavy well built man and he was keeping pace about 30 to 40 yards behind him and when Connor stopped there was one more step from his pursuer before silence. His follower had also stopped.

Connor smiled to himself, as if pleased with himself for working it out.

But that was it. Connor the young boy not yet 10 years of age, had indeed worked it out. But because he was so young and naive he didn't even realise what he had actually done.

He backed into a corner, into the shadows of total darkness

and waited for Cain to walk around the corner.

He was working it out in his head. How long it would be before Cain walked around the Corner.

He counted down from ten as the footsteps got louder and louder and louder still, it was if somebody was hitting a piece of wood next to Connor's ear, it was so loud, 4.... Nearly here, 3.... Just around the corner 2.....here he comes... 1....

Connor froze.

It wasn't Cain.

It was Bennett.

* * *

SILENCE IS DEAFENING

As Connor stood frozen solid with his back to a cold wet brick wall in the dark black shadow's, another of his senses had kicked in.

Fear.

Fight or flight.

To a young boy of nine the first word meant very little. To try and fight a well built man of over six foot tall, didn't come into the equation.

Flight.

That's what his instincts were now telling him to do. Run and run for your life. But something, he didn't know what, something was telling him to stay right where he was. If he ran, he knew that if he got away, every time from now on when he saw Bennett, he would have to run again and again, it would go on for ever.

He stayed where he was. He wasn't going to be running away from anybody.

Bennett wasn't moving now, he was standing stone still. Connor could hear his own heart pounding. It was so loud. So loud in fact that he was sure that Bennett could hear it from where he stood all but 10 yards away.

The silence was deafening.

But Bennett wasn't looking for Connor.

He was looking for Cain.

He had followed him through the alleyway when Cain had left the square but had lost him after only a couple of corners within the darkness of the back alleyways. He'd heard the footsteps of somebody ahead and he had followed presuming it was Cain.

It wasn't.

It was Connor. But Bennett didn't know that, he couldn't see him.

Cain had actually heard Bennett enter the alleyway behind him and had hidden in a gateway letting him pass before coming out behind him. He now stood watching Bennett, standing, looking towards the darkness in the distance.

Cain knew where Connor probably was, if he had done as he had been taught, he was stood in the shadows, backed up to the wall, standing absolutely dead still.

He was.

Cain stood there and waited, he wasn't going to do anything, it was still not the right time or place. Not unless he had too, anyway. More importantly though, he didn't need Connor seeing what he was capable of or what steps he was prepared to take for 'the cause'.

He stood, waiting. He knew Bennett would move first. He had it written all over him, impatience, wanting to get it over and done with.

Bennett moved, very slowly forward, walking straight towards Connor.

'Don't you move boy, do not move' thought Cain as he willed his foot soldier to use every bit of his training that he had now so patiently given him. If he moved now, then his usefulness would be over and done with before it had even begun.

Connor didn't move. But he could see Bennett getting closer and closer with each footstep.

3 yards from Connor, Bennett stopped. And listened.

Cain stopped, and watched.

Connor stopped breathing.

The silence….just deafening.

Bennett stood now, he was looking straight at Connor. But he couldn't see him. The shadow had wrapped around him like a thick black envelope.

As Bennett stepped forward Cain matched each step perfectly in time to drown out his own footsteps.

If he needed to react he needed to be there quickly.

But Bennett carried on, he walked passed Connor totally unaware of his presence barely three feet from him. As he continued through the alleyway and away, Cain walked silently up to where he knew Connor would be.

"Now is the time boy, this is it", whispered Cain towards the shadowy darkness.

"You follow him now lad and then you tell me where he goes".

As he watched, a cold shiver suddenly swept down Cain's spine. It was if the whole of the shadowy dark corner had got up and moved as one, as the blackness slowly walked passed him, silently following its prey.

✻ ✻ ✻

THE FIRST FOLLOW

It was as if it was what he had been put here to do.

It was a gift, there was no doubt about that.

As Connor followed Bennett through the winding narrow alleyways, it was as if he was tied to him on a piece of elastic that would stretch from 30 yards to no more than 40 yards long. If he was on a straight, he automatically dropped back ,stretching that elastic, when he knew there was a bend, he closed up. It was all done with no thought, just on instinct alone.

The rain was now lashing down, the tinny sound from the rain hitting the tin roofs on sheds echoed all around as they bounced off the walls, small streams were now forming on each alley, the water racing by him faster than he was walking. As they wound their way along the streets and alleyways Connor knew exactly where they were. Not by name, as he still couldn't read, but he knew where he was. He knew that the journey had turned slowly to the left and they were now travelling downhill and south west towards the Stonebridge pub and the bridge behind.

He was heading for the Bogmen estate.

As they approached the stone steps that led steeply down towards the bridge the storm had increased, causing the little street streams to become a fast flowing torrent down the steps and onwards towards the river. Connor knew that this was where he was going to be most vulnerable. The bridge that crossed the River Lee spanned 40 yards across. That meant it was 40 yards with little or no cover. It had a three foot ascent to the middle and the same descent on the opposite side. It was 10 foot wide with 3 foot high walls on both sides. The walls were two foot thick made of thick granite blocks bought over from Scotland almost 100 years ago. Two 5 foot pillars on each side stood at intervals 10 yards from either end of the bridge. Perfect cover for a nine year old boy. A single lamppost stood on either end of the bridge as though they were put there to define the size of it.

He saw the silhouette of Bennett slowly climbing the eastern side of the bridge. It was still very dark but he knew it was definitely him. His brain had sketched his size, shape and gate indelibly into his memory. There forever more if he should so need it.

As Bennett got half way across and into the darker centre of the bridge, Connor waited, he had sensed what Bennett was about to do. As he stood in the shadows of the tall north facing wall of the Stonebridge pub, he stood and watched as Bennett stopped, turned, and then walk towards the West side of the bridge and then lean on the wall, looking back towards where he had just come from. Connor stood deadly still as Bennett reached into his breast pocket and pulled out a cigarette and lit it, not taking his eyes from the East side of the bank. As Connor stood, the only thing he could hear was the rain and the fast flowing and swollen River Lee as it passed under the bridge before him. As he looked towards the man, it felt as if Bennett was staring straight back at him. In fact, he was doing just exactly that, but he couldn't see him. Connor knew that as well. He'd been taught well and had been told to trust his own decision making as to where to conceal himself. He was now doing just that, although it was still a little unnerving looking at somebody who appeared to be looking straight back at you from no more than 30 yards away. But a little over fifteen minutes ago he'd learnt one most important thing, that the darkness was now his friend.

Bennett stood, drawing on the last few remnants of his cigarette, happy that he was alone and nobody was following him.

He had been convinced that when he entered the alleyway Milburn was only a few yards in front of him. He was going to give him what he deserved. He was a devious catholic bastard and the word was that he was behind some of the attacks that had been carried out on some of his friends from the Bogmen. But where had he gone, he had followed him and he had heard him walking through the alleyway's just in front of him. But then he had just disappeared. Just vanished into thin air. No matter, he would get him another day in another dark alley. He flicked his cigarette over the wall and into the river and carried on towards the West side and home.

Connor had seen the red embers somersaulting into the river and watched as Bennett slowly descended the bridge on the far side. He moved, still in the shadows but towards the edge of the bridge. He moved fast but not running, towards the first pillar 10 yards in front of him. Then stopped and watched. He could see that Bennett had left the bridge and turned right and was now walking at some pace further into the Bogmen.

Connor walked to the far side of the bridge.

He paused.

He sensed it in himself.

Apprehension.

This was now totally uncharted territory for him. He couldn't rely on his brain to have memorised these streets, he had never been this side of the river before, let alone on the Bogmen estate. Should he turn back and if he did what would Cain say to him.

He moved on.

He could see that these streets were not as old as the East side of the river. The Bogmen estate was newer than the old town. There was still very little street lighting but where there was some, it was a different colour to that on the other side, it was more of an orange colour. The houses were only two storey's high and the streets, although still mostly cobbled, were a little wider. Connor silently closed on Bennett as he crossed the road towards another street off to the left. As he went along, his brain was now subconsciously memorising his every twist and turn that he took.

After 2 or 3 minutes and two more turns, one left and one right, Connor saw Bennett slow slightly, it wasn't much, just enough for Connor to sense that something was going to happen. Connor, 40 yards behind him, backed into a small gap between a wall and a hedge. Bennett continued to walk away from him but he waited, he didn't know why, he just did. After 5 more paces Bennett swung around facing back towards his direction and ran back towards him. Connor froze. 'He couldn't have seen me, it wasn't possible', he thought. But as Bennett reached the spot where he had just previously paused he turned to his left and banged on the front door of a small terraced house. After only seconds the door opened and Bennett walked inside closing the door quietly behind him.

He waited.

He waited for what seemed like hours before he dared to move. But it was in fact only 10 minutes before he slowly moved from his hiding place. He walked slowly on the opposite side of the street towards the house where Bennett had entered. As he got level with it he took the slightest glance and noted its number into his memory bank. It was a two and a one. He knew what numbers were and how to count but there it ended.

He carried on turned right then right again and made his way back to the bridge.

15 minutes or so later he was back on the edge of the square at the exit of The Siul . As he came out onto the square next to the Stonebridge pub he could see Cain about forty yards away, talking to four men, close to the entrance of 'the Point.'

As Cain saw him, Connor saw two things happen.

The first thing he saw was Cain speak to the men, who then all immediately turned and walked away, all in different directions.

The second thing he saw was a man in a long black coat and black hat standing 30 yards or so further on past 'The Point'. He was leaning against a wall and was watching Cain and the group of men. As the men turned away from Cain the man in the black turned left and walked away towards the North side of the square.

The man in black hadn't seen Connor.

And Cain hadn't seen the man in black.

As Connor walked towards Cain he couldn't help smiling at him as he felt really good about what he had just done, but Cain soon got rid of the smile.

"Where the fucking hell have you been boy", he snarled at Connor.

Connor shocked by Cain's reaction couldn't find the words to answer.

Cain carried on " You've been gone nearly 45 minutes, I was getting very worried about you, I have your Grandmother to answer too as you well know. Now get yourself on this cart and lets get you home before both of us end up in the shit, and get yourself under that cover before you die of pneumonia".

Connor climbed aboard and Cain set off at a faster pace than usual.

As they made their way back, Connor told him how he had followed Bennett into the Bogmen and he assured Cain that he hadn't been seen by Bennett or anybody else.

"Did you see which way he went when he went over the bridge" said Cain,

"Yes I did Mr Milburn, he turned right when he got to the other side".

Cain, now calming a little, after Connor's safe return was pleased with what Connor had done.

"Well thats good work lad I suppose, but you shouldn't have been away so long, we were getting a bit worried about where you had got too",

"We" said Connor shocked, "You haven't told my Nana have you, she'll go mad".

Cain quickly realising his mistake got out of it.

"No, no, I mean me and Duke here, we were worried about you thats all, and why didn't you come back through 'The Point', I told you that if you were in trouble you must always get back to there",

"Oh okay, but I wasn't in trouble Mr Milburn, so I didn't think that I needed to come back that way, I saw him go into number two and one and then I came straight back" said Connor.

Cain swung around in his seat "what did you just say",

"I said I hadn't done anything wrong so I didn't think",

"No no no" interrupted Cain "what did you say about two and one",

"Oh, that man Bennett went into a house with the number two and one on the door",

"You mean that you followed him all the way to his house" said Cain not quite believing what he had just heard.

"Yes" said Connor, 'he knocked on the door and was let in".

He then described his exact route to an astonished Cain. Cain got a piece of paper from under his seat and asked him to draw it. It soon became clear to Cain as to where Bennett could be found. If of course, that became necessary.

Cain now knew that Bennett lived at 21 Ballygenny Road.

He would soon be getting a visit.

Cain also knew that he now needed to write his messages differently.

No more numbers.

And so it began..........

One week later, the local paper announced that the body of David Bennett, a Protestant from Tralee had been found by his wife in their back yard at 7:30 on the morning of Saturday 1st of January 1916. it was thought that he had died due to head injuries received from several blows to the head with a heavy implement. The new years revelry and drunken celebrations, within the town, were thought to be a contributing factor.

But many believed the celebrations had absolutely nothing to do with it.

✽ ✽ ✽

TROUBLED TIMES

24th April 1916 Ireland

Irish Republican's had launched armed attacks in Dublin and other parts of Ireland and proclaimed an Irish Republic. The Easter uprising had begun. In the next few days the British, with much greater weaponry and numbers, would suppress the rising but not before it had brought Republicanism back to the forefront of Irish politics.

2 Days Later and 560 Miles Away.

26th April 1916 Vermelles Northern France.

Riley's war had at last begun. He had been in France almost 6 months, but had remarkably not seen any action, due mostly to the confusion of war. But that was about to all change, and not for the good. Within the next few days he was about to see things that would remain with him to the day he died.

He had gone, as he had told Daibbi in his letter, to the stabling yards in Vermelles, to start his new job, looking after army horses, or so he thought. On his arrival, he had been sent to see the commanding officer of the mounted section, Major Cassell.

As he waited in the corridor of the town hall, which had been commandeered as the Headquarters of the 16th, he sat and pondered what his future held for him in the coming weeks. He knew, from what he had heard that he was very near the front line now, but he had still not seen any action of any real kind.

As a tall wiry man approached him, Riley stood immediately to attention. "Gillian, I presume" smiled the man before him, "Yes Sir", Riley replied.

The man thrust out his hand "Major Cassell, very pleased to have you aboard".

They walked out to the rear of the building and into the courtyard. As the Major held his arms out wide he said,

"welcome to you new place of work, how long that will be for remains to be seen, but for now this is it".

He liked the Major from the off. He had a kind but authoritative manner about him, and rather surprisingly, thought Riley, in the current surroundings, a very sharp wit. The Major then took time to show him around the stables and introduced him to some of the other soldiers that were around.

"Ok Gillian, or shall I call you Riley" said the smiling Major Cassell.

"No, I think its definitely going to have to be Gillian, for if I shout Riley around here half the bloody regiment will turn around" laughed the Major.

They both laughed as they walked up to one of the horses stabled in the yard.

"Right Gillian, this beauty here is Blue, he's a fine lad, a bit of a handful but if you show him who's boss you'll be fine, throw his saddle on and we'll head on out".

Riley stood there a little confused but did as he was asked as the Major walked towards a second horse across the courtyard.

The Major shouted from across the cobbled square, "And this Gillian, is my boy, this is Jacko, and no matter whatever anybody tells you, he IS mine and nobody, that is, nobody, else's".

He smiled widely at Riley and then kissed Jacko on the side of his neck.

Five minutes later they rode out of the stable yard and paused briefly at the gate.

"Ok" said the Major pointing to his right "about 2 miles that way is Hulluch, and although it seems very quite this morning, I think we'll turn left and have a little ride, away from the drama for now".

Riley having only just arrived this very morning had no idea what the Major was talking about but was more than happy aboard his new friend Blue. He had looked in the horse's eye and could see a kind and calmness about him. He already knew that things would be fine. This 16'2 Irish draft, built like a pocket battleship was made for just this. War.

As they rode, the Major expertly explained the lay of the land around them, he was clearly not a Desk Major. He had obviously been out travelling these lanes for sometime. He told Riley they were now travelling West and away from the front line, which was about 3 miles to the East of the town hall and beyond the small village of Hulluch.

As they rode quietly through the small hedgerow lined lanes, twisting and turning through the beautiful countryside of Northern France, chatting as they went, it all seemed surreal, how could this be war. War was about death and destruction, blood and guts, kill or be killed. Riley had seen none of this. He didn't really want to see it. But he felt a fraud. This wasn't what he had in mind when he had joined up. He'd joined to fight to turn a wrong into a right. To avenge those poor women and children that had drowned abroad the cruise ship Lusitania.

He wouldn't be feeling a fraud before the day had done.

They'd been riding for just twenty minutes when........ Boom

"Here we go" said the Major "their late this morning , must be building up to something, its not usually this quiet".

Riley sat still, stunned by the noise of the blast, but what he was more astounded and shocked by, was his horse. Blue hadn't moved a muscle. He hadn't bucked or thrown him off, he hadn't jumped to the side or even shown the slightest concern as to what had just happened. It was like he was sitting in an armchair.

"Told you he'd be ok didn't I. He's rock solid is Blue, Davy loved him. They are all pretty sure though. Once they get used to the bangs and booms going on around them they won't throw you, unless one lands right next to them or they step on a mine".

Riley just looked at the Major, still in shock. It all seemed so matter of fact.

"I take it for the look on your face that you haven't seen much action so far Gillian".

"No sir, nothing at all, this is my first day anywhere near the front".

The Major looked at him in amazement "Nothing, you mean you haven't been shot at, bombed or gassed yet".

Riley just shook his head.

"My god Gillian, I'm sorry, I didn't know that, we better be gentle with you then, they say if you last the first week then your chance of survival increases somewhat".

"Lets hope so" said Riley.

They started to turn right along the lanes and Riley felt that they were going around in a circular route and were now more or less heading back in the direction to which they had come from.

Three loud explosions then boomed out from some distance in front of them followed by a horrible yellow cloud that slowly rose up and started billowing in the wind.

The Major went into battle mode in an instant "Gas, get your mask's and be quick about it, they are on the back of your saddle, put it on now, and then put Blues on" Yelled the Major.

Riley did as asked as the Major did the same.

They waited to see which way the gas cloud dispersed before they moved.

As the gas began to move to their right they remounted and the Major took them quickly on a half circular route to the left as the gas moved away from them. They crossed some uneven ground, all at a gallop. Now off the road, they began jumping hedges and gates, the Major turning occasionally to make sure Riley was still with him and also noting the excellent ability of his riding.

As they came back to a walk the Major looked at Riley and appeared deep in thought. As they rode on in silence it was the Major who eventually spoke "I think I might have just the job for you and Blue here".

Riley looked at him thoughtfully "I thought that I already had a job and that I was here to look after the horse's sir",

"No no, we need all the horsemen we can get. No Gillian, I think you and Blue here could become a very good team".

As they rode slowly back towards the stabling yard, the Major asked Riley where he was from and how had he become so accomplished on a horse. As they rode on Riley told him a brief history of his life, but he still had one burning question to ask the Major.

"Sir, my I ask a question"

"Yes Gillian of course, but if its, 'when do you think this war will be over', then the answer will be, as it always is, 'it will be earlier for some than it will be for others".

"No Sir, it wasn't that, I was just wondering who Davy was",

"Ah Davy".

The Major seemed to drift into somewhere else for a few seconds before he replied.

"Davy was a good soldier, he was also a true gentleman, and a very good friend",

"You speak sir, as if he is no longer here",

"Yes Gillian, your right, Davy is no longer with us, he is in fact sadly no longer in this world, and we all miss him dearly".

They both rode on in silence and soon they were back at the stabling yard.

"Gillian, if you would be so kind as to put Jacko in his stable, there is something I need to attend to as a matter of urgency. When you have done that, come to my quarters, and we will speak".

"Yes Sir" replied Riley and as he saluted the Major was already hurrying away.

An hour later Riley was led into the Quarters of Major Cassell.

Once shown inside, Riley saw that the room had in fact once been the town library.

Each wall, which was at least 12' high, had hundreds and hundreds of books stacked in neat rows on solid oak shelves to just below the ceiling. As he was marched across the polished oak floor the Major was sat at his leather topped desk. Sat to his right was another man who Riley had not yet met.

They both stood as Riley approached them and the Major said " now Riley let me introduce you to Corporal Hayworth".

Hayworth was a small stocky man with a ruddy complexion with a shock of thick blonde hair. He had the rugged appearance of a former boxer, and, thought Riley, ' not a very good one, judging by his very flat bent nose. Hayworth looked at Riley who at 6'1" towered over his own 5'6" frame, thrust out his arm and shook Riley's hand. His grip was more than vice like, and Riley wondered if it had been done on purpose to prove something of a point.

"Welcome to hell" said Hayworth, smiling at Riley and now showing him that he had lost at least three of his front teeth. 'definitely a boxer' thought Riley.

Riley smiled back at him "I'm sure it can't be that bad Corporal".

"I'll ask you in a week, thats if your'e still alive, and it's Harry " said Hayworth still smiling.

"Now then Harry" said the Major "lets not scare him to death, I'm sure Riley here is just as much hoping to stay alive as we all are. Now lets sit down and discuss what needs to be done".

The Major then went on to explain that since the death of Davy, they were short of a good horseman. He had explained to Hayworth that he wished to give Riley a go, he knew that he couldn't replace Davy but from what he had seen this morning he was more than happy with his riding skills and that given time and with the help from Hayworth, who would be his mentor, they could become an excellent team.

Riley looked at them both, he had to admit that it felt good to be part of something, but what that something was he still wasn't quite sure. "Sir I'm very pleased that you have shown your confidence in me, but I must ask, why me, and, what is it that I will actually be doing".

"Yes Riley, I'm sorry, please let me explain. Firstly, the reason, or should I say, reason's, as to why I have chosen you are these. One, as I have witnessed this morning, your riding skills are excellent, two, you look like you can look after yourself, and three, well, three is,…I haven't actually got anybody else".

The three of them broke into smiles and a little laughter echoed around the library walls, probably, for the first time in a while.

The Major and Hayworth then went on to explain that the vast majority of there work was done behind enemy lines. It was done, obviously, in total secrecy, and normally, in the dead of night. Almost all of it was done on horseback and sometimes it meant that they would be gone for days, using pigeons to communicate their information back to the intelligence department. No uniforms were worn and no identification papers were taken.

"You are on your own over there, just the two of you, if you are unlucky enough to be caught, then expect to be shot as a spy" said the Major.

Their job was to go behind enemy lines and mark the enemy's positions, their numbers, and where their weak spots were. They were to bring the information back or if that wasn't possible then they would send a pigeon back with it. It they met any trouble then guns were not to be used unless in the last resort. If you needed to defend yourself then knife, rope or bare hands were to be used. "And" said the Major almost in a whisper "we take no prisoners, do you understand".

Riley looked at the Major and just nodded his acknowledgement, he didn't need to speak.

The Major then went on to say that Davy had been doing the job with Hayworth for the last twelve months. They had been getting fantastic results and they had been looking to expand to at least two more teams. But Davy had been caught. He was caught three miles behind enemy lines close to some ammunition dumps in the Somme valley. Hayworth who had been with Davy at the time had managed to get away in the confusion and darkness and had managed to hide in amongst ammunition boxes as the four German soldiers had dragged Davy away. Hayworth had sometime later, in the early hours of the morning, been able to move to a nearby hedgerow, but had remained there in the hope that he could somehow free his colleague and then both escape back to the British lines in order to fight another day.

As daylight had approached, the horror of what was happening to Davy could now be seen by Hayworth who was still unable to move from his position just fifty yards away. Davy had been pegged out on the ground, on his back, in the shape of a horizontal crucifix. They, the German soldiers, were taking it in turns to kick him about the body, but one in particular, the tall one, seemed to like using Davy's head as a football. He, to the cheers of his fellow soldiers, had now started to take a run up to deliver his blow's. He could hear the groan's of Davy as each kick hit its target. This continued throughout the day, but the groan's had stopped sometime ago and the blows were now getting no response from the stricken British soldier. The German soldiers now getting bored, occasionally took a break to have a drink and sit laughing and smoking their cigarettes. Hayworth didn't know if Davy was still alive or not but it was still horrendous to watch. By the time the sun had set he was sure that Davy was now dead. As night turned into the early hours of the morning Hayworth knew that now was the time that he needed to get away. But he couldn't leave Davy. If he was dead or alive, he just couldn't do it. In the darkness, he had made his way across to where he had last seen him pegged to the ground. As he got there he could see his lifeless body, contorted in an obscene shape. He looked for the soldiers, but they were nowhere to be seen. He slowly crept over to Davy and he knew straight away that he was indeed dead. He skin felt like that of a dead fish, clammy and wet. He cut him from his ties and, though Davy was considerably bigger than himself, he threw him over his shoulder and began to carry him the four hundred yards back to where they had hidden their horses the day before. But after only fifty yards he had heard them.

The soldiers. They were over to his left somewhere.

He slowly lowered Davy's body to the ground and took out his knife. In the distance about 50 yards away, he saw the shadows of the four soldiers. They were all laughing and sounded quite drunk. As he had watched, he saw three of them turn away from him and walk back towards a small wooded area that was about sixty yards away which was silhouetted by the moonlit sky. The forth soldier had carried on walking, generally towards his direction but slightly to his left.

Hayworth could see it was the footballer and he knew exactly where he was going.

He was going to have his one last kick before bedtime.

Only this time he wouldn't be waking up.

As Hayworth crouched behind the hedgerow he let him walk on and when he was about ten yards away he followed him from behind, matching his stride. He closed on him with rapid steps and as he got two paces behind him, he grabbed his jaw, pulled his head to the side and slit his throat.

It was over in seconds.

Hayworth wasn't finished though. As the dying soldier

slumped to the floor he quietly followed him down, still holding on to his head, and stared into his flickering dying eyes. Without breaking his stare he reached back to the right boot of the dying soldier and pulled it off.

He then rammed it into his still gurgling mouth.

Two days later Hayworth rode into the camp with the body of Davy "Crockett" Jones laying over his saddle on the back of Blue.

Such are the horrors of war.

They all sat there in silence for a moment, as if it should be so, for Davy's sake.

Eventually the Major broke the stillness within the library.

He coughed slightly to clear his throat and with his voice, still a little shaky, he said "So Riley, I ask you this…..do you still want in".

Riley looked at the stern and saddened faces of the soldiers in front of him.

"Sir, it would be an honour".

※ ※ ※

IF ONLY THEY KNEW

The next day, Thursday 27th April 1916

Vermelles Northern France

Just before dawn, the dull thud of an explosion woke Riley from his restless sleep. He, as did the rest of the soldiers in their makeshift sleeping quarters in the Town Hall, dressed as quickly as they could and rushed outside. It was clear to see what had just happened. A large yellow gas cloud was billowing across the sky about a mile and a half away over the British held ground within the village of Hulluch. Many soldiers grabbed their gas masks and ran over to the two of the lorries that were already waiting to go. As Riley stood waiting and deciding what he should do he saw Corporal Harry Hayworth hurrying towards to him.

"Get Blue ready Riley, wer'e going out".

at 07:00hrs precisely, as Riley and Hayworth rode out on their mounts towards the southeastern side of the trenches of Hulluch, an unbelievable scene was unfolding back home in southern Dublin, Ireland.

The republican army had deployed men on bicycles to replenish stocks of ammunition to the men on the front line who were returning fire on the British army who, in turn, were dug in, in trenches, which they had dug the night before.

The first armed action of the Irish Republicans and the British had begun.

These initial skirmishes were not to last long due to the overpowering numbers of the British and their firepower.

This, as the Commanders of the republicans all knew, would have to change. The increase in the numbers of recruits wasn't going to be a problem. The feelings of many a man, especially in the south of Ireland, was that something needed to be done and it needed to be done now, drastic action was now required. Men were joining the republican movement in their thousands.

The problem was fire power. They had very little. What little they did have was old and unreliable. A shipment of arms, which had secretly been sent from Germany for the Republican cause, had been intercepted by the British just prior to the start of the uprising and it had been a massive blow to them.

The word had been put out to all senior leaders of the IRA to prioritise the procurement of arms, in whatever form they may be, bullets, sidearms, rifles, grenades, explosives. Anything that would help the cause, was to be obtained and secured. It was then to be hidden, and be readily accessible if and when it was required. Only a select few were to know the location of these stashes and if any of the arms was required only the ones in the know were to retrieve them and they intern were to pass it on to a third person for delivery.

08:30hrs Manor Farm Rossbridge

Cain was sat at his father's desk in the study. As he read the note, hand delivered to him that morning, a smile crept onto his face.

'At last' he thought something was beginning to happen. He had become frustrated at the lack of action that had been taken by his fellow republicans in the wake of attacks on his fellow men.

It didn't say it in words, but this was indeed his call to arms.

His father had now stood down as the man that everybody had to answer to in the West of Ireland, he had served his country well, but now it was time for change. A more ruthless measure of action was now required and he was the man to help this cause.

He was now to be second in command of the Western side of

Ireland. The Leader himself, had sent the letter congratulating him on his promotion and also on the success of the recent attacks in Tralee. It went on to say that from here on in there would be a more rigid rank structure, not only in this part of Ireland but covering the whole of Ireland, thus bringing more organisation, stability, and discipline to the organisation. Random attacks could still take place but if they were going to be of high profile then authority should be given by the local head of command before any action could be taken.

As he read that, Cain's smile broadened further. 'As far as he was concerned he shouldn't have any trouble getting things done'.

It also mentioned, that even more stealth should be used regarding meetings and any correspondence between members should be kept to a minimum.

Information had been received from an informant, that the police had now begun to use undercover officers. Therefor should any persons be identified or suspected of being one of these officers then it should immediately be brought to the attention of the higher command and a decision would be taken as to the plan of action.

The note then told the recipient to burn the letter and to ensure that nothing remained of it.

It was signed and sealed by the new Commander

Head of operations South West.

❋ ❋ ❋

HEAVEN AND HELL

08:30 Hulluch Northern France.

As Hayworth and Riley rode steadily out of Vermelles towards the village of Hulluch, the gas had now dispersed. The smell of the chloride was still in the air but it had lost its potency.

But it was the bodies, they were everywhere.

Riley had seen a dead body before but this was totally different.

The corpses of men lay distorted, as they had died, in pain gasping for the their breath, as their lungs burned a fire within them. A few horses lay alongside them who had also been dealt the same fate. Even a few cows in the fields had succumbed to the dreaded gas.

Hundreds and hundreds of bodies were laying in the fields, at the sides of the road, everywhere you looked, it was total death.

"Jesus" said Hayworth as he looked around stunned at the brutal barbaric scene in before them "there must be half of the regiment here, there's hundreds of them".

As they rode on through the mayhem and slaughter the feeling of being inadequate and totally useless began to overwhelm Riley. 'Surely there must be something that could be done for these poor souls'.

"This is not for us Riley" Said Hayworth in a respectful whisper.

"There is nothing here for us to do now. Somebody else will bury them, don't feel guilty. They wont know we have passed them by, they are in a better place now, let's leave em be". They nodded their heads to the dead and carried on they're way.

The two of them were dressed in civilian clothing to mirror those of farming stock, something which Riley felt comfortable with. But what he didn't feel comfortable with was the language. No matter how good he was at naturally being a farmer he was not at all natural at being a frenchman. He couldn't speak a word. He therefor felt somewhat reassured that, as Hayworth had already told him, he was fluent in french.

As they turned to the south east and moved parallel to the front line with it at its nearest, about a mile to their left, they could hear the sound of heavy shelling, the occasional gunshot and short burst of machine gun fire, but it was all at a distance too far away to worry them. They moved with cover for most of the time, not that Riley knew when they did have or didn't have it but he knew that he was in safe hands with Hayworth.

As they moved quietly through a small wood he could sense that Hayworth had relaxed slightly and he, for some reason, could sense it in Blue too. It was as if they all knew that for now, no harm would come their way.

"Soon we will soon be at the Deule" said Hayworth. The Deule was a canal that ran north to south and which occasionally broke into natural river.

"There is a small bridge that crosses it and from there we will follow it North for a time and then turn North west, from then Riley we will be on our own, we will be behind enemy lines. They have a small break in their defences, they will cover it soon I'm sure, but we have been through it five times in the last few months so let's go and see if its still there ".

They continued until early evening when they then held their position at the edge of a small copse and waited for nightfall.

With the horses well hidden, thirty yards or so further into the copse, Riley and Hayworth sat and ate what they had. As they did they quietly talked about many things, of how Hayworth had run away from home to join the army. He'd run away due to his alcoholic father's beating's, and how he had forever since felt guilty in leaving his younger brother and his mother to suffer in his absence. After three years away he had returned home to find that his Mother had left his father and was now living in America with her new husband. His brother had also left and had also joined the army. He knew that he joined the fusiliers and that he too was fighting somewhere in this war but where exactly, he didn't know. Riley had told him the reason's why he had eventually joined up and he had spoken about Daibbi, Connor and Aibbi, but didn't go into too much detail other than how much he missed them all and couldn't wait to get back home and see them all again. But in the end the conversation usually came back to Davy. Riley could see and hear in Hayworth's voice that the anger was still raw. But he could also see that Davy had been a truly inspirational figure in the life of not only Hayworth, but that of the whole regiment and no more so than that of their leader, Major Cassell. There was no doubt that Cassell, Hayworth and Davy had been a close knit team and Riley felt privileged that he should be asked to fill, what he felt was, his somewhat unfillable boots. But he would do his best. He liked Hayworth, he could tell that he could trust him and he liked to think that Hayworth felt the same.

As it approached midnight they had seen movement to their west of several platoons moving southwest towards the front. Hayworth had noted their position in his head, and due to their locality delayed their exit from the copse.

"We'll wait a while Riley I think, give till 01:00hrs then have another look, I'm not too happy moving till they have some ground away from us, what do you think".

The last four words had let Riley know that he had been truly accepted into the fold. Four words, but they were the best four words he had heard since getting to France that was for sure.

He had just one word for it.

Trust.

At a little past 01:00 they made their way quietly along the lane towards the Deule. As described by Hayworth, there it was, the small foot bridge, barely wide enough for the horses but they crossed it to the Eastern side without any problems.

As they moved silently on, they rode at a walk along the towpath, a six foot hedge giving them good cover. Hayworth took the lead with Riley and Blue, two strides behind them. They were to follow the canal for about two miles until they would cross back to the West side across a very small old bridge that had been built at least two hundred years previously, probably to service the local farm.

As they reached the bridge, Riley could already feel Blue becoming a little more tense, nothing drastic but he could definitely sense a change.

Hayworth had stopped just prior to the bridge.

"We need to put the mufflers on" said Hayworth.

They both dismounted and Riley held the two horses as Hayworth retrieved the eight small hessian sacks, four from his own rucksack and four from Riley's. He then filled each sack with straw from the field at the side of them. He then placed each hoof of the horse's into the sacks, tying them as to stop them falling off. The horse's didn't bat an eyelid as Hayworth went about his task with urgency but not at a panic. Riley had never seen it done before but then again why would he. Not many horses had ever been used to sneak about in the middle of the night.

As soon as they were ready they remounted and slowly

crossed to the bridge. Riley was amazed at the difference the 'mufflers' made. There was virtually no sound at all from the horse's hoofs as they hit the stone road beneath them.

They travelled along the track, tall thick ancient hedgerows on both sides keeping them in the shadows and shielding them from the moon shining brightly above. They continued in a westerly direction for about fifteen minutes until Hayworth turned abruptly to the left and straight down into a ditch. Blue followed them instinctively, he'd been here before, he knew exactly where they were going.

The ditch was at least six feet deep and around four feet wide with a small stream of water running along it. Hayworth got off his horse and silently gave his reins too Riley to hold. He walked past him and Riley turned to see Hayworth using a thick branch to brush the grass and mud to hide the fact that horse's had descended into the ditch. He smiled at Riley as he took his reins "your going to like the next bit, just follow me" whispered Hayworth.

He remounted and they moved forward along the ditch. Almost immediately they were in a tunnel, not one made of brick, but made of thick, bushy, prickly hedgerow and brambles. It was at least three foot thick on both sides and above . The branches above them, equally as thick, curved just over their heads. They were completely invisible to the outside. It was also totally pitch black. It was if a miner from a welsh coal mine had burrowed out a shaft in the French countryside for them to walk in, totally undetected from the outside. You wouldn't be seen in daylight let alone in the middle of the night. But moving through it at night was safer all round. But that wasn't all.

It went on, slowly weaving and climbing higher and higher northward for almost two miles.

Two miles deep into enemy territory, right under their very noses.

Riley was amazed. How on earth did Hayworth know that this existed.

They moved slowly on, every now and then there was a gentle sound of splashing water from one of the horses as the ditch got a little deeper. But other than that there was nothing to give them away.

After about forty minutes they stopped. Riley could see that they had come out into a small opening which then went into a large wooded area, most of which were huge oak tree's.

Hayworth repeated the process of hiding their tracks as they climbed out of the ditch and then they rode on through the wood, now turning in a southwesterly direction. Haworth then stopped and dismounted and signalled Riley to do so.

They tied the horses to some trees and then Riley heard Hayworth moving what sounded like bushes across the ground. They then both moved slowly forward to what Riley could see was the edge of the wood.

They crawled through some undergrowth for what seemed like forever until they eventually dropped down the edge of an embankment into a rocky clearing. they both then sat with their back's to a heavy oak tree looking down at a vast valley, the moonlight causing shadows over the rolling ground tumbling away from them. It was now 04:20.

"This will be our home for a day or two Riley, you'll see why when daylight breaks, but for now you better get some sleep. I'll keep watch, I will wake you at 07:00".

Riley nodded. He couldn't possibly sleep, his head was full of questions, but he'd try.

He slept.

He slept a deep sleep.

When he woke, it was with a start and for a moment he completely forgot where he was and what he was doing.

As he came to his senses and looked around him, he could see that he was in what appeared to be some sort of a shelter. It wasn't your normal type of shelter built out of rocks and wood with a steel roof, but it was a shelter all the same. The back of it had been carved out from the cliffside and was about five feet high from floor to ceiling. The ceiling itself then stretched out from the rear wall about six foot, it was made of a tapestry of weaved branches and ferns and was so thick you could see nothing through it. The shelter was as wide as it was deep, six foot square, ample room for two men. The sides were again dug out from the earth and rock, but the floor was of solid rock. Hanging from the left hand wall from a cut off branch were two gas masks. There was also one pair of binoculars and folded up in the corner was a telescope attached to a tripod.

He was in some sort of a man made hide.

Hayworth was sat leaning against the left hand wall and was looking forwards out the opening to the front which was about eighteen inches high and spanned the entire front of the shelter. Underneath the opening it had a two foot wall made from thick pivot branches which was attached to the walls at either end by twine tied to branches that grew from the side walls.

Hayworth had sensed his new housemate stirring.

Without turning around he spoke, not in a whisper, but still very quietly.

"Good morning my sleeping beauty, I didn't wake you as I thought you might need the rest".

"I'm so sorry Harry, I cant believe I've overslept, what time is it".

"Just after 08:00, but don't worry about it, we've got no appointments scheduled for the day" said a smiling Hayworth.

As Riley washed the sleep from his eyes Hayworth looked at the tattooed 'D, A and C' on Riley's inner left wrist, he watched as Riley gently kissed the letters in turn,

" You really are missing them aren't you".

" I am Harry, I really am, but I give them a kiss every morning and every night, they are in my heart".

" Well lets hope this is all over soon. Now, it's getting busy down there, so come up here and enjoy the view".

As Riley moved slowly forward, shuffling across the stone floor on his backside, the panoramic view that the hide had, started to come into view.

And .... Oh what a view it was.

As he leant on the opposite wall to Hayworth on the right hand side, he stared in disbelieve at the view before him. Their viewing platform was at least six hundred feet above the river that flowed below. The valley that stretched out either side of the river and dropped down beneath them, was at least two miles wide and they could see, from left to right, at least three miles in each direction.

He felt like he was an angel looking down at the beautiful earth below.

Only he was about to find out that the sprawling fields below was more like hell on earth to the poor souls that were down there.

As they both sat silently taking in the view, the clouds cast shadows that moved swiftly across the valley, changing its colours from greens to browns and yellows to reds, the fields separated by a patchwork of hedgerows that made it look like a chessboard that changed with each cloud that passed over it.

The river now sparkled in the new sun that had risen and had passed over the opposite ledge of the valley and started to reflect on its every tiny flow that hit a rock or crashed against the bank. It was as if somebody was floating hundreds of candles gently down the river. The peak of the ledge on the opposite to them was not even half as high as the ground which they were now on and didn't afford the fantastic view which they had.

"Impressive isn't it" said Hayworth.

"Where the hell are we Harry" said Riley, still looking around in total amazement at the unreal view that spread out before him.

'Riley, you are looking at the valley of death. Such a harsh name you may think, judging by the stunningly beautiful sight that spreads out before us. But I can assure you that within the hour my friend, you won't, and never will again, feel the same about the view that beholds you at this moment".

As they sat watching, Hayworth explained to them where they were.

On the other side of the valley to them were the British, now having pushed the Germans back, they held the ground to the west of the river. The Germans were on the East side of the valley.

" Yes Riley, I know what your next question is going to be, we are on the East side of the river, held by the Germans and we're surrounded by them, thankfully though, we know that, but they don't".

He then went on to explain that the ride up the enclosed ditch had actually took them, at some points, up to four miles behind enemy lines. They had found it by accident when he and Davy had needed to get off the road quickly on a previous deployment and had plunged into the ditch when they had heard German soldiers suddenly coming in their direction and had nowhere else to go. They had hidden in the ditch under the overhanging hedgerow while a number of German soldiers had made their way past them in broad daylight.

They had waited for an hour before they had dared to move. As they were about to turn around and climb back out of the ditch, Davy, who was in front on Blue, had moved on through a small covering of brambles and hawthorn and had found himself within a tunnel of part ditch and part natural hedgerow. As he continued to move further into the naturally created tunnel, he had started to wonder how far it actually carried on for. He had dismounted Blue and walked back to Hayworth quietly signalling for him to follow him into the covering. Once inside he could see the ditch was at least five foot deep, and even deeper in places. It was also, for most of the time three to four feet wide, it had a small stream flowing through it which for most of the year was no more than ten inches deep. They had then tied both of the horses up, still within the ditch, and had then made their way on foot for over two hours, clearing the way as they went, occasionally climbing out when the opportunity arose, to check on their progress and location. They knew, from the constant climb that they were climbing towards the top of the valley. But when they had actually got to the top and had come out into the wood, the view across the valley below was breathtaking but more importantly, the view of the battlefield was second to none. They could see far more, being at least four hundred feet higher than if they were sat at the top of the ledge on the opposite side. From their vantage point they could see gun batteries and ammunition dumps, they could see the weak points and the strong points in the German lines as well as their own. They could see the German trenches and where most of the troops were at any given time. They could see the movement of the troops on both sides and where the next attack was likely to come from.

They both knew immediately that they had stumbled on the biggest stroke of good fortune they could have ever wished for.

Over the next ten months they had used the tunnel, burrowing it out by slashing back the low lying privet branches and brambles above them and forming a thoroughfare beneath the hedgerow above, and the ditch below. They had become, and also the horses, so confident in it that they had used it several times during daylight hours and still hadn't been detected. The main problem they had, and always would have, was getting in and out of it. At these times they were always at their most vulnerable. Which is why, for most of the time, they moved within the hours of darkness.

"Where we are now Riley, we are surrounded by the enemy, they are mostly near to the bottom of the valley, but occasionally we have heard them nearby" said Hayworth

"They know, or they think they know, that we are over on their side somewhere, but they don't know where, and they definitely don't think that we are up here. You see, they hide their positions from anybody looking from the front, obvious really, but they don't bother to hide their whereabouts from anybody looking at them from behind, because we shouldn't be anywhere near here. This cliffside is surrounded by the Hun. It's of massive strategic importance. And because of that, they are so cock sure that there is nobody up here, they don't bother looking for us. But in truth, the only way in and out for us is the tunnel. If they find that, then it's a three mile gallop downhill dodging bullets all the way and I don't need to tell you the outcome of that".

Their conversation was halted by a loud blast coming from the far side, the British side, of the valley. A large plume of smoke had already floated several feet into the air from where, presumably, it had come from. Three seconds later a fireball exploded three hundred feet below them and about hundred yards to their right.

"Here we go" said Hayworth " our working day has now begun. When they return fire we need to remember where it comes from and log it on our map here".

As he waved a map towards Riley.

"We will send on the co-ordinates later, but if it goes to plan we are going to be here for at least two more days".

For the next eight or nine hours they watched as the two sides of the valley blasted each other to pieces. As it had started, in the early morning sunshine, Riley had felt each explosion on the British side with utter dread and sickness, fearing for his fellow soldiers down below, but as the day had moved on, and on each new explosion, no matter which side of the valley it had landed on, he had started to feel the same sadness every time. From far up above, on their magnificent vantage point, the true horrors of war were slowly unfolding yet again for this quiet man from Ireland. It didn't matter really which side you were on from up here. Whether you were British or German, all you could see was devastation and death. After a time he had begun to feel sorry not only for his own fellow soldiers, but also for the German soldiers on the receiving end of the onslaught from the far side of the valley. He knew then, at that very moment, that should he be fortunate enough to survive this horrendous belligerent waste of life, he would never be the same again. The scar's that he now already had, would never heal. They were burned into his brain forever.

Some people would describe their view as the best seats in the house.

They were right in some respects.

But if this was up in the heaven's. Then down below in the valley, and the river's of blood, it was hell on earth.

❈ ❈ ❈

THE QUIET OF NIGHT

As dusk fell onto the valley below, the sun was still shining on their higher vantage point. Until it dropped behind the opposite hill they couldn't move. It was as if the sun was showing exactly where they were and not only that, they were blinded by it as it shone, burning into their eyes.

As it dropped slowly at first behind the hill on the British side, once it had got passed halfway it seemed to disappear very quickly behind the silhouetted hillside. As it did so the temperature noticeably dropped immediately and a chill descended into their cliffside hideaway.

"Ok Riley, we move again, but don't worry we're not going too far" said Hayworth, "We just need to check on the horses before last light".

They grabbed their knives and slipped on their coats and Hayworth led the way out, crawling on hands and knees over the rear left hand-hand corner of their shelter and into thick bramble bushes. As they got onto what was the back of their roof, still on their hands and knees and still within the thick bramble bushes, they turned at ninety degrees to their left, paralleling the edge of the hillside just ten feet away to their nearside. They continued to crawl turning firstly right and then left again, almost in the reverse shape of a letter S, before eventually after two or three minutes, they emerged from the overgrowth and into a small clearing within the wood. As they crawled out they waited, kneeling on the edge of the edge of brambles and thicket, watching and listening for any movement or sound from further within the wood. The light was now fading and was considerably darker the further you looked into the dense assortment of trees.

When they had arrived here the previous night, Riley had sensed the twist and turns as they had made their way towards their hideaway, but he had had no idea that he was crawling through a secret pathway, which was exactly what it was. Once they felt assured that there was nobody within their immediate vicinity they both slowly stood. Riley looked back to where they had come from and could see nothing at all of their secret little hideaway. He felt one hundred percent confident that they would never be detected while in there. However, where they were now was a totally different prospect. He felt as if he was about to be lit up by a spotlight, as if on stage in a west end show, not that he had ever seen one, but he had seen the newspaper photographs. It didn't feel comfortable at all.

A thumbs up from Hayworth was the signal to move, in silence, towards the centre of the wood. As they slowly climbed they approached the thickest part and the summit of the hill and wood. Riley sensed movement ahead and dropped to a crouch, gripping his knife in his left hand. Hayworth, slightly in front and to his right sensed him dropping and turned to look at him and smiled as if to say 'its ok'. They carried on and as Hayworth walked towards a thick hedgerow Riley looked on in amazement as Hayworth grabbed the hedge and slowly pulled a six foot length of it back towards him to reveal a small clearing within and two silently grazing horses.

Blue looked up to see who the visitors were, but once happy that he knew who they were, he carried on, head down, chewing the lush grass of the green oasis.

"don't worry Riley, we have hidden the horses here for the last ten months on and off. But if anything does happen you need to know where to find them in case your on your own, you see that dark bush over there" Hayworth pointed towards a thick dark green holly bush on the opposite side of the crest.

"That is the entrance to the tunnel that we came through to get us up here. Just walk Blue towards it and he'll know where he's going, but hopefully I'll be with you" he smiled at Riley.

"That would be good" whispered Riley " I'd be scared on my own".

They both silently laughed at each other trying not to make too much noise.

After checking over the horses Hayworth opened one of the back packs that he had placed on the ground and hid in the hedgerow. He slowly placed his hand inside and as if he was a magician at a fair, he pulled out a pigeon and held it in his hand.

"let's go send a message".

They walked back in the direction they had come from but as they approached the entrance to the hide Hayworth veered off to the right and signalled to Riley to follow.

Once they had walked about fifty yards further on he took a small piece of paper hidden under his collar. He rolled it into a small scroll and placed it onto the pigeons leg.

They then moved towards the edge of the cliff and sat looking at the now virtually dark valley below.

"We have to do it from here, away from the hide" said Hayworth "the Germans sit and watch for Pigeons and try to shoot them in case they are carrier's. In two minutes time, at 20:08hrs to be precise, they should, providing everything is ok, fire a few shells to divert the eyes of the Hun, and hopefully, scare a few more pigeons, so we can send our boy here on his way home, its worked really well up to now, so fingers crossed".

They waited their two minutes. Then..... boom boom boom,

They hadn't let them down.

Off flew the pigeon and a few of his feathered friends also joined him in frightened flight.

With him on his way, they made their way back to the entrance to the hide and then silently slipped into the tunnel towards their beds for the night.

As Riley sat leaning on the wall looking out across the now dark valley, the full moon was casting shadows on the rock faces and the river sparkled again as if the candles had returned, floating gently down stream. As he slowly drifted into a light sleep the occasional gunshot woke him from his dreams before he drifted back again, and so it continued for the next couple of hours. By 0100hrs he had given up and decided to make himself a hot drink. Hayworth was asleep and in a very deep one judging by how heavy his breathing was. The temperature in their hide had dropped considerably and though they had blankets to keep them warm, the damp air had started to get through them. He restocked the small fire that they had on the stone floor and was about to light it but stopped as he heard movement from behind him, further into the wood but it sounded no more than thirty yards away.

Whatever it was it was getting nearer. It was more likely to be an animal, thought Riley, as it was now scratching at the ground. From some way off the howl of a wolf echoed across the valley. It was unusual to hear a wolf as they were few and far between in this part of France nowadays, but occasionally men had said they had heard them higher up in the hillside.

Riley jumped, startled by the howling reply from what seemed like no more than twenty yards away.

The scratching animal was a wolf.

It had also had the same effect on Hayworth who had sat up bolt upright and spinning around to grab his knife.

"Where the hell is it, it sounded like it was in here" whispered Hayworth.

"Don't worry Harry it's out there, about twenty or thirty yards away I think. I heard it first a few minutes ago scratching at the ground" said Riley, "What shall we do about it".

"Nothing" said Hayworth "if Mr wolf is about, I very much doubt Mr Hun will be. They tend to be scared of each other. If a wolf sees a man they run a mile and vice versa generally. Tonight Riley you can sleep happily in the knowledge that there wont be a German within a couple of miles of us at least. Now get your head down and try and get some rest, we will need it as tomorrow we may have to return to Vermelles".

Hayworth lay back down and within a few minutes his breathing returned to its heavy slow in and out routine, he was fast asleep.

Unlike Riley.

For the rest of the night he slept in fits and starts but rarely got into any sort of deep sleep. He lay and listened to the forest which now seemed more alive at night than it was in the day.

He heard deer, foxes, badgers, all sorts of birds and the occasional grunt of a wild boar and the slow heavy breathing of his friend carried on and on.

It was going to be a long night.

❋ ❋ ❋

A LETTER

Ireland June 1916

Daibbi had received regular letters from Riley over the last few months. All of them showing his frustration at not seeing any action of any sort, but they still had a positive feel and a happiness about them.

A new letter had now arrived.

This one was different.

My Dear Daibbi,

I hope you are well and that Connor is too.

I write to let you know that there is no news as to when this will all end. But I fear that from what I have recently seen, this will not be any time soon.

The horrors of what a man can do to his fellow man is beyond belief. I will not scar you with the details, but it is truly horrific.

I wonder that I will ever be rid of the sights that I have seen, for when I close my eyes, they stare back at me with unbelievable clarity.

I worry about you my darling, not because I think you can't cope because I know that you can, but I would not wish you to be on your own should anything happen to me.

I can face death, I do not fear it. But when you are with someone that is so full of life, such as you, you tend to want to share it with them.

The gift of life is a wondrous thing that all too many of us take for granted.

Nobody here takes it for granted anymore.

I hope to be able to write to you again soon, god willing.

I love you,

I miss you,

But only in my dreams can I kiss you.

I hope and prey that the day will come soon when I can be with you again.

Take care my love

Riley x x

She sobbed. No Riley, no Aibbi, all she had now was Connor. That wonderful little boy was her life, and for now that's all she had. She sat and tried to think of what to write back. Should she write and tell him that she still hadn't heard from Aibbi, should she tell him that Ireland was in a state of turmoil and was at war within itself. Or she could write back and tell him that Connor was doing well at school and had started his little job. She chose the latter.

How she carried on, sometimes even she didn't know, but she knew if she were to break, then this house would come tumbling down.

God what a mess.

※ ※ ※

NUMBER 19

Ireland September 1916

Cain Milburn was now a very busy man. His own farm, and the surrounding ones which his family also owned and rented out, were going from strength to strength. As was also the republican movement, which he was now very heavily involved in. The attacks had continued on both sides and not only on civilians but also on the police and British troops that had been put into several of the larger cities to the North.

As a result of this increase in violence, he had now had to become more secretive in his movements and actions. He now had to rely on the unknowing Connor to pass on all of his messages to his fellow republicans within the town of Tralee, for it was far too dangerous for him to do it himself.

It was now a year since Connor had started working on the milk round and eleven months since Cain had spotted his true potential and usefulness.

It was 05:30 in the morning and as they rode into the town, Cain was thinking hard about something that had come into his head a few days before.

He turned to look at Connor who had been promoted to driver for over a week now. As Connor gently held the reins, encouraging Duke on his way Cain smiled to himself, happy with his idea, it was going to be fine, he thought.

"This morning Connor lad I have a new job for you, and if it goes okay you might be in for a wage rise" said Cain.

"A wage rise, does that mean more money for Nana" said a rather excited Connor.

"Yes lad it does, but don't get too excited it wont be much. But now you have started driving us here and, if it goes alright today, we will see what we can do".

As they rode steadily on a heavy down poor blew in from the West soaking them in an instant and before Cain could pull the rain sheet over them that they used in bad weather.

As they got to the town, Cain got off the cart and took Connor over to 'the Point'.

"Right lad here's what I need you to do, I want you to take the milk today as normal but I also need you to go to the big house on Sheep Street, and take this note, it's his bill. You just post it through his letter box".

Connor knew which house that Cain meant. He'd been with him to it a few times before, and every time, he had felt very uneasy when they had walked up the narrow winding path within the grounds towards the front door. The house itself was set thirty yards back from the street in its own grounds with a small wall around it, on top of which stood seven foot high iron railings with large sharp spikes on the top. Within the front garden were a number of large trees which reached higher than the house itself, even in the middle of summer they imposed heavy dark shadows over the grounds and the building.

The house was three storey's high with a central front porch which had a thick oak panelled door painted black. On both sides of the door were two, five foot high windows. Four matching windows directly above the four on the ground floor, were on the first floor, and above that were two more windows on the second floor.

For some reason, and Connor didn't know why, he hated it. When he had gone up the path with Cain on previous occasions he couldn't wait to get back out onto the street. There were never any lights on at the front of the house and Connor had wondered if anybody actually lived there, but he assumed that somebody did as they had always took milk, and Cain had usually taken a folded note, with money in it, from a small hole in the wall at the side of the door and he would sometimes get Connor to put the bill through the letterbox.

That was another thing that Connor hated about the house.

The letterbox.

It was a large black thick cast iron letterbox with sharp decorative shapes on the edges. As you pushed it open, the springs inside pushed back, threatening to easily trap his tiny hand within it. The height of the letterbox didn't help either. It was eye level to a ten year old. The first early morning he had pushed it open, he gazed through it briefly and saw a long hallway lit by several flickering candles. On the right hand side was a coat stand which had a large black hooded cloak hanging from it. But it was the far wall facing him that had held him and almost frozen him to the spot where he stood.

A huge crucifix, standing at least three foot high, with the body of christ hanging from it, was lit from underneath by two more candles that stood on a table. In the middle of the table was a huge Black Bible.

It was one of the most frightening things he had ever seen in his short life.

He had also noticed the smell that came through the letter box from the inside.

The burning candles. He would remember that smell for the rest of his life.

"why do I have to go there, you always do that house" said a clearly worried Connor.

"Because Connor, I need you too. I have somebody that I need to go and see and, if you ever want to do this job on your own, then you have got to start going to all the houses that I deliver to, not just the ones that you like going to".

"Can I really do it on my own then" said Connor, not quite believing Cain.

"I don't see why not, but let's get this out the way first then we'll see. Now let's get going".

Cain held out the folded note for him to take. Connor noticed that it was folded in a strange way. It was sort of folded in on itself several times and if you held one of the pointed ends upwards, it reminded Connor of a diamond he had seen in a picture at school. As he took hold of it he could see that it didn't open but was held tightly shut by all the folds.

It also had two numbers written in pencil on the back of it.

19.

"Take this and put it through the letterbox, but until you get there put it inside your pocket and don't get it out until you get to the door".

"Why" said Connor.

"Why, why, why, never mind why Connor, just do as you are told. If it's in your pocket you wont lose it will you and if, when you get there, there is a note in the wall, put that in your pocket and bring it back to me".

"The money" said Connor.

"What about the money" said Cain.

"You mean the money is in the note in the wall" said Connor.

"Yes, yes, the money will be in the wall. Now go lad or you'll be late for school".

As Connor set off through 'the Point' the rain started to pour again, but once inside the alleyway he was sheltered from the most of it by the tall overhanging houses on both sides. He made his way around his round returning to the cart to refill his basket several times, and put the folded notes and the money under the seat. He'd noticed that Cain wasn't around at the cart, just Duke quietly standing half asleep waiting for his trip back. It wasn't unusual for Cain not to be there but normally the reason he wasn't was that he would be delivering the milk as well, not visiting people.

As Connor went back into 'the point' for the sixth time he knew that this time he had to go too 'the big house'. It was his last street on this side of the square that he needed to go too, and he was still dreading it.

As he turned the corner into Sheep Street he could see it immediately, 'the big house' fifty yards further down the street on the right. As he walked steadily on, just wanting to get it over and done with, the wind and rain had increased causing him to turn his head sideways so he could see where he was going. The fallen leaves were making little tornado's along the cobbled road swirling around on their unknown and unpredictable route.

As he got to the gate he paused looking through the swaying tree's that were now making dark shadows dance upon the front of the house. He looked at the windows on the first and second floor.

There was a light on.

He'd been to this house probably half a dozen times with Cain and apart from the lit candles in the hall, it had always been in total darkness.

But now, of all times, standing there on his own, there was a light on.

The window on the first floor immediately above and slightly to the left of the front door, had a very dim flickering light coming from within.

He stood looking at it.

Out the corner of his eye he saw, at least he thought he had, some movement.

A moving shadow, nothing more, in the window to the left of the one with the flickering light.

He watched.

He watched from window to window on the first floor but saw nothing more.

He had to do it.

If he didn't Cain wouldn't be happy, his Nana wouldn't be getting anymore money and he definitely wouldn't be getting the job on his own.

He had to do it and he had to do it now.

He set off at pace on his thirty yard sprint up the path, Cain had always told him not to run with bottles but there was no chance he was going to walk, not now. He sprinted up the path towards the front door. Took out a bottle and placed it on the concrete step.

He took out the note from his pocket, his hand now visibly shaking. He lowered his basket of empty bottles onto the step trying desperately not to make any noise. But the bottles couldn't help themselves. They clinked and rolled then clinked again against each other causing what seemed like the most horrendous din. His left hand went towards the letterbox, shaking almost uncontrollably now. He pushed at the opening trying to push it upwards.

It wouldn't go.

He pushed harder but it was as though the springs were fighting against him and were refusing to lose this little battle.

He pushed as hard as he could, it gave, it moved upwards about two inches.

That was enough.

He pushed the note forward with his right hand and placed it in the gap desperately trying not to get his hand caught by the black metal jaws of this ferocious black metal jaw of a tiger.

The note fell inside, he pulled his hand back as quickly as he could, grabbed his basket and ran. He ran as fast as his legs would take him, sprinting back down the path and out onto the street.

Out on the street he stopped. Breathing hard, but at least he had done it and it was over.

But it wasn't over.

He'd forgotten to get the note from the wall.

He had to go back.

He couldn't believe that he'd not checked to see if there was a note in the crack of the wall. He stood deciding what to do.

He could tell Cain there wasn't a note. But what if there was a note and Cain later spoke to the man who lived there and the man told him that he had left a note. Cain would know he had lied and he wouldn't like that. He would probably lose his job.

He had to go back.

He walked back to the gate and again looked at the house.

The flickering light had gone out.

He looked at all the windows, all ten of them. Each one totally black, it was as if somebody had painted black paint all over the glass.

Was somebody looking out of one of them.

It felt as if somebody was.

He watched.

Nothing.

But he could feel it. He could feel somebody watching him.

He didn't know why, but he knew somebody was up there watching him from one of the windows.

He placed his basket next to the gate. He wasn't going to take it with him, he didn't need it.

He ran. He ran faster than he had the last time. He got to the door and looked down to the left to where Cain had several times previously, pulled a note from a crack in the house wall.

There was a note.

Connor gently bent down and pulled the piece of folded paper from the gap.

He immediately noticed that it was folded in exactly the same way as the one which he had not more than two minutes ago, posted through the letterbox, it was also shaped like a diamond.

He placed the paper diamond securely in his pocket and ran back down the path, grabbed his basket and walked as fast as he could back towards 'the Point'.

As he exited 'the Point' the cart had gone. He looked across the square to the left of him and saw the back of the cart moving quite quickly backwards and forwards but he couldn't see the front as a market stall was blocking his view. He ran, thinking that Duke had probably wandered off and somebody was trying to hold him steady.

That wasn't the case.

As he turned the corner, around the edge of the market stall, he could see that Cain had hold of Duke's bridal and was hitting him with the large club that was usually hidden under the seat.

As Connor reached the cart he grabbed the whip from behind the seat and ran towards Cain, the anger already brewing up inside him.

"No!" Shouted Connor "Get away from him".

Connor now had the whip in front of him and stood just three feet away from Cain who had now spun around to see who was shouting at him.

He stared at Connor not quite believing for a moment what he was actually seeing.

"Put that down Connor, put it down now" he said quietly but in a very obviously stern tone.

"Not until you put that down" replied Connor his voice shaking with anger.

Cain looked around and could see that they were starting to draw some attention from the people near them.

"I'll put it down,..... but get on the cart lad, we need to be on our way".

Cain gave Connor a look and nodded as if to say 'Its alright'.

Connor climbed on the cart but still kept hold of the whip.

Cain walked around the cart and placed the club under the seat.

They set off in silence back towards Rossbridge.

Outside, Cain looked angry, but inside he was smiling.

Eventually it was Cain that broke the awkward silence.

"Are you going to put that whip down now lad"

Connor didn't look at him but answered quietly but confidently,

"I will, when you promise not too hit Duke again"

"He was being stubborn Connor, you weren't there, he wouldn't move".

"That's no reason to beat him Mr Milburn, Riley say's you shouldn't hit animals, animals are better than people, you can trust animals. If you look after them, they will always look after you".

"Is that so Connor. Well I will try and remember that the next time, how's that".

Connor looked at him and saw that Cain was smiling at him.

"You promise Mr Milburn that you wont hit him anymore"

"I promise, and it's 'Cain', there's no need for all that Mr Milburn stuff, you should call me Cain.

Now, was there a note for me".

Connor placed his hand into his pocket and handed him the diamond shaped note.

They rode on in silence once more and after a mile or so, Cain, pretending that he hadn't noticed, Connor quietly put the whip back behind the seat.

The boy had his mothers and Nana's guts that was for sure. He was going to need them. The mornings events had proven to Cain that Connor, a young boy of ten years old, was going to have what it takes.

❈ ❈ ❈

MY FREIND

Ireland

Christmas 1916

The week before Christmas the first snow had arrived in the West of Ireland. Not a lot, but enough to make any sort of journey a little more difficult.

It was just after 05:00 when Connor came down for breakfast.

Daibbi was always amazed at how happy he was even at that time of the morning.

"Nana, would it be alright if my friend came round to play later, after school" said Connor.

"Of course it would Connor, but which friend is this"

"Cal Moran, of course" said Connor.

"yes that's fine, but will his mother know"

"Yes Nana, she said he could come"

"Well it sound's to me that you have already got it all planned, so that should be fine".

Cal was from a local family that had lived at the other end of the village.

Daibbi knew his Mother, Emma, who still lived in the village, and had known her mother, Cal's grandma, Heather, for a long time. Heather now lived in Tralee. Daibbi had remembered when Cathal, he was christened Cathal but everybody called him Cal, had been born. His mother Emma had nearly died whilst in childbirth and she had comforted Heather when it looked as though she could possibly die. But happily it all turned out well in the end and they had remained friends to this day.

Many thought that Connor and Cal were brothers as they looked similar in both looks and build. Cal was slightly the taller but both had blonde hair and fair skin. The only thing noticeably different were that Cal had blue eyes as apposed to Connor's green, but from any distance it was difficult to tell them apart.

as Connor and his Nana sat there, the strangely muffled sound, due to the snow, of hoof's, were now coming from outside the front door, it was the signal for Connor to grab his school bag and run for the door.

"Connor" shouted Daibbi at the young boy now half way out the front door

"What have you forgotten".

Connor spun around and stood looking a little confused as to what it could be.

"I've got my bag Nana, I don't need anything else".

Daibbi stood looking at him with her finger to her pursed lips waiting for a kiss.

Connor ran back into the kitchen and kissed his Nana, turned and ran back out of the front door.

As they rode through the snow covered lanes towards Tralee Cain took out four 'diamond' shaped notes from his jacket pocket and waved them at Connor.

" Now lad, listen carefully. I need you to deliver these notes today to four different houses. You know them all as you have been to them before, but I have written on the back of them the number of the house. Now I know that you cant read but I will tell you which street they are on and all you have to do is match the number on the back to the number on the door".

"Alright" said Connor "But what if I get it wrong".

"You wont get it wrong, but if you do, don't worry, it wont matter"

It wouldn't matter because all the notes said the same thing.

Sunday 31st December 6pm The Holy Corner, Reindeer. Use the back door

Cain explained to Connor the house's which he wanted him to post the notes too.

The last of them was 19 Sheep Street.

As they rode on, the knot in Connor's stomach would get bigger and bigger.

'why do I have to go back to that horrible house again' thought Connor.

As they arrived on the edge of the Tralee, Cain told Connor to stop the cart.

" I'm off here lad, I will meet you in the square when your'e done. I have to go and see somebody, and don't forget those notes".

'How could I', thought Connor. He hadn't thought about anything else for the whole journey.

As Connor passed through 'the Point' his brain now automatically switched on to watching and listening mode.

For some reason Connor felt a little more apprehensive this morning. It must be down to the fact that shortly he would have to make the dreaded journey back up the path of number 19. But there was something else, something didn't feel right. He had also thought that Mr Milburn seemed a little different today as well. Maybe it was that, that he, Mr Milburn, had made him feel this way.

Within the hour he had nearly completed almost half of his round and, more importantly, he had posted three of the four notes.

He now had only the number 19 note left.

As he approached the corner of Sheep Street, the knot within his stomach had tightened even further. It was still only a little after 7 o'clock in the morning and most of the streets were deserted. The snow that lay at least a couple of inches deep in most places, had barely been touched by anybody throughout the round, but here, of all places, on Sheep Street, he was following footprints in the snow.

And they were fresh.

They were going in the same direction that he was.

And they were big.

As he got to the gate, they stopped.

They had vanished into thin air.

He looked back up the street to where he had come from.

He could see that there were now two sets of footprints, the smaller ones which were his, and another set much bigger than his, that belonged to whoever had been walking down the street not so long before him.

As Connor stood there, he suddenly realised where they had gone next.

He looked slowly over the gate to see the same large footprints disappearing into the darkness and into the grounds of number 19.

He was now visibly shaking, and it wasn't the cold.

He stood watching the house. No lights. No moving shadows. No sound.

The house itself appeared to be asleep, let alone anybody else that may or may not be in there.

He decided that his tactic should be the same as he had used the last time he was here.

He'd run. He would sprint for his life, there and back.

He gently placed his basket of bottles on the ground. Grabbed a full bottle. Took the diamond note from his pocket, and ran. He ran as fast as his feet dared take him in the slippery wet snow.

As he ran up the path he could see that the footsteps were still going in the same direction in which he was going, right up to the front door.

As he got to the door he placed the bottle of milk just to the side of it.

Now for the note.

He reached forward with his right hand and got ready to push the letterbox with all his might. He pushed as hard as he could.

The letterbox slammed open making the most almighty crash as it hit, metal on metal, on the inside.

It had been oiled.

He almost threw the note through the gap and let go of the letterbox. It slammed back shut, again causing another amount of noise that he really didn't want to make.

If anybody was asleep in the house, he very much doubted that they were now.

This time he didn't forget, he quickly bent down to look to see if there was a note, which there was, he grabbed it and ran back down the path grabbing his basket as he passed it and ran, he ran for another minute at least.

But as Connor had run back down the path, he had missed something.

He hadn't noticed the footprints.

The larger footprints in the snow that were now walking back down the footpath back towards the gate of number 19.

At the bottom of the path, at the gate, the footprints had turned right.

He hadn't seen them there either.

In his panic he had seen nothing at all of the maker of the footprints, the man that had been hiding within the bushes close to the front door, and then who had walked hurriedly back down the path before Connor made the return journey.

Connor needn't have worried, the man wasn't there to see what Connor was doing. He had been as shocked as Connor would have been, if he had seen him, to see the young boy delivering a bottle of milk.

The man was there to have a look at number 19 Sheep Street, nothing more.

He just needed to know who lived there.

He had been there since 3 o'clock in the morning, sat in the bushes just yards from the front door, but he had fallen asleep. The next thing he had heard was the crashing sound of the letterbox as the little boy delivering the milk had posted the bill through he front door.

He had panicked before realising what was going on and got out the bushes behind him and ran back down the path, through the gate, turned right and ran.

The man had been dressed all in black.

Still a little breathless, Connor had walked back through 'The Point' to be met with a scene that he hadn't at all expected.

It was the shouting that made him turn to his right to see what was going on.

He could see that two policemen were struggling to hold down a man that was shouting and spitting abuse at the two officers. The man had now managed to punch one of the officers full in the face causing him to lose his balance and fall backwards into the snow. This was met with instant retribution as the other officer gave the man a full blooded kick into his stomach causing a loud groan from the man on the ground.

The second policeman had managed to regain his composure and reigned in with some more heavy kicks to the man's legs and lower body. But it was the forearm smash into the man's face that ended it all. The man went limp and immediately stopped resisting. As the police officers grabbed an arm each they lifted him to his now unfeeling feet and dragged him towards a police horse drawn carriage.

Connor now stood open mouthed as he saw who the man was.

It was Cain Milburn.

He stood deciding what to do next.

He decided on nothing, because out the corner of his eye he had seen him again.

The man in black.

The man in black was stood watching the whole scene from the other side of the square.

Not taking his eyes from the Policemen, Cain, and the man in black, Connor walked slowly to where he had left Duke and quietly climbed aboard the cart, while still not averting his eyes, he took the notes he had collected from various houses from his pocket, and placed them under his seat.

There were four in all, all in the shape of a diamond.

He watched as the policemen took their still unconscious prisoner around the square and away towards the police station on the Northern Road.

The man in black followed them about fifty yards behind.

Connor gave them all a minute or so before he moved. Then he rode quietly around the square and back south towards Rossbridge and home.

As he approached Manor farm he needed to decide what to do. Should he leave Duke and the cart at the farm or should he carry on home and leave him there. He dare not take him to school. The teacher frowned on him enough as it was for working for the Milburn's.

He decided to take Duke home. He was sure he had time but only just.

He pulled into the yard to be met by his Nana.

" Now Connor, what have we here, your supposed to be at school in ten minutes" said Daibbi.

" Sorry Nana but I had to bring him home" said Connor jumping off and grabbing his bag.

" Whats happened, have you been promoted" said Daibbi laughing.

"Well, yes something like that, I need to go Nana, see you later"

And Connor raced out the yard before his Nana could reply.

Daibbi looked on in amazement as she now stood there alone. Alone that was apart from a very hungry and sleepy Duke.

" Well Duke my handsome boy, lets get you off this horrible cart and get you some nice hay for your very well earned breakfast"

She unhooked his bridal and led him to one of the stables. He'd be okay in there for now.

The day passed without any further falls of snow until around mid afternoon when it fell from the sky as if god had made double the snow that he had needed.

The drifts around Rose cottage were 2 foot high in places, and still it fell.

Daibbi's peace and quiet was broken as she heard the laughs of two young boys coming through the rear yard's squeaky gate.

A snowball crashed against the kitchen window followed by another hitting the kitchen door.

She looked out the window to see Cal throwing hand grenades, otherwise known as snowball's, towards a flat prone Connor laying apparently dead in the soft white snow in the yard.

As she walked out the kitchen door a white fluffy grenade exploded on the wall just to the right of her head.

" Watch out Nana, the Germans are on the attack" shouted Connor who had now made a miraculous recovery and was now throwing his own white hand grenades back towards the direction of the barn, and Cal, now hiding behind the stable door.

"Don't you go scaring Duke, he's still in there" daibbi said, looking towards the stable. "When is Cain fetching him".

" I don't know, when the police let him out of jail I suppose" Said Connor very matter of factly.

Daibbi spun back around and looked towards Connor.

"What did you just say, did you say the police, what's he doing in jail".

"The police took him this morning" smack, a grenade hit him at the side of his head.

"The police took him where" said a now shocked and somewhat intrigued Daibbi

" I told you, to jail".

" What for".

" I don't know Nana, he was fighting with them in the square, so they took him away".

She looked at him, 'oh to be so young'. She watched him as he and Cal raced around the yard, not a care in the world, oblivious to all the troubles that were now so prevalent in this now oh so violent world.

" Nana"

" Yes Connor"

" Do you think Riley has killed any German's with hand grenade's yet".

She silently shook her head and walked into the kitchen, she didn't want to think about that prospect at all, let alone answer him.

✳ ✳ ✳

THE MAN IN BLACK

The man in black was Declan McGann.

McGann was an undercover police officer.

He had joined the Irish Constabulary six years previously, aged just 22, in the hope that it would stop him being called up to the army. He hadn't really enjoyed his first three years and had often wondered if he was cut out for the role of a policeman. He hated confrontation and any sort of violence. The money was good compared to anything else that was available but the escalating violence that had now started had made him start to have a rethink about his future.

But then, two years ago, this job, had been offered to him.

They, the police, were in need of police officers who were willing to work undercover in plain clothes, and that were also willing to travel to other cities and towns, where they wouldn't be recognised. Their role was to watch and observe the growing numbers of men that were thought to be joining the Irish Republican movement, to report on their movements and activities and if possible and where necessary, to try and recruit informants from the catholic population of the town that they were currently working within.

Once they had been in the city or town a for a few weeks and they had been accepted by the local population, they were expected to stay and live for four or five times a week in order to build further friendships and acquaintances.

McGann had now been in Tralee, off and on, for over a year. He had managed to establish some good contacts within the local catholic population but had not really discovered anything of significance.

that was until now.

Shortly before last Christmas, a female that he had met one drunken evening in the Reindeer pub, had intimated that she knew of a family that were the rising force of the republicans in this area. She had slipped the name of Cain Milburn briefly into their drunken conversation. Was this the breakthrough that he needed. He had been watching Milburn, and other local men, for sometime now but had, up to now, drawn a complete blank.

He had filled out his report's and now, after almost a year, and also to his surprise and amazement, the powers that be had tasked him to target the Milburn family from the nearby village of Rossbridge. Milburn had been dragged in by the police last December but he had told them nothing and had been released with no charges other than to 'keep the peace'.

He was to gather as much information as he could about the Milburn's, their farms, who they associated with, and who worked for them.

McGann had subsequently moved into digs in Tralee. They were situated in a small terraced house on The Easpag on the East side of the city, about 80 or so yards back from the town square.

As this was now to be his permanent posting, he was to stay in the town at least four nights a week and he was requested to report back to the head of operations at Tralee police station. He was to use the rear entrance and only between the hours of 23:00 and 01:00. He was to come alone and to ensure, at all times, that he wasn't being followed.

McGann had always been a little cock sure of himself, he was sure that he needn't worry about being followed. He had been in this game along time now, two years, and he'd never had a problem. But he'd play the game. The bosses always knew best, well they thought they did. He had no respect for the hierarchy. They were all in it for themselves. The next promotion was all they were really interested in. He could do this job standing on his head.

He was soon to find out he hadn't done it for long enough.

Every man, even the strongest willed, have a weakness.

In no particular order, they were usually, gambling, drink, money or women.

The problem with McGann was that he had many.

His main problem was Women, Of which he had also had many. His tall dark handsome looks had helped him bed at least one woman in each town that he had recently been sent to work in. Tralee was no exception. His second problem was drink. He liked a drink. His job meant that he frequented many a drinking hole on most evenings. It was where he could pick up most of his information, and more importantly, his women.

But there he had a problem.

He couldn't drink.

That wasn't strictly true. He could drink quite excessively most evenings, but more often than not, it usually left him slumped unconscious in the corner of a pub or worse, flat out in the street. Most evening's went one way or the other. He would either end up in the bed of his latest conquest or in a gutter.

The only evenings that he stayed reasonably sober were those when he went in to the police station to fill out his weekly report, usually on a Sunday evening. But it hadn't been going well. When filling out his report's, he had been barely able to write more than a few lines.

He had spent hours watching Cain Milburn, hidden in the hillside around his various farms. He had watched him in the town of Tralee, around the square and meeting several other males, all of which he didn't know, and still didn't know. He had watched Milburn visit several houses and one in particular had aroused his suspicions. He had noticed that whenever Milburn went there he seemed different, wary of what was around him. Milburn would watch those close by and seemed edgy, almost worried at times.

The house was 19 Sheep Street.

But he didn't know anything about it, nothing at all. In fact, since he had been tasked with the Milburn job he had found out virtually no strong, hard, factual information at all.

He was convinced that Milburn was connected to many of the attacks and assaults that had taken place in Tralee over the last few months, but, he had absolutely no evidence or even good intelligence that this was the case.

So now, due to the pressures of needing some results, he had committed the most fatal sin in the world of intelligence gathering.

He has started to fabricate evidence.

In other words, he was making it up.

Little did he know that in some ways, what he was making up, was actually very near the mark. But it was all guess work. He had no actual evidence at all.

His last report had read that Cain Milburn had been seen with several males in clandestine meetings in dark alleys close to Tralee Square. He had also been seen to visit 19 Sheep Street and be met by a male who in turn went with him and met the other males.

Not one word of it was actually true. Not true, in respect that McGann had seen nothing that remotely resembled his report.

As a result of his fictitious report, his boss had tasked him with finding out who was living at 19 Sheep Street.

What McGann didn't know was that his boss had been tipped off about him drinking heavily and was also now fully aware of his shenanigans with various local women. A colleague had voiced his concerns having seen him on several occasions, totally drunk in various pubs around the town and he had also noticed the presence of his very loose tongue.

McGann's job was to watch, not be watched. His boss was not a happy man.

So now McGann had now found himself having to get up at the unearthly hour of 2 am to hide in the bushes in the front garden of 19 Sheep Street and wait for all the light to go out so he could have a snoop around.

The only time he had been still up at that time of the morning was when he was on his way home after bedding his latest conquest. And that almost certainly coincided with him being somewhat inebriated to some level or another.

It turned out to be a complete waste of his time.

All he had seen was the boy delivering milk.

He needed to get some results and fast.

At 05:00 the next morning Daibbi was woken by the squeaking back gate being opened. It was amazing how she was woken by it now. When Riley was here she was barely woken by it at all. It was always Riley that jumped out of bed to see if anything or anybody had opened it.

As she looked out of her bedroom window she saw that it was Cain bringing Duke out of his stable. She watched as he put his bridal on and attached him the cart and slowly rode out of the yard.

Just over a half an hour later he was back. The cart now full with milk bottles.

Connor, who had got up anyway, thinking he had to ride to Manor farm, finished his breakfast and grabbed his bag.

"You wait right there young man" Said Daibbi pointing at Connor to wait in his seat.

She went out the front door and was immediately stunned by what she saw. Cain was sat in the cart, clearly in pain judging by his contorted shape and holding the left side of his torso. As she got closer to him she could also see that he had two black eye's, his nose looked too have been broken and his top lip had a large gash in it.

" What in heavens name has happened to you" said Daibbi

pulling her coat around her as the wind blew a fresh flurry of snow towards her.

" I fell off a roof" said Cain,

" Really" said a mocking Daibbi, " and would that be the roof of Tralee Jail by any chance"

" He told you then" said Cain,

"He's ten years old Cain, he doesn't lie to his Nana, not yet anyway"

" I had a little disagreement with the officer's is all. Don't you worry about me"

" Oh Cain," she said somewhat sarcastically, "I can assure you I'm not worried about you at all, its my Grandson that I'm worried about, I really don't give a fuck about you".

Cain looked at her and half smiled although, even that hurt him.

" Do you ever not tell the truth Daibbi, have you no sympathy for me at all".

" For you Cain, no, none whats so ever. I'm sure that whatever has happened to you, then it was fully deserved. What I need to know is if this is likely to happen again, because if it is, then I'm sorry but I cannot and will not allow Connor to work for you anymore, he doesn't need to be seeing this sort of thing".

She sensed Connor at her side.

"But Nana" said Connor.

" But Nana nothing" said Daibbi not averting the stare that she was giving Cain.

" Do you understand what I'm saying Cain"

Cain looked at her and slowly nodded. He knew he couldn't argue. The child was his best weapon and he wasn't about to give it up.

" Don't worry Daibbi, I promise it wont happen again"

" Thank you Cain, make sure it doesn't".

She turned and stopped in the doorway of the front door

"You can go now Connor, but don't you be late for school".

She patted him on his head as he ran out the door.

As Cain and Connor rode into town Cain could sense Connor keep stealing a quick look at his battered and bruised face.

"You should see the other two lad" said Cain trying to force another smile.

" What the policemen, I saw them, they looked alright to me" said Connor.

" Not after I had finished with them lad".

Connor's face was a picture, his mouth open in shock of the thought that anybody dare hit a policeman.

" I'm only joking Connor, I didn't do anything to them don't worry. Now then, have you any notes for me".

Connor lent under the seat and pulled out the notes and money he had collected the previous day. He noticed that there were four in a diamond shape again.

✽ ✽ ✽

THE FOUR OF FIVE

The four notes were the replies from the four of the five men that formed the newly formed IRA council for County Kerry. The fifth man was second in command, Cain Milburn. The note's were the replies to the request from the Commander for an emergency meeting to be held at the Reindeer on Sunday evening on the 31st December 1916, News Years Eve.

There was no coincidence that it had been arranged for New Year's Eve.

Most of the police force would be on leave and the likelihood of anybody observing the meeting would be very small.

The meeting had been called because it had been bought to the attention of the Commander that they had a mole. Information was believed to be being leaked to the police about arms hides and there various routes into Ireland.

The seizure of quite a substantial amount of firearms being supplied by the Germans, had been a devastating blow to the republican movement.

It couldn't continue.

It wouldn't continue.

As Cain opened the four replies in turn, he smiled to himself. They were all positive. They would all be there.

Cain sat quietly pondering the thought of what the future held for the movement. It was gathering pace, and it was gathering strength. Now was the time, their time had come at last. He truly believed it.

At Rose Cottage, Christmas came and went. There was no news. There were no letters. There were no unexpected visitors.

Just tears.

Three days later they were back to work.

"Well Connor lad did Father Christmas pay you a visit"

"Yes Mr Milburn, he gave me a brand new bike and some soldiers"

" A bike eh, well you must have been good for him to bring you that"

" I'm always good Mr Milburn, my Nana thinks so anyway"

" And what did your lovely Nana get for Christmas"

Connor was quite for a moment.

" Well I know she didn't get what she really wanted, she really wanted a letter from Riley and my Mummy, I heard her asking god for it when I was in bed. I heard her crying too. I wish I could make her happy. I gave her some flowers and she said it was the best present she had ever had but I know what she really wanted".

Cain looked at the boy at his side. He couldn't help but like him.

They rode on arriving at Tralee a little after six.

It was a normal morning for Connor until just after 06:30.

As he walked back to 'the Point', to replenish his basket, he saw that the man was there again.

The Man in Black.

He was stood watching the cart. There was no sight of Cain, just Duke, standing patiently alone waiting for the journey home.

Connor held his position standing just inside 'the Point', in the darkness, leaning against the cold wet wall, looking upwards the North side of the square.

He didn't know what the man was doing, but he knew that he was probably waiting for Cain.

Since he had been working for Cain he must have seen him in

the square at least 5 or 6 times.

Whatever he was doing, Connor didn't think it was good.

Something was wrong.

So he waited.

After almost five minutes the man in Black still hadn't moved but Connor needed to get back to the cart.

Then from the far side of the square Connor spotted Cain as he appeared from The Eala on the East side of the square.

Connor watched the Man in Black, he had seen Cain that was for sure. His body language had altered immediately. He had tensed up. He turned to his left and started to walk towards the top of the Square, all the time Connor could see that he wasn't taking his eyes off of Cain, who was now walking up the East side of the square and then stopped just ten yards from The Eorna and then knocked on a green door of a terraced house that faced onto the square itself.

As Cain was let into the house Connor watched as the Man in Black took a notebook from his pocket and wrote something in it, he then put it back into his pocket and walked away to the North side of the square and disappeared into The Noafa.

Connor took the opportunity to walk to the cart and carried on with his round.

It was now 8:30 and some two hours later and Connor was back in the square.

And he wasn't the only one.

The Man in Black was now stood on the North side of the square and was looking directly at the front door that Cain had entered almost two hours ago.

Connor stood watching.

Ten minutes passed before Connor saw Cain exit the same green door as he had gone into.

The Man in Black stood watching, not taking his eyes away from Cain.

As Cain rounded the North Eastern corner of the square he saw Connor, almost 100 yards away, still standing in the shadows of the Point.

Cain knew immediately.

Something was wrong.

He didn't panic, he knew better than that, but Connor was stood just inside the alleyway and he wasn't coming out.

Connor watched Cain now walking along the North side towards the West side as he got halfway across he watched as the man in black slipped into a Butchers shop just twenty yards or so in front of him. Cain, seemingly oblivious to the man, carried on and as he turned the corner almost 40 yards from where Connor still stood, he locked eyes with him and tried to give him some assurance that 'it was all okay'.

As he got to the Point he didn't go in but stood just outside, sideways on to Connor who was now barely two foot away from him, but still hidden in the shadows. He sensed that Connor was concerned about something or someone else in the square as Connor kept averting his gaze from his and appeared to be looking beyond him over his shoulder.

"What is it lad" said Cain quietly and calmly, but looking straight ahead but not looking at Connor at all.

"Why is that man watching you" said Connor.

Cain turned slightly to his right to look at Connor, suddenly realising that this, whatever it was, was happening right here and right now.

" Now Connor, you listen to me, do not come out of that alleyway, don't point or look at him, just look at me". He saw Connor slowly nod his head.

"Now Connor lad, can he see you, if he cant, you stay right where you are".

Cain stood rock solid not moving knowing that his back was

towards the man, who ever that was that Connor was talking about.

" He cant see me"

" Okay thats good, now, I'm going to ask you some questions Connor, do not move your head, just keep looking at me and speak very slowly and quietly. Now, what does he look like".

Connor looked at Cain and answered the question in a quiet and calm voice.

"He is wearing a black hat and a black coat"

" Where is he now, do not look at him, is he behind me"

Connor slowly nodded his head.

As Cain moved his eyes to his right, he said

"Is he this side"

And then Cain moved his eyes to his left

"Or is he to this side"

Connor looked past Cain's right shoulder

"How far away is he"

"He's leaning against the wall at about half up the square before the top"

This was about 50 yards away.

Cain continued with the questions.

"How old is he"

"He looks a bit younger than you"

"How tall is he"

"Taller than you, but he's thin"

"Anything else"

Connor thought for a few moments his brain now feeding him with the information that was needed.

"Yes, when he walks, he seems to bend over a bit, and his coat looks too big for him"

" Thats really good lad, how long has he been there"

" Well today, he's been here nearly all morning"

Cain froze, stunned with the realisation that was now hitting home to him, his eyes seemed to bore into Connor as he snarled the next question.

" What do you mean, 'today', have you seen him watching me before".

Connor feared he was now in deep trouble for not telling Cain before, but he had to tell him the truth, Cain didn't like people telling him lies.

" I think I've seen him watching you about 5 or 6 times, but I didn't know why he was Mr Milburn honestly, he just turns up every now and then and watches you thats all, but I saw him today watching you go into that house and he wrote something down in his book, so I thought I better tell you, but I wished I hadn't now".

Cain tried to calm himself and then quietly tried to reassure Connor.

" No, no, Connor lad, you've done well"

Said Cain hoping to put Connor at some ease.

" I just wish you had told me before is all, but don't worry about that now we can sort this out. How long ago did you first see this man"

" Well, not long after I first started working for you I suppose but then I hadn't seen him for ages, until a few weeks ago".

It was the turn of Cain's brain to start to work overtime now.

'How long had this man been watching him, where had he seen him go, who had he seen him with, and who was he working for' all these questions would need answers that was for sure.

The movement was in grave danger if he knew only half what Cain had been up to within the last few months.

But he needn't have worried.

McGann knew next to nothing.

But Cain didn't know that.

He now needed to act fast, he needed to know who he was, where he lived and what he was doing.

He knew just the person that was now required.

He was stood next to him, barely two foot away, in the dark wet alleyway.

" Okay lad, here's whats going to happen now. I'm going to walk down to the bottom of the square and through the alleyway to the bridge. I want you to follow him, see where he goes. If he follows me, don't you worry I will know, but you keep following him until I give him the slip".

Cain looked at the slightly confused Connor " that means you keep following him until I lose him".

With that Cain was off and walking at pace downhill towards the bottom of the square.

Connor waited still in the alleyway but now further within and now on the opposite wall, hiding in the darkness.

A few seconds later, sure enough there he was. The Man in black walking briskly down the hill following Cain who was now about 50 yards in front of him.

As Cain approached and entered The Siul, that led to the stone bridge and the Bogmen estate beyond, Connor saw it immediately, the Man in Black hesitated. He could see that he clearly didn't want to go into that alleyway.

Connor stopped and leaned nonchalantly against a doorway, still holding his basket of empty bottles, watching him out of the corner of his eye. He knew he wasn't going to follow Cain into that funnel of trouble, once in, you were on your own and at the mercy of what fate had in store for you.

McGann, not completely stupid, knew it as well. There was no way on this earth that he was going to follow Milburn into an alleyway, not on his own, that was for sure.

He'd seen the body of the man called Bennett that had been

murdered on the Bogmen estate, and it hadn't been a pretty site. He strongly believed that Milburn had had some involvement in that murder but, as usual, he had no hard evidence, and until he had, there was no chance that his bosses would allow him to bring him in for questioning.

He turned to his left and walked towards the eastern side of the square.

Connor watched him go, gave him a few seconds, and then walked through the centre of the square and through the market stalls keeping McGann slightly in front him and to his right.

Occasionally he lost sight of him behind the throng of people now busy buying their goods within the market. But he knew where he was going. He was going to look at the green door which Cain had only just exited a short time ago.

Connor positioned himself still within the stalls but now with a perfect view of the green door.

Sure enough as McGann approached the door Connor saw him deliberately drop a piece of paper on the floor and stop to bend over to pick it up. As McGann slowly got up Connor saw him look through the window to the right of the front door.

McGann must have been happy with his work as he then moved off at pace towards the North side of the square and back towards The Naofa which Connor had seen him disappear into over two hours ago.

McGann actually wasn't happy, but at least he had something to go on and more importantly, something to write in his next report.

He walked away from the green door, it was 27 Market Street.

He knew what he needed to do next. He needed to make sure he wasn't being followed.

He had been taught how to combat being followed when he

had began his training for his present role as an undercover officer. Before you returned to a police station or back to your digs, you cleansed yourself. In other words you made sure that you were not being followed. The idea was that you led people through alleyways where you would either then turn around and walk back towards them or you took them into a dead end.

McGann didn't like dead ends.

It meant there was only one way out for him and that was back from where he had come from which also meant that he had to pass, or more than likely, fight his way past whoever it was that was following him.

He didn't like fighting. He wasn't very good at it.

But he was doing it, not because he thought he should be doing it, but because he'd been told to do it.

But he wasn't very good at doing that either.

He walked through the alleyway, turned right then left, walked twenty yard up a further alleyway and then stopped. He listened.

He could hear footsteps.

He carried on, quickening his pace.

The footsteps carried on behind him.

He turned right into another alleyway.

But now he had a problem.

He didn't know where he was, he had committed the fatal sin, he had already lost his bearings.

He carried on blindly up the alleyway and then he stopped.

It was a dead end.

The sweat was now beading on his forehead and trickling down his back.

'For god sake man calm yourself' he told himself.

He slowly turned around to face his foe.

It was the 'bloody kid' delivering the milk.

He heaved a big sigh of relief and walked briskly passed the milk boy and turned left towards the East side of the town.

Connor let him go. He'd tell Cain what had happened.

Cain was with him again in the square within minutes.

He had watched from within the alleyway as McGann had passed the entrance and carried on towards the eastern side of the square.

He, as Connor had done, had watched as McGann stopped at the front of number 27 and drop the piece of paper. He saw him look through the window. He saw him walk through The Naofa on the Northern side of the square. He saw Connor follow him into the alleyway, and then he saw McGann walk back out of the alleyway some minutes later, looking harassed and worried.

He then watched him return to the eastern side of the square and disappear into The Eorna.

It was the Friday 29th of December.

Connor was going to be working this weekend.

Saturday 30th December 1916

Persuading Daibbi to let Connor work over the weekend hadn't been the hardest part. What had been was persuading Connor to leave his new bike at home and not go out with Cal exploring the countryside.

Some gentle persuasion had resulted in Cain promising to buy a very small broach in the shape of a red rose.

Connor had begun to realise his worth to Cain.

He hadn't let on of course, but he knew. He knew that Cain now needed him probably as much as he needed to carrying on working for Cain.

Connor's innocence still told him that he was needed to do the milk round for Cain so that he could carry on working on all of his farms.

Cain had told Daibbi that Connor was needed to collect the empty bottles again before they all disappeared before the New Years eve celebrations.

Connor's brief had been to collect all the bottles and whilst he was doing that he was to keep a look out for the Man in Black. If he should see him, then he was to follow him to wherever he went. Cain had stressed to Connor, without trying to scare him, that it was really important that he should do his absolute best in trying to find out as much as he possibly could about the Man in Black.

His reward would be the beautiful rose broach made of gold.

The thing was, Connor would have done it anyway. He thrived on achieving the goals given by Mr Milburn, or anybody else for that matter. If he was asked to do something he always strived to complete his task that had been given to him. Praise, whether it be a little or heaps of it, meant the world to Connor.

Give him any whatsoever and he would return again and again and again for more and more.

And because of this, Connor set out a little after 09:00am to collect his bottles, but more importantly to complete his task.

To find the Man in Black.

His memory bank was informing him that the best place's to find him were the alleys to the North side of the square and also those to the East side.

Connor had seen him on at least two occasions disappearing into the The Naofa on the North side and Cain had told him that he had seen him walk into the Eorna on the East side.

He would concentrate on these two sides.

After six hard hours of looking It was now 3 o'clock in the afternoon.

There was to be no broach.

He hadn't found him.

As they rode home Connor sat in silence. Cain could see and feel the disappointment in the boy at his side.

" Don't worry lad, we try again tomorrow, thats all we can do. I'm sure you did your best and tomorrow we will start a bit earlier. I will pick you up at 07:00, now chin up and lets have a smile".

Connor turned to look at him and eventually he forced a smile.

He hated failure. He hated not achieving what he had been asked to do.

He would find him tomorrow that was for sure.

Sunday 31st December 1916 New Years Eve.

Connor's task was still the same.

But he also had another one.

He was to deliver four Diamond notes to the usual addresses, and they were to be the priority.

Once he had delivered them then he was to go looking for the Man in Black.

As was now the norm, Cain got off the cart on the outskirts of the town, leaving Connor to ride on alone.

As he entered the square he stopped the cart and set about completing his first task.

He had delivered two of the notes and was now moving on towards the third address. He pulled one of the notes from his pocket. He made sure it was the right one.

Number 27.

The note was open.

It hadn't been folded properly.

Should he fold it back up.

Should he leave it as it was.

He stood staring at it.

He could see part of a written note on the inside.

He opened it up further. His hand trembled slightly as he did so.

It read:

WE ARE BEING WATCHED.

BY WHO IS NOT YET CLEAR BUT IT IS IN HAND.

THE MEETING TONIGHT GOES AHEAD.

MAKE SURE YOU ARE NOT FOLLOWED.

IF YOU FEEL THAT YOU ARE, RETURN HOME

AND AWAIT FURTHER INSTRUCTIONS.

THE BOY WILL DELIVER AGAIN TOMORROW

But It didn't matter that the note was open, because Connor still couldn't read.

He folded the note back together as best he could and then walked across the empty market square and placed it through the green front door of number 27.

As he turned back to walk to the cart, he saw him.

The Man in Black was stood watching him from The Naofa.

Connor didn't look at him but casually walked along the eastern side of the square down the hill towards the southern side, collecting the bottles as he went.

As he got to The Easpag he slowly turned to his left and entered it and then once out of sight, he ran down it as fast as he could. He ran forty yards to the next alleyway and then turned left again. He ran another fifty yards and turned left again now on The Eala and now he was facing back towards the square.

He stood on the edge of The Eala just two yards from the

square itself, watching.

There he was. The Man in Black was now stood in the middle of the square looking, no longer at Connor, but now he was looking at the front door of number 27 Market Square.

And he was writing something in his little notebook again.

As Connor watched him the man seemed to be smiling to himself. Almost laughing. Whatever he was doing he seemed to be very happy with himself, thought Connor.

McGann was happy.

He was happy for two reasons.

He was happy because he had not long left the side of his latest conquest and once he had finished his little job for the day he was going back to his digs where she was still waiting for him to return.

The second thing he was happy about was that he had at last discovered something that might prove to be very useful in finally having something of consequence on Cain Milburn.

The Boy. The boy was connected, he felt sure of it.

As McGann placed the notebook into his coat pocket Connor watched him as he walked north back towards The Naofa. As he entered The Naofa, Connor sprinted across the square to the western side, he placed his basket on the cart and then ran and stood just inside The Balla. He wasn't going to need the basket from here, he knew exactly what McGann was going to do next.

Sure enough two minutes later, McGann exited The Naofa and turned left towards the eastern side of the square. He cut the North Eastern corner and walked down the hill and turned left into The Eala. Connor sprinted back across the square and into The Eorna, one alley north of The Eala.

As Connor got to the first crossroads of alleyways, Clog Istigh, (Inner Clock) he stopped and he listened.

He could hear footsteps.

They were going away from him. He slowly peered around the righthand corner and saw McGann now walking away from him in a clockwise direction along Clog Istigh towards The Easpag.

Connor crossed the alleyway and continued on down The Eorna to the next alleyway, Clog Seachtrach (outer clock). He stood waiting. He had a view of the junction's to the right of both The Eala and The Easpag. The Eala was about forty yards away and The Easpag was at least another forty, but he could see it clearly.

McGann crossed the Clog Seachtrach, and continued walking along The Easpag. Connor, now happy that McGann wasn't going to come back towards him, sprinted down the Clog Seachtrach towards The Easpag. He stopped as he got to the corner and knelt on the ground.

But now he had no choice now. He had to look around the corner.

He slowly moved his head now just six inches above the ground, towards the edge of the wall, half expecting McGann to be stood there waiting to kick him in the head.

He wasn't.

He was still walking along The Easpag now just thirty yards in front of him. He watched and saw the inevitable pause. Connor slowly pulled his head back behind the wall.

He waited five seconds.

And then he slowly moved his head back around the corner just in time to see the front door shutting of a house on the right hand side.

It had the number 33 on its red door.

33 The Easpag.

Now what should he do. Connor stood on the corner thinking.

Would Mr Milburn want him to go and tell him what he had found or would he want him to stay where he was.

He decided to stay watching the house with number 33 on it. However, he wasn't going to do it from where he was now. He ran back up the clog Seachtrach, back towards The Eala where he turned right and carried on running until he reached a further crossroads where he turned right again. He ran back down the hill towards The Easpag and stopped as he got to the corner. He slowly peered around the righthand corner and smiled to himself. He was now facing west, back towards the Square. The more likely route for anybody coming out of number 33, which he could just see about fifty yards away.

He waited, and waited some more.

It was now almost 11:00. He had been waiting for almost an hour and a half and not seen a soul.

He was beginning to wonder if the man had come out while he was running around the alleyways to get to the East side of the house.

He needn't have worried.

As Connor stood with his back to the alley wall he saw the door slowly start to open.

He moved quickly back into the alley away from view.

He listened.

He heard the door shut.

He waited.

Footsteps.

Not one pair but two.

Two people were walking along The Easpag..... and as the sound of the footsteps began to lessen he knew that they were going away from him towards the square.

He walked across the junction of the Easpag and looked to his right.

The man was now with a woman.

He watched as they walked away from him, her arm through his and he could see that she was clearly very happy with her lot.

She had long black hair and was at least a foot shorter in height than the man in black, who was still, the man in black. It was the woman that was wearing the colour, she was wearing a black coat, but had a yellow scarf around her head and shoulders and her long black hair hanging at least six inches out of the bottom.

Connor thought subconsciously that it was good that she was wearing a yellow scarf. Easier for him to follow.

He let them walk on for a moment and then followed them until he reached the Clog Seachtrach. He then turned left onto the Clog Seachtrach itself, and ran, now travelling south and then following the Clog Seachtrach around the south east corner in a clockwise direction, now running East to West, at almost six o'clock on the clock face, with the square to his right.

As he approached the first alleyway on the South side, The Sagart, he turned right and ran towards the Clog Istigh where he stopped and looked towards the Square, catching a brief glimpse of the woman and McGann walking across the southern edge of the Square towards The Siul.

They had moved apart now no longer arm in arm but still walking together, talking quietly as they went.

Connor turned left now along Clog Istigh and continued running towards the Saighead again stopping at the corner, he was there just in time to see the two of them walk into The Siul.

He continued running along the Clog Istigh, now running towards the Stonebridge pub. As he got to its back gate he backed into the yard and waited.

He'd guessed right.

They were heading for the Bogmen estate.

From his slightly raised vantage point, he watched as they crossed the bridge over the River Lee and carried on walking further into the estate itself. He then saw the man briefly kiss the woman who then carried on walking for another forty yards or so before entering a house on the corner, just off the main street. It had a number 4 on the front door.

Connor knew he was having a good day. Mr Milburn was going to be very pleased with his mornings work, he was sure of that.

For the next hour and a half Connor continued to follow the man back in and around the centre of Tralee until he did his usual thing and entered the Naofa. By the time he had exited back out onto the square, Connor was already ahead and waiting for him back at number 33 with the Red door.

He watched him turn around and look behind him just before he entered and closed the door behind him.

It was now almost 1 o'clock in the afternoon and it was time to find Mr Milburn.

He decided to make his way back to the square and Duke and the cart and then wait for Cain to come and find him, as the chances of him finding Cain were virtually none. As Connor walked along the Easpag towards the square, he walked towards the rear gate to the Reindeer public house, as he got level with it, a hand came out from behind the gate and grabbed his arm, pulling him into the yard.

" In here Boy".

It was Cain.

" Shit, Mr Milburn, you scared me"

Cain stood there barely able to contain himself from Connor's response.

" What did you just say Connor lad, did I hear what I thought I heard"

" I'm really sorry Mr Milburn but you really scared me, I

thought it was the man"

Cain looked at him and his face slowly broke into a smile.

" You found him didn't you"

" Yes Mr Milburn I did, and he lives just down there"

As he pointed behind him back up The Easpag.

Connor then went on to tell Cain how he had followed the man through the square then eventually to the red door with the number 33 on it. As he was about to go on and tell him about the woman Cain interrupted him.

" Well done lad, I knew you would find him".

As Cain put his hand into his jacket pocket Connor watched as he pulled out a small red box.

" And I believe in keeping my promises so, here it is".

Cain had been so sure that Connor would achieve his task that he had gone and bought the broach the day before from the small jewellers in the square.

Connor stood open mouthed as he placed the box in his tiny hand.

" Is this really it Mr Milburn, is it really mine"

"why don't you open it and have a look"

Connor slowly opened the box and smiled from ear to ear as he saw that it was indeed what he had been promised.

" Now put it in your pocket and don't lose it, else your girlfriend wont be happy will she".

Connor now going bright red said,

" It's not for my girlfriend, I haven't got one, it's for my Nana for a late Christmas present"

" Well" said Cain " I'm sure she will like it, but don't tell her that I got it for you else she will throw it back in your face"

They both laughed a little and started walking towards the square until Cain stopped as though he had just thought of something.

" Hold on boy, there's something I need to show you" Cain turned around and the two of them walked back towards the rear yard of the Reindeer.

The day wasn't done, not just yet.

As Cain led him into the yard Connor could hear laughter and shouting coming from inside the pub. It was Sunday lunch time on News Year's Eve and it was heaving with bodies.

" Now lad listen carefully because what I am going to tell you is very important and if I need you to do something you are going to have to do it right, do you understand me"

" Yes Mr Miburn I understand" said Connor still overjoyed with his prize now safely in his pocket.

" Okay, tonight, well, to be more precise, at six o'clock, me and some friends of mine are going to meet in this pub here and have a drink. What I need to know is if that man down there" he pointed to number 33 " is anywhere near this pub, and, if he does come near it and looks like he might come in or is watching it from the outside, I need you to let me know, do you understand me so far".

Connor nodded confidently trying his best to assure Cain that he could trust him to do whatever was required.

" Okay, now obviously you are not allowed into the pub so here's what you are going to do if you need to signal to me that the man is here, you see that window over there".

He pointed to a 3 foot square window about 5 foot from the ground with bullseye glass panes in each one of the nine square window panes that looked out onto the Easpag.

" I will be sitting inside, just the other side of that window" Cain now walked towards the window, as Connor followed behind, he then stopped to pick up half a house brick from some rubble on the ground.

" If he comes anywhere near this pub or is watching, you throw this brick through this window".

Connor stared at him in disbelief, the look of total shock was all over his face. He'd been told off by his Nana on numerous occasions for throwing stones and now here was somebody, and an adult at that, actually telling him to throw a brick through a window.

" I can't do that Mr Milburn, I'm really sorry, but I can't throw a brick through a window, my Nana will kill me".

" I'm giving you permission to do it Connor so don't worry about it"

" You cant give me permission Mr Milburn it's not your window and it's not your pub and if my Nana finds out that I have done it"

Cain held up his hand to stop him and began nodding his head at him as he said

" Connor, your Nana, I can absolutely promise you, will not find out anything about it, no more so than she wont find out anything about that little burst of blasphemy earlier on".

Connor looked down at the floor embarrassed that he had said, or more like, having been caught saying such a word.

" Do I make myself clear"

" Yes Mr Milburn, but if I do throw it through the window, can I run off, because I really don't want to get caught"

" Connor you can run as fast as you like and to where you like as long as you send this brick through this window. Okay, now what I need you to do is to take Duke back to Rose cottage and then come back here for five o'clock. I'm going to be watching our Mr Man in Black until you come back. Tell your Nana you have been sent home for some tea and then you have to come back to me until about 8 o'clock tonight, got it ?"

" Got it" said Connor.

" And I hope she likes the broach " smiled Cain

" Now get going or you will be coming back before you get there".

As Connor rode back towards home his thoughts drifted to his Grandad Riley. He had actually been the last person to tell him off for throwing stones. He had thrown one towards an apple hanging from a tree one day in their back garden, missing it by several feet, and it hit the kitchen window cracking the glass but not completely breaking it. His Nana had spotted it several weeks later and Riley had put the blame on an imaginary black bird that had flown into the window some days before.

As he sat gently rocking back and forth on the cart, he wondered how he was. He missed him terribly, he knew that his Nana did too, he was their rock, his idol and most of all, his best friend.

He hoped that his little present would cheer his Nana up a little.

As he entered Rose cottage yard there was no sign of her. He tied up Duke and walked into the kitchen.

His Nana was sat at the kitchen table and she had a beautiful smile on her face.

As she saw Connor walk through the door her smile seemed to widen even further.

"I've had a letter from your Mummy Connor".

❋ ❋ ❋

GUILTY HAPPINESS

As Connor sat at the table beside her, she smiled at him.
His face full of anticipation and innocence.
"Would you like me to read it to you"
Connor didn't say a word, just nodded as if his head were about to fall off
Daibbi began to read,
"My dear Mother, Riley" she looked at Connor and nodded "and of course Connor,
I hope with all my heart that you are all well.
I hope my boy is doing well at school and perhaps he could write me a letter himself sometime, wouldn't that be lovely."
She looked at Connor over her spectacles but said nothing, but Connor got the message.
She continued on.
" For a change I have some good news to send you.
As you know I have been working at the Gaiety Theatre for some time now,
Well, the leading lady in the latest play, ' The Waining Moon' has taken ill. Unfortunately her being ill has been my gain and they gave me the part.
MY NAME IS UP IN LIGHTS !!!!

Obviously I had to have a stage name and I hope that you and my dear Riley wouldn't mind but I chose my name shown in the attached newspaper cutting.

Would you believe it !!

I promise to keep in touch and if all goes well would you and Riley come to see me one day, that would be so nice. I could take you back stage to meet everyone and then you could watch the show later on,

THE BEST SEATS IN THE HOUSE OF COURSE.

If it is possible, you could bring Connor with you too but he wouldn't be able to watch the show as he's too young but I have a friend he could stop with for a while, that would be so perfect, oh please let it happen.

I promise as always !! to keep in touch, please give my lovely boy a big kiss from me and I hope to see you all soon

All my love

Aibbi

(Ellen Gillian) ha ha x x x

Daibbi then showed the newspaper cutting from the Dublin Times, of the picture of Aibbi dressed in a beautiful floral dress, her hand to her head as if in distress. The words printed in bold above the picture read

' ELLEN GILLIAN, A STAR IS BORN'

Daibbi sat almost bursting with pride.

"That, is your mummy Connor, doesn't she look beautiful"

"Is it Nana, are you sure it's her. she hasn't got the same name has she, you said her name was Helen"

"its not Helen, its Ellen and yes its definitely your mother"

"then why has she got a different name, why isn't she called Aibbi because thats her name"

" Because Connor thats what you do when you are an actress,

you choose a different name from your own, and she has chosen the perfect name for herself, it's a wonderful gesture to her grandmother, my mother, her name was Ellen".

Connor still confused by the whole situation was having none of it,

" Well how do people know who you are then if you don't use your own name, and whats the point anyway"

" Thats just what actor's and actresses do Connor, you should be very proud of your mother, she's doing very well"

"Oh Nana I am, I'm very very proud I cant wait to go and tell my friends at school but because she has a different name they wont believe me will they"

" Connor they will believe you and if they don't then you send them to me"

Connor looked at his Nana. It was the first time in a long time since he had seen her smiling and happy.

He smiled back as he put his hand in his pocket suddenly remembering his late Christmas present.

" Oh Nana, I nearly forgot to give you this".

He pulled out the small box from his pocket and placed it onto the table in front of her.

"Its a late Christmas present, I'm sorry its late but I had to wait for Mr Milburn to give me my money"

As Daibbi stared at the small box before her she said softly to Connor

"What do you mean you had to wait"

" I asked Mr Milburn to save me some money from my wages so I could get you a Christmas present but he only gave it to me yesterday so here it is"

He knew it wasn't quite the truth but he also knew that he'd earn't it.

"You shouldn't have done this Connor, wasting your money on me"

" Its not a waste of money Nana, I love you very much and I wanted to show you how much"

She smiled at Connor, her Wonderful sweet little boy who she would quite willingly die for.

" Well then" she said " let's see what Father Christmas has bought me shall we".

She slowly opened the box and gasped with shock as she saw the small but perfectly formed gold broach with the blood red rose and gold petals and tiny emerald green leaves around the bottom.

" Connor, my dear darling Connor, its beautiful, truly beautiful"

"I thought you'd like it Nana, I know that you like roses"

" Oh Connor, I love it. I will treasure it for the rest of my life. Its the best Christmas present ever"

She knew that it wasn't quite the truth, it wasn't quite the best. That present was impossible to bring.

The whole family together was all she really wanted but that would have to wait.

So now as she sat here, with a warm glow of happiness enveloping her, the guilt now began to swell up within and overwhelm her.

Riley, where was her dearest Riley.

A tear slowly rolled down her cheek, but she smiled, a huge broad smile at the little scruffy boy who was sat next to her, staring at the picture on the newspaper cutting which he held out in front of him with both hands.

*** * ***

THE COUNCIL

Connor had returned to the square as he had been instructed.

It was a little after 5 O'clock in the evening and he had found a spot on a front door step of a closed store within the square to sit on. it had a view of both the front of the Raindeer, and also of the alley 'the Easpag'.

He watched quietly taking it all in again without realising that he was memorising almost each and every persons movements that he thought might be of significance.

as her sat he logged within his brain, four men, he remembered that he had seen at least three of them before. They had been stood with Cain within the square when he had first seen the man in black. He watched as in turn, each of the three men walked towards the front of the Reindeer and as they got to the steps at the front door, slowly turn around to see if they were being watched or followed and then in turn, each one enter the Inn.

The fourth man that drew his eye was new to him.

His brain told him that he had never seen him before but his brain also told him that there was something about him that made him look as if he was of Importance.

He watched him cross the square after he had exited 'The Point' and slowly, but with a purpose, walk towards the same front door, the same pause and turn as the others, and then he walked inside.

But there was one significant difference in his appearance.

This man was a Priest.

Inside, the four men had greeted each other and walked over to the table in the left hand corner, below the square window with nine bulls eye glass pains and where the fifth man was already seated.

The fifth man was Cain Milburn, second in command of the

Tralee IRA council.

He stood and smiled as the four men walked over and joined him at the table.

It was a quiet corner. Well, not exactly quiet, but considerably less noisy than the rest of the bar.

It was known to most of the locals as The Holy Corner.

It had been called the Holy Corner for as long as most people could remember. Legend said that in the early 1800's, a local Priest had tripped and fell in the town square whilst walking across it with a fellow Priest. He was then carried, unconscious, to the Reindeer and placed on a table in this very corner, where he was given the last rights by the other Priest who had been visiting him at the time. After a short time, the stricken Priest had awoken from his death bed and declared that during his sleep he had been visited by the virgin Mary who declared to him that his work here on earth was not yet done and she had sent him back to complete his reason for being here.

What had slowly been forgotten over the last two hundred years was that many had recalled the two Priest's staggering from an Inn at the top of the square, which had long since vanished, barely able to stand due to the fact that they had been in the public house all day and had been there for at least the three days before since the visiting Priest had first arrived.

But it was a good story and since then it had been known as the Holy Corner.

For the last half a century the local Priest would hold court and perform quiet personal confessions to those that felt they needed one, away from the church.

Nobody else ever sat in 'the Priest's Chair'. It was unofficially reserved for gods Head Servant. If you wanted to see the Priest then you sat at the table and waited for him to arrive, if he didn't arrive then you came back the next day.

For the last year or so It was now also used to hold meetings such as the one that was about to take place.

In Ireland, as in many Catholic Countries, the Priest was a man who was not only respected but also held a great deal of power.

However, The Priest that reigned supreme over the Holy Corner at this moment in time held the most powerful seat for miles around. And it wasn't just of the cloth.

The man was Father Henry Milburn.

The eldest son of Edmond Milburn, older brother of Cain Milburn.

Father Henry Milburn, Commander of the west of Ireland and Tralee IRA council.

The five men all sat at the round table, Cain sat with his back to the window and his brother, Father Henry, was sat to his right, in 'the Priest's chair', and although the table was round, he somehow had the aura about him that made him appear to be sat at the head of the table.

They all exchanged the basic pleasantries and then fell into a natural silence waiting for Father Henry to open proceedings.

They all watched as Father Henry raised his glass in a silent toast, all of them knowing exactly what he meant and raising their glass in reply.

As Father Henry lowered his glass it was already half empty, it had been a hard day and it was far from over.

"Ok gentlemen shall we begin" said Father Henry.

"We have a lot to talk about this evening and as always, I cannot say how Important it is that what is said, here and now, it is not repeated to anybody, and I mean anybody, is that clear".

The four other men each nodded their reply in solemn recognition of the importance of it all and then raised their glass again to swallow another two mouthfuls of ale.

"Now Cain, I trust that you have the latest problem under control ".

Cain looked at his brother and slowly nodded his response.

" Yes Henry, I'm hopeful that he wont be a problem for much longer, lets say that our youngest member of the cause has it all under control".

"Ah the messenger boy, yes, he's still working for us then, how is that boy of yours doing" said Henry.

"He's doing very well, in fact he's watched you all come in here tonight.

"Well I didn't see him" said Byrne.

" Well that Mr Byrne, is exactly the reason why I'm using him, and I can assure you that he will have seen every single one of you come into this establishment, he will remember from which direction you have come from, and not only that, he will also remember exactly what each and every one of you is wearing from head to toe".

They all looked at each other.

It was Father Henry that broke the silence and he broke it with laughter.

Within a few seconds the rest of them were laughing and chinking glasses with each other over the table.

The three other men were, Dermot Brady who was in charge of recruitment, Niall Ramsey, intelligence and informants and Lany Byrne weapons and purchasing.

Lany Byrne lived at 27 Market Square.

" And" said Cain "He is still out there and will be out there until we leave, just in case he needs to warn us that we are being watched ".

Cain pointed to the window behind him with his thumb and he quietly said

" If that window should be broken, then our problem is either coming in here or he's watching from outside".

As the fiddle and drum started to play from within further

into the bar, the singing of 'follow me up to Carlow' began to resonate throughout the whole of the building, the beat hardening with the tapping of the feet and the clapping of the hand from the throng within, almost becoming hypnotic in its constant and repetitive rhythm.

As the music got louder and louder the five men sat bent over all leaning toward the centre of the table, talking in loud whisper's. Discussing the matters in hand, drinking beer, and slowly but surely driving each other into a fervid frenzy of excitement and anger.

Over an hour and a half later Connor was still sat in the same space but now due to the darkness, his attention had now moved to watching the Easpag and more importantly, and luckily, a well lit part of the alley in the area of the Red door.

The door was along way from where he sat, over 150 yards away at least, but he was happy that he would see any movement, and if he did then he would move towards the Reindeer should he need to do so.

It wasn't long before he had too.

He saw the woman first. She came from where the door would be and stood in the centre of the Easpag looking back at the door as if she was waiting for somebody.

And she was still wearing her yellow headscarf.

A few seconds later McGann appeared.

The two of them started walking towards the square, and more importantly towards Connor, and the Reindeer.

Connor began to walk across the square towards them but slightly to their right to give himself some cover.

They were now about fifty yards from the rear yard of the Reindeer.

Connor was sixty yards.

If they went in that way he wasn't going to make it.

He quickened his pace.

They were now only thirty yards apart and as Connor watched them he saw McGann, very briefly, look over in his direction.

'Had he just looked at me, why would he do that' thought Connor.

They were now level with the yard, Connor now stood at the side of the entrance to the Easpag away from their view in a house doorway. He stood completely still.

They hadn't gone into the yard.

They continued out into the square swerving around the ever increasing number of people now moving from one place to another across the square.

Connor breathed in a sigh of relief, he wasn't going to have to throw the brick.

He'd breathed 'it' a little too soon.

He saw them pause. He watched as they had a quiet conversation. She looked as if she didn't want to go across the square, she had turned to face McGann and she was pointing towards the Reindeer.

He saw McGann look at his watch.

He saw the woman mouth the word 'please'.

He saw the shoulders of McGann give in.

He felt the knot of his stomach tighten.

They were going to go into the Reindeer.

As they climbed the steps to the front door Connor raced around into the Easpag and into the rear yard.

McGann was in a good mood. He'd had a really good day.

He had bedded his woman twice. Which wasn't factually correct, as she wasn't his woman. She, Mary Donnelly, was married with two young children. But all the same he had had a nice time.

He had also made some substantial progress, or so he thought, into the workings of Mr Cain Milburn and his associates. He knew that one of them lived at 27 Market Square. He knew that one of them lived somewhere on the South Road on the outskirts of the town as he had seen Milburn getting off the cart on the way to town. He had seen Milburn visit a house on Sheep Street and he had now seen a small boy appear to be delivering notes to at least two of the houses. Was it just coincidental or was the boy not just delivering milk but also notes for Milburn. He felt confident that it was probably the latter. But would his boss.

Anyway he'd had a lovely afternoon with Mrs Donnelly at his digs and now it was time to take her back home to her children. He had to be careful as her husband would be finished work and would now be waiting for her to return so he could go out. As they had left 33 The Easpag he had forgotten his little notebook and returned inside to get it. He'd need it later as he needed to go to the police station to update his report. He couldn't put it off any longer.

He smiled as he knew that he had a lot of good information to put in it.

As they walked towards the square arm in arm, life was good, they laughed and joked about their day and other little things. His attention was suddenly drawn to a boy walking towards them from the square.

"In here" said Mary

McGann turned to Mary and said

"sorry what"

"I said in here"

He turned back to look where the boy had gone.

He'd disappeared, gone, just vanished into thin air.

'Was that him' thought McGann 'was that the same boy that he had seen earlier pushing the note through the door of number 27'.

"Come on Declan, I don't want to go back yet, lets have a drink in the Reindeer".

McGann, his mind now set on other things, wanted to go looking for the boy "What now, what about your kids".

" Don't you worry about them, my ma will be there getting their tea ready, come on let's drink",

She paused and looked at him with the eyes that made him melt.

"I will make it worth your while" raising her eyebrows.

She knew that she would have him with that.

McGann scanned the square but it was no good, the boy had completely vanished.

She grabbed his hand and pulled him up the steps and into the noisy, vibrant, heaving bar.

Connor was in the yard. The brick, now in his small trembling hand,

'Oh god, oh please god, don't let my Nana find out about this'

He thought.

He knew he had to do it, and he had to do it right now.

As a result of his one action two things then happened at the same time.

One ; As Connor let the brick fly, he closed his eyes and waited for the sound of breaking glass. He didn't know it but he had been very lucky. He had managed to hit the window pane in the bottom right hand corner causing it to shatter and send glass flying into the bar and, as instructed, into the Holy Corner. A few inches to the left and the brick would have just bounced back at him due to the toughness of the glass. Hearing the sound that he needed to hear, he ran, and he ran as fast as his feet would take him across the square and into 'the Point'. But he kept on running, he couldn't stop. He had never done anything so bad in his life.

At the Clog Istigh he stopped and turned around. There was nobody there.

two; The brick had come through the window causing the five men to instinctively duck further down towards the table, lower than they already were. They automatically spun around scanning the bar to see if they were about to be attacked or worse, were the police arriving.

Neither was happening but Cain had seen him.

McGann was walking through the bar towards the far side away from where the council were sat. And he was with a woman.

As Cain watched the two of them walking happily through the bar he knew that the five of them and more importantly, the movement, were now in serious trouble. He needed to act and he needed to do it as soon as possible.

There was one other thing that should have happened but hadn't.

What should have happened was that McGann and Mary should have seen the five men sat in the corner watching them.

But McGann and Mary had been oblivious to the whole scenario.

They hadn't seen the window break.

They hadn't seen the panic over in the Holy Corner.

They hadn't seen Cain watching them walk across the bar.

And they hadn't seen the other four men sat around the table,

The Leader of the IRA in county Kerry,

The Second in Command,

The man in Charge of recruitment,

The man in Charge of intelligence and informants,

and the man in Charge of weapons.

They just wanted a drink. Nothing else, not yet anyway, just a drink and some fun. McGann knew that he should really be going to the police station to write his report but, as always, it could wait. He would do it later tonight. The night was young, and so were they.

They bought a drink and settled in the far opposite corner to Cain and the other four.

The bar was full.

Neither could see either.

They, the five, would wait until he moved. He couldn't do anything in here.

At a little past 8:15 pm McGann and Mary got up to leave. As they passed the bar heading towards the front door Cain saw them.

They didn't see Cain.

Cain lent over to Henry and whispered in his ear that he would be back.

He grabbed Byrne by the arm signalling that he was to come with him.

As they exited the bar, Cain scanned the market square.

" There they are towards the Siul" said Byrne.

But Cain wasn't looking for them.

" I know where they are, I'm not looking for them".

And then Cain caught sight of Connor following them about fifty yards behind.

" Okay, he's got them, come on Byrny boy lets go, I think you are going to enjoy this".

They watched Connor and followed him through the Siul and towards the bridge that crossed the Lee.

As they exited the Siul at the edge of the Lee, Cain and Byrne stopped dead.

They had disappeared.

No McGann and no Mary.

And no Connor.

Cain's eye shot towards the River Lee. He ran to the railings and peered into the darkness. The river was flowing fast and angry, swelling in wallowy waves rushing by from left to right.

He couldn't see anything.

Cain placed both his hands on top of his head and slowly ran his fingers back through his hair in anguish and despair.

A soft voice from behind him.

Cain span around.

It came again.

"Mr Milburn".

"Connor".

"I'm here, Mr Milburn".

Cain looked into the dark shadow of the wall as Connor moved out from it, causing Byrne to slightly jump in surprise.

"Jesus, Connor, I thought.... Never mind".

"Why are you not following the man".

Connor looked puzzled and then a little worried as he had never spoken about what he did for Cain in front of anybody before.

He stood looking at Cain and then at the other man wondering what to say.

"It's okay Connor, this is Mr Byrne and you don't need to worry about him, now what's going on".

Connor still looking a little unsure, explained to Cain that he had followed McGann and the woman earlier that day and had seen them enter a house, he described its location and that it was number 4. He then told him that the woman had remained in the house and that the man in black had come out on his own and had returned back to his digs on the Easpag.

"So Mr Milburn, because I knew where he was going I thought you wouldn't need me to do it again" said Connor, still wondering if he had done wrong,

Cain looked at Byrne with a huge smile on his face.

"I told you this boy was good didn't I".

Cain stood thinking about what to do next.

" Okay Connor here's what I need you to do now. You go and watch the house with the number 4 on it and when anybody comes out you make sure that you beat him across this bridge and we will be waiting right here".

Connor nodded his response and ran across the bridge towards the Bogmen estate.

Caine turned to Byrne.

"Go and fetch Ramsey".

As Connor got to the house he could hear shouting coming from inside. It was a man's voice but he could hear a woman screaming and then he could hear her crying.

He moved back into the shadows as the door suddenly opened and a man came charging out. The woman came out after him trying to pull him back but he swung his arm away and as he swung back around to face her, Connor saw that he had a thick wooden walking stick in his right hand, he swung it at her hitting her on the arm and then with his other hand he punched her in the face causing her nose to explode with blood.

The man then briskly walked away passing Connor barely 3' from him.

It wasn't the man in black.

He watched as the man continued to walk quickly in the direction of the bridge, subconsciously noting what he looked like, his height, his build, what he was wearing.

As Connor stood thinking what to do next, he saw another man move out of the alley from his right hand side just slightly in front of him.

He'd been lucky, if he had gone just ten more yards towards the house, the man would have seen him.

It was McGann.

He watched as McGann looked back down the street in the direction of where the man from the house had gone. McGann then ran towards the house.

He also must have seen and heard what Connor had just witnessed.

He saw McGann enter the house and close the door behind him.

He needed to tell Cain.

He sprinted back to the bridge and less than five minutes later a breathless Connor walked up to the darkness where a short time ago he had left Cain.

As he got there Cain appeared out of the shadows.

Connor couldn't see the other men but he could feel them, they were there in the darkness that was for sure.

As he explained to Cain what he had just seen, Cain stood working out what had happened.

" So Connor, what did the man look like that came out',

"He was a bit taller than you but thinner, he had a black cap on and a brown jacket with a white shirt on underneath and he had a thick wooden walking stick"

" Phelan Donnelly" whispered a voice from the darkness.

"Shut the fuck up" snarled Cain at the unseen figure behind him.

" Ok Connor good work, now you go and get yourself on that cart and get yourself home".

"But what about you Mr Milburn" said Connor.

"Don't you worry about me lad, I will see you in the morning now get yourself gone".

McGann had been waiting outside for Mary's husband, Phelan Donnelly to leave for the pub. He'd been promised a special treat for taking Mary to the pub for one last drink.

He really hadn't got the time but another half an hour wouldn't matter.

He had stood and waited patiently in the darkness looking forward to his reward when he had heard her screaming. He thought about walking away, but women sometimes scream over nothing so he waited.

He saw the door open and walked back around the corner and into the darkness out of view.

He then heard some sort of commotion but didn't see it. He then watched as Phelan walked past him towards the bridge. He gave it a few minutes then made his way hurriedly towards the house and his prize.

The scent of a woman had led many a man to his death.

He was in the kitchen still tending to his latest conquests bloody nose when the three men burst in through the back door.

Just after midnight, on his arrival back home, a very drunk Phelan Donnelly staggered up the central staircase to bed.

He was still there the next morning when the police broke into the house following a report of children screaming from within.

Three days later Phelan Donnelly was charged with the murder of his wife, Mary Donnelly and an as yet, unidentified man.

The police obviously knew who the unidentified male was, but due to the sensitivity of his work it was decided that his identity would not be released to the newspapers.

The main witness to the double murder was the Donnelly's next door neighbour, Mrs O'Rourke. O'Rourke had heard the shouting and screaming from within number 4 Lee Street at around 8:30pm. This wasn't an unusual occurrence, it had happened several times, 'Mary had had several beatings from her husband in the past' she had told them, but it had seemed a little more frenzied than normal. She had then heard a lot of banging and what sounded like a muffled scream about half an hour later.

It had then gone completely quiet until she heard the screams of the children at around 7:30 the next morning.

She had gone and knocked on the front door as she was worried about the children and found that it was unlocked. So she entered to discover the gruesome sight of the two body's in the kitchen, with pools of blood all around them.

She had taken the two children to her house and left them with her husband while she went to find a policeman.

The policeman had entered the house with his colleague and on confirming that the male and female were dead, they went upstairs to find the still unconscious Phelan Donnelly in his bed. The officers had noted that Donnelly had several deep scratches to his face and neck, and large bruises on his upper arm.

Around ten hours earlier as McGann had lay unconscious and dying on the Kitchen floor of 4 Lee street, Cain Milburn had searched his pockets. He knew what he was looking for.

He found it in the black coat's inside pocket.

The small black hardback notebook was in one way a priceless treasure to help the cause, but in other ways it asked more questions than it gave answers.

A few days later, as Cain sat in the study at Manor farm, reading the contents, he sat shaking his head, trying as best he could to think of the positives, the consequences of it's disclosure were too dreadful to even think about.

As he flicked through the numbered pages he noted that some of the pages were missing. He continued through, as he did so he stopped and read the notes trying to judge the damage that they may have caused.

The first few pages were scribbled notes of, what he thought, insignificant conjecture.

Then he turned to page 11.

Page 11

Suspect one

Cain Milburn

Manor Farm.

40-45 years, 6' tall, black wavy hair, stocky build

Milk round

Bennett Murder ?

The last line didn't worry him too much. He was always going to be a suspect in any sort of trouble that occurred in the town. It was the line before that which concerned him.

Milk round.

What did McGann know about the milk round.

He read on.

Page 17

19 Sheep St

Important place ? Doesn't go often but he's different when he goes there.

3 males with Milburn

Male 1

45-50 years 5'8" tall, medium build, red hair.

Male 2

30-35 years 6'2" tall large build, quiet man doesn't say much !!!

Male 3

40-45 years, 5' 8" stocky build, scar on left cheek.'

What did he mean by that, 'he's different when he goes there'

Did he mean him, he very rarely went there, or did he mean Connor. Did he know about Connor.

And what did he mean about ' different'.

The descriptions were clearly describing Byrne, Ramsey and Brady.

He carried on,

Page 28

19 Sheep street.

Kid, milk.

11 River Walk, early visit again , scar man stays sometimes.

This wasn't good.

What did he know about his brother.

What had made him go there, Sheep Street, how had he found out about that.

Connor again was mentioned, but more importantly in conjunction with the word 'milk'.

11 River Walk, This was Ramsey's house, did he know that Ramsey was one of his men, he definitely knew where he lived.

But it was the last page he was about to read that turned him ice cold and pale.

Page 31

27 Market Square red hair man,

The kid is posting note's !!!!.

' The kid is posting note's'.

As he read it he knew.

He now knew that McGann had been on to them in a big way. But who else knew, and how much did they know.

If they did know about it, Cain knew he could expect a visit very soon. He also knew that Connor would be getting one too.

But McGann had been unprofessional to the end.

He had spent too much of his time womanising and drinking and not enough time writing his reports and doing his job, that he had been very well paid for.

His boss had washed his hands of him. The husband had given him what he had deserved. He probably hadn't meant to kill him but as most of these things do, it had gotten out of hand.

The Milburn file was placed to the back of the cabinet.

Cain never received a visit.

And neither did Connor.

The scent of a woman.

It would be on August 2oth 1917 that Phelan Donnelly would be hanged for the Murder of his wife, Mary Donnelly, and that of the still unidentified male.

He screamed all the way to the gallows that he was an innocent man.

The rest of Tralee didn't believe him, but five men and five men only, knew the truth.

* * *

A DEAD MAN'S BOOK

September 1917

Against his better judgment, and that also of his brother, Cain had kept the little black book that he had taken from McGann.

Henry had looked at the book and told him to burn it.

But he hadn't.

He didn't know why he hadn't, but he had kept it. He had hidden it in the roof of the cow shed behind Manor Farm. But now it was time to get rid of it. His brother had been right, It held too much information and if found, it would bring down their fight that was for sure.

So now as he sat in the sitting room of the Manor House, he read through the pages for the last time. As he read them he tore the page out and threw it on the first fire of the dying summer burning away in front of him.

There was nothing more to read. He had read it from front to back, back to front, several times now.

But as he tore out the last page, he saw it.

As he had ripped out the very last page, the corner of it had been glued to the hardback cover, and there, in the top left corner, he could see that a small piece of paper had been slipped behind the glued back page.

It had writing on it.

He placed the book down and slowly stood and then walked across to the small oak bureau, opened the draw and pulled out a small Ivory handled letter opener. He walked back to his chair and picked up the book. He slipped the letter opener behind the ripped page and very carefully ran it around the edge until he could fold it back.

The small piece of paper that had been hidden behind fell to the floor. As he looked down at it he could already see what it was.

He bent to pick it up and then slowly looked down the page.

It now all fell into place.

He whispered to himself " Oh Mr McGann what a silly man you were".

McGann had been a policeman, and he hadn't been an ordinary one either.

Cain had heard that the constabulary had started using undercover police officers but it had never crossed his mind that the man in black could be one of them.

McGann had written down his own police number and also that of the name of his Boss.

Cain knew the man well.

But what he wasn't so well acquainted with was the rest of the names.

McGann had kindly written the names and numbers of 16 other officers, and each name had an Irish city or town written against it.

He folded the small piece of paper and placed it inside the bible which was sat on his table in front of him and threw the remnants of the black book onto the fire.

As he watched it slowly catch fire, the smile had returned to Cain Milburn's face. He looked up to the ceiling and quietly thanked the lord he hadn't burnt it when he should have.

❊ ❊ ❊

THE GHOST OF A MAN

February 1918

It was cold, very cold. But dry. As Daibbi looked out of her bedroom window into the rear yard the ice had formed on the outside of the glass making appear as though she was looking through an opaque window . She heard the sound of a horses hoof's outside of the front of the house and walked out onto the landing to see who it was. It couldn't have been Connor returning, it was far too early for that. It was a little after 730 and he would be at least another hour if not two.

As she looked out she saw a horse drawn carriage turning around and heading back south from where she presumed it had come from.

She then heard the distinctive sound of the back gate being opened.

She went downstairs and through the kitchen and as she got to the back door she peered through the small pain of frost covered glass into the rear yard. she saw the shape of what appeared to be a man walking very slowly towards her.

She froze. 'It couldn't be' she flung open the kitchen door and there he stood.

"Hello my beautiful Daibbi, I've come home"

"Riley".

That was all she could say as she held him in her arms trying hard not to believe that it was all a dream and she was about to wake up again in her lonely bed.

Eventually she let him go and stared at the face of a man that she could see had changed, and not just in his appearance.

The man that had left had been a well built muscular fit man in his early forties, with smiling eyes and a happy smile.

This was the same man, he had the same name and the same wavy hair but there it ended. This was a beaten man. A man that seemed devoid of emotion and if he hadn't been breathing she would have thought him to be dead.

As she slowly looked at him she realised that he was on crutches and his left leg was held out in front of him and was heavily bandaged from toe to just above the knee.

As she slowly came to her senses she spoke.

"My god Riley, what have they done to you, let's get you inside".

She picked up the case at his side and helped him through the door and then led him towards the chair at the kitchen table.

He sank heavily into the seat and she saw a brief wince of pain across his face as he did so.

She held his hand and waited. She could wait all day. He could speak when he wanted to.

He was home and that was all that mattered.

They sat in silence for almost ten minutes before Riley spoke.

"How's the boy I thought he would be here, is he still in bed"

"No Riley he is still helping Cain Milburn with the milk round, he's been working for him for some time now. He loves it Riley, its given him some independence"

"Well thats good then" said Riley.

He drifted back into silence and Daibbi felt that she needed to keep the conversation going, for Riley's sake if nothing else.

"Ive had some letters from Aibbi" she said and lent behind her and passed him two envelopes.

As he began to read them she could see that the words were not going in. There was no emotion, no hint or sign of recognition of what it contained, it was as if he was still somewhere else. His mind probably was.

This was going to take a long time. But she had the time, she had all the time in the world for this man. She would get him better. Time was a healer they say.

It was going to have to be.

" Let's get those horrible dirty clothes off you and get you into something clean and fresh" said Daibbi.

As Riley went to stand Daibbi put her hand to his shoulder.

She said " You wait there I'll go upstairs and fetch you some clothes".

A few minutes later she came back down with his clothes and entered the kitchen.

The suitcase was now on the table and lay open. Riley was nowhere to be seen, but she had a good idea where he was.

She walked out into the yard and crossed towards the barn and towards The Bear's stable.

As Daibbi got to the barn she could see the Bear standing, his head not quite outside the door but close to it. She was a little surprised to see Riley not with him but further towards the back of the stable on his knees at the wooden tack box, the lid still open and Riley looking inside of it.

"Your not taking him out if thats what you're thinking" said Daibbi.

Riley turned and looked at her, a small smile on his face thought Daibbi, just a small one but yes, it was definitely there.

"No Daibbi I just wanted to give him a brush".

She helped him to his feet and as The Bear stood patiently chewing on a net of hay they groomed him, top to bottom, front to back.

After almost an hour she thought it was the right time, if ever there was one, to ask a question that needed to be asked.

"Riley,"

He looked at her, he knew what was coming.

" What do we need to do about your leg, do you need to see a doctor or go to a hospital"

He shook his head "No Daibbi, it's healing, but I've been told that I need to rest it as much as possible. I can't walk on it for at least another 6 weeks but they are pleased with how its going".

As they carried on brushing and thoroughly spoiling the horse before them, Riley knew he had to tell her, and so he sat, and then, warts and all, he told her exactly what had happened to him.

She listened, she didn't ask him any questions, she didn't interrupt him, she didn't react, she just listened. He needed to tell her and she was going to listen to him for as long as it took.

It took a long while.

He started from the beginning, about how for the first few months he saw nothing of the war itself. He heard stories from injured soldiers on their way back from the front before returning to England about what was happening but it never really prepared him for what lay ahead.

As he began to tell her about his eventual secondment to the very secret unit ran by Major Cassell, Daibbi saw and felt the immense pride that Riley had for where he had been.

He went on to tell her about how he had gone on horse back, several times behind enemy lines and then hid for several days on a hill side and how they had fed the information back to the

British intelligence unit using carrier pigeons.

As he told her all about his friend Corporal Harry Hayworth, she saw his eyes fill with tears and as they slowly slid down his cheeks she knelt down before him and gently held his hands.

"Its ok Riley you can stop now if its all too much"

"No Daibbi, I need to tell you now, they said it would do me good to share it with somebody"

As he looked at her, seeking her approval to carry on, she squeezed his hands and gently nodded for him to continue,

He carried on.......

They had been back to their hide several times over the last few months in between travelling to other area's, and each time they returned, they felt that it was getting more difficult to get there unseen. There route in along the ditch was fine as it was summer and the thickness of it had deepened and they were virtually almost totally invisible from the outside. It had been getting to the the ditch that had become the problem. The Germans, due to their own intelligence, had become increasingly suspicious that their were British troops behind their lines. It had shown that somebody was feeding information back to the British about their troop movements and numbers. From what information had been sent back, it was clear to them that the only way they could have known this information was that they had seen it with their own eyes. What had confirmed their suspicions was that a dead pigeon had been found by a German soldier who had spotted a small capsule tide to its leg. He had opened the capsule and had seen several lines of tiny numbers written on a piece of paper. He had immediately passed it on to his sergeant who, on examining it, knew exactly what they were. They were grid references and times.

They subsequently increased the numbers of infantry on the likely routes that somebody would use to get behind the lines and they, he and Harry, almost every time over the last six or seven deployments, had had to take evasive action to prevent their detection.

On the last trip they made they knew deep down that this was probably going to be the last time they could do it.

As they made their way in total darkness, it was just after midnight, along the canal, they had heard gunfire ahead no more than half a mile away. They had never heard it from that area before as they were almost two miles behind enemy lines.

They knew that there should be no other British troops in this area as they were the only two that should be there. They had a choice to make.

Carry on to the hide on top of the hill or turn back for home. They couldn't stay where they were it would be getting light in around 4 1/2 hours and then they would be out in the open with nowhere to go.

They had backed into the hedgerow with the horses trying to decide what to do.

Another crack of gunfire, much nearer this time, made their-mind's up.

They had to turn around and start to make their way back home, and that was where it all started to go horribly wrong.

Some horses, not all, but some, don't like going back from where they have just come from. They like riding out, which is why many people that ride horses, when they can, they ride a circular route, that way the horse remains quite happy with his life and doesn't realise he's home until it's too late to worry about it.

Blue was fine about turning around but Harry's horse, Cyril, didn't like it, far from that, he was having none of it what so ever.

The more Harry tried to turn him around the more noise he was making.

A third crack of gunfire seemed too, in some ways, help the

situation, it was so near that it couldn't have been more than two hundred yards from them and it appeared to be from further up the canal.

Harry leapt on Cyril and smacked him hard on his backside and they took off at a canter along the canal away from where the gunshot had come from, Riley on Blue just yards behind him. The need for quietness had gone, they needed to be away from where they were and fast.

As they raced along the footpath more shots rang out from behind them and in the reflection of the moonlight on the water Riley saw two splashes caused by bullets slightly to his right.

They'd been seen.

Another crack but no water splash this time. It hit him in the back of his right knee making him scream in pain.

Harry hearing Riley scream, lept the hedge to his left and put Cyril into a gallop. Blue instinctively followed the horse in front and also leapt the hedge, Riley hanging on for his life.

They were on open ground now heading west across a newly cut wheat field lit up by a half moon.

Up ahead and about six hundred yards away, they could see the silhouette of a large wood. They needed to get in there and then they would have a chance, not much of one but a better chance than they had now.

More shots rained down on them.

They both knew what they had to do. They needed to split up.

Harry went right and Riley turned Blue to his left.

The gunfire had now become incessant as Riley weaved and turned trying to dodge the incoming fire. He was now about 100 hundred yards from the wood and he turned to his right to see Harry no more than 60 yards from the edge of the tree line and then it happened.

Another gunshot.

Harry's head exploded.

His already lifeless body waved from side to side across Cyril's back. He stayed on for another ten yards or so before his body crashed to the floor rolling over and over in the dirt.

Riley knew Harry was dead. There was no life left in that body.

The pain in his leg was horrendous, but as he crashed into the woods he carried on, he knew that the deeper he got into the woods the better chance he had.

He slowed his pace as both he and Blue gasped trying to get their breath back.

Eventually they came to a stop and he slowly looked around him.

The wood was dense. Which was good in someways as it gave him good cover. But his manoeuvrability was not so good. He also knew that if he got off Blue, he was going to have great difficulty in getting back on. He looked down at his leg.

It wasn't good.

The blood was dripping onto his boot and his foot was off at a funny angle.

He was bought back to his senses by men shouting. They were German voices and they were coming from behind him and over to his right. They were over where he had last seen the stricken body of Harry.

He heard two more shots.

He knew that his friend was definitely dead now.

He was starting to feel faint. He needed to keep moving. He carried on the way he was going away from the shouting and the open ground and moved further into the wood.

He must have passed out. He slowly came around but he was now laying on the floor.

As he looked around him he realised that it was now daylight. It was still early morning, the sun had only just come over the horizon.

and then he sensed he wasn't alone. Blue was standing a few

feet away to his side. As he slowly turned his head he saw the soldiers boots.

This was it then. This was how he was going to die.

In a wood somewhere in eastern France.

A bullet in the head.

As he slowly sat up he shuffled backwards and placed his back to a tree. He looked up at the young blonde haired German soldier standing before him.

Quietly he said "If your'e going to kill me, can I ask you one thing. Will you take my horse and make sure he gets looked after."

The soldier looks at him and took Blue's reigns, and replied in very good English.

"Was the man your friend,"

"Yes he was"

"He had no identity"

Riley looked at him

"Is he dead"

"Yes he is".

Riley paused, his heart sinking to a depth he had rarely known and replied.

"Then his name was Corporal Harry Hayworth and yes, he was my friend".

The soldier looked at him.

"Can you stand"

Riley struggled to his feet. The pain etched all over his face as he leant against the tree, now standing on his one good leg.

The soldier held out the reigns in front of him and offered them too Riley.

"Can you get on"

"Not without your help".

The soldier took hold of Riley's left leg and lifted him on.
Riley looked at the young soldier.
"Thank you".
The Soldier smiled at him and held out his hand and they shook.
The soldier pointed south west " You need to go this way for just over one kilometre and then you must turn right and follow the railway line, stay on the left hand side of it and you will be in cover and back on your own side after another 500 metres"
"You sound like you have been there before".
"One or two times ", he smiled knowingly, "you do it, we do it".
"Don't worry, I will make sure the Corporal is dealt with properly".
Riley nodded his approval and thanked him again.
As Riley rode off, it crossed his mind he might be shot in the back.
But the shot never came.
The soldier had been true to his word. The route back had been safe and he made his way back undetected.
'You do it, we do it' he had said.
Whilst he and Harry had been behind the German lines, the soldier, had undoubtedly been hidden in some whole looking back across the valley of death behind the British lines. He had smiled to himself and shook his head. By mid day he had managed to make his way back and was taken straight to hospital.
He had a shattered kneecap and broken tibia.
He wouldn't be coming back to the war.

Later that morning Connor returned from his milk round and Daibbi saw a smile on her man's face that warmed her heart.

It was going to be alright.

Over the coming months Riley told her stories and tales from his time in France, but there were some things that the demons in his head wouldn't let go. He couldn't tell her everything.

Riley had also sat for hours talking to Connor about the war. Connor would sit listening intently to his stories, of what he had done behind enemy lines, and where they had hidden themselves and watched the battles fought out in front of them. He talked of the wondrous flying machines that carried men and how they would watch them fly around the skies fighting each other and dropping bombs onto the soldiers below. Connor was fascinated by the danger and excitement that it had involved. He was almost sponge like in his need for information and detail. He seemed to log the places and names within his brain for storage, and when Riley would speak of them again Connor would recite almost word perfect the sight of its location and what he had done there. Riley though, would only tell him as much as he thought a 12 year old boy should hear, but nothing more. Like Daibbi, there were somethings that Connor didn't need to know.

They, were for his own torment, and his only.

※ ※ ※

USE IT, THEN LOSE IT

May 1918

Riley was on the mend. His knee was never going to be as it was. He would have a limp till the day he died, but his break had mended. The crutches had been cast aside and he was at last getting back to some normality. There was now a couple of things he needed to do.

The first was to get back on Bear. He hadn't ridden since that fatal day and he knew that if he was going to get back to work, he needed to start riding again.

As he left the kitchen he casually looked around him then walked across the sun drenched yard towards the stable's, as he walked into the Bear's stable he softly stroked the horse's velvet like nose.

"Yes boy we're going out, but first I need to do something else".

The something else was a Webley Mark VI Revolver.

He'd hidden it in the Bear's tack box on the day he returned and due to his injury's he hadn't been fit enough to find a safer place for it, but now he was fit enough and he knew exactly where he was going to put it.

Most soldiers that had returned from the war had bought back a firearm of some description. Not all legitimately of course, and Riley's was definitely not that, but he'd heard before his return that back home, things were not good.

He'd decided there and then that he would, if at all possible, bring something back with him. And so he had, along with forty bullets. Hidden away inside a pair of socks in his suitcase.

He hadn't told Daibbi, he knew she would fret about it, and hopefully, there would be no need to use it anyway but if he did need it, it was there.

He climbed the ladder up into the hayloft. It was where he had stored old tools and some worn out saddlery.

As he walked, bent over under the low hanging roof, he could feel the warmth of the sun on the inside of the slate. There was nothing like the smell of warming hay, he thought. It reminded him of home and always had. In France, when he had needed to, he would walk into the hay barn and just stand and breath. The flip side to that was now he was thinking about his time back in Vermelles.

As he got to the far corner he knelt down quietly and unrolled the rags that were wrapped around his secret contraband.

He felt its weight in his hand and turned it over, examining it, checking its movements. It was habit. He'd done it hundreds of times before because he'd had to, but now he didn't need to do it but he had anyway. Some habits die hard.

As he rolled it back up in its cloth he sensed some movement over to his left. He turned quickly and saw Connor sitting in the right hand corner of the hayloft behind a couple of boxes.

"God Boy, what are you doing there you made me jump" said Riley quietly,

"Sorry Riley, but this is my den, I always come here, I hide things here too" said Connor smiling,

"Who say's I'm hiding anything" said Riley,

"Well I saw you looking at the gun and rolling it up in that cloth, and then I saw you put behind that old tool box".

Riley smiled back at him, fair enough he'd been had.

He sat, thinking. He could hide it somewhere else, but he knew Connor.

If he hid it somewhere else Connor would spend the rest of his days trying to find it.

"Your right lad, I am hiding it but I'm not hiding it from you. I'm hiding it from your Nana. She doesn't like guns so she doesn't need to know that its here, do you understand",

Connor looked at him and tapped his nose twice in acknowledgement.

Riley shook his head smiling.

"Could I have a look at it Riley" said Connor,

"Why",

"Well I've never seen a gun like that before",

"I should hope you haven't" said Riley,

"Come over here".

Connor crawled over to him and Riley took out the rolled up weapon of destruction.

As he unrolled the cloth Riley took out the gun and held it in his hand.

"Do you want to hold it" said Riley,

Connor nodded back silently.

" You hold it by the handle, its okay you can pull the trigger, theres no bullets in it, but you never ever point it at somebody, unless, you need to" he looked at Connor,

'Do you understand what I'm saying".

Connor nodded again and took the gun from him and immediately almost dropped it, somewhat surprised by its weight.

He placed his left index finger on the trigger and pulled, but he couldn't do it. It was too stiff.

"You will need to hold it with two hands lad, its a bit stiff",

He placed his right hand on the handle and tried the trigger with two fingers. It clicked, the barrel turned.

"Well done, you did it, now you listen to me" he looked Connor in the eye as he said,

"I'm going to put it back here and here it will stay, along with the bullets. I'm trusting you not to move it or take it. It stays here unless you, or I need it. Do you understand".

Connor nodded his silent response for a third time.

"We only get this out when we really have to. You or I will know when that is. But if ever you do need to use it, I tell you this. You use it and then you get rid of it. Do you understand, you throw it in the river, you use it and then you lose it",

"Okay Riley I promise" said Connor, bursting inside with pride because he had been trusted with such an important thing.

Riley placed the gun back in its hiding place.

it would stay there for the next five years.

❄ ❄ ❄

THE IMPORTANCE OF SECRECY

Saturday 7th September 1918

The summer had been a long hot one. The farmers were now busy making hay. It was long days and little sleep. The busiest time for many farmers and it was no different for Cain Milburn. He'd been very busy on his farms, his father's health had deteriorated dramatically over the last two months and the doctor had told him to prepare for the worst. There was never a good time to lose your father but now was definitely not the right time.

The movement, the cause, whatever you wanted to call it, had grown legs, and lots of them. The political party of the IRA was Sin Fein and it was firmly believed that come the election in December they would win. Cain was now a wanted man and not only wanted in the adoring eyes of the Irish.

He was also 'wanted' but for totally different reasons, by the not so adoring eyes of the British.

The suspicion that he was high up the the chain of command of the IRA was not some whimsical outlandish guess of some political opponent or a local police officer in Tralee. This was now the belief of some very powerful people in the British government.

The suspicion had gained momentum following the now increasing numbers of undercover police officers, throughout Ireland, mysteriously disappearing, never to be seen again. A total of 17 had now vanished into thin air and the ones that were still out there were worried men, very worried.

Although they didn't often associate with each other, because if they did it was something they they all knew could sign their own death warrant, they occasionally met in secret to discuss intelligence, information and tactics.

They knew, all of them, what each other were capable of. What their limits were.

And they also knew that of the 17 that had already disappeared only 2 of them would be likely to walk away and disappear. The rest were there for the right reasons, and there for the fight. They wouldn't be running away, it wasn't what they would do.

17 men had disappeared, 2 of them had probably walked away.

Which meant 15 of them were more than likely dead.

And it had all started in Tralee with the death of Mcgann.

If ever there was a turning point for the movement, the murder of McGann had been a massive one. His death had been the single pivotal event that would probably mean win or lose, first or second, life or death. The British government would never know how close they had come to winning this particular war but with his death they had lost and they had lost without even knowing about it.

As normal, Connor left the Yard at just after 05:30, but not so normal was the fact that he was now more often than not, working alone. Cain had not been out with him for some weeks now. Connor felt quite proud that he should be trusted in getting on with the round on his own.

He wasn't just delivering the milk.

He was still delivering Cains notes.

And he still couldn't read.

This morning was slightly different that instead of turning left out the yard and towards Tralee Connor pulled the reins of Duke to turn him right, a move that Duke wasn't too impressed with as it was against the norm and Duke didn't normally take kindly to doing different things. As Connor pulled harder to stop Duke turning back to the left he said "No boy, we have to go this way first this morning".

They travelled on towards the village of Rossbridge and as the entered the small green in the middle Connor bought Duke around to face back to where they had come from, for which he seemed much happier about. He bought the cart to a stop and waited. It was a nice morning still some warmth in the air and not a cloud in the sky, it was going to be a lovely day that was for sure, thought Connor.

A few minutes later the passenger for which Connor had been

waiting for came running around the corner.

"Morning Cal, you still look asleep, climb aboard my friend",

Cal replied somewhat wearily

" I am still asleep Connor, how can you get up at this time everyday, its still the middle of the night to me".

They both laughed as Cal lay down on the bench of the cart and pretended to go back to sleep.

Connor had promised Cal the previous day that he would take him to his Nan's house in Tralee first thing in the morning to stop him having to walk the 2 1/2 miles that he usually had to do. But the down side to it was that he would have to be ready a little after 5:30 in the morning. As they climbed the hill towards Manor farm the two of them chatted and laughed as any two best friends would.

As they rounded the bend the large imposing front of the Manor House came into view, the sun had just come over the horizon and was reflecting back at them from the upstairs windows.

"That place always gives me the creeps" said Cal as he stared at the big oak doorway,

Connor smiled and looked towards the house as well and laughed,

" dont worry Cal we're not going in there, I'm fully loaded up".

And as he turned away one of the upstairs windows caught his eye, was that the curtain moving or was it just the reflection of the newly rising sun, thought Connor.

He hoped it was just the latter for if it had been somebody at the window he'd have some answering to do if they had seen Cal on the cart.

Cain didn't like anybody new around the place and made sure that everybody was aware of that by telling everybody that worked for him that they should keep their work private whatever that may be, nobody needed to know, it was none of their business.

As they carried on and left the farm behind them Connor hoped that if it had been somebody that they wouldn't tell Cain.

It had been somebody. And they had seen them. But they wouldn't be telling Cain.

It was Cain that had seen them.

Connor was in trouble.

As Connor entered the town of Tralee, he wished his friend a good day and they arranged to meet up later in the afternoon. It was a Saturday and that meant no school.

As Connor went about his round he delivered his notes and messages, as usual, he'd been his cautious self. Nobody had followed him and there had been nobody to be concerned about.

He made his way steadily back to Manor Farm and as he turned into the yard he bought the cart to a halt, took the harness off Duke and led him to the paddock at the side of the stables. As he walked slowly back he saw him, he knew straight away that he was in trouble. He also knew that he had been seen.

" I'm really sorry Mr Milburn but he needed a lift",

"Shut the fuck up boy" said Cain in nothing more than a whisper.

He pointed to the stable and followed Connor inside.

As they stood there Cain closed the stable door behind him.

" Now boy, what the fuck do you think you were doing, you know what the rules are, we keep ourselves to ourselves, its not some bloody passenger service, its a milk round, and who the hell is he anyway" said Cain no longer in a whisper but more in a throaty growl,

" He's my best friend and he needed a lift to his Nan's in Tralee. I promise Mr Milburn that I wont do it again",

" Oh that's alright then" said Cain sarcastically.

He walked across to Connor and lowered his face so that now he was just inches away from him. So close that Connor could smell the stale cigar smoke on Cain's breath.

He stared him in the eye and now snarled in a low voice.

" Oh too fucking right right you wont be doing it again, because if you do boy you'll be gone, do you understand, you wont have a fucking job, you wont have a house, you'll have nothing, I'll fucking finish you and your Nana and her fucking soldier man, do I make myself clear".

As Cain now moved his head away slightly, he couldn't help but notice that Connor hadn't moved an inch. He knew that he was scared but he also knew that he had balls.

He liked that. As much as he was a bully he always had some respect to anybody that didn't back down or run and hide. Connor was a chip off the old block that was sure.

" So tell me again, who is this friend of yours",

"His name is Cathal Moran but everybody calls him Cal, and he wanted to go and see his Nan who lives in Tralee, so I said I would give him a lift, I didn't think it would matter, but I'm sorry".

Cain raised his hand to silence him.

" Whats done is done and there's not a lot that can be done now, but now let me just explain one thing to you",

As Cain stared at him, he lowered his voice again and said,

"Its the importance of secrecy " said Cain,

Cain looked Connor in the eye and said,

" How many people live in your village Connor"

Connor, confusion written across his face, looked at him,

" I'm not sure Mr Milburn" Said Connor,

" Well have a guess",

" I don't know probably about 60",

"Okay" said Cain,

"so yes, let's say 60. So, on the first day, I tell you a secret.

So then on the second day at least two people will know it. That's me and that's you Connor.

On the Sunday of that week, I tell you this, four people will know it.

After two weeks ten people will know it.

And in one month, half the village will know it."

He paused nodding his head at Connor and then continued

"And so Connor, within two months, the whole of the village will know my secret, and you, my boy, will be dead.

Do I make myself clear lad",

Connor looked at him and slowly nodded his head,

"Yes Mr Milburn you do"

"Then thats good" said Cain, and then trying to relieve the tension a little he said,

"Now lad, If you need company on your round then why don't you take your dog with you, and the last I knew, dogs were very very good at keeping a secret".

He smiled at Connor and Connor nodded and smiled back.

"Now off you go boy and say hello to your lovely Nana for me would you",

"I will" said Connor laughing "but she still doesn't like you".

Cain chuckled to himself and went inside.

He didn't chuckle for long.

His 90 year old Father was laying dead on the study floor.

The following week the funeral of was held at the church in Rossbridge. Many people from far and wide attended. All the brothers helped carry the coffin, but Henry didn't take the service. He didn't go to the wake at Manor Farm either. He, now head of the family, felt that he needed to distance himself a little from the people that had gathered for the day, as most of them were now members of the IRA. He hadn't wanted them to attend but it had been decided it would look strange if they had been told that they couldn't go.

And so just before he made his way back to Tralee, he shook their hands and said his goodbyes.

He was the new Lord of the Manor and he was loving every minute of it.

Out on the farm Riley had been drafted in for the day to help with the cattle as most of the farmhands had attended the funeral.

It was early evening as he made his way towards the feed barn. Although he was 60 yards or more from the house, he could still hear the singing and shouting from the throng within. 'It sounded more like a birthday party or a wedding than a funeral' he thought to himself.

He entered the barn through the 12 foot high wooden door and climbed up the ladder onto the feed floor some 20 feet above the ground. As he got to the back, close to the eaves, he found the bag he was looking for and began to pull back towards the ladder.

It was then that he heard the voices of 4 men coming into the barn.

He didn't know why, but he froze and crouched down close to the floor. For some reason he felt that he would be in trouble if they saw him. So he stayed where he was and didn't move.

After what he was about to hear he would have wished he had moved.

All four of the men then walked over to where he was and stopped directly underneath him, he was only 14 foot or so above them on the creaky dusty wooden floor.

He couldn't move an inch.

For the next hour he heard the four men talk in hushed tones.

But he could hear every single word. He might as well have been stood right next to them.

But the more he heard, the more he knew he couldn't move.

He listened in horror as they talked about two murders, one he had heard of, Bennett, and one he hadn't, somebody called McGann.

They had all spoke very descriptively of what they had done to both the men and how they had enjoyed themselves whilst doing it.

As he now lay completely prone on the wooden floor, he barely dared to breath let alone move for fear of them either seeing or hearing him, because he knew that if they did then he would surely be a dead man.

As the men continued talking and digging themselves, or more likely, himself, further into a very big whole, he prayed that they would just stop.

But they didn't.

He then heard the names of six different men, all of whom he had never heard of, but all had been described as 'undercover coppers'.

But it was the next the sentence of the male, that seemed to be leading the conversations and who was obviously in charge, that chilled him to the bone.

"Henry wanted them killed and I agreed with him, we needed to send out a message".

As he listened to the other three men whispering their agreement, it hadn't been the words as such that had shocked him, it was the fact that he knew who the voice belonged to.

It was Cain Milburn.

He had no doubt in his mind.

When he heard Cain say the name "Henry" it had all fell into place.

He hadn't heard anything of Henry for years. He had thought he had long since left the area and always felt that the family had disowned him. He hadn't any hard proof that was indeed the case but whenever his name was mentioned it was with a dismissive tone as if nobody had anything to do with him anymore. It could of course, been another Henry that they had meant, but Riley felt for some reason that it was Henry Milburn, the eldest son of Edmond Milburn, that Cain was talking about.

He didn't know who the other three men were, he couldn't see them and he didn't recognise any of their voices, and there was no way he was going to move to try and sneak a look.

At last the conversation seemed to be coming to a close. It was ended by Cain who stressed that secrecy should be paramount in their minds and to stay low for a week or two.

"The Brits will be expecting us to carry on the fight but now we wait, let's be patient, our time will come".

He heard the four men walk out the barn, closing the door behind them.

He lay there for the next half an hour still not daring to move, drenched in sweat and shaking like a leaf.

Oh how he wished he had come down.

He had been right about one of the males being Cain Milburn but he had no idea the three others were Byrne, Ramsey, and Brady.

And so, over the next two weeks, Riley's emotions and nerves were slowly torn to shreds. He knew that he had to do something.

But It was the 'something' that was the problem.

Should he go to the police and tell them. Something which he was very reluctant to do, due to the ultimate consequences which would inevitably follow.

He knew that if he chose to do just that, he would have no

house, no job, and wouldn't be employed for miles around, all this was of course subject to him remaining alive which in all probability would be very doubtful. And it wasn't just his life that would be in danger, they wouldn't stop there, he had Daibbi and Connor to think of.

He knew deep down that that wasn't an option at all.

Another option was that he could front up and speak to Cain himself, but again, what good would that do, it would lead to exactly the same conclusion.

You crossed The Milburn's at your peril.

He hadn't told a soul of what he had heard that day, and that included Daibbi, but she knew that something was wrong, she wasn't stupid. He had put it down to his injured leg but he knew that she didn't believe him.

But as the days and now weeks moved on he knew that he had to do something and he had now decided what that something was going to be.

He was going to tell a man his secret because a problem shared is a problem halved, and he knew that the man he was going to tell was not allowed to share his secret with anybody, apart from that is, god.

He was going to go to confession.

※ ※ ※

WHEN I MEET GOD.

Not being a religious man, Riley hadn't attended a mass or confession for over 25 years. Whilst in the army he had gone to a few services on the odd Sunday, but this was generally down to him having nothing else to do. But now he felt that if he did tell a Priest, it would release some of the guilt that was building up inside of him, and if the Priest felt the need to tell the police then that was up to him, but he knew that the Priest would not be giving the details to the police of who had actually passed the information to him.

'Yes' he thought to himself 'thats what I'm going to do'.

And so on the Friday evening in the late September sun, he set out on The Bear and rode to Tralee.

As he rode towards the Saint Michaels church on the northern corner of Sheep Street he saw people walking in to it. He tied Bear up and slowly walked up the cobbled path towards the big oak door. It felt as though he was stepping back in time. He had been just 18 years of age the last time he had walked along this path but it felt like only yesterday.

As he slowly opened the creaking wooden door the smell of the candles took him back again further to when he used to stand at the front as a child, his mother proudly standing behind him as he read the lords prayer aloud and alone.

The Priest stood in the doorway welcoming the congregation. It wasn't really much of a congregation though, more like twenty or may be a couple more.

He was a little surprised by the Priest though.

A young man, no more than 25, but looked a lot younger. He was over 6' tall and powerfully built. His thick blonde hair neatly combed to the side. His shook Riley's hand and welcomed him, a somewhat delicate handshake from such a big man.

Riley sat down on one of the pews towards the back. A few people turned to look at him and smile their welcome, but most sat looking toward the front, or down on one knee giving the sign of the cross.

He heard the big oak door shut behind him and then the young Priest made his way to the front and climbed the pulpit.

He welcomed everyone again and apologised on behalf of Father Henry, and explained that he couldn't attend due to illness.

Riley then saw the woman in front of him lean over to the lady at her side and whisper something in her ear. The other lady raised her eyebrows in acknowledgment. Riley thought he heard her say something like " ill my arse" but he couldn't be sure. He smiled to himself and listened to the Priest as the service commenced. Riley thought he seemed a nice man. His voice was soft and quite relaxing in a way.

It a little under 30 minutes it was all over and the throng began to leave by the same big oak door. Riley watched and waited until they had all left.

He turned to see if he could get the Priest's attention but he had gone.

He looked over towards the confession box and could see that the door was slightly open.

He hesitated slightly, wondering if he was about to do the right thing, but he thought that the Priest seemed like a receptive man so he walked on and opened the door, he sat down on the old wooden bench and left the door ajar.

The confession box in this church was unusual in that the Priest would sit to the side. Probably due to the fact that the door from which the Priest entered was from within the wall to which the box was attached to, meaning that when the Priest entered, persons sitting outside would not see him doing so. The latticed wooden window was to his right and as he turned to look through it he felt sure that it was the same Burgundy coloured curtain that had been there so many years before. It certainly smelled like it, musty and damp.

The window seemed different though. The wholes seemed smaller and the view through the window seemed more obscure. Perhaps it was because he was so much younger then.

As he looked at the shelf in front of him, a battered old bible sat there along side the same old bell you rang to inform the Priest that you were there.

Again he hesitated. He knew that once he rang that bell there would be no turning back.

He lent forward and picked it up.

And then he rang the bell.

It was a few minutes before anybody came. He was just wondering if he should ring the bell again or just walk away. But then he heard footsteps on the concrete floor somewhere from his righthand side. He then felt a draft through the lattice work and heard the door on the other side close again.

He then saw, through the lattice, the shape of a man dressed in black sit heavily on the chair, accompanied by a small groan as if he was in some sort of pain.

'This wasn't the same Priest that had just took the service', thought Riley, 'it must be the Father Henry that the young Priest had just mentioned'.

Both men sat in silence, Riley, unsure about the etiquette as to who spoke first, he waited, but then as the silence continued he decided to speak.

He spoke softly but not in a whisper, he remembered that the Priest that had listened to his last confession, all those years ago, was extremely deaf and when you told him your sins, the whole congregation outside would hear them as well, which, he seemed to recall, all seemed a bit of a waste of time actually going in the box.

"Good evening Father" said Riley,

A softly spoken but slightly muffled voice came back to him in immediate response.

"Good evening to you too, how can I help you this evening, do you need to repent your sins",

"No father I don't, but I seek your advice and help in a matter that concerns me",

" I see, well thats what I'm here for too, and it sometimes makes a pleasant change from peoples wrong doings".

Another moment of silence as Riley for the last time decided if he should continue, and then he carried on.

"I have heard something Father that has disturbed me greatly, and I just don't know what to do about it",

"Well we are all god's children and a problem shared is a problem halved. So they say",

"It is Father, thats what I thought too, so I thought I might share it with you if you didn't mind",

" Carry on, lets see if I can help, I'm sure I will able to somehow",

"I hope so Father, I really do",

"It happened just over two weeks ago when I was at work. I overheard a conversation between four men. They were talking about something bad they had done".

Henry, who had not been particularly interested and was generally going through the motions became slightly more interested.

"And what might that be", he said,

Again a short spell of silence and then Riley said it.

"A murder".

Henry, now a lot more interested, took his turn to be quiet for a moment before asking the confessor to continue.

"Carry on".

" I heard the men talking about a man that they had killed and how they had enjoyed doing it".

Henry was now not only very interested but also worried about where this conversation was going to go next. But he knew one thing for sure, he didn't want anybody else listening to this. He lowered his voice and whispered,

"Would you just close your door".

Riley did as he was asked.

"Continue".

" Well, they carried on talking and after a while, I then heard them describe how they had killed a second man".

"When was this".

" do you mean when I heard it or when did the murder happen, because I only know when Bennett was killed but not the other man".

Henry almost coughed and choked when he heard the name of Bennett.

'Who on earth was his on other side of the Lattice' he thought to himself.

Henry pulled himself together and said.

" I meant when did you hear this conversation and where were you",

" I heard it just over two weeks ago and I was at the funeral of Edmund Milburn, he owns, or should I say, did own, Manor farm in Rossbridge, do you know it, and sorry I may have confused you, I mean't that I was at the farm but I didn't go to the funeral itself".

' Shit' thought Henry this was bad, really bad but he needed to know more.

" I am aware of the farm yes, please continue",

" They talked about the second man but I had never heard the name before, I presumed that he must not have been from around here. But I knew Bennett, he lived on the Bogmen estate",

"The name of the second man, did you say you heard it" asked Henry,

"Yes, sorry Father, it was McGann". whispered back Riley.

This was now big trouble. A whole world of shit had just landed right here on the floor of St Michaels church of Tralee.

"And what part did you play in this conversation" asked a now desperate Henry,

There was silence for a moment.

"What do you mean by that Father",

"I mean, you were there, so what did you say, did you take any part in it at all",

"No father I didn't. They didn't know I was there, the men I mean, I was in the feed area of the barn, up in the roof, I had gone to get some feed for the cattle".

Henry couldn't believe what he was hearing. The world he knew was falling in around him but he still had more question's to ask.

"Do you know who these men were",

"I couldn't see them".

'Thank god' thought Henry but then Riley continued.

"But I recognised one of the men's voices........... It was Cain.... Cain Milburn, Edmond's middle son".

'Fuck, fuck, fuck' thought Henry his head now completely in a spin. He tried to calm himself but his voice was trembling and if Riley could have seen him he would have seen him shaking too.

He had been wrong, he thought he had asked his last question but then he had a thought.

"Have you told the Police about this".

Silence.

Silence, that to Henry seemed to go on forever.

He asked again

"Have you".

more silence, until........

"No Father I'm sorry. I couldn't do it. I know that if I did, then, well, there would be consequences".

Henry breathed heavily.

'Too fucking right there would be consequences, and there still will be, don't you worry about that' he thought to himself.

It had led then to another question.

"Does anybody else know about any of this, your wife for instance, have you told her",

"No Daibbi knows nothing, I have told nobody, only you".

Henry smiled to himself.

He knew who the Confessor was.

"Then leave this with me, I will speak to the police tomorrow, and you have my word that your identity will remain anonymous. Come to see me in the holy corner in the reindeer on Sunday night at 7pm and we will talk again",

"Thank you father, I really appreciate you listening to me" said Riley,

" No thank you, its no problem at all, and remember, god loves us all in different ways, god be with you",

"And also with you".

As Riley came out of the door of the church he felt as if an enormous weight had been lifted from his heavy shoulders. As he climbed on the Bear he rode home feeling much happier about life.

'A problem shared', he smiled to himself, he'd made the right decision he was sure of it.

Father Henry wasn't feeling so happy about his life. In fact, he was feeling distinctly unhappy about the events of the last hour.

He was also hurting.

He was black and blue from head to toe.

But that was definitely not a problem to be shared.

'It could have been worse' he thought to himself 'but not much'.

He now needed to get hold of Cain, and fast. This problem needed sorting out as a matter of urgency.

'The Cause' was hanging by the flimsiest of thread that you could ever imagine.

❋ ❋ ❋

SENTENCE OF DEATH

By 10pm that evening Cain had made aware of the situation. It was left for the next morning before they would decide what should and would, be done.

At 5:30am Connor made his way into the stable to get Duke ready. As he led him out he was a little surprised to see Cain standing in the yard waiting for him.

" Morning lad, I've got some things for you to deliver today. A few more than normal and there's a few of them that you will have to go back to. I need the replies, I'm sorry about it Connor but unfortunately I need them today, they cant wait until tomorrow",

"Okay Mr Milburn" said Connor "do you want me to bring back the replies when I'm done",

"No leave them on the cart, I will get them from there",

"Okay" said Connor, a little surprised.

Cain then put his hand inside his jacket pocket and pulled out what looked like at least 10 diamond shaped notes.

'He was right' thought Connor, he'd never had this many notes before.

"There's a few of them that need to go to the same houses, I've written the numbers on the front, but you have been to them all before",

"Okay" said Connor again, he was okay with numbers, to a degree, but still couldn't read or right a single word.

He set off on his travels and was soon on the edge of Tralee and the first of his note deliveries.

Number 6 Gallow Street, the home address of Dermot Brady, Connor had been here several times before.

He posted two diamond shaped notes through the letter box, both had the number 6 on the front. And walked slowly back to the cart. He doubted as to whether Brady would be there as he often stayed at Ramsey's house but as he was turning around Brady came out of the front door and shouted to him.

"Boy, you wait" and with that he went back into his house.

Connor had never liked Brady very much. He didn't really know why but on the occasions that he had met him he always seemed a little aggressive, unnecessarily so, Connor had thought, the scar on his left cheek didn't help either, more than likely down to a skirmish sometime in the past.

A few minutes passed before Brady came back out his front door and was now holding a folded up piece of paper, which Connor took from him and placed it under the seat into the basket.

His next note delivery was 11 River Walk. The home address of Niall Ramsey, Connor couldn't recall ever hearing him speak. He was a huge man but very quiet. Again he posted 2 diamond notes through the letterbox only this time he waited.

He had been right to wait, for after no more than a minute, Ramsey ran out of his front door and was somewhat surprised to see Connor still waiting there. He passed him a note and just said the one word of "Thanks", nodded his head, and returned back inside.

It was sometime before he posted anymore notes but soon he had only three left which were all for number 27 Market Square, the home of Lanny Byrne.

He posted them through his letterbox and again waited outside. his round was now done, Market Square was where his round always ended. Today was no different.

That was up until he was about to leave.

Having taken a note from Byrne, Connor set off on his return journey and as he left the southern edge of the square Cain came out of nowhere from his left and jumped onto the cart.

"Keep going lad I'll tell you when stop",

Cain then bent down and removed the notes from the basket.

As they turned the corner Cain very quietly said,

"Wait here".

He then jumped off and ran into the alleyway, the Saighead, and disappeared.

None of this wasn't really like anything that hadn't happened before. But Connor thought that Cain did seem a little more worried than usual. Probably nothing to worry about though, it was Saturday after all and he just wanted to get home and finished.

He waited for over 15 minutes before Cain ran back out of the Saighead. He jumped on the cart and handed him back four more notes, three of them were to take back to where he had just been, Gallow Street, River Walk and Market Square.

The fourth one didn't have a number on.

But then Cain told him where to take it.

He had been there a few times with school but never to deliver a note.

It was to go to Saint Michaels church.

"I need you to take it into the church and give it to the Priest. Then you must wait for his reply and bring it back to me at the Manor" Said Cain,

"Okay, but will that be it then, because it's Saturday and I was supposed to be meeting Cal" said Connor, who now was getting a little fed up, the days work was getting longer and longer.

"You'll be done when I say your done and the longer you sit here moaning about it the longer it will be before your home".

And with that he was gone, back down the Saighead.

Connor decided to leave the note for the Priest until last, no particular reason other than it was the last one that Cain had given to him.

Having delivered the three other notes he had had just one reply from Byrne the other two had just said "okay" and returned into their homes.

And now as he walked up the cobbled path towards the church door the feeling like he didn't want to be here came over him again.

'Its this street, the place gives me the creeps' he said to himself.

He opened the door and walked into the deserted church.

There was not a soul inside.

He stood there contemplating whether to just leave the note on the alter at the front and walk out when a voice came from over near the confession box.

"In here boy" said the voice softly "bring it over here".

Connor walked over and slowly pulled open the wooden door.

Having never been in a confession box before, he was a little surprised to find that he actually couldn't see the Priest, he was hidden behind a wooden screen with small holes in it. He lent forward and peered through one of the holes and saw the Priest sitting down just inches away from him.

He then noticed that he had two black eyes and his cheek was very swollen.

The Priest, a little surprised also, to see the eye of the boy peering at him through one of the holes, instinctively held the palm of his hand over the whole to try and stop him seeing what a state he was in.

"I believe you may have something for me boy" said Henry,

"Yes Father I do" replied Connor,

"Then place it under that shelf there between us".

Connor did as he was asked and then watched again, less obviously this time, through another hole as the Priest read the note. As he finished reading he saw a small smile come over his and then heard him say,

"Good, thats good",

As he looked up again, Connor looked away quickly not wanting to upset the Priest any further.

"Would you wait there boy while I get a pencil, I wont be a moment",

"Okay Father".

'More waiting' thought Connor, it was going to be midnight before I'm home.

A few minutes later the Priest returned and passed a note

under the shelf.

Connor took it, his good manners getting the the better of him as he said,

"Thank you Father".

The Priest, a little surprised by the good manners shown by the boy, said,

"No my son, I must thank you, and remember, god loves us all in different ways",

"Thank you Father, may I go now",

"You may, have a safe journey home"

and with that Connor was gone.

Ramsey's note had been an instruction to make a bomb.

Not any ordinary one but one that would detonate at a specific time. They had been used in the past but with varying success or failure. One such failure had resulted in three republicans being killed whilst planting their bomb in London.

But things had now moved on somewhat and their success rate was rapidly improving.

Byrne's note's were one for himself, telling him to take the second note to the landlord of the Raindeer. The Landlord was told that he should take his family away for a few days and if anybody should ask why, he was to say that his mother had taken seriously ill and he had to return home to Killarney. He was sworn to secrecy and if he told anybody of the note there would be consequences and he knew what those would be. His third note was to take to a man named Gorse. He lived on the outskirts of town to the North. Most of the weapons were buried on his land and he was the only one who knew where they were.

In all of the notes the recipients were told to stay away from the Raindeer from 5pm Sunday evening.

By late Saturday evening the plan had been passed and agreed by all it concerned with the final instruction to simply write a one worded note the next day saying if it was a 'YES' or a 'NO' to the bomb being used. If anybody had any doubt's that the plan, or they themselves, had been compromised, then they should write 'NO' nothing more. These notes were to be collected the next day, Sunday, around 4pm.

And so as Connor rode towards the town of Tralee on a beautiful sunny late afternoon he hadn't a care in the world.

But then, what he didn't know was that by 8pm that evening his life would never be the same again.

As he rode around the town collecting the notes from where Cain had instructed him to go, he placed them all under his seat. Within an hour he rode back towards home and a little before 5pm as he crossed the brow of the hill he saw Cain standing at the gates to Manor Farm.

"Evening Boy" said a smiling Cain "have you got anything for me",

Connor leaned under his seat and pulled out the notes.

"Thanks lad, now you get Duke in there and I'll sort out the cart, then you can get yourself home",

"Thanks Mr Milburn" said Connor.

Cain walked into the house and pulled the notes from his pocket.

10 notes.

10 yes's.

By 5:30pm Connor made his way out of the barn and began to walk down the hill towards Rose Cottage. As he slowly walked along pulling at the long grasses at the side of the road and sucking on the stem, he heard the sound of hoofs coming towards him, as he looked up he was a little surprised to see Riley riding towards him on the Bear.

"Evening Connor, your Nana is threatening to throw your tea to the dog".

Connor knew he was joking by the smile on his face.

"Going out at this time of night on a Sunday, you'll be the one in trouble not me, where are you going" said Connor returning the smile.

"Off to Tralee to see a friend, would you like to come" Riley knowing full well that Connor wouldn't say yes.

"If its okay with you I will carry on home and have that tea before the dog has it",

"Please yourself" said Riley and rubbed to top of Connor's head.

"See you in the Morning".

And with that Riley put the Bear into an effortless trot and was gone.

About an hour later Connor sat eating his dinner with his Nana.

At exactly the same time, Riley entered the bar of the Reindeer pub.

He was surprised at how quiet it was. He wasn't a regular by any means but the times that he had been in the place it was usually packed to the rafters.

The young barman busied himself, thriving on his new found self importance, and was sweeping the floor. He looked up to see Riley standing there and dropped the brush and rushed over.

"Sorry sir, I didn't see you come in" said the Barman,

"Not a problem" said Riley "I'm in no rush, I'm here to see the Priest but I'm a little early",

"Oh he comes in around 7 normally, you have a seat over there in the Holy Corner and I will bring a pint over to you",

"Very kind, thank you" said Riley and walked over to the table to where the barman had indicated.

For the next twenty minute he sat there, two more people came in but neither was the Priest, but he had been twenty minutes early after all.

He didn't hear the blast and he didn't feel it either. Neither did the five others that were killed, one of which being the young barmen. All of them blown to pieces at precisely 7pm, along with a horse that had been tied up outside.

Their success rate was rapidly improving.

The police visited Rose cottage to tell them of the death of Riley.

Diabbi sat in silence, Connor sat in shock.

Neither spoke hardly a word.

Just total devastation.

Over the coming months the blame was laid firmly at the door of the Protestants from the Bogman estate. The Stonebridge public house was set on fire 3 times in retaliation, suffering some severe damage but was rebuilt each time out of defiance if nothing else.

Diabbi and Connor wept quietly together every night, their silent grief a private one.

Aibbi had sent her mother a reply from her new home in America wishing that she could attend the funeral but would never get over in time. Diabbi wrote back telling her not to worry she understood and told her that Connor was fine.

He wasn't.

The fire had started within him and it would burn until he

gained revenge.

And so

The end Of 1918 came and went, the turn of the year was very difficult for Daibbi and Connor. They had been assured by Cain that they could stay at Rose Cottage for as long as they wanted. Connor was given a wage rise and Daibbi agreed to clean at Manor farm four times a week.

Their fortunes were in total contrast to a full of hope Ireland.

Sinn Fein had heavily defeated the Nationalist Irish Parliamentary Party and was now the ruling party. And just as significantly, in Ulster, the Unionist party had prevailed.

It had been an election for the people. For the first time women over the age of 30 and men over the age of 21 could vote.

The split of Ireland had moved on somewhat. The Unionist's of Ulster, almost entirely Protestant, apposed home rule where as, Sinn Fein, almost completely Catholic, wanted separation from the British and, at all costs, to establish an independent republic.

Over the next two years, the killings continued,

The battle raged on, the hatred festered, and then it grew, and it grew, and then it grew some more.

On the 21st Jan 1919 Ireland formed a breakaway government and declared independence from Britain. On the same day two members of the armed police force, the Royal Irish Constabulary, were shot dead in County Tipperary by the IRA. This to many was seen as the beginning of the conflict but it wasn't really, it had been festering in the townships for years. Catholic's and Protestant's both readily first to blame each other but both equally responsible for the increase in tensions.

For most of 1919 the IRA worked on capturing weapons and freeing republican prisoners.

In September 1919 the British government outlawed Sinn Fein thus further intensifying the conflicts.

The IRA then began ambushing RIC and British army patrols and attacking barracks causing some remote barracks to be abandoned.

The British government then took the step of bolstering the RIC with recruits from Britain..... the black and tans, Who became notorious for reprisal attacks on the civilian population thus creating the The Tan war.

The Black and Tans were officially the Royal Irish Constabulary Special Reserve. They were temporary constables that had been recruited to assist the RIC. It had been the brain child of Winston Churchill, the then British secretary of state. Many of the black and tans were British army veterans of ww1. Their role was mainly to fight the IRA but not only them. Their nickname had come from the colour of their uniforms. They became infamous for their attacks on civilians and civilian property.

And then.............

On Bloody Sunday 21 November 1920, 14 British intelligence officers were assassinated in Dublin.

The RIC opened fire at football crowd killing 14 and injuring many more.

The Black and Tans then besieged Tralee in revenge for the abduction and killing of 2 local RIC men. They closed all businesses for a week and shot dead 3 locals.

This stunningly beautiful country of Ireland, the Emerald Isle, gods garden, was too many, hell on earth and ugly to its core.

❋ ❋ ❋

GET RID OF THE BOY

DECEMBER 1920

Connor now 14 years of age, had been left to run the milk round on his own. He had almost doubled the amount of customers and consequently virtually doubled the amount of milk that was required. This had led to yet another increase in his wage which had pleased and also helped his Nana immensely. It was good to see him getting some independence and, following the death of Riley, some of his confidence back. Connor had been very withdrawn and quiet since the awful events at the Raindeer. He was still a boy but was growing up fast, and Daibbi, due to her own grief, was struggling to keep him from going a little off the rails. A number of times, too many in fact, she had had to drag him from his bed in the morning to get him to go to work. But they rarely fell out, Connor loved his Nana dearly and his tempers were quietly dealt with, not with chastisement but with a loving arm around his shoulder. Because of this though, Daibbi had barely been able to greave herself. She had nobody to turn or talk too. She understood that Aibbi had a fantastic career now in America but she longed for her to return just for a small visit, anything would do.

Connor rarely asked about her but Daibbi knew that he also longed to see his mother again. She would often hear him crying in his sleep and would go into him to sooth his dreams and nightmares. In turn Connor would lay in bed at night unable to sleep and hear his Nana gently sobbing longing for the man that she had loved so dearly, and for the return of Aibbi.

They both knew of each others heartache but rarely said so to each other. They lives were slowly being ripped apart in front of each other's sad and tearful eyes. But neither knew what to do to stop it.

And so life moved sadly on.

Connor still delivered the milk and the messages.

He now took Aggie with him almost everyday. She would sit at the side of him on the cart curled up into a ball to keep warm and on their arrival on the outskirts of Tralee she would sit up and stretch. It was almost uncanny as to how she knew where she was. One minute she would be fast asleep and the next minute she would be sitting up ready to jump off.

Unbeknown to Connor rumours had begun to surface that messages were being passed between individuals belonging to the IRA by a young blonde boy. Its origins were unknown but none the less they had increased and the rumour had found its way to the ear of Cain Milburn and consequently to the ear of his elder brother, Henry. So much so that Henry had left a note for Connor to take to his brother, Cain, summoning him to attend Sheep Street that evening.

It was something that never happened and Cain knew it must be something extremely serious.

And it was.

As he walked along Sheep Street up to the gate he took a brief look behind him to check he hadn't been followed and then walked up the path to the front door.

He could see why all those years ago, Connor hadn't liked coming here, and, why he still didn't.

It was an extremely daunting building to walk up to. As he stood at the door he didn't knock he knew his brothers housekeeper, the aptly named Dower, it was spelt differently to Dour but was said the same, would be there to open the door.

He had been at his brother's side for as long as he could remember. He had always wondered about his brothers relationship with him but had never said anything to him. Nobody did, it was something that was better not said.

His suspicions had been confirmed though, as far as he was concerned, at their mother's funeral when he caught a brief glimpse of Dower gently squeezing his brother's hand, giving him support as Henry wept quietly in the corner of the church.

It hadn't been much but he knew.

But he didn't know everything.

What he wasn't aware of was that Dower was a very dominant man. He had regularly beaten Henry over the years and some of the beatings were so severe that Henry would not be seen for days. But Henry relied upon him totally and would not hear of any bad word said against him.

The confession box hid a lot of secrets and they were not just verbal ones.

As the door slowly opened, the tall slim figure of a smiling George Dower came into view and ushered him inside.

The soft southern Irish drawl welcomed him,

"good evening Cain, it's good to see you again, your brother is in his study, he's expecting you",

Cain looked at him, he hated the way that Dower always had a way of making him feel inferior to him whenever they met.

" I know he's expecting me Dower, because that's exactly why I'm fucking here",

Dower wasn't finished though, he smiled at him again and said with just a hint of sarcasm,

"Then please go through",

Cain brushed by him attempting to ignore his demeaning attitude but he couldn't hide his disdain for the man. He didn't care for what he and his brother got up to, but his hatred for him festered deep within and it wouldn't take long for it to come to the boil.

As he entered the study Henry was sat at the side of the fire with an open bible on his lap. Cain stood in front of him and but Henry didn't look up or even acknowledge him being there, but after a few moments he just very quietly said,

"Sit down".

Of all the brothers, everyone said that Henry was the most like Edmond, their Father. To some degree they were right, Cain could see his father in him, but he had always thought he was more like their Mother. He had a nastiness in him that matched hers, and some. He could cut anybody dead with just one vile outburst of fury.

No, he was definitely his mother's son of that there was no doubt.

Henry gently closed the bible and placed it on the small table at his side and eventually he looked up at Cain.

"We have a problem".

Cain gave it a few seconds before replying

"And what might that be Henry".

Henry's face changed immediately into the snarling rapid dog, his teeth now showing and as he began to speak his next sentence, the spit began to flow.

'Their mother had arrived' thought Cain.

"You know exactly what that might be Cain. You've heard the fucking whispers the same as I have",

"But that's all they are Henry, just whispers",

The snarling dog continued.

"My god Cain, sometimes you're so fucking thick. It doesn't matter whether they are true or whether they are not. But somebody out there is putting it about that the boy is carrying our messages, and please correct me if I'm wrong, but the boy is actually doing just that, he's delivering our secrets, each and every one of them",

"Yes he is Henry, but there is nothing in the messages that gives anything away. If they caught him nothing could be proven".

His snarl now turned into whisper but the phlegm still flowed.

"That's not the fucking point is it. Somebody somewhere knows what we are doing. Wherever the rumour is coming from we need to stop it and we need to stop it right now".

The study door opened and Dower came in carrying a tray of tea.

Henry ignored the entrance and carried on.

"It will be that fucking book I tell you, you shouldn't have kept it, I told you to burn it and be rid of it, but you had to keep it didn't you. The boy is compromised and he needs to go, I don't want you to use him anymore, you can find another way, just do what I pay you to do".

Cain averted his gaze from Henry and looked at Dower.

"Henry, with all due respect, we shouldn't be speaking of this in front of him".

Henry, now completely enraged, turned on him with with all the vitriol vile abuse he could muster.

"I will speak of what I fucking want to speak of, when and where I want to, Do you understand".

He pointed his finger at Dower, who had not moved and was now looking like he was really enjoying the moment.

"I trust this man more than I trust any of you lot put together and in case you have forgotten little brother, I'm the one that's fucking in charge here".

He stopped and turned his back on Cain and walked towards the bookcase and as he did so he said,

"Get rid of the boy",

Cain turned and walked towards the door and as he opened it he heard Henry say it again.

"And I mean it Cain, you get rid of him, understand. You've got a week, now fucking get out".

As Cain opened the door he felt Dower move behind him as he began to follow him out.

As he passed him he said,

"Let me show you out Cain"

"I know the fucking way out" said Cain,

"Now get out of my way and go back to your boyfriend before I say something else I may regret".

Cain placed his hand on Dower's bony chest, pushed him away and walked out the front door leaving it wide open.

' That man was living on dangerous ground, very dangerous', thought Cain, but he would have to be very careful with this one, he had a lot to lose if it went wrong. First though he had a much more important thing to be dealing with.

How to save Connor's life, and more importantly to him, how to keep the best weapon he had.

As the week wore on, Cain had decided that he was going to have to send the boy away. To where and how it was going to happen, he didn't know, but he needed to buy some time because what time he did have was running out fast.

As Connor rode back in on the Wednesday morning Cain was waiting for him in the yard.

"Morning boy, hows business" said Cain,

"Business is good thanks" beamed the smiling Connor,

"I've had two more new customers this week",

" Good lad thats what I like to hear. I've been meaning to have a word with you because I think you deserve a bit of a holiday, being that you have more or less doubled the number of customers."

"Really" said Connor "I've not actually ever had a holiday before",

"Well all the more reason to have one then, how would you like to go to a friend of mine who lives by the sea at Tullaree, you could go this weekend and come back Monday, or I could perhaps spread it to Tuesday if you like, you would like it there, there are loads of animals".

Connor face was a picture 'A holiday, a real holiday, he must be dreaming' he thought to himself but then he remembered. He had promised Cal that he would meet him in Tralee when he had finished his round on Friday as they didn't have school that day and it was also Cal's birthday. They had planned to go into the town and meet some other friends and spend some time down by the river. They were then going to camp near to the river over the weekend and try to catch some fish for their tea. He'd been looking forward to it for weeks.

"I don't suppose I could go next weekend could I" said Connor

Cain looked at him with surprise,

"You mean your turning down a free Holiday" said Cain,

"No, no, I'm not turning it down at all, I just cant go this weekend as I've promised Cal that I will spend the weekend with him as its his birthday",

Cain looked at him shaking his head "Okay, let's see what I can do".

As Cain walked away he hoped that he might have bought himself a few more days, the weekend at least. Connor wasn't going to be at work and even better still he wasn't going to be at home.

By Thursday evening Cain had been given a name of a Protestant man who lived just three doors away from Niall Ramsey, at 17 River Walk, Tralee.

His name was Kieran Duggan.

Duggan had apparently seen a blonde haired boy post notes through the front door of Ramsey's address several times and not liking Ramsey very much, due to his beliefs, he had taken upon himself to inform the police of such happenings.

The police in turn had filed it for a time before somebody of rank had decided that they should look at it.

* * *

SOME GOOD FORTUNE SOME BAD LUCK

Friday came and Connor was looking forward to the long weekend off from school. He had also been given the weekend off by Mr Milburn. So as he left Manor farm on his round with Aggie at his side, he felt happy, tired but happy. He had got up a little late, not actually wanting to go but his Nana had dragged him out of his bed and sent him on his way, he was late but he wasn't too worried, he had been late many times before and had always managed to make the time up, all apart from on one occasion when he had been far too late to go to school and had then had to feign sickness to his Nana so he wouldn't have to go. But there was no school today so it didn't matter too much.

By the time he had got to the edge of the town he had virtually made up his time and was only about five minutes behind. But then a mini disaster happened. It was all down to him rushing, he had been told many years ago by Mr Milburn that when he had milk bottles in his hands he should never run. A rule that he had generally stood by, apart from on occasions such as these. As he set off at speed with a milk bottle in each hand, Aggie, as usual, jumped off the cart and ran behind him.

Connor hadn't seen the discarded beer bottle in front of him and as he stepped full on it, it rolled under his foot causing him to fall heavily onto his back, the two milk bottles that were in his hands both smashed into the ground breaking instantly and then as Aggie ran past her spread eagled master, her front left paw was cut wide open by a 3" shard of milk bottle, causing the now flowing white milk to turn a bloody pink.

As she yelped she came to an immediate halt, holding the dripping bloody paw out in front of her.

Connor climbed to his feet and made his way over to his now three legged dog.

It wasn't good.

Her paw had a gash at least 2 inches long and half an inch deep and was leaking a lot of blood.

He quickly took off his shoe and slipped off a sock. He then wrapped it around her paw.

As he stood deciding what to do next, he heard footsteps coming from behind him. It was only little before 8am and was still fairly dark but he recognised the owner of the footsteps immediately.

"What have we here lad, it looks like somebody's in the wars",

" Morning Mr Milburn, its Aggie she's cut her foot",

"I can see" said Cain "and it looks like she smashed some milk bottles".

Connor looked down at the milky pink fluid now running towards the gutter and immediately leapt to Aggies defence.

"It wasn't Aggie Mr Milburn, it was all my fault, I......."

Cain looked at him knowingly.

" You were running Connor, what have I told you about running",

"I'm sorry Mr Milburn, but........"

"But you were late" said Cain,

Connor looked at him, his face full of guilt.

"How do you know where I am and what I'm doing, all of the time, its like your there and watching whatever I do",

"Correct" said Cain " I know exactly where you are and what your doing all of the time, so don't you go doing anything you shouldn't be doing, will you boy".

He smiled at him and Connor smiled back.

Connor felt relieved.

And Cain had just had an idea.

"Now lad if I'm not mistaken, thats Mill Street over there and isn't that where your friends Nan lives. Why don't you take Aggie here, round to their house and get them to take her to the vet when it opens, and don't worry about how much it costs I'll pay, just tell them to make sure the vet puts it down to me. Now get going lad or you will be late for school".

As Connor walked away with the three legged Aggie he punched the air and shouted back at Cain,

" no school today we're off"

Cain nodded and smiled at him.

He already knew that. It hadn't been a coincidence.

'I know where you are and what you are doing all of the time'.

By 11am that morning the police had been tipped off by an informant, that the blonde haired boy that was working for the IRA lived in a house on Mill Street and they were also told that he had a lurcher dog that had hurt its leg.

By mid day that information had been passed to the commander of the Royal Irish Constabulary Special Reserve, otherwise known as the Black and Tans.

By 2pm that afternoon number 18 Mill Street had been raided by 12 Black and Tan soldiers.

At 3:35pm, hoping to collect his dog, Connor walked towards the house of his best friend's Nana.

He was stopped fifty yards short by a policeman who was stopping everybody wanting to go into the street.

As he watched wondering what was going on, he was, along with the now gathering crowd, moved to the side in order to let an ambulance pass by. As it made its way towards the front of number 18 it stopped and two men got out. They made the way inside carrying two wooden stretchers.

Nothing happened then for another 20 minutes until the front door opened and the same two men came out now carrying a stretcher with somebody on it. He couldn't see who it was as the body was completely covered over with a blanket, but he could see that it was an adult and that due to the head being covered, they were probably dead.

They slid the stretcher into the back of the ambulance and returned back inside the house.

He, along with the crowd, carried on watching.

Ten minutes later the door opened again. The same two men came out carrying another stretcher, again the body was covered over.

Only this time it wasn't an adult.

Connor watched in disbelief.

What was happening. He knew that Cal's nan lived there alone. He knew that the only grandchild she had was Cal.

'Please oh please god don't let it be them' he thought to himself.

As the ambulance moved away the police officer would still not let the crowd go through. As tempers started to flair the officer shouted for two more officers, who were now stood at the front door, to join him.

Eventually a man dressed in a dark brown coat and matching trilby hat came out of the front door.

He looked very solemn and as he spoke to another policeman who had exited with him, he briefly looked over towards the crowd.

For a moment he looked like he was going to come over to speak to them but then thought better of it and turned and walked the other way with the police officer.

Two more officers then left the front door and locked it behind them. As they walked over towards the crowd a woman from the back shouted at them.

"Murdering Bastards".

Connor swung around to see who the woman was. He didn't know her. A man who was stood at the side of him started to walk towards them, his fists clenched, ready for trouble.

"You fucking Murdering Bastards, he was but a boy " said the man.

The last officer to leave the house held out his hands with his palms out defensively. He spoke to the crowd.

"It wasn't our doing, this is nothing to do with us",

The man that had been stood next to him wasn't finished.

"Then who the fuck was it then".

Another voice from the back shouted,

"The black and tans, it was the black and tans, I saw them coming out about two hours ago, there was loads of them".

A tremor went around the the crowd and then people began shouting and pushing.

Connor felt it was time to leave.

He walked away in a daze. Was this really happening. Had his best friend and his nan actually been murdered.

He was nearly half way home before he suddenly realised that Aggie must still be in the house.

He turned in a panic and began to run back towards the town.

As he got to the town's edge, he saw the cart being pulled by Duke coming towards him with Cain driving it.

As it pulled up at his side he saw Aggie curled upon the front seat, her paw now properly bandaged.

He looked at Cain and saw that he was deathly white. He had never seen him look so bad. He looked at Connor and in a low whisper he said,

"Get in boy".

They rode on in silence until they reached Rose Cottage.

As Connor jumped off, Aggie gingerly followed him and then Connor turned expecting Cain to turn the cart around and go, but he didn't. He jumped off with him and walked at the side of Connor and for the first time ever, Cain showed a glimpse of affection towards him as he briefly put his hand on his shoulder.

"I need to see your Nana, something bad has happened".

For the next hour Connor listened in shock as Cain told his Nana that Cal and his Nan had been brutally murdered by the black and tans in their house in Tralee. He said that Connor should take some time off work for at least a week and then if and when he felt okay he should let him know.

As Cain rode off back towards Manor Farm he sat in silence. He hadn't meant for this to happen. How could they kill a young boy and a woman. He thought they might rough them up a bit or worse lock them up for a day or two but not this. Not cold blooded murder. Somebody would pay for this, he would make it his mission to find out who had done it and who had ordered it to be done. He also needed to see Ramsey and Byrne, they needed to clear up another outstanding problem.

Duggan.

But as he turned into the gate of his farm the real Cain Milburn began to surface and a small grin came over his face.

The Black and Tans had inadvertently saved the life of his number one foot soldier.

Something good will always come out of something bad.

The messenger boy was dead.

Long live the messenger boy.

The next evening Cain went back to Sheep Street to see Henry.

Luckily for Cain, his mother wasn't there, Henry was in a good mood.

For the next two hours they discussed the events of the previous day and of the consequences of them. Cain also told him about a man called Duggan who, it had appeared, had been the instigator of the rumour. He explained that Duggan was now resting with the fishes at the bottom of the River Lee and wouldn't therefor be causing them anymore problems.

At the end of the talking they both agreed that Connor was in the clear and could continue to do his work.

"It had been a gift from the devil himself" Said Henry with huge smile on his face.

"Those stupid British bastards have a way of making it difficult for themselves don't they. I want you to find out who was responsible, we need to make the most of their ineptitude and brutality and show what we ourselves are capable of",

"Don't you worry Brother, It's already being done" said Cain.

Within a week of the terrible events of Mill Street, people talking through the dark spidery web of informants and grasses, had led to Cain not only having the names of the soldiers present, he also had the names of the two who had delivered the killer blows. Private Carl Stevens and Private David Rogers.

Just six weeks later a huge explosion devastated the bar area of the Stonebridge public house killing 8 Protestant men and two off duty soldiers by the name of Stevens and Rogers. Connor had witnessed it all from the market square, just over fifty yards away.

The following months became the most bloody and savage ever on the streets of southern Ireland.

And so, when all seemed lost and no end insight to the turmoil, on the 11th July 1921, a somewhat surprised Ireland woke to the news of an agreed truce, and, as a consequence, the Country of Northern Ireland was created.

For the next few years, on the surface anyway, the truce held and the violence decreased. But lift the carpet, and you would see the ugly little creatures scurrying about continuing to kill and maim. Most people were happy not to lift the carpet, what went on underneath there was none of their business.

They were happy to ignore and believe in the future.

But the sadness and tears would never leave Rose Cottage.

※ ※ ※

THE BOY NOW A MAN.
September 1924

Connor was happy. Well he was happier than he had been for a long time.

He still had his moments, still tortured by the death of his grandad Riley, and he still swore to himself that one day, revenge would be his.

But, yes, he was happier in himself.

Molly had given him hope and kindness and now, having been seeing each other for nearly a year and a half he was beginning to feel normal again.

He was beginning to feel to be able to love and be loved.

He loved his Nana dearly but this was different.

He had met Molly one dark February evening in a dark street of Tralee. He had bumped into her when he had been collecting his empty bottles one Friday evening to stop them getting smashed and on turning the corner they had collided, causing the basket to fall to the floor, smashing the entire contents.

He had been surprised by her reaction as she has told him 'to watch where he was bloody going, you stupid man'.

He hadn't known if it was her calling him a 'man', nobody had called him that ever before, or whether it had been those beautiful brown smiling eyes, full of mischief and happiness.

Molly was just a month younger than him and was working at their old school, training to be a teacher.

His Nana had long since given her approval. She loved Molly dearly and knew that she had had a profound effect on the uplift in Connor's new found confidence and positivity. She gave them as much space and time together as she possibly could, but because of it, she found herself becoming increasingly lonely. She tried to meet people and make new friends but Daibbi had always been her own woman. She hadn't needed anybody when she had Riley and when he had been killed she had focussed her life on continuing to bring Connor up as best she could. But now, at eighteen, he was a man, and a strapping one at that. 6' tall broad shoulders, solid muscle, but lean, he hadn't an ounce of fat on him.

In the evenings she would sit in the front room knitting or making a small piece of furniture and would listen to the two of them talking in the kitchen.

She didn't pry but she would hear Molly trying to teach Connor how to read and write. It was a struggle still, but she had a way about her and she could tell that he was progressing further than he had ever done before.

As Connor set out for work he shouted goodbye to his Nana, she didn't reply, but that was nothing new, she was probably busy doing chores before heading off to work at Manor Farm.

He climbed the hill steadily, running as usual but slower, he was early for a change.

At the farm he loaded his cart. There was no sign of Cain this morning and no notes left to be delivered. Not unusual for a Thursday morning, the notes now seemed to be sent out on Fridays and Mondays.

He completed his round and by one o'clock in the afternoon he was making his way back home, complete with some vegetables from the market that his Nana had asked him to get the night before. He was a little pleased with himself for actually remembering them, more often than not he had to return to Tralee or 'borrow' them from Manor Farm.

As he rode into the farm he saw Cain through the window of the study.

Cain saw him and waved at him telling him to wait.

A few minutes later Cain came out.

"Afternoon lad, everything okay",

" Yes Mr Milburn, everything's fine",

"Good to hear, how's that Nan of yours, is she okay because she didn't come to clean today".

Connor looked at him a little surprised. It wasn't like his Nana to miss a days work. In fact he couldn't ever remember her missing a day before.

"She was okay when I left this morning",

His mind went back to when he had left.

'She hadn't answered him'.

"I'll see you in the morning Mr Milburn".

He waved and ran out the gate.

He ran down the hill.

Faster than when he had ran up it that morning.

As he ran through the back gate he knew immediately something wasn't right.

The cattle were still in their stable.

He quickly walked into the kitchen and shouted his Nana.

There was no reply.

He ran back out into the yard and across to the barn and stable but there was no sign of her.

And then he looked up to her bedroom window.

The curtains were still drawn.

He ran inside and raced up the stairs.

There she lay on her bed. Still with her covers pulled up to her chin as though still asleep. She was asleep, but in a sleep that wouldn't be woken.

The doctor arrived shortly after and pronounced her dead.

'She had died of a broken heart' he had said.

At the funeral the whole town of Rossbridge turned out to pay their respects, including Cain Milburn.

They left Rose cottage and made their way slowly towards Rossbridge church. Rain now gently falling from the grey skies above. 'Gods tears' his Nana used to say.

Connor walked alone behind the horse drawn cart but Molly was only yards behind him should he need her.

Cain had let him use the milk cart and Duke to carry her. Connor thought his Nana would have liked that.

The service wasn't a long drawn out affair, just a few simple words about a woman who had led a simple life.

As they left the church the congregation respectfully bowed their heads and then quietly followed the coffin outside.

As Cain rode away on the cart, twenty or so mourners joined Connor and Molly as they slowly walked into the graveyard at the side of the church and towards the freshly dug hole in the ground on the far side.

The young Priest, along with the others bowed their heads in prayer and as he ended the prayer Connor slowly raised his head.

His attention was drawn to a woman who was now over to his left, where she had appeared from he didn't know. She stood about 10 yards away, alone under a large oak tree, with a black umbrella held over her head to help shelter her from the rain.

Connor looked at her, she in turn was already looking at him.

He gently nodded his head and smiled.

Molly, standing next to him, saw the gentle fleeting acknowledgement between them and whispered quietly her question to him.

"Who's that",

Connor's gaze, still transfixed to the woman as if he had been hypnotised, didn't move, but just replied with two quiet words.

"My Mother".

A few more words were spoken by the Priest before Daibheid Gillian was slowly given up to god and lowered into the ground. The Priest then invited Connor to drop soil onto the coffin.

It was then that the first tear appeared in Connor's eyes. As he looked sadly over to his mother he held out his slightly shaking hand.

She looked at her boy. A man now of course, but he was still her little boy.

The tears now flowed softly down her cheeks, tears of not just sorrow but that also out of guilt. Guilt of her abandonment of her one and only child all those years ago.

He held his hand out still and slowly nodded his head to tell her 'it was okay, it will all be alright'.

She gently placed the umbrella onto the wet ground and walked slowly over to her son. As they met together at the side of her mother's grave, she held the hand of her little boy for the first time in almost sixteen years.

Together again at last, her Mother, his Nana, would have liked that.

An hour later the three of them, Connor, Molly and Aibbi sat at the kitchen table in Rose Cottage.

There they sat and they cried, and they laughed, and they talked.

But one thing remained the same all evening.

Connor held his mother's hand..... and he didn't let go.

After a while Molly made her excuses and left, she felt they needed some time together.

They talked for hours. They talked about Daibbi and how she and Riley had brought him up.

They spoke of what she now was, a famous actress and what he now was, in charge of a milk round.

They spoke of all the lost years between them.

And then, inevitably, they spoke of Connor's father.

"He was a lovely boy, your father" said Aibbi,

"Do you know, the last time I saw him, he was barely as old as you are now",

Connor looked at her, he hadn't ever thought of it like that before. It hit him like running into a brick wall. His father, Mally hadn't even lived to be nineteen years old.

And so they sat........They both had questions to ask, some more important than others.

But Connor had one he had wanted to ask since he could remember and was so desperately in need of an answer. It was a question he had dreamt of, thought of and often asked of, but had never had a real answer from anybody, and now, at last, sat with his mother, it was time to ask it one last time.

"Mother",

Aibbi looked at him, her eyes now suddenly filling with tears of absolute joy.

She had just been called by the name she had so much longed to be called but never had.

'Mother', he had called her Mother.

Oh how good that had felt. It was like her life was now complete but she knew that it wasn't, but for now it would do.

But then all too quickly, the sorrow and sadness welled up from her stomach because she knew what the question was to be.

Connor looked her in the eye.

And she looked straight back at him, …. Waiting.

"What exactly happened to my Father",

She squeezed the hand that still gripped hers, as if trying to rid it of all the blood that was in it. Her eyes now streaming with tears.

"My darling little boy, I have been dreading this question since the day that I left you, but it is your right to ask it. He was your father and he would have loved and adored you dearly, but please believe me when I say I do not truly know what happened. But ……there is one thing I do know for sure and that is that, you're father is dead. I dearly, with all my heart, wish, that I could tell you that he is still alive and that one day you may see him, but he is not. I am so sorry that I cannot give you the wish that you so longed for, but I cant".

He looked at her, now at last, he knew the truth. His father was dead.

He watched her place her hand into her small handbag and she took out a small white envelope.

She passed it to him and he looked at it.

"Do you know what it says on the front" she looked at him waiting for the answer.

"Its for me, its says Connor",

"You can read ?",

"I can read more than I could, Molly has been teaching me",

"That's very kind of her, she's a nice girl",

"I think so too",

She looked back at the envelope and said,

"Within this letter is what happened to your father and I, on that dreadful day over eighteen years ago. When you read it, I hope you will understand why I had to run away and stay away. I wasn't, and still I am not, proud of what I did, but I had no choice. I ask you not to judge me until you have read it. But …… I ask you to promise me one thing, you alone must read it, for if anybody else sees it, then they will be signing their own death warrant".

She looked at him and he nodded his head.

They carried on talking until the early hours of the morning.

She promised that she would write and he in turn promised that he would go to visit her in America. She insisted that she would pay the fare to which he eventually and reluctantly agreed.

"Connor, I have the money, you don't, you could come and stop with me and if you wanted to bring Molly then that would be lovely too" she said,

"Do you live on your own" said Connor,

She smiled at him knowing what he was thinking.

"No, I live with George, and I'm sure that you would get on fine".

Without thinking they both found themselves looking at his mother's left hand which was resting on the table showing her wedding finger that held a wedding ring and another which held a huge diamond.

They both looked up at each other and grinned like two Cheshire cats.

"You will like him, I promise",

"I'm sure I will Mother".

The next morning they were both up early, Aibbi had to leave to return to America that same day. They said their sad farewells but both knew that they would see each other again.

What they didn't know was that it would be much sooner than they thought.

※ ※ ※

NEVER LOOK BACK

Christmas Eve 1924

Connor was looking forward to four whole days off.

He couldn't remember the last time he had had that much time off before. But because Christmas Eve fell on a Wednesday, Cain had told him he could have the time off until the following Monday. So as he set off a little after 05:30am on a very cold and snowy morning, he felt good. He was looking forward to the break and more time to spend with Molly.

He still hadn't read his mothers letter, he had placed it with the others that his Nana had saved for him and now, fearing what his mother had said, he had placed them all in his hiding place, in the loft of the barn.

He couldn't bring himself to read them, not yet, the time

wasn't write. Something was holding him back. It was as if he didn't want to know the truth of what had happened all those years ago. He would read them when he was ready.

Connor liked Christmas Eve, as was tradition within Tralee, a small gift was left for the likes of the milkmen and other traders that delivered their wears to the houses. Sometimes, at the rich and wealthy premises, small amounts of money was also left. Small amounts they may have been, but it all added up. Last year Connor had more than doubled his wage for the week.

And so as he made his way around Tralee he placed the gifts of small tins of biscuits and bottles of beer under his seat. The money went into his jacket pocket. He wasn't as trusting of some of the residents of Tralee.

On his return, he didn't turn into, but rode on past Manor farm and carried on towards Rose Cottage. He had too many gifts to carry back home, so he turned into the yard, tied Duke up and started to take the gifts from under the seat. As he did so some coins fell from his jacket pocket and rolled further under the seat.

He got down onto his hands and knees and felt around for the them but couldn't find them. He gave up and then carried on removing the gifts, taking them inside to the kitchen, placing them on the table.

He returned to the cart and as he was about to untie Duke he saw two of the coins had rolled right to the back, under the seat. Once again he got down on his hands and knees, this time placing his head sideways onto the floor of the cart and looking towards the back of the underside of the seat. He saw the coins, he reached out with his arm and grabbed them.

It was then that he saw something else, it was off white in colour standing on its end and partially hidden behind the box that usually held the notes and the wooden club.

He knew immediately what it was.

It was a diamond shaped note and it had the number 27 written on the front of it.

He reached to the back and pulled it with his fingers but as he did so, it started to unfold. As he got slowly onto his feet he looked down at the dusty, dirty piece of paper in his hand. He could see part of the inside and saw one written word.

It said '8 o'clock'.

He stood. He stood for what seemed like forever before he did anything else.

And then he opened the note that had been under his seat for over four years.

And then he read it.

It said 'It's happening tonight at 8 o'clock, stay away from the Stonebridge'.

He stood still, his brain had gone into overdrive, and there was no room left for a message to tell him to move, it was too busy working out what all this meant.

A few moments later it had done.

It came with a flash back from within his brain which was four years old, as he remembered standing in Tralee market square as the right hand side of the Stonebridge pub disappeared before his very eyes and then the blast knocking completely off his feet. It continued then with the screaming and crying of grown men laying all around him. Blood pouring from dismembered limbs and the smell of burning flesh. It was something he couldn't and wouldn't ever forget.

He walked into the barn and climbed the ladder.

He bent down into his own little corner and gently pulled out all the letters from their hiding place.

For now was the time to read them.

He sat with his back to the wall, looked at the dates stamped onto the front of the envelope, and then started from the beginning.

For the next two hours he read. He read all the letters that his mother had sent from when she was in Dublin to when she was in America.

The tears slowly began to stream down his face and then finally, he came to the last one. The one that she had given to him the day they buried his Nana.

He opened the envelope and unfolded the letter and then he read it.

It read.

'My darling Connor,

I hope when you read this letter we have already spoken together and you have been able to forgive me for what I did when abandoning you all those years ago.

What I write here has never been told to anybody before. Not a single soul. This includes both your Grandmother and Riley, I have never told anyone until now.

I need to start from before you were born and tell you what happened on that dreadful day in Donnell's wood and why it changed our lives forever.

Your Father, Mally, and I had gone into the wood, like we had done so many times before. I remember it had been snowing but it had stopped.

It was the day Cain Milburn found us in the wood.

He was with a farm worker known as Parrot. They both had shotguns and an argument started between us about us poaching.

There was not any love lost between the Milburn's and I, but to accuse us of being poachers was just an excuse to create an argument. The argument soon escalated into more than just words and it soon developed into a very dangerous situation.

Your father, obviously worried about what was going happen next, managed to distract them and shouted at me to run away, which I did.

But your father didn't get away.

I then I heard one of the shotguns go off, and then, what seemed like seconds later, another shot. I didn't know what to do but my mind was made up for me when I heard a third shot followed by the blast shattering the branch just above my head.

There was no doubt in my mind that the third shot was meant to hit me, and there was also no doubt that the other shots I had heard before that one, were the ones that killed your father.

I then heard Cain Milburn shout to Parrot to come back to him but he obviously didn't.

I managed to get into the stream and I thought that I had managed to escape but then I heard somebody walking in the stream behind me.

It was Parrot. He saw me and I felt sure that he was going to shoot me so I hit him on the head with a rock.

I killed him Connor. I killed a man. But I swear I killed him in self defence.

It was the next morning when I ran away to Dublin. I knew that if I stayed in Rossbridge then I too would soon be dead.

Over the next few months I realised that I was pregnant and all the time I hoped and prayed that your father was still alive and that he would come and find me, but he didn't.

And so, as you know, when you were two years old I returned with you to Rose cottage to confirm if you father was still alive but I soon knew that he wasn't.

I knew then that I couldn't stay and that I now had a terrible decision to make.

Should I take you back to Dublin to live again in squaller or should I leave you with my Mother and Riley.

It was a decision that broke my heart but I still believe that it was the right one and the only one I could make.

They raised you well and I am so proud of the man that you have become but now I worry about your safety.

Some time ago I returned very briefly to Dublin and one evening whilst at a party with some friends I was told of a story of a boy that was working for the IRA. He was known only as 'The Messenger Boy'.

I thought little of it until your Grandmother sent me a letter about the awful death of your friend Cathal and his Grandmother. She told me that the Black and Tans had killed them.

Connor, they killed them thinking he was the Messenger Boy, but I know, as well as you do that it wasn't him.

It was you Connor that they wanted to kill. Whether you know it or not, you were, and still are the Messenger Boy.

There has been so many tragedies that have happened recently over the years and sadly we have been connected to too many of them. I don't believe that any of them have been bad luck or just coincidence. Cain has had a hand in most of them I'm sure of it, but he answers to somebody else.

Do you think that it was just a coincidence that your Grandad Riley was in the Reindeer pub when that bomb went off. Riley hadn't been in that place for years, he didn't drink. They killed him too, I'm certain of it.

Please believe me son when I say that when they don't need you anymore then you too will be in grave danger.

I also beg you to believe me and forgive me. But I had, and still have no choice.

I will love you for ever more,

Mother x x x x

Connor sat looking up to the roof of the barn. His face now

soaked through with tears.

Because he now realised the awful truth.

He had been the one that had delivered the notes that had led to the murder's of so many people, but so tragically, he had also delivered the messages that led to the death of his Grandad.

He collected up all of the letters and put them in a pile. All apart from the one from his mother, he placed that back behind the timber and into his hiding place, 'he couldn't burn that one, his mother had written it just for him'.

He moved over to his right and placed his hand into the hiding place. But not 'his' hiding place.

This time it was Riley's.

'Use it and lose it' Riley had said.

It was time to use it.

He walked across the yard and into the kitchen and threw the remaining letters onto the fire. He went to the cupboard and found a pencil and a piece of paper then wrote a note and placed it on the kitchen table.

Five minutes later he was riding back up the hill in the gently falling snow towards Manor Farm.

As he turned into the yard there was no sign of Cain. There was no sign of anybody at all. The place seemed deserted.

He took Duke off the cart, let him out into his paddock and threw half a bale of hay on to the snow.

He looked across the fields in front of him and down into the valley below.

He looked down towards Donnell's wood. He imagined his mother, running for her life, through the tree's and then down into the stream.

'It had been snowing, but had stopped' she had said. It must have been a day much like today he thought to himself. Apart from today, the snow hadn't stopped, it was still falling gently.

And then from somewhere within Donnell's wood he heard a gunshot. And then another.

A shiver ran through his bones. This all seemed so real. It was like he was being took back in time.

He watched, waiting for something to happen.

And then he saw them.

Cain and his younger brother Glendon coming out of the woods and walking through the field and up the hill towards him.

They were both carrying dead rabbits, pheasants ……….and shotguns.

They were almost halfway through the field and about 60 yards away, before they saw him.

He watched them and he saw Cain say something to Glendon but couldn't hear what. Whatever it had been it made Glendon look towards him and then back towards the wood.

Connor waited for them. He didn't want Glendon there. This had nothing to do with him.

As they came through the gate Cain looked at him. He knew straight away that something was wrong. He'd seen it in Connor's eyes many times before.

"And what brings you out in this weather Connor lad" said Cain,

"Cain, I need to speak to you".

'Cain… he called me Cain', he thought. 'He has never called me Cain before, not once'.

"Okay, shall we go inside" said Cain,

"I'd rather not, I would rather stay out here, and I need to speak to you alone",

"Connor, ...I don't think you need to worry about Glendon here",

"I'm not worried about him at all Cain, but I need to speak to you alone",

'He'd said it again, Cain', now a little concerned Cain thought to himself, 'where was this going'.

"Okay have it your way", he looked at Glendon, "take the game inside, I will be in shortly".

Glendon hesitated and looked back at Cain, seeking his assurance.

Cain nodded at him and said "put the kettle on the stove".

Glendon walked slowly past them taking the dead rabbits and pheasants from Cain as he passed. He waited for his brother to get inside and then he asked Connor.

"Whats this all about, you seem a little worried about something",

"I'm not worried" said Connor,

"Okay, so your'e not worried..... and I'm not a fucking mind reader, so would you just get on and tell me what it is your here about before I get frostbite in my fucking feet".

Connor reached behind him with his left hand to his back trouser pocket and pulled out the opened diamond shaped note.

"I found this on the cart" he held it out in front of him, waiting for Cain to take it from him.

Cain looked at it. He knew what it was, it was one of his notes, but he had written hundreds of them over the years and hadn't a clue what the message was inside. He stepped two paces forward and leant towards Connor and slowly held out his hand and took it off him and then took three paces back.

"Thank you, is that it, or is there something else that's bothering you",

"Aren't you going to read it",

"Do I need too",

"I want you too",

"You do do you, and why would you want me to do that",

"Because I want to see your face when you do",

Cain looked at Connor and then down at the note and slowly unfolded it.

"Okay I've looked at it, is my face okay.....now what do you want me to do" said Cain,

"Can you remember what it was for" said Connor,

"No Connor I can't, perhaps you could enlighten me, oh forgive me I forgot, you cant read can you",

"I know what it was for",

"Oh really and how the fuck do you know that Mr Sherlock Holmes",

"I can read".

Cain looked at him. He looked past him at the kitchen window. Glendon, watching from inside, standing next to the stove, he nodded at him.

"Don't be stupid Connor, even if you could read, and you can't, you wouldn't know what this was all about, it was years ago",

"It was nearly four years ago Cain, you probably cant remember, but I was there".

Cain's mind drifted back to that day. He remembered hearing that Connor had been close to the pub when the bomb went off and was so relieved when he heard that he had not been badly injured.

Cain slowly slid the shotgun from his shoulder, which went not unnoticed by Connor. It Also went not unnoticed by Glendon.

"Who read it to you Connor because whatever they told you it said, I can promise you it doesn't",

"I told you, I read it myself and now I have worked it out for myself, I know what I've been doing for you all these years."

Cain laughed, a cynical laugh full of contempt.

"You don't know fucking anything",

"But I do Cain, I do know, I know that I have delivered notes that has led to many people being killed and I also know that I delivered the notes when you organised the murder of my Grandad".

Glendon had now quietly slipped out from the kitchen and was stood 20 yards behind the seemingly unsuspecting Connor.

Cain slowly raised the shotgun, not to head height but to just below the height of Connor's waist and slightly to his left. Not openly threatening, not yet. But not far off.

Cain looked back over the shoulder of Connor.

Connor knew Glendon was there. He'd seen the snow over to his right darken just a little.

"Go to Henry, go now" said Cain.

'He answers to someone else' the letter had said.

Connor heard Glendon run across the snow towards the barn, he turned to look and watched as seconds later he came out on his horse and ride quickly out the gate. As he slowly turned back to face Cain, he saw that the shotgun was now chest high and now no longer slightly to his left but straight at him, about five yards away.

"Now Connor, it's just me and you and now I have a problem. You see, you have been a good servant to me and the cause, the best I've ever had but this, all this, makes you a dead man. You understand that don't you, I can't let you go from this".

Connor looked at him and then did something that Cain wasn't expecting at all.

He smiled at him.

He knew now who was in control, and it wasn't Cain.

"You've got your Mother's balls lad thats for sure".

Connor ignored him.

"Why did you have to kill my Father" said Connor.

Cain looked at the boy, the boy who was now a man, he'd watched him grow up, he'd helped him grow up, but here and now, he was going to have to kill him.

"That was a big crock of shit that went from bad to worse Connor. It is something that shouldn't of happened, but it did",

"Where is his body," as Connor looked over Cain's shoulder towards the wood he asked him "Is it down there",

Cain slowly nodded his head.

"Your Mother, I take it she is still alive and well then, she told you this didn't she, it could only have come from her",

"Yes she did, she wrote me a letter".

Connor again reached back behind himself towards his back pocket.

Cain looked at him and waved his left hand shaking it in a 'no' motion, which made his right arm naturally move slightly out to the right.

"Connor no, I don't need to read it",

Connor bought his left hand back around.

There was no letter.

He pulled the trigger, shooting him in the head.

Cain was dead before he hit the floor.

Connor calmly looked at him. The blood gurgling from his open mouth and the splashes of blood and brain dotted in the snow around his now lifeless body, their redness against the blinding white snow made it appear like it had rained hot strawberries from up above.

He took hold of the shotgun, now half trapped under the body and pulled it free. He picked it up and placed the barrel into Cains mouth, grabbed hold of Cains right hand and placed his index finger on the trigger. Connor then turned his head away, pressed down on the finger and squeezed the trigger, blowing what was left of his head completely apart. More hot strawberry's appeared, falling into the snow, fizzing as they did so.

Connor was surprised at himself, how unemotional his was about what had just happened. He felt nothing, no sadness, no guilt, no happiness, no sense of redemption. Nothing.

Connor placed his own gun back into his waistband and walked slowly into the Manor House.

He walked into the study and over to the book shelf.

He pulled out the last book on the left of the second highest shelf and opened the small 8" x 6" door that was hidden behind it and reached inside.

He'd seen Cain hide money in there many years ago and had never forgotten it.

He pulled out all the money that was inside, which was a quite substantial amount and placed it in his pockets.

He calmly walked back outside and into the barn, carried a bale of straw back into the study and threw it onto the Chesterfield settee. He grabbed a handful of the dry straw from it and held one end into the open fire until it was burning, then threw it onto the settee and walked back outside into the now heavily falling snow.

He walked past the body of Cain, now starting to get covered in the soft white snow and walked into the field where Duke stood gently eating his hay. He stood in front of him and grabbed him around his neck and gently kissed him on his forehead and whispered to him "Goodbye my beautiful friend, I will love you forever".

As he turned left out of the gate he didn't look back, 'never look back'.

He was going to Tralee.

He needed to go to confession.

As he got to the edge of the town he watched as the horse drawn fire engine sped by in the opposite direction. He knew where they were going. You could see it as well. Grey smoke billowing up into the snow filled sky, 3 miles to the South.

'There wouldn't be much left of it' he thought. He hoped so anyway.

As the darkness descended on Tralee he made his way through the now deserted streets towards Sheep Street and Saint Michael's church. Firstly though, he was calling at Number 19.

As he got to the gate he noticed the now partly snow covered hoof prints.

He walked up the path towards the front door, he didn't know why but he felt different from the last time he had made a visit here, he just didn't feel the way he usually felt. There was no knotting of his stomach, no dread, and no apprehension whatsoever. A calmness had come over him like he had never felt before.

He grabbed the metal knocker and gave three heavy knocks.

There was no answer.

So he gave it three more.

Through the small window pain above his head he noticed the light change slightly within.

So he placed his left hand in the rear of his waistband.

The bolts slid back behind the door and then it was slowly opened.

A tall thin man stood in front of him. 'This wasn't the Priest that Connor had seen and who he now knew was Father Henry, Cains eldest brother.

Dower looked at him, he didn't speak, he was waiting for the question.

Connor looked back at him.

"Good evening, may I speak with the Father please",

"He's not here at the moment, can I be of any assistance" said Dower.

"No sir, I'm sorry I need to speak to Father Henry, do you know where I may find him",

"Well lad, he went out in a hurry about half an hour ago, he may well be at the church, that would be my best bet, I should try there",

"Thank you sir I will, sorry to trouble you",

"Its not a problem, you have a nice evening",

"I will thanks".

As Connor turned to walk away he stopped and looked back at the tall thin man who was slowly closing the door, he said,

"Why do you beat him",

Dower looked at him slightly shocked by the question, but he eventually replied,

"I beg your pardon, what did you just say",

"I said why do you beat him, the Father I mean, why do you beat him, does he beat you",

Dower was again quiet for a moment.

"No he doesn't beat me",

"Then why do you beat him if he doesn't beat you".

Connor stared at the silent Dower and then carried on.

"It wont happen anymore anyway, where he's going you wont be able to hit him ever again".

Connor turned at walked away and then the door closed silently behind him.

As he got to the church he noticed that the lights were on within. Not unusual, it was Christmas Eve after all. There would be all sorts of events going on throughout the day and evening. He opened the large oak door and walked in.

It was empty.

It was surprisingly warm inside. The candles at the alter, flickered gently in the draughty air while the smell of the burning wax filled the building with the familiar aroma.

The walls were filled with the Christmas decorations and a large Christmas tree stood in the far left hand corner adorned with its own.

He walked over to the confession box, it was time to get on with what he was here to do.

The door to it was closed. He couldn't see if there was anybody inside. He slowly put his head to the door and listened. It was quiet. He pulled the door open and looked inside. It was empty. He stepped inside and closed the door behind him.

And then he took the gun from his waistband. He placed it on his lap and then he rang the bell.

Nobody came.

So he rang it again, only louder.

This time somebody heard it.

He felt the familiar draft from the other side of the lattice.

He picked up the gun with his left hand, pulled back the trigger with his right thumb and then held it with both hands down between his knees.

As somebody moved into the other side of the lattice it caused a shadow to form within the confessor's side and then it sat down.

Connor slowly raised the gun and looked through the holes in the wood. He could see the black top and then the white of the dog collar on the top, but he couldn't see the face. Was it him, was it Father Henry, he pointed the gun towards the wooden window and slowly and gently squeezed the trigger.... And then the shadow spoke.

"Good evening sorry if I kept you but I was getting wood for the fire, how can I help ".

It wasn't Father Henry.

It was a younger Priest.

Connor slowly lowered the gun back down between his knees.

"I'm sorry Father but I need to speak with Father Henry it's quite urgent, is he here",

"I'm very sorry but no, that won't be possible this evening, Father Henry has been called way on urgent business and wont be back for sometime".

Connor wasn't happy with the answer, was the young Priest hiding something, he couldn't see his eyes, he always knew when somebody was lying by looking at their eyes, it was something that had never failed him so far, so he had to ask instead.

"Are you sure of that",

"I beg your pardon" replied the young Priest,

" Are you sure that he wont be back, where has he gone, what can be so urgent on a Christmas eve",

"I can assure you that he has gone away. I saw him get picked up outside but 10 minutes ago. He was off to the railway station with his brother Glendon and they were in a rush",

"I'm sure they were" muttered Connor.

"I'm sorry what was that" said the Priest,

"I said, tell Father Henry when you see him that Connor will catch up with you at some point",

"Okay, yes I will, is there anything else I could help you with"

"No Father, not tonight, sorry for troubling you".

And with that he was gone.

Molly found her letter on Christmas Day, it was not the present she had been hoping for. In it, he explained that he needed to go away for a time, he hoped that she could forgive him but he couldn't tell her why.

But it didn't take much working out why.

She had seen with her own eyes the burnt out building that

had once been the Manor House. It was beyond repair and would have to be demolished. She had also been told that it appeared that Cain Milburn had taken his own life. But she had her own thoughts on the recent events.

Over the next few months Connor hunted Southern Ireland for his prey but to no avail. Both Henry and Glendon had vanished. Nobody knew of their whereabouts or at least nobody was telling him where they were.

And so……

On the 7th May 1925 in Queenstown Ireland RMS Andania sailing from Hamburg, docked to pick up passengers bound for New York.

Curtesy of the Miburn Family, Connor Gillian was climbing aboard.

He was going to see his mother.

❋ ❋ ❋

NO MORE SECRETS

October 1941

After much sole searching and his heart ruling his head and

vice-versa, Connor had decided to join the British army in February the previous year. He had many reasons for not joining, but the one reason to sign up far outweighed those against.

He'd had some first hand combat almost immediately and it wasn't long before his speciality for concealment and the uncanny ability to covertly follow people or even better, follow whole German divisions, had been noticed, but following the evacuation at Dunkirk he had returned to England. But his name had been noted and it wasn't long before his name was being talked about in some very high places.

And so as a consequence, he was summonsed to Snettisham old Hall, a secluded Manor House in Snettisham in the county of Norfolk. There he was to be introduced to his new boss, Colonel Richard Southall.

As Connor approached the building along the tree lined gravelled drive, the memories of Manor House farm in Rossbridge came flooding back to him. Some good, some bad, but it was the bad ones that stirred the anger deep within him. He had it nearly always it under control, but when things stirred the memory pot, it bubbled deep within.

Somethings you can never forget, and somethings had to be evened out.

'But wait a while and it will come', he thought to himself.

He was calm and relatively happy again by the time the driver stopped outside the front door. He thanked him and grabbed his small case and walked across the gravel.

As Connor walked towards the large oak door it was opened for him by an army sergeant who then led him into the entrance hall. People bustled about going this way and that, carrying papers or briefcases that contained more papers.

Nobody looked at him and smiled or acknowledged him in anyway. They were all far too busy doing what they were doing.

'Secret stuff' thought Connor 'don't tell anyone your secret, or you will be dead lad' came whistling back into his head.

They walked down an oak panelled corridor, more people passed him in a hurry, with more papers, and more briefcases carrying more papers. The corridor must have been 60 yards long, as they got to the end and couldn't go any further the sergeant gently tapped on the door in front of them.

A shout of 'Enter' came from within and the sergeant opened the door and stood aside letting Connor go in.

Colonel Southall was a tall, muscular well built man. He was closing in on his 50th birthday but he had looked after himself you could tell. His blonde hair was in decline and what was left was shaven close to his suntanned head. If you didn't know he was a colonel in the British army you would have taken him for an American GI.

But when he spoke there was no mistake, he was as English as roast beef. Softly spoken but with an authoritativeness that shone out. He didn't demand or expect respect, he didn't need to because he got it from those that knew and worked for him by the bucket load.

A man's man, a natural born leader of men.

Connor liked him from the moment he met him.

The Colonel greeted him with a handshake and then offered him a seat inside his study.

By the time the meeting was to be over, some two hours later, Connor had been promoted to Captain, had a staff of one, that being Sergeant Hunt and had been told to be ready to be flown out of the country by 22:00 hours the following evening.

During the meeting Colonel Southall had explained to him what sort of work SOE carried out. It was dangerous, very dangerous work, mostly if not all done behind enemy lines, and mostly if not all, done on your own.

" We like to work on our own Gillian as you are less likely to be caught. On our own we have fifty percent chance of buggering it up compared to if there's two of you, if you understand what

I mean" said the Colonel.

" I only work on my own anyway Sir" said Connor, possibly a little too self assuredly thought to himself immediately after saying it, but was put at ease by the Colonel straight the way.

" Good, I like that. Somebody who is confident in themselves brings confidence to others. I like that a lot".

" Now we need to go through some details about what we need you to be doing whilst your out there" said the Colonel,

Connor looked at the Colonel.

" where exactly is 'out there' said Connor smiling,

" good point" laughed the Colonel,

"You will be working in Northern France gathering intelligence on German troops and armoured divisions. I will go into more detail tomorrow morning but all I will say is this, it's a very dangerous job. We have lost a few operatives already due mainly to some bad luck but my gut feeling is that we have a bad apple over there who is tipping the Germans off."

He looked at Connor as if he was going to ask him something but then thought better of it.

"Okay that's enough about what we need you to do, for now anyway. What I would like to know is more about you Gillian",

said the Colonel , his eyes narrowing slightly as if to accentuate the total lack of their knowledge about him and his past,

"Where the hell have you come from and more importantly, where did you learn about what you do",

"No secrets" said Connor as in asking a question,

" no secrets and no lies" said the Colonel shaking his head.

Connor nodded, and said,

"I don't tell lie's, ...but I have many secrets".

He took a breath and started his story.

" Okay, I was born in a small village in the south west of Ireland called Rossbridge to a Protestant father and a Catholic mother".

The Colonel didn't react at all, 'unusual', thought Connor, he carried on.

"When I was very young my mother had to run away and I was bought up by my grandparents",

"I take it that's them on your wrist",

Without knowing it, Connor had subconsciously been rubbing the 'DRA' tattoo on his wrist.

A slightly embarrassed Connor nodded his response and continued.

"My grandad worked on a local farm owned by the Milburn family but he then went to fight for the British in the first war and when he returned he told me many things, some good, but mostly bad".

"Whilst he was there I was given a job on a milk round by the Milburn's. They were a big farming family, they owned most of the farms around that area.

When I started working for them I was just six years old. By the time I was eleven I was doing the round on my own. They were troubled times in Ireland at that time, much worse than now".

Connor was silent for a moment subconsciously deciding if he should go on.

He did.

"When my grandad returned from the war he had been injured when fleeing from behind enemy lines, you see, that was his job too. He taught me a lot",

"So then, we have to thank your grandfather for all of your skills do we" said the Colonel,

Connor paused and looked him in the eye and said slowly and softly,

"Not entirely Sir, no",

"Then who else do we need to thank".

Connor paused then sat back in his chair and said something he had never said before in his life.

"The Irish Republican Army sir",

For the first time the Colonel showed a small glimpse of a reaction.

"You were taught by the IRA",

"Yes sir, I was ".

Connor looked at the Colonel seeking his permission to carry on. The Colonel nodded for him to continue.

"They taught me virtually everything I know about concealment and how to follow and watch people covertly".

The Colonel looked at him, studying him almost.

"And exactly how long have you been working for them, as in the IRA, when were you recruited",

" I don't work for them anymore Sir if that's what your worried about, and when I did, I didn't know that I did, if you understand my meaning",

The colonel looked at him quizzically and Connor could see that for the first time the Colonel wasn't quite sure what was coming next.

"They recruited me, if that's what you want to call it, from an early age",

" I see, so exactly how old were you then",

" I was eight years old".

It was now the Colonel's turn to sit back in his chair.

"Eight..... Your telling me that the IRA recruited you and trained you from the age of eight, my god Gillian".

The Colonel stopped talking and looked at him deeply as if something was now making sense.

They sat in silence for a moment before the Colonel spoke.

"I think I know who you are",

He studied Connor's face for a reaction but there wasn't one.

"Your'e the messenger boy aren't you",

Still no reaction.

" Here am I, a Colonel from the British army sat opposite a member of the IRA, about to give him a job. The same man, or should I say, boy, who was partly responsible for the murder of 15 under cover Irish police officers".

Connor looked at the Colonel to make sure he had finished, this was not the time to interrupt.

"Sir, firstly can I say that I never was, knowingly that is, a member of the IRA. Secondly when I was 'working for them', I didn't know that I was, as you would say, 'working for them'. Yes I delivered their messages and yes I followed people for them, but I didn't know what the messages were or what they meant and I certainly didn't know why I was following anyone",

" Didn't you read the messages Gillian, surely if you had read them you would have known what they were",

" The first one that I ever read, was the last one I ever read, and by then I was eighteen years old",

"Gillian, your telling me, that from the age of eight, you delivered your, or should I say, their death messages until the age of eighteen and you never read one note, not a single one".

Connor stared at the Colonel and then he finally spoke.

" Sir.....I didn't read them. I didn't read them because I couldn't"

He paused,

"By that Sir, I mean that I couldn't read or write ".

The Colonel looked at him now understanding a little better, bit by bit it was unfolding, he nodded for him to continue.

Connor carried on.

"When I was seventeen I met a girl, Molly, and for some time I didn't tell her that I couldn't read or write, but eventually she worked it out for herself. So when we could, we would sit at night and she would teach me how to read and how to write. It took me over a year to learn but eventually I got it.

Then one day, I found an old diamond note underneath the seat on the milk cart, it had been there a long while".

Connor saw that the Colonel was about to ask what he meant.

" Sorry sir, let me explain, he, Cain Milburn, folded all the notes in a certain way, they were folded over and over into the shape of a diamond and they didn't come undone unless you pulled them apart. On this occasion though, as I pulled it from the back of the bench, it came undone",

"What was the message, can you remember".

Connor paused. He knew he had to carry on but he felt he was now at the point of no return. After a long pause he said,

"Yes I can remember, it said 'It's happening tonight, 8 o'clock, stay away from the Stonebridge",

The Colonel nodded and waved his hand for him to continue.

" I had been there, at the Stonebridge, four years prior to finding that note, that night in January 1921 , I can remember it now as though it was yesterday, I saw it with my own eyes when at 8 o'clock in the evening, the bomb went off in the Stonebridge public house in Tralee, killing 10 people, all Protestant's, members of a gang who were taking the fight to the Milburn people, and two off duty British soldiers".

He paused again for a few moments.

"And so, four years on and now being able to read, I knew that I had been the one delivering the messages that organised and led to that bombing and also to other bombs that were planted and that, yes, I had been the messenger boy, and in a way, i had been responsible for the murder of tens of people if not more",

" Is that why you left the IRA",

" No sir it wasn't. Like I say, I never knew that I was in it in the first place but, 'I left' if thats what you want to call it, for other reasons".

Connor stopped again, this was hard. He had never told this to anybody in his life and now he he was telling somebody he barely knew, his life long secrets, secrets he thought were his for ever.

"Carry on" said the Colonel,

" I left, ... I left because they killed my grandad, ...

and I,.....

I had delivered the note that had killed him".

For the first time in years Connor felt tears welling in his eyes, they trickled down his cheek and they dropped onto his lap.

The Colonel let him stop for a while before he spoke again.

" When you say they, who are 'they' ".

Connor explained that 'they' were the Milburn family. That Cain was his boss and that Father Henry, the local Priest was Cain's older brother and also the head of the IRA for that area.

He looked at Connor nodding his understanding and asked,

" Where are Cain and his brother, Father Henry now",

The Colonel saw a look come over Connor that up until now he hadn't seen in him before. It was almost a smile on his face but not quite, more like a satisfactory half grin.

" Cain is dead",

" I see, and you know that for certain do you".

He looked at Connor,

Who nodded his response,

The Colonel continued,

" how"

" I know and yes I'm certain,......... because I killed him",

The Colonel, unfazed by the response carried on

"And what of his brother Henry",

" He is alive and is believed to have been in France working for the British army as a Priest, but I presume that he must have come back with the rest of us",

"Is that why you joined the British army Gillian, to kill the Priest",

"Yes Sir it is".

They carried on talking for an hour or more.

How the Milburn's had murdered the father he had never known. How they had killed his grandad and consequently his beloved Nana dying of a broken heart. How they had driven his mother away, fearing for her life, and how the British, the black and tans, had killed his best friend Cal, who they had mistaken for him.

" I take it then that the IRA are no friends of yours now then",

Connor sat looking at the Colonel, it was a while before he spoke again.

"Sir, I have no ill feelings at all towards the IRA. You may find that hard to believe having what's happened to members of my family, but you need to understand that when I was growing up in Ireland, they were hard times. People, my people, Irish people, we were starving to death, the movement, if that's what we can call it, was desperate measures, by desperate people, in desperate times. The British didn't cover themselves in glory Sir, no, not at all. They murdered, we murdered. I say 'we' because I'm a proud Irishman, so, …..no Sir, if that is your question, no, ….my fight is not with the IRA, it never has been and never will be, but nor is it with the British army.

My fight is with the people that, yes, were highly ranked members of the IRA, but my fight has nothing to do with that, it is because and only because they killed my Family".

The Colonel looked at him, imagining him as a young boy walking around the streets of Tralee, in the shadows, hiding, watching, following.

"Do you know that the British intelligence service's had suspected that a young boy was helping pass messages for the IRA, and also that he had identified and followed an undercover police officer who was found murdered, and at the time, a dead woman's husband was found guilty and hanged for that crime."

Connor nodded,

" Yes Sir, I have heard this, but I learnt of this some years after the event's you are talking about, from my mother. She also told me many things within a note, when I met her at my Nana's funeral some years a go",

" Do you know that many people believed that you, as in 'the messenger boy' were dead, but the myth, the myth said that you were actually still alive",

" Yes Sir, I have heard this story also, but again some many years after. I think, well I now know, that when they killed my Cal, they thought, and they thought for some years, that they had killed me, 'the Messenger Boy' if you like, but Cal was never 'the Messenger Boy', no, he was just a young boy, a lovely true friend, ...the last one I ever had",

The Colonel shook his head

"have you never had another friend Connor",

" No sir I haven't, being friends with me is a dangerous pastime".

They smiled each other, a cruel joke, but very true in some respects.

A dead father, a dead grandfather, a dead Nana, and a dead best friend.

Dangerous pastime indeed.

As the meeting drew to a close Colonel Southall thanked Connor for his honesty and had one more thing to say,

"For this to work we need to have complete trust in each other Connor, do you agree",

" Yes sir, we must, but, if I didn't trust you I wouldn't have told you any of this",

" I know, and likewise I wouldn't be promoting you to Captain and sending you on your journey, would you agree",

"Yes sir I would",

"Good, then lets keep the contents of this conversation to ourselves, nobody else need know, if you understand my meaning",

"Completely",

" and" said the Colonel with a knowing look,

" If, or should I say, when, you do find the Priest, I need to know," said the Colonel,

Connor nodded,

"Of course Sir",

"Dead or alive that is",

" Without saying Sir",

The Colonel stared at Connor his eyes narrowing slightly and almost in a whisper he asked the question he had wanted to ask much earlier,

"And if you happen to meet a bad apple",

"Same applies Sir",

"Good, see you in the morning",

they looked at each other knowingly, shook hands again and wished each other goodnight.

Connor slept a restless night.

When he slept he dreamt of his mother and Cal.

Most of it good but some of it bad.

Connor rose early the next morning. By 7am he had eaten breakfast and headed out of the grounds for a walk. As he walked along the country lanes he eventually came to Snettisham beach. It was a fresh morning with not a cloud in the sky.

One of those Indian summers his Nana had loved so much he thought.

As he strolled along the deserted beach, with its gravelly sand and grassy dunes, he looked at his watch. It was 8:40am.

He would have to make his way back. He took a gentle jog back the way he had come, as usual, he had subconsciously mapped the route in his brain, and just before 10am he jogged up the path of the Manor House.

As he walked towards the front door it swung open quickly and was a little surprised to see Sgt Hunt stood looking a little flustered and in a slight panic.

"Sir, the Colonel has asked me to tell you that you are required to attend his office immediately",

"Certainly Sgt, but have I got time to take a quick bath or wash",

The Sgt who had been looking for Connor for almost 30 minutes already, now looked at him in an even bigger panic, said,

"No Sir, definitely not, he wanted you sometime ago but I couldn't find you, I was beginning to think that you had done one, as in buggered off Sir",

Connor smiled at him and laughing said,

"No Sgt, I haven't 'done one', okay let's go and see the boss".

The building was alive with people, walking about with a purpose and all still in a hurry.

They quickly walked along the corridors that led to his office, they eventually arrived and the Sgt knocked and walked straight in.

"Ah the wanderer returns" laughed the Colonel,

"Come in Gillian there's somebody I want you to meet",

Connor looked to the man stood to the right of the Colonel.

He could see that he was a General. A small man, late fifties he thought, swept back grey hair with piercing blue eyes.

Connor saluted them both and the Colonel said,

"Captain Gillian I would like you to meet General Todd".

The voice didn't match the man. His welcome literally boomed out from the small lithe body.

"Please to meet you Gillian, I've heard a lot about you, welcome to SOE",

Connor stole a brief glance at the Colonel and the Colonel knowing what his concerns were, put him at ease immediately,

"Yes Gillian I've updated the General on your work for us so far, and he's mightily impressed",

"I am indeed Gillian, some of your work has been outstanding and this job is made for you that's for sure",

"Thank you Sir that's very kind of you" said Connor,

The General looked at him, his blue eyes seemed to be trying to see into Connor's head.

"Whoever taught you taught you well, and your bravery is truly commendable, we are very lucky to have you on our side Gillian",

"I thank you again Sir" said Connor to the General,

"but with respect Sir, I'm not on anybody's side",

The blue eyes now narrowed but before the General could ask his question Connor answered it for him.

"Sir, I fight for the right against the wrong, nothing more",

The General smiled at him and then said,

"Then today must be our lucky day then",

Connor smiled back,

"Yes Sir it must".

For the next three and a half hours the three men sat and went through what was required of Connor.

He was to be parachuted in that evening flying from Langham airfield, a relatively small base close to the seaside port of

Blakeney in Norfolk. The base was used by Coastal Command but the occasional SOE flight went from there, usually in the hours of darkness.

On the way he would be picking up four friends, the only friends he would have for the next two to three months at least.

His drop zone was to be to the south of the northern French town of Bayeux. There he was to make his way, on his own, to observe and watch any military activities in and around the portal towns of Northern France. Whatever he saw and only if he felt it important enough, he was to get a message back to their headquarters as a matter of urgency. This was to be done by one of his friends taking it back, or he left a message at a dead drop. The dead drops were specific locations throughout the area he had been asked to operate in. They were places where he could leave or collect information. They were in a variety of places such as, holes at the bottom of a specific tree, in certain farm buildings, train station toilets. Connor was told of over twenty of them and he memorised them all. But If it could wait until he returned to Britain then it should. He was to stay over there for at least ten weeks but may be longer.

He was given the address of a safe house in Bayeux, he was also given the name of a fishing boat, Le Rouge Gitan, that fished from the port of Honfleur and if and when he needed to return, whenever that may be, he was to make contact with Captain Henri Distan.

"Captain Distan, who is also on our side" smiled the Colonel "knows that somebody may contact him, but he knows nothing about you or what you look like, we just need to know a name you will use",

"Billy" replied Connor,

"Sounds good to me, then Billy it is. There are a few more things you need to know, the Captain, he is 60 years old, grey hair, grey beard and wears a blue cap. If it's safe for you to approach the Rouge Gitan then the captain will always wear the blue cap. If he is wearing a red one it's not safe for you to approach. You wait until the blue cap is on. The boat has a small bell at the very top of its mast and the bell is painted yellow. He fishes everyday apart from Sunday's and he leaves the harbour at around 04:30hrs, dependant on tides and weather of course, but he would prefer you to make yourself known the night before. If that's not possible, due to the curfew, which I know you shouldn't have a problem with, is 22:00hrs until 05:00hrs, but he says it's sometimes quiet in the port around that time and you might struggle getting aboard without someone seeing you. But I'm sure you will manage it somehow."

He flashed Connor a knowing look.

He handed Connor an envelope.

"You will find some of your papers in there. Your identification papers will be ready shortly now we have a name, there is a letter from your wife, and some money."

Connor looked at the Colonel.

"Sir, with respect I travel with nothing. I don't carry paperwork. What I find remains in my head, I don't write anything down. If I find anything that is urgent then you will know don't worry, all I ask is that when I return, you have somebody available that I can unload my brain on and write it down as I speak. I can assure you that everything that needs to be remembered will be."

"Understood said the Colonel, but all 'I' ask, is that on this occasion, you do carry papers. The Germans are holding or shooting any person not carrying them, and so because of this, I insist".

Connor held out his hand and took the envelope.

The General and Colonel shook his hand and wished him good luck. He'd need it thought the Colonel, he felt like never before that he was sending someone to his death.

....

As Connor lay on his bed, he looked at the mantle clock on the wooden draws. It was a few minutes after 10pm . He lay there listening. The ticking reminded him of the clock in the kitchen at Rose Cottage. It was a gentle tick-tock, soft, not clinical, it sounded like it was about to stop but it didn't. He pictured his lovely Nana busying herself around the kitchen, crashing the pots and pans, she was never quiet, she went about her work with gusto. Things would get broken things would get smashed. He remembered once when she broke a little brown jug when it slipped from the shelve because she had put it on there in a rush and was wanting to get on and do something else. It had lost its balance and fell, breaking in to small pieces. He remembered that she had cried because the jug had been her mother's. And then he remembered the ticking of the clock as they sat in silence, whilst he held her hand.

He had been no more than 6 years old.

Thirty years ago.

It felt like yesterday.

He got off his bed and grabbed his small bag.

He looked around the room to make sure he had everything he needed.

Nothing had been left...........

Apart from an envelope thrown in the bin next to the door. It's contents intact, minus only the money.

'I travel with nothing'.

Connor walked out into the courtyard where Sgt Hunt was waiting with their car. Just 30 minutes later they were nearing the Langham base, 200 yards prior to it they turned left and drove down a gravel track, their restricted headlights barely showing the way ahead and after travelling 300 yards they came into a clearing and in the darkness in front of them was the silhouetted shape of a large wooden barn. Sgt Hunt stopped the car outside the wooden door. They both got out and walked across the pea gravelled drive. It was deadly quite apart from the crunching steps taken by the two men. As they got to the door it was slowly opened from within. They both stepped inside. It was dark, there was no lights above, just a very small wall light in the far distance, about 60 yards away, it was warm but damp and the air had a very musty smell to it. The occupants were sleeping but as Connor and Sgt Hunt followed the man who had opened the door down the passageway they started to stir having been woken by the new visitors.

The barn held over 2000 homing pigeons.

Connor was here to collect his four friends.

The Wellington took off at 23:20hrs it was going to take up to 2 1/2 hours for it to get to its drop zone just over 300 miles away, due south of Bayeux and a mile North of the small village of Saint Andre, Normandy. 'just past a small wood shaped like a heeled boot, "cant miss it" laughed the bomb aimer to Connor as he helped strap him in.

For the next two hours Connor slept, the flight over eastern England had been relatively smooth but as they approached the English Chanel, slightly to the left of Bognor Regis, Connor felt the plane make a rapid descent. 'Things might start to get a little interesting for a while now', he thought.

Flying at almost 200 miles an hour at a little over 50ft above the sea took some concentration and Connor had the utmost respect for the pilot and his crew.

They were taking a man into enemy territory, to deposit him, as best they could, to a specified place. They didn't know him, they didn't know what he was doing, they hadn't a clue why they were doing it, but doing it they were, and they were doing it very well.

The bomb aimer, who was redundant for today's mission, signalled to him that he had ten minutes before they kicked him out. Connor gave him the thumbs up and stood and checked his parachute fixings.

He felt the turbulence as the giant bomber crossed the French coast which was almost immediately followed by the a huge bang as the first flack was thrown in their direction. The pilot put the Wellington into a steep climb, not to get away from the flack, but to get some height for their passenger to be able to jump out. Another bang and flash then another and another, the plane turning left and right causing Connor to lose his balance before managing to grab hold of a rail.

The bomb aimer opened the door and the air and noise rushed in to greet them both.

A thumbs up from the bomb aimer and out he went, into the black.

His shoot opened almost immediately and he watched as the plane continued on its journey before it turned sharply to the left, the flack following it as if to help light the way.

He watched it, dancing almost, left and right, right and left and then it was gone.

Safe journey home he thought.

He looked down now to see if he could see a safe area to land, at least to try to avoid landing in the wooded heeled boot, but it was total darkness. He couldn't even see the ground let alone a safe place.

And then there it was.

The ground.

It seemed to rush up to meet him. He landed, somewhat heavily, not his best landing that was for sure. His knees hitting him in the chest and winding him. But he was in one piece.

No broken bones, no twisted ankles.

No dead pigeons.

He lay on the ground waiting for his lungs to feel like they were his again before he moved.

As his eyes became accustomed to the dark he could see that he had landed in a field, close to a small wood about 100 yards to his north. Not bad he thought. He rolled up his parachute and ran quietly to the wood.

Now it was time to wait.

Watch, listen, smell, assess, react.

He wouldn't move until daylight.

* * *

TO WATCH THE WATCHER

As the sun rose in the east across to his left he looked out onto the field where he had landed some 5 hours before.

He now sat in the wood about 10 foot in from the edge in thick undergrowth on the southern perimeter. He loved being outside again. This was his world. Out in nature, he loved the smell of the earth, the smell of the ferns, the rotting wood, it was where he belonged.

It was quite. Just the birds and the odd cow calling its wayward calf somewhere in the far distance. He sensed movement from his left. It wasn't far away, just a few feet. He saw it, before it, saw him. A young Roe deer. It's wet nose moving and twitching trying to sniff out what was there. Connor didn't move a muscle. Just his eyes, very slowly to his left. As he met its gaze they looked at each other in the eye. But the deer still hadn't quite worked out what it was looking at.

Connor had been busy since walking into the wood and had

built his hide. He now sat with his back to a tree, surrounded by branches and foliage that he had placed around him. His hide was about 4 feet wide and 3 foot deep. It had a roof that would be virtually shower proof, and a floor with a base made of parachute, covered by dry leaves.

All the roe deer could see of him was his eyes. But it could smell him.

More movement further to the left.

The roe didn't move.

So Connor didn't either.

If it had been a danger, the roe would have been gone in an instant, but it hadn't ran. It had stayed where it was.

A few seconds later Connor smiled to himself as he saw the reason why.

Mother Roe came into view and stood next to her fledgling.

Her nose, also wet, and also twitching, and she knew he was there as well, but she knew that this was not the time to be hanging about. She leapt over the 3 foot high bush in front of her with ease, and ran, the youngster instinctively followed her, Leaping over the same bush. Within seconds they were gone.

It gave a confidence of sort.

If a wild animal couldn't see him then a human being had virtually no chance at all. What gave a human being away to almost most animals, humans included, was movement and smell. Being detected by a human by smell was rare, unless you had really bad body odour or you were dead. Movement was the killer when being hunted for by fellow man.

This was where Connor excelled. His movement, to move covertly, had been sent from above. You couldn't teach it. It was a gift. You could either do it or you couldn't and Connor was the best. Many a fellow soldier had marvelled at his ability to get so close to the enemy without them seeing him or even suspecting that he was there.

By the time they saw him it was too late. Before they could react, they were either dead or dying.

As he sat, deadly still, he watched, he listened, he breathed in through his nose.

Nothing.

No movement. No sound. No smell, apart from the smell of the earth and trees and the recently farmed pumpkin field in front of him, abandoned pumpkins dotted about the field like severed heads.

Time to move.

He slowly got out of his hide, stood and stretched his cramped up limbs, then moved to the edge of the wood.

He waited a few more minutes before he was happy and then stepped out into the field. As he turned right he walked keeping the wood to his right before briefly looking behind him to note, within his brain, the position of his hide. He would be back at some point for sure. His four friends would be waiting fo him.

Within 15 minutes he had reached the corner of the wood and he turned right again now travelling north. It was easy going, the ground was still reasonably hard, the French summer had been a long hot one and the ground needed some rain. Not yet though thought Connor, not yet.

After an hour or so, he could see a town in the distance. He recognised it immediately, it was Bayeux. He had been shown pictures of the Cathedral the previous day and there about a mile and a half away was its unmistakable spire. 'Well done boys' he thought to himself. Right on the money.

As he entered the city from the south he was surprised by the lack of any visible army. The streets were busy with people but they were locals not soldiers. He continued towards the centre and as normal, again subconsciously mapping the route within his brain.

As he walked along the Rue Saint-loup his mind briefly went back to the cobbled streets of Tralee. The town of Bayeux seemed bigger but there were some similarities between the two. It was certainly more undulating, the streets were like waves on a swelling sea.

He carried on towards the cathedral, which looked quite majestic in foreground and as he rounded the corner, he saw his first German soldier of the day. It wasn't just one though, there was at least twenty of them marching two abreast their boots in time hitting heavily on the cobbled stones. He stood in the doorway of a bakery as they marched by, he watched them go and then walked into the shop.

Time to eat.

As he sat in the park eating his newly baked pastries, close to the cathedral, he looked around his surroundings. You would struggle to see that this country was at war he thought to himself. The park was surrounded by huge oak trees, there leaves starting to go the red and golden brown in the warm autumn sun.

People were sat on the grass quietly talking among themselves. He sat close too, but not with, a group of four middle aged people, two men two women, if somebody had looked at them it would look as though he was sat with them. Connor was good at blending in. He listened to their conversation. He had learnt some French on his previous trips to France and would nod in the right places, he would smile and laugh when they did, but they didn't notice, but anybody watching him would see five people, talking, relaxing, socialising in the morning sunshine.

He stayed there for an hour or so and then as they got up and walked away he waited for a moment then waved them goodbye.

They didn't see the farewell wave, but everybody else would have.

He walked in the opposite direction and continued through the park towards the cathedral.

A lone woman walking on her own. He walked just fractionally in front of her, mouthing silent words as if talking to her.

She didn't see it, but everybody else would have.

When she turned and walked away on the edge of the park and went behind the tree line, he spoke his silent words and waved to her, she didn't see it, he then blew her a kiss, she didn't see that either, but anybody else would have.

He was alone, but not alone.

He was friends to all that came near to him, they just didn't know it.

The day passed without incident and as evening approached he made his way across to the western side of the city. He wanted to have a look at something, number 7 Impasse des Sangles, the safe house.

He wasn't going in.

He just wanted to watch.

He watched for the next 5 hours. Nobody went in and nobody came out.

But a man walked by it 4 times.

Connor had seen enough.

He decided to stay in the city. He'd felt reasonably safe and it would be more risky heading back to his hide. He had passed a small guest house on the way, it had been in a small street called the Rue Royale, it looked as good a place as any and he didn't need to be wandering about the streets in the early hours, all of his 'new friends' would be tucked up in their beds.

He booked into the guest house with no real drama's. The only problem he had had was identification. He didn't have any, but as with most places in France since the occupation, money was tight. The lady on the desk had taken his money and given him the keys to a room, number 13, on the third floor, the top floor, and facing the back. He wasn't worried, he wasn't a suspicious man.

"The fire escape is out of your window, if you should need it", she had told him.

He climbed into bed and slept immediately, he would need it. He would have a busy day ahead tomorrow.

The next morning he woke early. He lifted his sash window and leaned out to see where the fire escape went to.

He was a little surprised, and pleased, to see that not only did it descend into the rear communal courtyard but also went up to the roof. Two escape routes were always better than one he thought to himself.

The courtyard was about 50 metres square and was surrounded by further buildings on the three other sides, the tallest of which faced his window. This building was two floors higher than the guest house and the roof sloped down to meet his building to his left. From there he couldn't see anything at all. No matter, he would have a look at his surroundings once he had done what he needed to do.

And what he needed to do was go back to the safe house.

He took a different route than the day before. Not because it was quicker, but because he just didn't like to repeat his movements unless it was absolutely necessary, and for now, it wasn't.

He had watched the safe house from the south the previous evening, today he would watch it from the north.

He decided to watch it from a small cafe, so he sat at a table inside reading a book.

He had found the book in the hat stand at his guest house and thought it might be useful. It was called, Clochemerle, he hadn't known what the book was about but he liked the burnt orange book cover. As he sat he flicked through it. He wasn't completely fluent in French but could get by. An irony came over him as he realised it was a comical book about a fictional village in France that had installed a urinal in the village square and had caused problems between the Catholics and republicans. 'We can even fall out over a toilet' he smiled to himself.

And then out the corner of his eye he saw him.

It was the man from the previous evening who had walked by four times, no doubt about it.

He was around 50 years old, tall, at least 6', wiry, with greying greasy hair. His big ears sticking out had the grey hair hanging over them.

His clothes had once been smart but they were past their best now.

Connor watched as Mr Wiry walked towards him along the Impasse des Sangles about 50 metres away and closing. As he got to number 7 he saw it, the giveaway pause. Just a slight hesitation but it was there no doubt about it.

He'd seen it before, several times through his life. It was a dead giveaway, and dead being the operative word.

The man carried on.

And walked into the cafe.

Instincts.

'Wonderful things your instincts' Cain Milburn had once told him, 'trust them as if your life depended on them, because one day, they might' he had said.

He did trust them.

His instincts were telling him not to move and to stay right where he was.

So he stayed right where he was.

Mr Wiry waved at the girl behind the counter and sat down at the table next to Connor's. Side on to him, with his back to the counter, looking straight out of the window.

He had to sit there to get the view of the house.

Connor carried on reading his book.

He sensed the man looking at him but he didn't look up. He would look up when he was ready. He wasn't worried about getting into conversation but he just didn't want to speak to him right now. He would speak when he was ready.

The girl came over to Mr Wiry and placed a cup of coffee in front of him. She smiled at him as she said "Good morning Monsuir Pavell and how are you this morning",

The man didn't look at her but continued looking out of the window and rather gruffly replied "Je ne me sens pas bien" Connor understood that the man didn't feel well. He didn't look well either, thought Connor, in fact he looked more dead than alive. He didn't smell too good either. Since he had been sitting there Connor kept getting a whiff of something very unpleasant.

The girl turned and looked at Connor and raised her eyes and shook her head. Connor smiled back at her and asked for another coffee.

Connor knew that by him speaking, it would result in the man to start to speak to him. It nearly always did. When someone wants to get into conversation with someone they invariably join in somebody else's conversation.

The man didn't let him down.

He spoke softly in French and asked him "Is the book good",

Connor looked him in the eye for the first time and replied in French,

"I've read better",

He nodded at Connor and continued,

"What is it about",

"A toilet",

The man gave a throaty laugh and said,

"You could say then that it is shit",

Connor smiled,

"Yes I suppose you could",

Then the man got on to what he really wanted to know.

"Do you like books" he asked,

"Yes I do, I find reading relaxing",

"Then I take it you go to our library",

Connor's memory bank immediately clicked in, he remembered passing the library on the eastern side of the cathedral the day before.

"Of course, I was there just yesterday, getting a book and sitting in the park next door, in the shadows of the cathedral, my perfect day".

Mr Pavell was checking him out.

"Yesterday, why I thought it was closed yesterday",

" Well yes you are right but It was closed in the morning but then it opens in the afternoon".

He knew he was right he'd remembered the sign on the big wooden door.

"Oh yes of course".

Connor looked back down and began to read his book again, that was enough conversation for now.

The man sat and sipped his coffee alternating his gaze occasionally between the house and Connor.

Connor had been watching the man's feet from over the top of his book.

He had learnt over the years that feet often gave away the possibility of movement.

He carried on reading, the man carried on watching.

And then.........

He saw the mans right foot suddenly turn to the right.

He was going to get up.

He did.

Connor watched out the corner of his eye as the man left the cafe in a hurry, taking most of his smell with him but leaving behind just enough to let you know that he'd been there.

Connor knew where he was going.

He had also seen the man exit the safe house and turn left and walk away from them along the passage to towards south.

Mr Wiry, Monsuir Pavell, walked briskly after the man. Connor watched them both go and then stayed where he was.

'The safe house was definitely not safe'.

He stayed in the cafe for the next hour.

He saw nothing, because nothing happened.

The girl came over and asked him if he would like another drink, he politely declined but took the opportunity to ask a question because to ask a question when you have been already asked a question never seems to give the impression, or as much anyway, that your being nosy.

"He doesn't seem a well man, he needs to go to the doctor" said Connor looking at the empty chair as if Mr Wiry was still sat there.

"I don't know about seeing a doctor, but I know he needs to be seeing a bath. The smell makes me feel sick and when he goes it lingers for hours. It's even worse in the summer when it's hot",

"Oh dear, I cant remember seeing him before but I take it he comes here a lot then",

"He was here a lot during the summer but then I didn't see him for weeks, I supposed it was because he was ill or something but then he turned up here again a couple of weeks ago and has been stinking the place out everyday since",

"He went very quickly didn't he, I thought I may have upset him or something",

"No" she replied "he does it quite often, one minute he's talking to you quite normally, but the next minute, he's gone",

"Is he from round here, like I say, I've never seen him before",

"Oh yes, he's from the town, he lives at the top of Rue Saint floxel, the house matches the man if you know what I mean",

She nodded her head as if she was agreeing to her own question,

"Ah yes" said Connor "I know the one, my friends and I call it the jungle",

He'd actually never seen it before but he could imagine and it helped him to pretend he had.

"A very good description" she said "go in there and you would be lucky to come out alive",

He laughed and said "good day madam, I may see you again tomorrow",

She smiled back, "good" she said "it's nice to see you again".

Connor had never seen her before in his life.

He was good at blending in.

As he left the cafe he took a brief look towards the safe house. He wasn't going to go to it, and he wasn't going to go to the Rue Saint Floxel either.

He had somewhere else he needed to go.

He was going to the Cathedral to sit in the park.

It was early evening before he saw him again.

As Connor sat on a bench, reading his book, he saw Pavell come around the walled entrance to the rear of the cathedral and towards the park.

He knew he would come. And he also knew that he, Pavell, had been to tell his boss about the safe house and that he had also told him that there was a newcomer in town who he had met in the cafe. He knew that his boss would have told him to follow the new man in town and see where he lived.

Connor wasn't going to let Mr Pavell, or his boss down.

He would see where he was staying, he was going to make sure of that.

He didn't really care too much as to where Pavell lived, but what he did care about was where his boss lived. And he would find out tonight and if not tonight, then tomorrow.

To watch the watcher.

Connor remained on the bench happily reading his comical book. He laughed occasionally to himself, it wasn't hard to do, not entirely because of the book though, but because of Pavell's surveillance expertise, or lack of them.

Pavell was stood around the corner of the street on the far side of the park some 60 or so metres away and every minute or two he would peer around the corner to see if Connor was still there.

He felt like playing a game with him but decided against it as he might lose him altogether and he really didn't want to do that.

He wanted Pavell to see exactly where he was going.

After about an hour he felt the need to put Pavell out of his misery. A chill was also in the air and the light was fading and to stay out any longer would have appeared a little odd.

But he needed it to be dusk.

He stood up from the bench and stretched his limbs. He didn't look at him, if Pavell missed him then it was his own fault he couldn't make it any easier for him.

He put his book inside his jacket pocket and walked slowly towards the north west corner of the park. He turned right and walked along the Rue Royale towards the Rue Saint Patrice. As he got about fifty metres from his guest house he crossed the road from the off side to near and as he did so he looked into the rear window of a lonely Citroen Avant parked on the street and saw in the reflection, the lonely figure of Pavell, blowing hard, following him up the hill.

As he got to the guest house he climbed the 3 steps to the front door, opened it and stepped inside.

He immediately raced to the first floor, jumping the stairs two or three at a time, and then stepped onto the landing. Facing him were the two doors that belonged to the rooms that looked out onto the front of the house. He needed one to be unlocked.

He gently tried the one on the left, it had the number 5 painted in black on the off white coloured door.

Locked.

He moved to the one on the right, number 6.

Also locked.

He turned and sprinted up the stairs to the second floor.

Again ignoring the doors to the rear facing rooms, he walked to the doors to rooms facing the front, identical to the floor below.

He tried the one on the left, number 9.

It was open.

He quietly leaned just inside the doorway and switched the light on, he waited 4 or 5 seconds then whispered the word 'pardon' and turned it off again.

He ran up the last flight of stairs to the top floor, opened his room with a key, closed the door behind him, quickly locked it and walked across to the sash window. He slid it open and climbed out, and then closed it again behind him. He walked, as fast as he dare, down the black rusting fire escape, feeling that he might get to the bottom rather quicker than he actually wanted too as it had seen much better days.

As he got to the cobbled rear courtyard he had a choice, he could turn left towards an alleyway which was back to where he had last seen Pavell, or he could turn right and walk 40 metres or so towards a further alleyway. He turned right.

Pavell having left the cafe earlier, had followed the man, who had left the house, into the centre of the town. He had followed him because he had been tasked by his boss to watch a house on Empasse de Sangles and to follow anybody that left it. Once that person had gone anywhere of significance, he was to report back immediately.

Some months previously the German intelligence unit for the Normandy area had targeted Pavell when, one dark rainy March evening, he was noticed stealing petrol from a German military vehicle which had been parked close to Pavell's address. He had been dragged away kicking and screaming and was then locked up for the evening. The next morning an officer from the SS had paid him a visit in his cell. Within an hour he had sworn his allegiance to Germany and Adolf Hitler, and had then been passed back to the intelligence unit where he was to be pardoned for his crime, but in return he was to work for them. He would receive an amount of cash for any information he gained providing it proved to be useful. He was generally tasked with specific places or persons to watch but received a bonus if, off his own back, he saw anything suspicious which again, proved to be useful.

He had had some success with the latter when one evening, he had overheard just one word, spoken in English, but with a Scottish accent.

The word had been 'Lancaster'.

He had been walking home one evening and was behind 2

males who were walking generally in the same direction, when he heard the taller man speak. From just the one heard word, he knew immediately that the man was Scottish.

Pavell's uncle had been from Fife in Scotland and had had a broad Scottish accent. He had prided himself from a very young age by learning English from his uncle.

And so, had decided to follow the 2 men and saw them enter a house just 500 metres from his own. He had reported the information back to his contact at the intelligence unit.

At 5am the following morning German soldiers stormed the building and shortly after, two RAF pilots were among those taken away never to be seen again.

One of them was a certain Flt Lt Gordon McDonnell, from Kirkcaldy in Fife, Scotland.

Now, Pavell had been a little suspicious of the new man he had seen in the cafe. He couldn't quite put his finger on it, but there was something he wasn't happy about. He had gone to his German contact officer and spoke to him about the new man in town, and, because of his recent success, he was told to follow him and report back, and so he had, and when seeing Connor go into the guest house, he stopped on the corner of a small street on his right about 30 yards prior to the guest house. He watched the house and after a few minutes he saw the light briefly come on in the right hand bedroom window of the second floor.

'Got him' he had thought to himself. He decided to wait a few minutes to see if he came back out. He could see almost all the front of the guest house before the building line gently curved following the street to the left. No matter he could see the front door and slightly to the left of the front door, a gated alleyway that presumably led to the rear.

'I'll give it the lucky 5 minutes' he thought to himself, but then it would be off to see the commandant to inform him of the man's whereabouts.

It wasn't going to be a lucky five minutes.

Connor now walked along the dark and damp alleyway., the curved brick roof barely a few inches above his head. His footsteps, no matter how hard he tried, softly echoing on the cobbled floor. He got to the gate and stopped.

He listened.

Nothing.

He gently pulled open the gate. If Pavell was there he would just walk off. He'd have no trouble losing him.

He stepped out onto the street. Nobody to his left.

He looked to his right, to where he thought Pavell would be but saw that the building line went around to the right slightly blocking his view.

He smiled to himself,

It was also blocking Pavell's view.

He turned left and followed the corner round to his left. He walked about 40 metres, then, with a gentle look behind him, he crossed the road, knowing he was still out of Pavell's view, and turned right into a small side street. He walked a short distance before turning right again. He was now walking back towards the guest house but on the street that ran parallel to it.

He got to the next corner and if he turned right again, he would walk back towards the Rue Royale.

He didn't.

He crossed the street and as he did so he glanced to his right and there he was.

Pavell was stood on the corner with of the Rue Royale with his back to him, looking towards the guest house.

……..To watch the watcher.

It was his turn to wait now.

He didn't have to wait for long.

Just 2 whole minutes in fact.

He watched from the shadow of a garden hedge as Pavell, now happy that his prey had settled in for the night turned and walked back from the direction he had come.

It was time for Connor to do what he does best.

He followed him on a parallel route. He had memorised the streets and his brain was telling him that Pavell had no escape routes for at least 40 metres. Connor made his way down towards the park.

He increased his pace. It was almost fully dark now and he wanted to be on the park and in the blackness of the shadows from the oak trees before Pavell got there.

He made it in plenty of time. He watched as Pavell carried on walking southwards, keeping the park to his left.

But he stayed where he.

Because 2 german soldiers were walking straight towards Pavell.

He watched from the blackness barely 30 metres away. He heard one of the soldiers say "papers", he saw Pavell place his hand inside his jacket pocket and he pulled out a white peice of paper.

The soldier looked at it, looked quizzically at Pavell, then passed it to the other soldier who also looked at it, he shrugged his shoulders, muttered something and gave it back to Pavell. He then heard the first soldier say "who" and then heard Pavell say two words, "Commandant Mulder" he then saw the German soldier nod his head in response and then they smiled before they all continued on their respective ways.

Pavell turned then left into the Rue de la Poterie and quickened his pace.

Connor, noting the quickening pace, began to follow him again, he knew they would soon be nearing their destination. At the Rue Saint Loup, Pavell turned left and then right along the Rue Tardif towards a large 4 storey building on the right hand side of the road.

Connor crossed the road to the left hand side, 40 metres back in the shadows of a 10 foot high wall.

He watched as Pavell climbed the 6 concrete steps towards the 2 large wooden front doors. He watched as he gently pulled back the cast iron knocker and give two, somewhat surprisingly, light taps.

The right hand door was opened almost immediately and Pavell stepped inside, the door shutting again behind him.

Connor stayed where he was. From his position he could see most of the windows to the front and all of the windows on the right hand side of the building.

The building itself was a large box, symmetrically square with four windows on each floor, giving a total of 16 on the two sides that he could see. He was sure that the 2 sides he couldn't see, the back and the left hand side, would be identical. The building was probably at least 100 years old but could have been older.

Ornamental iron railings were bent around each window giving the impression that each room had a balcony, but you wouldn't want to stand on them.

Of the rooms that he could see, most were in darkness, but a few had lights on, dotted here and there. He scanned them all trying to see movement.

Nothing of significance. No real movement, no changes in the light.

Just two of the sash windows were open. One on the bottom left facing the front, and one on the right hand side of the building on the second floor.

Then, over to the right, towards the rear of the right hand side of the square box, on the second floor, he saw a man stand up. He was in the middle of the window and further into the room. Connor got the impression that he had just got up from a desk.

'Yes' he had definitely been sat at a desk. As the man walked towards the window he could see his right arm to just above his wrist, the man swivelled around the corner, his right arm taking the weight as if he was leaning on something, most likely the desk, and he continued walking out of Connor's view.

He waited.

A few seconds later the same man walked back across the window and did the same manoeuvre, only this time with his left hand as he swivelled around and faced back towards where he had just come from.

He then waved his hand as if asking someone to sit down.

He could see he was talking to someone, but whoever it was, was further into the room.

Was this Commandant Mulder, or was the unseen guest Mulder, or was it Pavell.

'It might not be any of them' thought Connor.

But he'd wager a bet if he had been a betting man that it was.

He watched.

The man sat at the desk was listening to somebody. He saw him nod occasionally and then say a few words but the person out of view was doing most of the talking.

It continued for nearly an hour, and then the seated man stood up.

He lent on the desk with both hands and then he pushed his right hand forward, 'he was going to shake someone's hand' thought Connor.

Connor crossed the road at pace. He felt vulnerable out there in the open, but he needed to see who the other hand shaker was.

He should have had a bet.

The scruffy grey hair over the big ears came briefly into view and shook the German officers hand over the desk.

And then something else happened.

The German officer shook another hand. Connor couldn't see who it belonged to. Pavell was blocking his view.

He then saw the German officer stand to attention and salute.

Pavell didn't move.

But the other person did. He saw the arm raise up in a salute.

The other person, was also a German soldier and more than likely, due to the shake of the hand, he was an officer.

Time to get back into the shadows and wait.

Five minutes had passed before anything else happened.

And then two things happened at the same time.

Pavell left via the front door.

And then the light came on in the room on the ground floor on the far left corner on the front, the one with the open window.

He let Pavell go.

He had something else to do.

From his current position he couldn't see into the ground floor room at all. The room was virtually at right angles to him. All he could see was the dark coloured curtain that was slowly being drawn.

He now had two choices, three really if you counted walking away and coming back tomorrow but that wasn't really an option.

He could stay where he was and wait for someone to come out of the doors or he could move more towards the front of the building and try to get a view directly into the room.

He knew that the curtains were drawn but that could change, especially if there was a noise outside to investigate.

But he decided on the latter.

He moved out into the street. He knew and he sensed the fact that he was now in a very vulnerable and dangerous position. It was now past 10 o'clock and most of the streets were now deserted, and worst of all he had no cover, and no shadows to hide in. The houses on his left faced out straight onto the street. A 12ft high wall was on the other side of the street and ran the forty or so metres up to the square building.

He walked as quick as he dared on the left skimming the house fronts hoping and praying that nobody stepped out of their front door. He carried on towards the building.

And then he had a bit of luck.

'He was Irish after all' he smiled to himself.

The row of houses on the left that faced directly out onto the street stopped and the building line moved back about ten feet. The next ten houses or so which were still joined to the previous ones, had a small wall with railings on top, and behind the wall, they had a 10ft long garden in front of them. 'built for the rich ones' thought Connor.

He was now almost directly in front of the window he needed to watch, just fifteen or so yards across the street. He could also see the two large doors.

He hopped over the wall and backed into the corner, just where the poor met the rich.

'Perfect'.

As he looked at the window, he could see, through a tiny crack in the curtains, that the light remained on within, but he couldn't see anybody inside.

But he could smell cigars.

He stayed there for the next 2 hours.

Nothing happened.

Know one came out, and know one went in.

No lights came on, no lights went off.

Nothing.

And then one of the huge two front doors opened.

Decision.

There was not one but two men. Two German officers.

They stood on top of the steps. The tallest of the two bent down as the smaller man gave him a light.

They stood about 60 foot away from him. He could hear every word they spoke.

Connor's German wasn't as good as his French.

But he could tell they were talking about women.

It didn't matter where in the world you were, what language you spoke, when two men talked together 'of women' they would sneer, be crude, vulgar and tease each other. They were doing all of these things and more.

The two officers shook hands and he heard the taller one say 'have a good time my friend, and say hello to Angelina for me. They both laughed And then they walked off.

In different directions.

Decision.

Which one should he follow.

He looked back through the small crack in the curtains.

The light was still on. And he could still smell cigars.

So he didn't follow either of them.

He stayed right where he was.

He stayed there, in his dark space for over another hour. His journey back to his guest house was going to be risky. But he had little choice. He couldn't stay where he was and he definitely couldn't go back to his hide.

He would give it another 45 minutes or so up to midnight and then he would have to go. Besides he needed to be up early in the morning.

Somebody downstairs from his room, could be getting a visit.

The night was quiet, deadly quiet. He could hear himself breathing, it sounded so uncomfortably loud. And then he heard a sound that he hadn't heard for over 25 years.

A very tiny clink, metal on metal. He knew exactly what it was.

It was the distinct sound of a cigar clipper.

His mind went straight back to the last time he had heard it. It had been at Manor farm whilst stood outside the study of old man Milburn. It was then, as it was now, followed by the distinct smell of a freshly lit cigar.

Five minutes later the sash window was lowered, but not quite shut, by an unseen person from the inside. The curtain moved barely an inch.

Then ten minutes later the light went out.

Ten minutes after that, he could hear the heavy breathing of someone in a deep sleep. Whoever they were, they weren't coming out tonight.

Keeping in the shadows he made his way back to the guest house.

As he walked up the hill towards the front door, he walked straight past it, rounded the left hand corner swiftly opened the gate and stepped into the alleyway shutting it just as quickly behind him.

He walked as quietly as he could into the courtyard at the rear and then climbed the shaky fire escape. Within 5 minutes he was asleep.

At 430 the next morning he was awake and out. Same route as before, down the fire escape and out the alleyway, taking the parallel route to the park where he stopped and waited.

A short while later he watched from the shadows of the oak trees as 6 German soldiers marched quietly up the hill.

At 5am the front door of the guest house was kicked in.

At 5:05am the male occupant of room number 9, on the second floor, facing the front, was led screaming his innocence from the building and marched back down the hill to a waiting lorry.

'Collateral damage' thought Connor. They would let him go once they realised they had the wrong man.

But Connor was aiming to eliminate that possibility.

They, the man at the desk, and the man shaking his hand, didn't need to know that they indeed, had the wrong man.

Pavell was the one and only person who could tell the Germans that the man they had arrested was in fact an innocent man, and that, the man they wanted was still at large.

But in order for that to happen they needed to speak to Pavell.

That wasn't going to happen.

Connor would be making sure of that.

He carried on towards the Rue Tardif.

Pavell could wait for now. He wouldn't be going anywhere this early.

As he stood back in the now semi blackness where the rich met the poor, he knew that he hadn't much time.

The darkness was his friend.

The light was his enemy.

At around 6:30 am, the curtains opened on the ground floor room on the far left hand side.

The man, now dressed in his German officers uniform looked straight at Connor, just 15 yards in front of him across the road, but he couldn't see him.

His friend, 'the dark', was still wrapped around him, but only just.

Connor looked back across the street and watched as the German officer raised his sash window.

Connor smiled to himself.

Was he Mulder, he still didn't know, but what he did know, was that he had seen him before.

He'd seen him just three days ago at Snettisham Manor.

He watched as the man put on a thick overcoat and then the light in the room was turned off.

He was coming out.

He had to wait only a couple of minutes. The large door to the front of the building was slowly opened and the man walked out, stopping briefly to light a new cigar. Connor watched as the man looked up and down the street before turning right and began to walk towards him.

Connor backed as far as he could back into the shadow and waited for him to pass.

As he walked by, he saw that the man was a Major and from what he seen over the last few hours, he now had a strong suspicion that he probably worked for the German department known as The Abwehr, an intelligence department very similar to that of the British version that he now worked for, SOE.

The Abwehr were known to have offices spread far and wide, but their exact whereabouts were generally unknown, that was until now, Connor was convinced that the box building on the Rue Tardif was indeed one of those offices, it was the only thing it could be.

Throughout his life he had met or had seen people that he had the utmost respect for, whether that had been members of the IRA, the British army, or the Nazi's. Friend or foe, it didn't matter, people were brave on both sides, he had often felt an admiration for a number of German officers. They were fighting for what they believed in and as far as Connor was concerned, that was how it should be, 'all is fair in love and war' they shouldn't be criticised for it if that's what they truly felt in their hearts, for it was exactly how he felt, but, on this occasion, he was on the opposite side to the man he was now following.

This man, who's name he still did'nt know, had travelled across the channel, by what means, nobody knew. He had walked around buildings that supposedly had the best security the British had to offer, without giving away the slightest sign of his true identity, he had moved and talked within circles of top brass officers, and now here he was, walking 40 yards in front of him, totally unaware that he was being followed.

As he walked on behind him, Connor watched his movement, his gate, his stance, everything about him he subconsciously took in. He noticed that his head lent slightly to the left, as if on a tilt, his left foot pointed very slightly to the left, unlike the right, which was straight as he walked, he also saw that his fingers on his left hand were constantly opening and closing, 'a stress sign' he thought. But still, as he took all of this information in, he couldn't help but think that this was one brave man.

And then Connor had a thought, was he in fact a double agent. Was he in fact, working for the Allies. Was he following one of his own.

But as he watched the Major walk along the tree lined street, he knew one thing for certain, If he was working against the British.

He would have to kill him.

In love and war, there were never any winners....... only losers.

At the Rue Larcher he saw him turn left and and they continued walking towards the Cathedral.

Connor now had another decision to make and he needed to make it quite quickly.

Should he carry on following him or let him go.

This man was far more important than Pavell, but .... If the Germans got hold of Pavell before he did, then the odds against him being able to continue his work diminished considerably.

He watched as the Major walked beyond the Cathedral towards the Hospital on the Rue de Nesmond.

He had already worked out in his brain that this would be a route that could be taken to Rue Saint Floxel, Pavell's house. If the Major was going there then he needed to get there before him.

Connor carried straight up the hill to the North, walking a parallel route to the west of the Major. He couldn't run, he didn't want to draw any attention to himself. So he leapfrogged people, walking with them if any soldier came into view.

As he got to the small square with Rue des Bouchers he looked across towards where the bridge crossed the river L'Aure and then right there, crossing it and walking towards him, was Pavell. Connor knew immediately what he needed to do. Spinning on his heels, he walked back the way he had come, but he needed Pavell to see him. He carried on walking still on his return route and as he approached the stores on the Rue Marechal Foch, he took a quick look in the reflection of their windows.

Pavell had seen him.

'Well done Mr Pavell' he thought. He continued along Marechal Foch still walking the opposite way to which he had come some minutes before, checking every now and then to make sure Pavell was still with him.

He was.

As he got to the Rue Larcher he could see that Pavell was struggling to keep up and was blowing hard, so he walked into the bakery to his left.

As Connor came out now freshly stocked with his pastries he saw that Pavell had at last caught him up and was stood in the doorway next to the Deportation Memorial.

Connor knew exactly where he was going to take him.

As he got to Rue de Desmond he turned left and walked very

slowly towards the river. He could see that the water was flowing quickly and swirls of under current made small whirlpools beneath the surface, the river rising and falling as the huge flow of water swept by. As he got to the water mill wheel, he turned towards it and crossed the river over the small wooden bridge behind it.

And then he disappeared.

Pavell couldn't see him, he had seen him cross the wooden bridge but then he had just disappeared. He hesitated. He knew he needed to see where he was but he didn't like this bit at all. 'He should have been arrested this morning, thats what Mulder and Major Klass had told him last night' he thought to himself.

'He had to follow him, there would be another big bonus waiting for him, just like last time' but he really didn't want to. He had no choice and the money would be useful.

He walked slowly across the bridge.

Connor heard him coming.

As Pavell got to the building line on the other side of the river, Connor thrust his arm out from the bushes that he was hid within and grabbed the trouser belt of the startled Pavell and pulled him with immense strength and speed back into the bushes.

"Good morning Mr Pavell, fancy meeting you here" said Connor smiling at the now trembling Pavell.

" Let me go, please I beg you, please let me go" whispered Pavell,

"And why would I do that Pavell",

"Because you will be in trouble if you don't",

"I'm already in trouble Pavell, thanks to your early morning call you arranged for me this morning",

"Then all the reason for letting me go, I swear I wont tell a soul of this, please I beg you, let me go",

"Your doing a lot of begging Pavell, do you really expect me to take pity on you after what you have done. But perhaps you may be able to help me",

" I will Sir, I will, if I can help you in anyway I will I promise you",

Said Pavell now visibly trembling.

Connor looked at him and in a quiet calm voice he said,

" well you see Pavell, I've been troubled by something since the last time we met, so please tell me, how did you know, that is, how did you know to go to the authorities about me and to tell Mulder".

He saw the surprise in the eyes of Pavell at the word of 'Mulder'.

Pavell looked at him, his eyes almost popping out of his head, desperately trying to rescue the bad situation that he had now found himself in.

"Sir, it was when I spoke to you in the cafe. I hadn't seen you before but when you spoke, I knew you were from Scotland, I didn't notice at the time but it came to me later, you see, my uncle was from Scotland and you said the word 'toilet' exactly how he used to say it".

Connor nodded his response and smiled,

"Very good Pavell, but your slightly off course, I'm from across the water from Ireland, but thats close enough I suppose, close enough to have me shot".

He tightened his grip on Pavell's neck causing him to gasp.

"They will catch you, you know that don't you, you wont get away with killing me, Mulder and the Major will see to that" said Pavell,

"Mr Pavell, do you really think that Mulder and Major.... " he paused as if he had forgotten his name,

"Klass, it's Major Klass" said Pavell,

Connor smiled at him again and laughed a little.

"Ah yes of course it is, thank you Mr Pavell, but your really not very good at this are you".

Connor looked at him in the eyes. He didn't like what he had to do next, but that, was exactly it, he had to do it.

"I'm sorry" said Connor.

He snapped his neck, killing him instantly, pulled him the two yards out of the bushes to the bridge and dropped him over the edge into the waiting river.

Connor watched him briefly float away before he disappeared below the wheel of the mill.

Bad apple's don't float.

It was after 21:00 before Connor finally arrived back at his hide which he had left only 3 days ago. If felt a lot longer.

His first job was to check on his four little friends, they seemed happy enough, and as they pecked seed from his hand he replenished their small bowl of water.

His next job was to write the message, which he wrote in the smallest writing he could possibly do.

It read,

S H ISN'T. SOME BAD APPLES. ONE DEALT WITH. NEED TO RETURN. CHANGE THE BLUE TO YELLOW, THE YELLOW TO RED AND THE RED TO BLUE. BE WITH HIM IN 2 DAYS. B

He rolled it up and placed it in its holder around the chosen pigeons leg.

He'd wait until just before first light before sending the bird on its way, it needed to have more food and water to give it some strength. It had over 300 miles to fly to get back home which would take anything up to between 6 to 12 hours, depending on wind strength and direction, for it to get to its home, the possibilities of it getting there were good, but things sometimes went wrong and it wasn't a definite that it would succeed in its quest. But Connor felt confident it of its chances.

Now though he needed to sleep.

* * *

LE ROUGE GITAN (The Red Gypsy)

He woke just before first light, having had the best nights sleep since he been flown in.

He had woke just the once and when he had, he'd had a thought about his four friends. He had decided they would all be going home. There was no need to leave any of them here. He wasn't aiming to return within the next few days. He had also decided to put exactly the same message on a second pigeon. Two chances were better than one, and then he had also decided not to put the message on all four. In his complicated mind, especially when in the middle of the night, he thought that meant double the chance of one of them getting caught.

He climbed out of his hide, stretched his limbs. He covered over the entrance and threw a few freshly fallen leaves to cover his foot prints. He then placed a thin twig, about 8 inches long, on top of the leaves as a marker to show him, if he returned, if anybody had been there whilst he was away. He had always used this method and he had always had a 100 percent success rate with it. He always placed the twig facing east and he always pulled a tiny piece of bark off the top end and then placed it back on putting the loose bark face down. This meant that if somebody found the hide and moved the twig, no matter how good they were at putting the twig back, they never saw that the small piece of bark had fallen off. Having done it, he moved slowly to the edge of the wood. As he looked out onto the field, the severed heads were now starting to look a little sorry for themselves, especially today. The rain was falling hard from the dark grey sky, the wind blowing in from the southwest wasn't very pleasant either, 'not a good day for a walk' he thought to himself. But it was an excellent day for flying, the wind direction was almost perfect.

He let his four friends go, one by one, watching them all briefly fly south before their inner compass kicked in and they turned a full 180 degrees and headed north.

"Safe journey, hope to see you in a few days" he said, and then walked quietly back to his hide. He grabbed what food he had left, checked his temporary home over one last time, and then walked back to the edge of the wood. It was time to get wet.

He'd already planned the route to Honfluer in his head after viewing maps at Snettisham, but things usually changed. This journey was by far, no exception.

He had numerous routes he could take but each and every one had the same, somewhat big, problem.

It was Caen.

Caen was heaving with germans.

He had to go past it to get to The port of Honfleur.

He could go above it, he could go below it.

He could, which would normally be unlikely, go through it.

Whichever way he chose had its own problems, some worse than others, some, very much worse than others.

He had initially decided to go by train. Safer in some respects but much more dangerous in others. He wasn't planning to use a passenger train, he preferred the cargo option. The cargo train was preferable due to the less likelihood of being discovered, however, cargo was being heavily targeted by the

RAF.

He'd take his chance though if it arose.

He needed to move in daylight because he needed to be arriving in Honfluer in darkness, he had little choice.

He headed east, he needed to get to the village of Condé-sur-Seulles, which, as the crow flies, and also the direction he would walk across the fields, was about 6 kilometres away. Once there he would aim to board a freight train. He'd picked this location specifically because of the the sharp left turn the rail track took just south of the village. The trains approaching would need to slow to barely above a slight jog for the turn, making it much easier for him to climb onto one of the wagons.

He made his way to the outskirts of the village in just under two hours. It had been an uneventful journey so far, that though would almost certainly change.

He had heard at least two trains, both travelling west, within the last thirty minutes. Both were no good too him, he was travelling east.

He moved around the southern edge of the village and headed for the track. He couldn't see it but he knew where it was.

The hedgerow that flanked the siding gave it away. As he made his way through the thicket the bank suddenly started to descend rapidly. He began to slip down the muddy wet ground, grabbing trees as he went to stop an uncontrollable fall towards the railway track. The branches were bending and whipping back slapping him in the face and chest but eventually he regained control and came to a stop. He looked down to the track, still another 12 feet below him. It was a single track and it was just starting the bend to the left.

He slowly climbed down the remaining 12 feet and stopped just inside the hedgerow. He looked out first to the left and then to the right. No movement, no sound. He climbed out the brush and walked onto the track. As he looked to his left he could see for at least 500 yards, he turned and looked to his right. The left hand curve turned sharply away from view and after only 50 yards or so the track disappeared around the bend, the hedgerow following it as if it was cocooning it, protecting it in someway.

It was an ideal spot to board a train thought Connor. When the engine had cleared the corner and providing the train was long enough, he could climb onto one of the rear carriages completely out of view of the driver and if he got on halfway around the bend he would also be out of view of the guard at the rear carriage. All of this of course was providing that the train didn't have German soldiers riding shotgun on the roofs.

He walked along the track towards the bend and then stopped when he met the spot where he could just see the end of the straight, he needed to see the train approaching. He wasn't getting on if there were soldiers on the roof.

He waited.

Nothing went east and nothing went west.

There were no further trains all morning. The allies must have been getting some success he thought.

And then shortly after midday he heard it. A train coming from the west. It was moving quite quickly. In the far distance he watched as the thick black smoke billowed above the tree line probably nearly a mile and a half away. He climbed a short way up the bank and sat leaning on a tree watching for the train to come onto the straight.

It was another five minutes before he saw it. It was already beginning to slow as it descended the slight hill towards him, the squeal of brakes now giving away the fact that it was slowing rapidly.

At 300 yards he saw them.

The outriders on the roofs.

At 100 yards he could see that some were facing towards him and some had their backs to him. He felt sorry for them. The rain was still pouring out of the grey skies. They must have been soaked to the skin.

As the engine passed him he felt the ground moving beneath his feet. The driver was looking out of the left hand doorway his back to Connor who was on the opposite side.

He heard as the engine was asked to increase the pace as it reached the point where the bend straightened out again.

It was a long train. And it also had a precious cargo, thought Connor. There must have been at least 30 cargo trucks behind the engine, and there was a German soldier on every other one.

He wasn't getting on this one.

He watched it disappear around the bend and listened as it slowly went away from him.

And then nothing went east and nothing went west.

Wait a while and it will come.

He was generally a patient man but today was stretching even his. It was now early evening and the sun, which had briefly emerged from the rain clouds, was slowly setting. It had long since past behind the trees over to his left but now the light was fading. Not a bad thing but once it was completely dark it made it difficult to determine if the train had any roof passengers.

It was a decision he would have to take when the time came.

The time came an hour and a half later. And it was dark.

The brand new waxing moon was giving nothing away.

He could hear the train approaching from the west, but he couldn't see it. He heard the train begin to slow as it descended the small hill and then the giveaway screech on the brakes, at one hundred yards he saw it for the first time. Seeing it was a slight exaggeration. All he could see were the red sparks and embers flying out of the funnel. The odd flame briefly lit up the top of the engine but that was it.

As the engine passed him he briefly saw the driver, lit up by the orange glow from within the footplate as the stoker, getting ready for the increase in speed, threw shovels of coke into the fire, and then he was gone. He quickly moved out from the trees and began jogging along side the fifth cargo wagon. It was moving much quicker than the last train that passed, which he thought was a good sign, the train was lighter and therefor it was probably empty, which meant no outriders. He tried pulling on the sliding door but it wouldn't budge. He slowed his pace then quickened it again as the sixth wagon drew level with him, again the same result, it wouldn't move, lucky seven he thought, it wasn't, same result. He was now running out of both time and energy. He heard the engine increase its speed, he grabbed the handle of the eighth.

It moved, but not much, just barely a foot. He pulled himself up and climbed onto the wagon placing his left foot into the gap between the open door and the frame and pushed on the door with his other foot.

It moved about the same again, he pulled himself forward propelling himself into the wagon and he fell onto his back exhausted. As he regained his breath he slowly pulled the door back towards him, just leaving a couple of inches gap so he could see outside. He settled down and sat on the floor with his left shoulder against the frame of the doorway.

The smell of engine oil drifted throughout the wagon. It looked empty now but had obviously had some sort of machinery in it not so long ago. As his eyes got used to the darkness he got up and moved around trying to see if there was anything of use to him inside but there was nothing. He returned to the doorway and looked outside, he needed to see where he was.

He was watching for the river.

Within the first fifteen minutes he felt the train begin to slow and then it slowed some more until it came to a complete stop. He could hear the engine up ahead, now resting slightly, getting ready for the next pull.

From towards the back of the train he heard voices. Not one but two. Speaking in German. Then he heard a French voice followed by another voice that was speaking in broken French. 'A German soldier speaking to the train guard' thought Connor. He slowly pulled the door towards him leaving it with just a half an inch gap for him to look out of.

The voices got louder but they were now just speaking in German.

He heard them as they walked past him and then they carried on towards the front of the train. Cigarette smoke wafted into his wagon. There was no mistake, Connor recognised the smell immediately, they were Atikah cigarettes, a popular brand with German soldiers.

A few moments later he heard the same voice speaking the same broken French, only this time he was talking to the driver, who was clearly not happy with the question he'd been asked. He began shouting, presumably at the Soldier, explaining the reason why they had stopped, due to a signal telling them to do exactly that, stop. The soldier was now shouting back at the driver telling him to start moving again but the driver was having none of it.

Connor sensed from the soldiers response that they were fearing an attack from either the air or, much more likely, from the French resistance. He had seen reports while at Snettisham that the resistance movement was prevalent in this area and had been getting some good results in the past few months.

He could understand why the soldier was feeling nervous. He was a little concerned himself because if the bullets started to fly the 1" thick wooden wall he was hiding behind wasn't going to help him much.

the train had now been stationary for over ten minutes. Something was wrong that was for sure.

And then he heard it.

The unmistakable sound of an air raid, in the far distance. Probably seven or eight miles away but the bangs and booms were still distinctive.

After no more than two minutes they had stopped and the quietness once more descended around him. Almost immediately he felt the carriage jolt.

They were on the move again.

They began to pick up some speed as they passed along a very long stretch of, what felt like, a completely straight piece of track. Connor knew where he was. The river couldn't be far away now.

He pulled the door open a little again and just two minutes later he felt both the track change as well as the sound, which was now no longer coming echoing back at him from the trees, as they passed over the river Orne.

They were entering Caen.

And it was on fire.

What he needed was for the train to carry on straight through, passing the burning city and carrying on east, but he knew deep down that it wouldn't.

He was right.

It didn't.

It began to slow and as Connor peered out his small gap he saw why. The train depot, including the station, was ablaze. large flames were billowing out from large buildings, he saw three locomotives on fire, one of which had been blown clean of the tracks and was laying on its side, as if it was slowly dying.

He quietly thanked his unknown train driver, who without his bravery in standing firm against the German soldier, they would have been in the middle of all this mayhem. He wondered if the soldier felt the same, he doubted it.

In some respects, what had just happened was more of a help than a hindrance. The germans were more occupied trying to put the fires out and saving vital war equipment than looking for people getting a free lift on a train.

He felt the train come to a stop and he waited.

After a couple of minutes he slowly pulled back the door, the full devastation of the raid was plain to see, and it was just that, devastating. Trains, wagons, tracks and buildings had been blown to smithereens, nothing had escaped the metal birds from above, least of all mankind. In amongst all of the mangled metal and wood lay bodies, dead or dying, bodies with missing limbs, limbs with missing bodies.

The smell of blood mingled with the cordite.

He seen it too many times in recent months, but it still bought on a sickness within his stomach. Nobody could ever get used to this.

But you hardened to some things.

As he stepped out over the tracks he walked over to what was left of a dead track worker. The bottom half of his body was completely missing but the top half of him was almost unmarked except for a whole in his left arm. Connor grabbed the right hand sleeve of his thick woollen black coat, he wasn't going to need it anymore, and then pulled it off his arm. On doing this, it made the torso roll over, making it much easier to release the bloody and savaged, left arm. He quickly put on the jacket, complete with the whole in the left sleeve and along with the still wet blood soaked into the wool. He ran his fingers through the damp cloth and then ran them down his face leaving the blood running from the top of his head down across his cheek.

Connor, the newly arrived badly injured French track worker, looked in a bad way.

He knew he would have nobody bothering him now. No German soldier would want to help an injured frenchman, not amongst this mayhem. They were far too busy, firstly looking after themselves and secondly looking after any of their own.

He needed to find an engine facing east that had carriages behind it and preferably empty ones.

He moved along the centre tracks, there were five to his left and three to his right and as he walked east he could see that they slowly emerged into just two tracks about 700 to 800 yards in front of him.

There were engines everywhere some facing west, but not many, and much more, facing east. Some had wagons on the back and some were stood looking sorry fo themselves, standing alone and abandoned.

Fires raged everywhere, people, soldiers and rail workers ran in a totally inn-orderly manner. Utter panic and chaos reigned.

'This was easy' Connor thought to himself.

He wandered about acting a little confused and injured and nobody gave him a second look. He walked up to wagons and looked inside them, he walked up to engines and onto the footplate. Nothing, nobody bothered him at all. As he looked around in the hope that something was moving he climbed onto a footplate and suddenly realised that the engine was stood idling and was ready too go.

And then he heard it, the dreaded sound of an air raid siren.

They were coming again.

The second wave.

The temptation to pull some levers and turn some wheels was immense. He resisted and was about to climb back down when suddenly a man jumped up onto the footplate and screamed at him "allons-y allons-y (lets go, lets go!!!).

The driver, 'that was all he could be', thought Connor, began turning the wheels and pulling the handles that just thirty seconds before, Connor had thought about pulling himself.

The train lurched forward and soon picked up some speed. Connor realised that the engineer was either on instruction to get the engine out of the danger area or he just wanted to get away himself, either way Connor had dropped onto a lucky machine.

He was heading east.

The driver having pulled on the throttle lever, slid open the fire door and urged Connor to start throwing in the coke. Connor scanned the footplate looking desperately for the shovel. As he turned around behind him and saw the handle of the shovel hanging out of the coal bunker. He grabbed it and began throwing it in as fast as he could.

A huge blast from behind them followed a split second later by the shock wave lifted him off his feet. The Engineer was flung forward smashing his head against one the valves splitting his forehead wide open. Another blast then another, they were landing all around them. Huge balls of flames exploded as some of the bombs hit fuel pipes and tankers. They headed out of the yard, smoke billowing behind them as they passed through it. The Engineer, now bleeding heavily from his head, leaned out of his left hand window scanning the track ahead to see if anything was blocking their way. Within just a couple of minutes they were clear of the fires and destruction and were now slowly heading south east. But the blasts carried on. Anybody left in there wouldn't be coming out.

As they continued on Connor ran through the route within his brain. He knew that he was heading east and that this was, generally speaking, the wrong direction, he wanted to go north, but to get to where he wanted to go, Hornfleur, he had to travel east on the railway to Lisieux. Once there he had two choices, to travel on by rail, hoping that the train having continued on past Lisieux, some twenty miles, would then turn left at the split just south of Serquigny. If it did then it was a straight run in to the fishing port of Honfluer.

If it didn't, then he was a long way from getting there before tomorrow night.

He couldn't risk that. Twenty miles was too far out. If he got to Lisieux he would have to bail out and make his way north using another mode of transport.

In the meantime he had to help the driver. He was now in a bad way and the blood flow from his head wasn't stopping. Connor grabbed a cloth that had been wrapped around one of the pipes and made him sit down. He wrapped the cloth around his wound and told the driver to tell him what to do.

Connor continued to throw coal into the fire and then returned to increasing or decreasing the throttle depending on what the instruction was.

After ten minutes the driver waved to Connor to say that it was okay,

"We should be okay now",

Connor looked at him, he was in a bad way and was on the verge of passing out.

" No you need a doctor urgently, we carry on to Lisieux, we stop there".

The driver wasn't arguing, he nodded his now badly injured head and began to now struggle to stay sitting upright.

"How long", said Connor.

The driver peered out of the door trying to see where they were but he couldn't see anything.

Connor shouted at him,

"We have just passed Mezidon",

"Okay, through the tunnel then ten minutes", said the driver.

Connor continued to throw in the coal and as they went round a long right hand bend he felt the engine begin to struggle as it started to climb. A few moments later the world went black as they entered the tunnel. The noise was totally deafening and the smoke and steam began to fill the foot plate. Connor prayed that there wasn't another train coming in the opposite direction. He'd ignored all the signals since leaving the yard at Caen but up to now he had felt reasonably safe, surely they wouldn't send trains towards a disaster zone. But the tunnel had only a single track, anything coming the other way and they were dead men. But to be honest the driver was almost all ready there.

Almost a minute later, which had felt very much longer, they came out of the other side. As Connor turned to look at the driver he saw that he had now collapsed onto the floor. He grabbed him by the arms and sat him back up leaning him against the edge of the coal bunker.

Within ten minutes Connor could see the edge of Lisieux approaching, the buildings were now on both sides of the train and he pulled the brake lever to slow the train.

As it came to a stop some fifty yards too early Connor jumped from the train and ran towards the station shouting " M'aider, M'aider (help me, help me) " a guard walking along the platform turned to look to see where the shouting was coming from and saw Connor running along the track. As he got close to him he saw that Connor was covered in blood and thinking it was him that needed the help he grabbed him by the arm. Connor shouted at him " no no, le Ingénieur and pointed back down the track and the train. The guard ran down the track towards the train. Connor ran the other way, he hoped that the driver was going to be okay, he doubted it but there was no more he could do for him now.

As he got to the exit he stopped running and walked off the platform. Outside he saw his next mode of transport. Two wheels, no engine, only pedals.

Beggars were not to be choosers.

It was now a little past half past nine in the evening. He had around 25 miles to travel to the port of Hornfleur. A journey which would under normal circumstances take no more than two and a half hours. These though were not normal circumstances. The streets around Lisieux were full of German soldiers and vehicles. The place was alive with them. Like ants around freshly spilt sugar. And the curfew was just thirty minutes away.

He had dumped his blood soaked jacket and had washed his face in a stream but that still didn't prevent him being under suspicion. This was a whole new different place. They suspected everything and everybody. You could be stopped on every corner there were that many of them.

This was going to take some time.

He decided to take the back roads. Most of them ran parallel of the main roads but were much less busy and some had virtually no traffic on them at all. But he couldn't be complacent. Around every corner lurked danger. Troop numbers has diminished slightly due to them being sent to the eastern front and the ones that were replacing them had come in the opposite direction and were there for some unofficial recuperation. This made it a little easier for Connor as most of the soldiers were on wind down but he had to be careful, he didn't need to make it easy for them.

After two hours and just over halfway, things were going quite well. He seen only small numbers of troops and most of them had been well on the way to falling over. But he always expected the unexpected, and it wasn't long before it came.

As he started to climb a steep hill he entered the edge of the Foret de Saint-Gatien just north of Vieux-Bourg. The new moon having risen a little higher was lighting his way slightly and reflected on the stones on the track, and then he saw it. The reflection of the moon briefly catching the metal edge of something about fifty mitres ahead of him. He saw it move rapidly upwards and knew what it was immediately, it was a rifle. And now it was going to be pointing straight at him.

Two choices.

Crash straight into the woods.

Or.

Pretend you hadn't seen it.

He went for for the second option, he didn't need the noise.

He slowly peddled on, waiting for the challenge …….or the shot.

He got the challenge.

He heard the bolt of the rifle first, followed by the words "stehen bleiben oder ich schieße" 'stop or I'll shoot'.

He took his hands straight off the handle bars and placed them in the air, and slowly wobbled to a halt.

Make yourself appear to be no threat at all, and do that as fast as you possibly can. Put the aggressor at ease, then he becomes the vulnerable one.

Connor waited, looking all around him, as if he didn't know whereabouts the voice was coming from. What he was actually doing was checking that the soldier was on his own.

He was.

The soldier was now 10 metres in front of him slightly to his left at around the 11 o'clock position. Connor moved his head to the right as if looking towards the 3 o'clock, but, knowing full well that in this light the soldier couldn't see his eyes, they remained fixed on the soldier.

He watched as the soldier slowly moved forward breaking his cover. In front of him was a fallen tree which the soldier would have to step over to get on to the track. Connor knew that this would be his first opportunity.

When inexperienced, people that carried weapons would nearly always do the same two things when stepping over something.

One, they look down at whatever it was the were climbing over, and two, they raised the weapon slightly upwards.

The soldier didn't let him down. He did both.

As he stepped over the tree barely 8 foot in front of him, Connor rushed him hitting him at speed and knocking him backwards back over the tree and onto his back.

The soldier froze briefly in shock before he started to kick out at Connor who was now diving down towards him and grabbing the rifles barrel.

It was over in a matter of seconds. Strangled by his own rifle barrel across his throat.

As Connor got up from the now lifeless body he knelt down while he regained his breath.

He began to search the dead soldiers pockets to see if he had anything useful.

He found a small amount of money and a packet of cigarettes, 'both useful', he thought.

Around his neck was a leather strap. Connor followed the strap and discovered that they were attached to a pair of Ziess Artl binoculars, 'very useful'.

He carried on down his body and found a sheathed knife which he took and placed in the back of his waistband. Round to the other side, he found a holster. It was empty.

Connor searched the area around the body, looking for the missing gun, but found nothing.

He walked towards where he had first seen the soldier but again, found nothing.

He had the rifle but decided on leaving that behind, 'Too big and visible'.

His search now complete, he grabbed the body by the shoulders and pulled him back into the trees and hid him within a bramble bush. Nobody liked brambles. He'd be there for while before anybody found him.

He threw the rifle into it as well.

He then pulled the bike further into the trees and hid that

beneath a young conifer tree, covering the wheels with fallen leaves. He stepped back and made a mental note of its position in case he needed it again, he doubted it but you never know.

He wasn't going to risk travelling any further down the track, the young German soldier had obviously been on guard for a reason and Connor needed to know what that was.

He set off north on foot now, through the trees, watching, listening, smelling.

He'd see them, before they would see him.

It was the smell that alerted him first. Smoke. Something was burning not far in front of him and coming from slightly to his right.

He stopped and listened. Nothing.

He carried on, conscious that even though he was being very careful, he was was still making noise, not much, but enough to give himself away if he got too close to somebody.

He followed his nose and headed towards the source of the smell.

And then he saw it. The small glow of the lit fire about 50 metres in front of him.

Where there was fire there were people.

So he stopped and watched and listened. It could have been the dead soldiers fire, but he doubted it.

And then he heard the giveaway sound of a sleeping man.

A snore, followed by another, and then the second snore caught up with the first snore.

Two people at least.

He slowly moved around to his left now skirting the central fire in a clockwise direction.

And then a very large black shadow suddenly loomed up from the ground over to his right about 30 metres in front of him.

It was a Panzer III tank. Which Connor knew, had a crew of five.

One was dead, two were sleeping. The other two were now his problem.

He knew where one should be. Further up the track beyond the tank, to spot anybody coming from the north. Therefor the remaining one would be split between the two, west of the tank, to protect anything or anybody coming from the 9 o'clock position, through the woods.

Which right now, was exactly where he stood.

He slowly dropped to his knees.

He reached behind him and pulled the knife from its sheath. He had been hoping he wouldn't need to use it so soon.

As he scanned the darkness, he saw the silhouette of crewman number 4. He was over to his left, about 15 metres away, facing towards the west, sat with his back to him and leaning at an angle against a tree. The angle, was that of someone asleep.

Connor slowly stood and began to walk North. Keeping sleeping beauty in his sights over to his left.

He could quite easily have crept over to him and slit his throat but he had done Connor no harm. When he woke he wouldn't even know he had been there. No, he had had enough of death for today.

He carried on north always keeping a watchful eye over towards the track and crewman number 5.

He had round 15 kilometres to go before he reached Honfleur, he was making good time.

And so, at just over half an hour past midnight, having had no further problems, Connor walked through the trees of a small wood and out onto the Cote de Grace. The panoramic view of the harbour some 500 feet down below stretched out before him at just over 200 metres away. He raised his newly found binoculars up to his eyes and began to scan the harbour from left to right.

Change the blue to yellow, the yellow to red and the red to

blue.

He took a brief look for a red bell but it was too dark.

He walked back into the wood behind him and as before, at the boot shaped wood, he built his hide. A different construction this time as there was little back cover behind him, and so he had to go into the ground. It took him 2 hours of hard graft, he dug a whole nearly 3 feet deep, 3 foot wide by 8 foot long, it had a roof made of fallen branches and was then covered with fallen leaves and moss. He called it his coffin. He had a small observation whole at the front, which looked down onto the harbour below, and a flap at the rear to get out of, but now it was time to sleep again.

He slept a good sleep. Probably due to the lack of it since he had arrived in France.

He woke still laying down flat on his stomach he raised his binoculars and scanned the harbour again. He could see much better now, it was 07:30 in the morning and it was a beautiful cloudless day, the sun now coming over the horizon and hitting the harbour down below him. The Harbour or Basin as it was better known, was of oblong shape, at least 100 metres long maybe more and 60 metres wide. The entrance to it was on the north wall which also had The Luietenancy' 'guarding the way. On the east, south and west sides, the 7 storey houses that boxed the basin in, shone out in their beautiful and full spectrum of different colours. It was as if god had sent down a rainbow and had left it there, forgetting to take it back.

But for now there was no red bell, and, more reassuringly, no yellow one either.

'Probably still out getting his catch' he thought.

That thought made him feel hungry, he hadn't eaten since midday yesterday, but he had managed to drink from a stream the previous evening. But his stomach would have to wait, he needed to see where the Rouge Gitan moored herself, providing of course, if and when it came into port.

He lay and watched the world go by, which wasn't much. On the hill road directly in front of him he saw two troop carriers, a couple of pedal cyclists and a man walking his dog. He didn't like dogs, a statement that wasn't really true, he actually loved dogs, he had enjoyed their companionship throughout his life, but he didn't like them when in his present situation. They had a terrible habit of sniffing you out. Not too bad if you were in a sitting position because you had the opportunity of fighting or running away, laying face down was a totally different situation and one that usually didn't go well for either you or the dog. The were ways to get around it, particularly if you had preparation time. An open tin of sardines tipped over to let the juice trickle out was an excellent way of putting them off your scent.

Once you had made your hide the trick was to get out and trickle your smelly fish juice some yards away in an arc around your den and carry it on beyond for some 30 or 40 yards or so. By the time the dog had lost the scent of the fish he would be well past you and would carry on. He'd used this method several times in the past, once using a very bad smelling pair of socks, borrowed from a fellow trooper. He'd ask Captain Distan when he met him, he may have something spare. Fish preferably, not old socks.

The harbour down below was much busier. People moved about the port carrying boxes and baskets, a few fishing boats were still making their way out but none were coming in.

There was also quite a lot of troop activity. Troop carriers, probably the same ones that had passed him sometime earlier, had stopped on the quayside and at least 10 soldiers had got off each one. He watched as they disappeared, marching 2 abreast, further into the town.

It was a little after midday before anything of significance happened. He had drifted in and out of of a light sleep throughout the morning for no more than a few minutes at a time but the rest was doing him good.

As he now watched the way in and out to sea along the estuary, he could see some small boats beginning to return from their mornings activities.

He peered through his binoculars as they slowly made their way in.

No red bell, and no yellow one either.

He watched the boats come in, 22 in all. Not one red or yellow bell in sight.

And then they stopped.

It was now late evening and the light was fading fast, he doubted that Le Rouge Gitan would be coming in now. No matter, he would have to wait another day. But now he needed to get out of his coffin, he legs had long since left his body and he was desperate for some food. He would wait though for darkness before he ventured out.

At 21:30, his legs now having returned, he stood on the edge of the small wood and looked out across the harbour. The wind had now got up and was having an effect on the sea. It was much rougher than the mill pond from earlier in the day. The odd candle light from within some of the boats flickered and bobbed up and down in time with the swell of the sea. But it was the noise of the ropes hitting the mast's that drew Connor's attention. The gentle instrumental song was almost hypnotic as they beat out a totally random tune down below him. It was if a hundred wind chimes had gathered together in the watery amphitheater below, to perform as one.

But now It was time to go and have a wander, mainly to get some food but also to see what else was about.

Three and a half hours later he returned from his successful trip with bread, milk and two bars of chocolate that he had managed to steal from an unmanned sentry post close to the edge of the port. He had originally looked in it with the hope of finding a discarded weapon or the like, but was just as happy with his find of chocolate. A very unhappy German soldier would soon return, no doubt having been very much looking forward to his little feast.

Having eaten, he quickly fell asleep and slept a sleep full of dreams and nightmares.

He dreamt of his mother.

It was the same dream he had had so many, many, times before in his younger years.

In it, he is a young boy, around ten years old, his mother has come to see him, as, in the dream, she has done so many times, paying a him a surprise visit but when she arrives, he is never at home. When he walks into the back yard of Rose cottage he hears a horse drawn carriage going past the gate behind him and turns to see his mother on the back of the carriage being taken away from him. He would then chase after them trying to shout but no words, no matter how hard he seemed to shout, would ever come out and his legs as though dressed in lead, would never run fast enough. She would then ride away into the distance totally unaware of him running after her behind the carriage. Sometimes in the dream she would be crying, he knew that she was because he could see her putting a handkerchief to her face. But, as in every dream he ever had about his mother, he never saw her from the front, he never saw her face.

He knew why that was.

It was because he couldn't remember what she looked like........

Was it any wonder that he wanted to kill the man that was responsible for all of this.

When he woke from these nightmares he would always feel unhappy for the rest of the day. Not wanting the night to come for fear of having the same dream again.

This morning was no different.

When he woke he was crying. Not loud but a gentle sob, and tears, real tears, trickled down his face. His right hand was slowly and very gently, stroking the inside of the palm of his left hand with his own fingertips, it was something his Nana would do to get him back to sleep.

He could hear her trying to comfort him and telling him, as she always did,

' you shouldn't eat so late my boy, it always gives you nightmares'.

Maybe tonight he should eat a little earlier.

He looked down upon the harbour which looked like a totally different place from the morning before. The sunshine and the rainbow of colours had long gone and had been replaced by dark grey buildings covered with dark grey rain filled skies which seemed to hover just a few feet above the hill of which he was perched upon.

He raised his binoculars and scanned the harbour.

No red bell and no yellow one either.

He decided to treat himself to the remainder of the bread and finished it off with the second bar of chocolate.

a short time later the man with the dog walked by, looking like he really didn't want to be out in this foul weather and the dog looking even more like he didn't want to be out in this foul weather.

Shortly after midday the boats began to return and he watched them one by one struggling to reach the safe haven of the port.

He had counted 18 of them when he saw it.

Swaying left and right, the mast seemed to have a mind of its own and seemed to move at least 45 degrees in both directions. And then there it was on top of the mast, the bell, at times it almost seemed to be struggling to hang on to the top, but he could see that it was a red one.

He looked down to the front of the boat to see if he could see the name but the swell of the sea seemed to be playing a game of hide and seek with him.

He moved his binoculars to look at the cabin but the rain, now lashing down, completely obscured his view.

As it entered the port it was if somebody had turned the waves off as the boat now seemed to float calmly into the harbour and made its way towards the harbour wall furthest away from him.

As it came to a stop he saw one of the crew throw a rope up onto the wall and then watched him jump onto the ladder that ran down from the top.

He raced up the ladder as if he was running up a set of stairs and grabbed the rope pulling the boat in and tying it fast.

He then looked at the stern which now faced him and saw the words.

'Le Rouge Gitan',

'good' he thought.

She was a medium sized trawler, a 60 foot long drifter powered by a diesel engine but still had masts for the sails which were used when fishing to keep the boat from going side on to the waves.

Connor looked towards the cabin doors, and then he saw the Captain walk out onto the stern.

He was wearing a blue cap.

'Change the blue to yellow, the yellow to red and the red to blue.'

'Damn, thats not good' he thought.

He lowered the binoculars and looked at the boat, two more of the crew had now come onto the deck and were throwing baskets up to a man on the wall.

He couldn't go anywhere near the boat while the captain was wearing the blue hat. Something must be be wrong, but he really did need to get back to England, sooner rather than later.

He raised the binoculars again he saw the captain start to

climb the ladder. As he got to the top he saw him stand and look out over the harbour back towards Connor's direction. If Connor hadn't known better he would have thought that he was looking straight at him, but that wasn't possible, not from that distance. The captain then took off his cap, brushed his hand through his grey hair, and slowly replaced the cap.

And then he saw it.

A yellow ribbon tied around the hat.

'Thank you Captain Distan, There must be a shortage of yellow caps' thought a now smiling Connor.

His day was feeling a little better already.

He lay and watched the rest of the afternoon go by from the comforts of his coffin, and then at a little after 11pm he climbed out and closed the makeshift door behind him. He threw some fallen leaves over where he had left signage of himself, then left his usual trip mark and walked to the edge of the wood.

The rain had now stopped but the roads were still shiny and wet, and the wind hadn't ceased at all. Which was good in some respects but not in others. They wouldn't hear him but he wouldn't hear them either.

No matter, he would see them before they saw him.

He walked out onto the Cote de Grace and looked out onto the Vieux Bassin below, some 300 hundred metres as the crow would fly, in front of him. It looked such a straight forward journey to the Rouge Gitan, only he wasn't a crow. He would have to walk at least 5 times that amount through the twisting winding, steeply descending cobbled streets. The moon, still waxing and now giving more light than the night before, would light his way, in between the darkness caused by the fast moving clouds that were rushing by quickly above him.

His ultimate destination for this evening was of course the Rouge Gitan but first he had to get to the harbour itself and then he had to get to the area of the 'Lieutenancy'.

The Lieutenancy was a large 4 storey building on the very edge of the harbour, with a huge wooden door that faced out onto the harbour itself and also led into the main body of the ground floor. To the right of the door were wooden steps that led up to the parapet that gave a view over the harbour from the ramparts.

Built the seventeenth century, it had once been the home of the Lieutenant to King Louis XIV, but now, 300 years later, it was full of Germans. As Connor had lay and watched earlier in the day, he had wondered why, 'of all places' did Captain Distan moor his boat so close to a building swarming with germans.

But as the evening wore on it became apparent that the Captain knew exactly what he was doing. Throughout the evening the building had slowly leaked out all of its German soldiers. Disappearing two by two, as if leaving the Ark, and out into the port and the surrounding streets. A small skeleton staff remained inside but only now and then did anybody venture out, only given away by the orange glow from their cigarette.

He started on his way, making a note in his head, to take an alternative route from the night before. He didn't need to be going near the sentry post. The chocolateless soldier was sure to be lying in wait for the thief to return.

The journey downhill was remarkably uneventful. The few soldiers he saw were very relaxed, but then again, he had seen them, but they hadn't seen him.

As he reached the 'Lieutenancy' he moved back into the shadows beneath the steps that led up to the ramparts. He needed to wait for a while and watch the Rouge Gitan.

He needed to know that there was nobody left aboard.

As he awaited, two soldiers returned to the Lieutenancy. They walked up the steps and entered the big oak door, closing it behind them. It was a little after 02:00hrs now and the harbour was at its quietest. The wind had dropped and the sea was back to the mill pond it was before.

Connor looked at the Rouge Gitan barely 50 metres in front of him. No lights or sounds from within.

He listened to the sounds from his surroundings.

He could hear only natures sounds. The wind and the sea. The only man made sound was still the hypnotic chimes of the ropes on the masts, much louder now that he was stood next to them.

He stepped out onto the cobbled path of the quay.

He walked slowly to the boat and stepped aboard, the tide was reasonably high, he opened the small door to the cabin area and stepped inside.

It was over two hours later before he heard anything else.

Voices.

One French, and one German who was speaking very poor French.

He heard the word's 'Bon Matin' and then 'Capitan'.

It was time to introduce himself.

He felt the boat slightly tilt to his right as he sensed somebody climbing aboard and he waited for the cabin door to open.

He didn't have to wait for long as seconds later Captain Distan stepped inside.

He couldn't see Connor as it was pitch black inside but as he looked at the silhouette of the Captain stood in the doorway he sensed that he knew somebody else was inside the cabin.

Connor decided to let him know.

"Bonjour Captain Distan",

The captain stood still and looked into the blackness.

" Bonjour, may I ask who is there",

"Certainly Captain, you may, its Billy,"

" I see" said the Captain and continued.

" And what is the colour of my hat Billy",

"Its blue but has a yellow ribbon around it",

" Then its a pleasure to meet you Billy",

" And Sir, its an absolute pleasure to meet you too'" said Connor.

The captain stepped inside and lit a small candle on the table between them.

He held out his hand and Connor held out his and as they shook hands no more words were spoken just a nod of the heads in respect of each other.

Both men knew that what they were doing was not only risking their own life but was also risking that of the other.

If either one of them was caught then the chances were that they would both be killed along with all the crew as well.

Trust.

There was no other word for it.

After a while the other crew members arrived. They all ignored him as if he wasn't there. The captain explained to him that they weren't being rude it was just safer not to speak to him for if they were caught they couldn't tell the germans anything that they didn't already know. Connor accepted that but knew that deep down, if they were caught, the fact that they didn't know anything wouldn't wash with the Germans, they would kill them anyway, but he decided not to say anything, it was something they didn't need to know.

At around 04:30 they set out to sea.

The tide was on the turn but it was slow going escaping the estuary.

Two hours later they went through the usual routine. they still had to catch fish after all. If they went back without a catch then questions, and not very nice ones, would certainly be asked.

As they threw the nets over board Connor watched. but he

wasn't watching them.

He was waiting for the big fish to surface.

And a few minutes later there it was. Rising out of the sea as if the Loch Ness monster had got lost and had made its way out into the English Channel.

The monster was in fact HMS P 36, a U class submarine of the British navy.

His ride home had arrived.

By 08:00 hrs that morning he was back on British soil and on a train heading north.

But It was just after 23:30hrs when he eventually climbed the drainpipe up onto a small flat roof at the rear of Snettisham hall.

He had someone he needed to see and he didn't want to be announced.

❋ ❋ ❋

NOBODY LIKES BAD NEWS

It was late, too late thought Colonel Southall. He had an early start in the morning, he had to go to London and needed to be there by midday. He should never had agreed to have gone to the mess, and now, well past midnight and with a heavy head to go with it, he unlocked his door to his room.

As he walked into the living area he sat down in his big brown leather chesterfield and slipped of his shoes. It wasn't worth going to bed.

As he sat back into the chair the spot light flared on from his desk in front of him, blinding him temporarily.

And then a voice came from directly behind the blinding lamp.

"Sir, I'm very sorry, I truly am, but I have two questions I need to ask and I need to see your face".

The Colonel, now sitting bolt upright and very rapidly becoming sober, recognised the voice immediately, he said calmly,

"Carry on",

"Do you know a German officer ranked higher than a Major with the last name of Mulder",

"Yes",

After a slight pause Connor continued,

"Do you know a German officer, called Major Klass"

"No",

"Does Major Klass work for SOE",

The Colonel looked back at the shining lamp, sank back into his chair and slowly and very deliberately said,

" Connor, thats three questions and the answer is still no, I've never heard of him, and now it's my turn to ask a question.

"Okay",

" Do you have a gun",

"No",

"Then turn that fucking light off".

Connor did as he was asked as the Colonel walked back to the door and switched the room light on.

" I'd like to say Connor that its good to see you again, but I'm not so sure it is".

Connor looked at him a little embarrassed and replied.

" I'm sorry sir but I really did need to know",

"Thats okay, and so I take it you are happy with my reaction to your questions",

" Yes sir I am",

" Of course you are" smiled the Colonel,

" Because if you hadn't been I'd have been dead by now wouldn't I",

"Connor shrugged his shoulders and smiled back.

The Colonel walked forward and shook Connors hand.

" It is good to see you Connor, now lets sit down and see what all this is about".

They sat and talked for the next hour about what Connor had seen at the safe house and about how he had met and then followed Pavell. He told him about the possibility that the building belonged to the Abwehr and that he had seen the two German officers meeting Pavell within the same building.

" So Connor, where is our Mr Pavell now",

" He's dead",

" Ah, the bad apple I presume",

"Yes, but there are other's, I take it one of my friends made it back then",

"All four of them" smiled the Colonel,

" thats good" said Connor,

" It is" said the Colonel,

" But lets get to the main point and discuss why you had to come back in such a hurry, tell me what do you know about Commandant Mulder",

"I know very little" said Connor "but what I do know is that he works in that building in Bayeux and that Major Klass works for him",

"and Pavell",

" he worked for them both",

" Interesting" replied the Colonel " but who is this Major Klass, as I've said, I've never heard of him",

Connor leant forward and lowered his voice.

" Sir, you may not of heard 'of him', but I'm almost certain you have actually 'heard' him".

The colonel looked at him a little confused and said,

"And what exactly to you mean by that",

" What I mean sir is that you have almost certainly met him, Major Klass, if that is indeed his real name, is working here".

The Colonel, surprised by the reply looked at Connor for some sort of clarification and said,

" You mean he's working here, in this country, how do you know that, have you seen him",

"Yes Sir I have, and he's not just working in this country, I think I may have misled you, when I say that he's working here, I actually mean right here, in this building, for SOE."

The Colonel's mouth gaped open in utter shock, he shook his head as if to pull himself together but eventually he said,

"You've seen this Major Klass in this building, when exactly was this, and how do you know its definitely the same person",

"Sir, Its definitely the same person and I saw him here the day before I left, walking along the corridor in the opposite direction, coming from the area of your office as I walked towards it with Sgt Hunt",

" What did he look like",

Connors photographic memory kicked in.

"Mid forties, fair greying hair, tall, slim, sharp features",

"Anything else",

" When he walks his head leans slightly to the left, as if on a tilt, his left foot points out very slightly to the left, unlike the right foot, which is straight as he walks, and his fingers on his left hand constantly open and close, a stress sign, I would imagine, and he smokes cigar's".

The Colonel jumped up from his chair and said quickly,

" Wait right there" and then he ran out of the room.

Five minutes later the breathless Colonel burst back into the room now holding a brown folder.

He handed it to Connor.

Connor looked at the front cover. It had three words on it.

Captain James Plowman.

Connor saw that a paper clip was holding something inside the front cover.

As he turned the page he saw that it held a photograph.

Connor looked at it for just a brief moment and then he said

"Captain Plowman, Major Klass" nodded Connor.

"Shit" shouted the Colonel,

" Come with me, right now",

They both raced out of the room and headed out of the building.

It was a cold night and the breath of both men blew out of their expanding lungs as they raced across the grass towards the officers quarters that presumably, thought Connor, housed the man pertaining to be a certain Captain Plowman.

As they approached the door the sentry on duty, who, rather surprisingly was not asleep, confronted them and shouted them to halt. The Colonel bellowed at him.

" Private Davis, Its me, now let us in and then come with us, right now, and grab anybody else thats about, whereabout's is Captain Plowman's room ",

"Top floor sir, room 9, the Belvior suite".

Private Davis unlocked the door and the three of them ran up the stairs.

As they got to the room Colonel Southall instructed Davis to break down the door, which he did with one kick from his right boot.

The colonel was in first holding his browning pistol out in front of him.

"shit, shit, shit" growled Southall.

They were too late.

The room was empty.

"He was hear just two days ago" said Southall "I saw him in the mess, he'd just come back up from London, well, that's where I thought he had been".

"I think you'll find he had come from further a field than from London,

Southwell, now looking distinctly pale, slowly nodded his response.

He sent Davis for some staff and over the next hour, the room was thoroughly searched, but they found nothing.

As the sun rose on a new day Colonel Southall knew he wasn't going to be going to London.

He knew that Connor should be being sent back to France.

But he also knew that this time would be much more dangerous than his previous journey. He had felt that he had sent him to his death the last time, he wasn't sure if he should do it again.

He also knew that shit travelled downwards, and the way things were turning out, his command here wouldn't be for much longer.

✳ ✳ ✳

IN FOR A PENNY

The next morning Colonel Southall was up much earlier than he had really wanted to be.

He went to the mess for breakfast shortly after 07:00 but was surprised to see the place virtually empty.

He had arranged to meet Connor there and had also instructed Private Davis to have his breakfast with them as there were things to discuss.

'Damage limitation' Connor had called it.

It was a little after 0800 before he saw either of them.

And It wasn't Connor.

Private Davis poked his head around the mess door and was immediately seen by Southall.

Colonel Southall nodded at him and ushered him in.

"Your late Davis, I said 7 o'clock",

"I'm very sorry Sir, but...." Said a breathless Davis,

The Colonel interrupted him.

"Never mind Davis, where the hell Is Gillian, have you seen him",

Davis looked at the Colonel.

'Shit travelled downwards'.

"Well" said the Colonel "have you".

Davis didn't say a word but passed over a folded piece of paper in the shape of a diamond.

The colonel knew immediately who it was from and also had a very good idea of its contents. He slowly unfolded the note

and then he read it....
'Boss,
Sorry had to go.
Bad apples calling.
Be in touch as before.
Keep it tight.
Give me 5 days.
Regards
Billy'

His decision had been made for him.

A few hours previously, Connor, on getting back to his room, had briefly laid on his bed, deep in thought.
Which ever way you looked at it, it hadn't been good, so he had decided to take matters into his own hands. If he stayed and did nothing then his boss was done for. Which probably meant, he was too. He owed the Colonel one last go if nothing else.
In for a penny.
And so, getting up from his bed, he had gone back outside and told Davis to take him to Langham. Within an hour he had been flown out of the country aboard the same Wellington, with the same crew.
The paperwork had been forged.
A photographic memory had helped, but a friendship made was the difference.
As he had entered the hanger at Coastal Command Langham, he had been in luck.
Virtually the same crew that had flown him out previously, the week before, were all sat in the hanger, some sleeping, some reading, but the pilot and the redundant bomb aimer

were wide awake and held in conversation.

As they turned and saw him, the bomb aimer, clearly surprised, smiled and laughing he said,

"Blimey mate, have you got a twin or are you back for more",

Connor smiled at him and replied,

"In for a penny in for a pound, cant get enough me, you lot ready",

The pilot smiled and laughed as Connor handed over the paperwork,

" I'm sorry Sir, I didn't realise we were down for taking you back over" said the pilot,

" No worries Captain, its a last minute job and I need to get back over pretty damn quick",

"No problem, let me call ops and see which way we're going",

"Okay, but I know I need dropping in the same area, but I will leave that up to you".

Half an hour later the Captain emerged from the office, somewhat frustrated.

"Ops are saying they no nothing of it Captain, I'm not sure we are going anywhere tonight",

Connor looked at him.

" With all due respect Captain, due to it being needed on the hurry up, their probably not going to know a thing about it, this is all down to, as you can see, by the paperwork, Colonel Southhall. But I will leave it up to you, its your call",

"Bugger it, paperwork, its all bollocks, lets go boys, Jack get hold of the tower lets go flying"

Twenty minutes later the wheels left the ground.

Major Klass would be getting a visitor.

....

Colonel Southwell looked at Davis.

"What time did he leave",

Davis, knowing that he was almost certainly on a charge, looked down at the floor.

"Just after 02:30hrs Sir",

"Do you know where he went",

"I took him to Langham, stopping for some birds on the way Sir".

Southwell did the math in his head. He was either there or almost. Providing that is, he hadn't been shot down.

"Ok Davis, you tell nobody of this, understand, now get yourself off for some breakfast".

A very relieved Davis saluted the Colonel and walked away.

Southwell made the way to his office, he had a phone call to make.

4 hours later he received the call to say that the Wellington had safely returned. He had apologised for the sudden arrival of his Captain but it was a matter of utmost urgency,

"No problem at all" had come the reply, "glad we could be of assistance".

The flight, or though reasonably uneventful, had been a rough one.

They had flown, under the instruction of the forged paperwork, at low level the entire journey.

Connor had felt that the lower they were, the less likely they would be detected, not only by the enemy, but also by the allies.

Remarkably, his feet eventually rejoined the earth just over two miles to the south east of his previous landing. Within 40 minutes he was back at his hide and after placing his four new friends in their temporary accommodation he made his way towards Bayeux.

In some respects he was happy to be back. He was in his element, it was what he was born to do. But now, having come back, he knew that they would be waiting for him.

They also knew what he was born to do.

And It was never as easy when they knew.

But..... He had no choice.

There was a bait to be laid and for it to work and be totally successful, the bait needed to be bitten and bitten hard.

For the next three days he revisited the park, the guest house, the cathedral and the library. All of them proved to be fruitless. Major Klass was nowhere to be seen.

On each evening he also visited the building that housed the Abwehr on the Rue Tardif but each night had had the same result, the curtains were drawn, no light was turned on within and there was no smell of any cigars.

On his fourth morning he decided to visit the cafe again.

As he opened the door, the smile that greeted him from the waitress was very pleasing, but not as pleasing as the double take from the man sat at the table nearest the window.

' the new Mr Pavell' thought Connor and he was right.

....

It was time to place the worm on the hook.

Connor walked over to the counter and smiled to the waitress.

"Good morning sir, I haven't seen you for a few days, I hope you are well" she said,

"Good morning to you too, yes I'm well thank you ,and how are you",

"I'm very good thank you, I thought that you may have been unwell, caught something off our friend Pavell",

" No, no, I'm good thank you, and I see our friend isn't here",

"He's not been in for days, I presumed he had taken a turn for the worse",

Connor gave her a rye smile.

"More than likely Mademoiselle, he was never in the best of health was he".

Connor sensed the eyes burning into the back of his head from the man sat at the table behind him.

He ordered his coffee and went and sat over by the window, two table's to the right of the new Mr Pavell. He nodded a hello but didn't get one in reply.

Connor opened out his newspaper and began to read its contents. He read it properly as in the past, he had noted that to pretend to read was very difficult and would often be noticed by somebody if they were experienced in field of surveillance.

Connor could see that the new Mr Pavell was much more astute than his predecessor. He wasn't looking directly at Connor, just keeping him in his periferal vision over to his right. He'd caught his eye just once, a brief glimpse, but the man hadn't looked away quickly, he just turned his gaze back to the window and carried on watching the world go by.

Connor stayed for an hour and then decided that it was time to go. He took his coffee cup back to the counter.

"See you soon" said Connor to the waitress.

"Your'e off are you, hope to see you soon too",

"I hope so, I'm going away for a few days but should be back for the weekend, I don't suppose you fancy going out for a drink or something when I'm back do you",

She looked at him and smiled,

"We will see, call in when your back, it would be nice",

"Great, see you then".

As he walked past the new Pavell and towards the exit, he winked at him.

The new Pavell didn't respond.

'No problem' thought Connor 'he'd catch up with him later no doubt'.

He decided to walk to the Cathedral, there were plenty of opportunities on that route to see if he was being followed, windows, doors, sharp turns and dead end streets.

Within a little under half an hour he was sat at a bench within the park next to the Cathedral. He had looked in the windows and doors, he had walked down dead end streets and now he sat on the bench sheltered by one of the big oak trees and he had seen nothing. Not one glimpse of his new friend.

'He was either very good, or he wasn't who he thought he might be' thought Connor. 'No, that double take was the killer give away. He was definitely his new Pavell, no doubt about it.'

Just wait then wait some more.

He waited some more and nothing happened.

As dusk came and went he decided to play his last card.

He walked away from the park and headed for the guest house on the Rue Royal. As he got outside he briefly looked through the window. 'Good' he thought 'there was nobody at the desk'. He climbed up the steps stepped inside and raced up the stairs to the top floor. He gently knocked on the door of number 13. There was no answer, he tried the handle.

It was locked.

He needed to get in.

He lent on the door with his shoulder, turned the handle and pushed hard.

The door flew open and he fell inside. The room was empty. He ran over to the window and climbed outside.

'As he climbed out of the window 'This fire escape would'nt take much more of this' he thought to himself.

Somewhat relieved as he got to the ground floor, he turned right and walked swiftly down the alleyway and stepped out onto the Rue Royal. He turned left, briefly ran down the road and then crossed it and walked into an alleyway between two buildings.

He'd remembered seeing it a few days before.

The building on the right had looked like it had been empty for sometime.

He'd been right.

Again, he put his shoulder to the door and forced his way inside. Cobwebs and dust were everywhere. Nobody had been in here for months, possibly longer. He quietly climbed the stairs and slowly pushed open the first door in front of him. The room had a bed and over by the window, a small dressing table. He walked over to the window and slowly looked outside.

Perfect.

It looked directly out onto the street and just 30 metres to his left was the guest house.

Time to sit and watch.

He watched for the next 5 hours.

Nothing happened.

No one walked by, nobody entered the guest house, and nobody, including the new Mr Pavell, appeared to be watching it either.

Either he had got it wrong or this man was good.

It was late, so he decided to make the most of the bed and went to sleep.

He was woken just four and a half hours later with the sound of a large bang followed by the screams and shouting of people from a building further down the street. He stepped from the bed and as quietly as he could and walked over to the window.

As he looked out to his left he saw a German soldier was stood on guard on the front steps of the guest house.

He had been hoping that this hadn't been the response. He was hoping that they would decide to follow him to see where "going away for a few days' might be, not drag him out kicking and screaming from a guest house.

But it had been worth a try.

He watched for the next twenty minutes, not a lot happened, but then he saw the man who he was least expecting, step out from the front door.

It was Major Klass.

Connor watched him standing on the top step and then lighting a cigar. He was smartly dressed in a cream Mac and wearing a black trilby style hat. He watched him turn, as he began looking up and down the street. At one point he appeared to be looking directly at the window that he was hiding behind. He also noted that Klass was smiling and looked to be nodding his head. 'A little odd' he thought. But then, it was just a game after all, a deadly one, but just a game, and they both surely knew how it usually ended.

Although he hadn't been expecting it, Klass himself attending the scene, he knew why he was there, that was obvious.

He was looking for him.

He'd been tipped off by the man from the cafe, who had somehow seen him enter the guest house just hours before.

But the presence of Major Klass actually being part of the search team showed to Connor how desperate they were to find him.

Klass had indeed been tipped off by the new Pavell. His name was in fact Fredric Walter, a French national of German decent. He had been in the French army but, on their capitulation he had quickly defected to help his mother land. He had been trained by the french in how to covertly follow and how to watch people. And he knew he was good. They had told him so.

As Connor carried on watching out of the window he thought to himself that It was good that Klass had turned up. At least he now knew that he was here. But now he had a problem, and a dangerous one at that.

He now had two people looking for him.

Klass and his new hunter.

To follow Klass was now going to be very difficult. To catch him and get him back to England was going to be even harder, it would test all his experience and expertise to the maximum.

But he had a plan. And he was going to enjoy it.

It was what he was born to do.

* * *

TWO MEN TWO SIDES

Klass was a pragmatic man.

He knew that the chances of catching his man were no more than 50/50.

He also knew that the winner would most likely be standing over the dead body of the other.

War.

It was a very small word for something that bought total and utter devastation to all those that were involved in it.

But he enjoyed it. He revelled in the challenges that came his way and this latest one, he was absolutely and utterly determined to win it.

He didn't like losing. A statement which in theory wasn't actually factual, the reason being that he had never lost a battle in his life, so too lose was an unknown entity for him. It was more like, he didn't enjoy the thought of losing.

As he had stood on the steps of the guest house, he had looked up and down the street. He knew that his nemesis, prey, apponent, whatever people would call him, was out there somewhere, he could feel it, and he had been told so by his new man, Walter, that he was probably watching him right there and then. He had smiled to himself and slowly nodded his head towards his invisible adversary in a gesture of admiration.

But he had a plan and he was going to enjoy it. He felt that it was something that he was born to do.

"Okay, have it your way. Lets see where you take us then shall we".

He had muttered to himself under his breath.

Connor had watched as the soldiers slowly left the building. This time they were empty handed. There had been no sign of the new Pavell, Walter, but he knew that he had been the one responsible for the rude awakening.

He went back to sleep for two more hours before he got up and made his way into the centre of the town. All the time looking for both his hunters.

He saw nothing of either and decided to make his way towards the Abwehr.

It turned out to be the right decision.

Within 20 minutes the worm had been bitten once more.

Connor had walked quickly passed the front doors to the building and on turning onto the Rue Larcher he crossed quickly into the park.

It had worked. As he exited the park on the far side he saw Major Klass enter where he had about a minute previously.

Now all he had to do was convince them that he needed to be followed and not caught. He had planned for that of course, but the bait still needed to be taken in order for it to work. He wanted to let Klass and his new assistant follow him all the way to Hornfleur.

He walked on towards the the Cathedral turned quickly left and ran along the Passage Flachat, turned right again towards the Rue Laitiere and then right again back onto the Rue Larcher, a complete square circle but now he was walking back in the opposite direction and hopefully towards Klass. He wanted to see if his able assistant was with him.

He was.

He watched them unknowingly walking briskly towards him, Klass, in a little of a panic having lost sight of his prey. Walter was walking 30 yards behind Klass. The new man was good, but not perfect, not by anybody's stretch of anybody's imagination. He had already fallen into the fatal fault of the back up man, he was watching Klass, not where he should have been watching, 30 to 40 yards in front of him, looking for their man.

He felt a little happier about the situation. It was still going to be difficult but the new man had already shown a floored technique, he wasn't a natural, more manufactured, plus, he always had the other option.

Take out the new man.

He was happy for now though. He thought he'd have some fun first.

Connor carried on watching, now stood inside a fruit and vegetable store, fifty to sixty yards in front of them. He'd wait until they got a little closer and then carry on walking.

Two hours later Connor was very happy. He walked around the town and they had followed him the whole time. They could have had him arrested several times but they hadn't. They had carried on following him and now as he sat on a wooden bench at the train station, he knew he was going to win, because he now knew they wanted to know where he was going, how he was getting back to England.

'Don't worry Major Klass' thought Connor ' you will soon see how I get back to England, and you will be coming with me'.

A short while later he heard the train approaching and slowly stood up.

He had spoken to the ticket clerk knowing full well that Klass or the new man would ask where he had bought a ticket for.

So, not wanting to disappoint them he had asked for 'Honfleur please'.

He climbed aboard the train and made his way to the carriages that held the six seater compartments.

He made himself comfortable on the window seat facing forward, he was expecting a visitor at some time soon but wasn't sure which one it would be, but it didn't matter, he wasn't going to move until they entered the tunnel.

He didn't have to wait for long.

As the train began to slowly move off, the 'new man' entered his carriage. His brown trilby hat pulled down over his eyes, he sat down opposite him but in the middle seat.

The train rattled on, stopping at stations, the steam blowing past the windows sometimes on the left, sometimes on the right and then it would disappear altogether.

Connor closed his eyes and rested. Nobody else entered their carriage, 'which was good' thought Connor.

They stopped at Caen which was interesting. Only in the fact that it was good to see it in the daylight. Some of the dead steam trains still lay on their side but thankfully that was all.

None of the arms and legs had been left behind.

It wasn't long before they were moving again so Connor again closed his eyes.

A short time later, the noise of his carriage door opening made him open them again. He caught a glimpse of the 'new man' closing it behind him, then walk left towards the front of the train. 'Probably off to report to Klass' thought Connor. 'No problem he'd be back shortly'.

He took the opportunity to stand up and disconnect the bulb above the door.

As Connor sat watching out the window again he felt the train begin to slow and then he saw the station sign.

'Mezidon'.

'The 'new man' better hurry back' he thought.

The train came to a stop and Connor watched as people got off and less so, got on.

The 'new man' had indeed been to see his boss, in the first carriage. Walter had told Klass he had found their man in the fourth carriage and that he had joined him in the same compartment and that there was nobody else with them. Klass was happy with that and said he would stay in the front carriage and continue looking out onto the platform as the train stopped at each of the stations.

"If our man gets out, you stay in the carriage until the train is about to move off and I will follow him until you catch up" said Klass,

"Understood" said Walter.

It stayed in the station for no more than 2 minutes and then it was off again, picking up speed very quickly.

Connor was now waiting for the right hand bend.

He didn't have to wait for long.

First he felt the train begin to slow ever so slightly but just noticeable, and then he felt the train begin to move around the right hand bend and start the slow climb.

They were nearly there.

Almost thirty seconds later two things happened at the same time.

The 'new man' came back to the carriage and slid open the compartment door.

And the train went into the tunnel and into the pitch black.

And then a third thing happened a split second later.

In the blackness, Connor leapt to his feet grabbed the new man in a neck hold, opened the outer door of the carriage and threw him out into the tunnel. It happened so quick that Walter had no time at all to react.

Connor didn't enjoy doing it, but the plan had changed. He couldn't risk being followed by the two of them anymore and he had promised Southall that he would be bringing Klass back alive. So the choice hadn't been his to throw him out but it didn't make him feel any better about it.

30 seconds later the train exited the tunnel and the sunlight streamed back in through the windows.

There was no sign of any struggle that had just occurred apart from a discarded brown trilby laying on the floor.

Connor picked it up and placed it on his head, went out of the carriage into the passageway and turned right, towards the back of the train.

He needed a coat.

As he walked along the narrow passageway, he occasionally bumped into the compartment windows, caused by the rocking of the train. Each time he did, he took the opportunity to see who was inside. He wasn't looking for Klass, he already knew that he was probably somewhere towards the front of the train. He needed to find a sleeping man and preferably one sat on his own. He passed people coming the other way, causing him to stand sideways on to let them pass. As he got to the last 2 carriages a man and a woman came through the doors from the last carriage and walked towards him. The train was still rocking, but that wasn't the reason as to why they could hardly stand up, it was because they were both heavily under the influence of alcohol. They staggered past him laughing and giggling as they did so, Connor turned and watched them as they approached the toilet. The man looked around, smiled at Connor, pushed the woman inside and followed her in, locking the door behind him.

Connor smiled to himself.

The man hadn't been wearing a coat.

He walked along quickly entering the last carriage and looking into each separate 6 seater compartment and then he found the now empty one that the man and woman had obviously just been in. His jacket was thrown onto the seat and the woman's coat had slipped onto the floor.

He opened the door, quickly picked up the mans jacket and put it on. He then picked up the woman coat and threw it out the top window.

He hoped that they would spend the rest of the journey looking for their lost compartment, never mind their coats.

He went back through the train passing the toilet, which was still locked, and then waited for for the train to stop at the next station, Lisieux.

He was getting off.

As the train came slowly to a stop he waited. He waited at the edge of the door waiting for the train to start moving again. He knew that as the train left the station it went around a right hand bend. He didn't want the front carriage to be in his view when he got off.

He felt the train jerk forward and slowly start to move. As the train started to bend around to the right he slowly opened the door and jumped down onto the very end or the platform, and walked back towards the exit. As he got to the door he turned and watched the train moving slowly away in the distance, he tipped his hat and said to himself.

'Okay Major Klass, lets see how good you are on your own'.

It was time to find another bike.

Just over 2 1/2 hours later he was back in his hide and taking the binoculars from where he had hung them inside. There was no sign of him and no sign of anybody being in, or around his hide. He would look for Klass again in the morning. First though he had some work to do in the dark.

He needed to find an empty boat.

At half an hour past midnight he made his way out into the shadows and down to the harbour.

The journey down was uneventful. But to move around the harbour undetected was going to be testing to say the least. He had counted at least 8 soldiers, working in two's patrolling the harbour wall and the Quay. It was a lot different to a few days previously when they seemed to be concentrating on the town.

He quickly climbed down the ladder in the southwestern corner and as gently as he could, jumped on the first boat and worked from boat to boat where he could along the south side. He hopped from one to the next, looking inside them to see if they looked occupied or in use. On the second he found a roll of rope which was about half an inch thick and at least ten foot long. He placed his right arm through it and carried it on his shoulder. For the first seven boats he had no luck, they all seemed in use. But then as he jumped onto the eighth he noticed that the floor was much greasier than the previous seven. The deck hadn't been washed for sometime, he also saw that the rope that tethered it to the wall looked old and frayed. As he looked at the rope rising up toward the 'pile' to which it was tied, he noted that the rope had green moss and seaweed either growing or trapped in it. This boat had obviously been here a while.

'This will do', he thought.

He searched around the inside to see if he could find anything useful, and found nothing, apart from a large knife which was at least 8 inches long and was very rusty but very sharp.

He placed it, along with the rope, in the rear of the cupboard that ran along the stern.

The boat itself was called Le Dauphin (The Dolphin). It was a small fishing boat, some 20 feet shorter than the Rouge Gitan, but the cabin was big enough. Big enough for what he needed it for anyway.

He climbed back off the boat and travelled along back the way he had come.

He now needed to get to the Rouge Gitan, which was a problem.

It was moored on the opposite side of the harbour, the north side, about 100 metres away.

As he got back to the first of the seven he waited and watched and listened.

The tide was on the way out which meant that all the boats were sitting at least 12 feet below the harbour wall, gently bobbing up and down in the calmness of the basin. Which was good in one way, it meant that the soldiers that were on patrol and walking around the harbour would have difficulty in seeing him twelve foot below in the darkness.

But not good in the fact that unless the soldiers that walked by the side of his current location, walked next to the edge, he wouldn't see them either.

So he listened. There was nothing, just the gentle melodic sound of the ropes on the masts playing their happy tunes.

The ladder that he had come down on, was now just slightly to his left, about four feet away. He moved over to it and grabbed the rail and pulled himself up onto it.

He watched across to the other side and could see two soldiers walking on the eastern wall but they were walking away from him towards the outer wall.

He slowly climbed the ladder. It was slippy and wet and he struggled to grip the rails. As he got 2 rungs from the top he stopped again. He listened.

Footsteps, two sets, and getting louder, he moved his feet off the rung and let his hands loosen slightly causing him to slip quickly back down the ladder, and then at the last moment quickly bringing his feet back towards the ladder and at the same time gripping hard with his hands, he came to a shuddering stop, just a foot above the boat.

He waited listening hard and holding his breath.

The footsteps passed and got quieter until he couldn't hear them at all. He quickly climbed back up the ladder to where he had been before and stopped.

Silence.

He moved to the top, it was clear. He stepped onto the slippy cobbled footpath and ran silently across the ten yards before he reached one the seven storey high houses on the south side that looked out onto the harbour. He tried the wooden gate to the side of a window. It was open he stepped inside. He found himself in a damp cobbled alleyway. The curved brick roof just a foot from the top of his head. He walked slowly away from the gate and towards the back of house's.

He was in luck.

The rear of the house's opened out into a communal courtyard. He turned right and quickly walked about fifty yards, towards what he hoped was the far end house in the southwest corner. As he arrived he saw that he had been right. He then ran along the western side, still behind the house's, running parallel with the Rue du Dauphin to his left behind a seven foot high brick wall, all the way to the far end. Another damp cold alleyway, the same as the last, led back towards the harbour. As he very slowly opened the gate that led out into the street, he saw just 40 metres in front of him was the Rouge Gitan.

But so was the building, 'The Lueitenancy'.

He stayed in the darkness with the gate open to just halfway, watched and waited again.

As he looked out he could see three pairs of soldiers. All walking away from him, but where were the other two.

He stepped out and stopped.

Silence.

He walked quickly over to the shadows formed by the old building and stopped again.

Silence.

He sprinted towards the Gitan. Grabbed the top of the ladder above it and slid straight down.

Two minutes later he was back off the Gitan and into the shadows of the streets.

He'd left the captain a note.

'Moor close to Le Dauphin. B'

※ ※ ※

TO WIN OR LOSE

He woke early the next morning.

He had things to do.

He grabbed his binoculars from their hanger and looked down onto the harbour below. It was a fine October day. The sun, now rising above the horizon was shining brightly and not a cloud was in the sky.

He watched until just after midday and saw nothing of the man that he had hoped to see.

He was contemplating going down to the harbour to see if he could tempt him out into the open. 'He might not even be here, I might be giving him too much credit' he thought to himself.

And then he saw a man dressed in a cream Mac and black hat.

'Well done Major, you made it then' thought Connor.

He followed him with his binoculars walking around the harbour until he went from his view in front of the house's on the western side that had their backs to him. Two minutes later he very briefly came back into view before slipping behind the front of 'The Liuetenancy'.

A minute later he was back in view again as he reached the

outer wall beyond the Leuitenancy. He watched him looking at all the boats that were moored, held firm by their ropes tied to the 'piles'. He then stopped and lit a cigar.

A feeling of 'deja vu' waved over Connor.

It didn't stop.

He smiled to himself as Klass looked at one the house's over to his left on the western side, the row that faced directly out towards the estuary, on the very inside of the basin. He watched as he slowly took off his hat as if tipping it towards his invisible foe.

' Well Major' thought Connor, 'you had me right the last time, but this time your way off, I'm not in there. but I might be later'.

Klass replaced his hat and walked back towards 'The Liuetenancy' and out of view.

Connor didn't see him again all day.

But he saw Le Rouge Gitan. Captain Distan had moored it next to Le Dauphin.

As darkness fell, Connor slept. It was hopefully the last bit of sleep he would get for while. He woke a little after 01:00hrs and crept out of his whole. He made his way down to the harbour, a different route of course.

He knew that Klass was either watching from 'The Liuetenancy' or from one of the houses that fronted out onto the harbour. He'd make sure that Klass would catch a glimpse of him, not too obvious, but just something to get him interested.

As he got to the edge of the Harbour he stopped 40 metres short and climbed over the six foot wall to the rear of the last house that was on the northwest corner. It was the same house that he had walked down the alleyway towards the Rouge Gitan on the previous evening. He headed towards the south side along the same walled alley next to the Rue du Dauphin.

If he was a betting man Klass would be in one of the three at the far end of this row or the row that faced back towards 'The Leuitenancy' on the south side.

He walked along the rear of the houses, as usual keeping in the blackness where he could. As he got to the first of the last three he stopped and looked at the building. There were no lights on in any of them.

He carried on to the end of the row.

It was deathly quiet. No sound at all. No wind at all to help the bobbing boats play a tune. Nothing.

He turned the corner and slipped down behind the buildings on the south side.

Same result.

He moved back into the shadows right on the southwest corner and watched the rear of all the building in front of him, waiting, 'wait a while and it will come'.

He waited for almost an hour before anything happened, and then it was just a very brief glimpse of a very small flash of a dim light.

It had come from a fourth floor window of the second house on the southwest corner over to his right on the southern side.

It was a possibility. It would have an excellent view of all the harbour.

But then nothing.

He mapped the position of where it had been and worked it out where it would be when looking at the front of the same premise, because that was where he was going to next.

He moved around to the western side and tried the back door of the first house. It was locked and the door felt very sturdy, he put his shoulder to it, it didn't budge at all.

He moved to the next one.

Same result.

The third and fourth were the same.

He moved to the fifth.

Same again.

But not quite.

His attention had been drawn to a metal plant stand to the left of the door, hanging on the wall, or more specifically to the plant pot on the far left of the four that it held.

It wasn't resting on the bottom. something was propping it up.

He slowly lifted it up and placed his hand in the whole where it had been.

He found what he was looking for.

He placed the damp wet slightly muddy key in the door and turned it slowly, unlocking the door.

He quietly stepped inside and closed the door behind him, leaving it unlocked. Cain came straight into his head, he could hear him telling him,

'Never lock yourself in lad, you will find its much safer if you lock yourself out'.

He stopped at the bottom of the stairs, between the kitchen and the front room and listened.

The house was asleep.

He moved slowly through to the front room and towards the front door and stopped again, listening, not just for the inside but also for the outside.

Nothing.

The front door was solid oak, no window to look out of, he moved to the front window, he had wanted to move the curtain slightly to the side anyway.

Because he needed somebody to see it.

He went back to the door and slid back the bolts to unlock it, there was no key but that didn't matter.

He half opened it and listened.

Silence.

He stepped out pulling the door to behind him but not locking it, he couldn't, there was no key.

But to somebody watching from a fourth storey window, it would probably appear to be locked.

He looked around him, no soldiers, the quay was empty.

He ran across the cobbles and grabbed the top of the ladder and dropped straight down onto the first of the seven.

The tide was just on the turn and so the boats were barely six feet below the cobbled street.

Easy for anybody watching from a fourth storey window to see into them.

He jumped from boat to boat until he reached Le Dauphin and paused briefly to look behind him and towards the house's to his left.

But he eyes weren't looking towards the left.

To somebody looking from a fourth storey window his head might have been looking towards the left.

But his eyes were looking towards the right and towards the fourth floor of the second house from the end.

The curtain on the window on the fourth floor of the second house in, moved, a very slight, almost an inconceivable move, but it moved all the same.

It could, of course, have been the wind......

But there wasn't any wind.

'Got you' he thought to himself.

Now he needed to get back into the house.

He waited a few minutes then made his way back across the seven and up the ladder.

Stopped and looked.

Nothing.

He crossed the street and placed an invisible key towards the lock as if letting himself back in to the same front door of where he had left just a few minutes before, walked inside, locked it behind him and made his way through the house to the back door.

He crept outside and did the same, locked it behind him and placed the key back to where he had found it under the damp muddy plant pot and went back to his original hiding place, watching the house from the rear.

He was going to watch the rear of the houses because that was the way Klass would go.

He didn't have to wait for long. Just over half an hour later he heard a door very quietly open and close over to his right. It was 03:30 in the morning.

And then he watched as a man in a cream coat and black hat walked by him barely five foot away, smoking a cigar. He watched him walk all the way to the north-west corner and turn right towards the Leuitenancy.

He knew that he now had about a minute to get back to the Dolphin.

He ran around to the rear of the south side and turned right to run along the covered alley between the third and fourth houses. As he got to the gate that led out onto the quay he paused briefly before opening it.

Still no soldiers and still no sign of anybody watching from the Leuitenancy, but this was now definetly not the time for walking across the cobbles as he had done barely thirty minutes earlier, no, now was the time to use the blackness.

He'd seen where he needed to cross earlier on in the evening but he hadn't used it because he had needed to be seen, he wanted Klass to see where he was going. This time though he didn't want anybody to see him, not a soul.

Over to his right about fifty metres away, on the south side of the quay, the black shadow of the church's steeple above, crossed from the buildings and stretched all the way across the cobbled quayside and beyond into the water itself. The shadow was over 15 feet wide at its widest point. In its centre he would be invisible, total darkness. He walked along the house line keeping as close as he could remaining in the shadow of the house's until he met the shadow of the tallest building for miles around. And then he walked slowly down the middle of it, across the cobbles and jumped straight down over the edge and landed on number seven.

The one next door to number eight.

Le Dauphin.

He climbed aboard his abandoned boat and went to the stern. The small window at the rear looked out onto the harbour and towards the Leuitenancy. He was going to watch it but deep down he knew what was going to happen next. But he would watch it all the same.

Because it was exactly when it was going to happen that he still wasn't sure about.

Ten minutes earlier, Klass had been on the fourth floor of the second house from the southwest corner of the harbour. He had in fact, been there for a few hours, watching and waiting for his foe to move. He knew, or he thought it was most likely, that his man was within the buildings on the western side, or possibly on one of the boats.

In effect, he'd been right on both counts.

At around 03:10hrs he'd seen the briefest glimpse of a shadowy figure emerge from the front door of a house just 30 to forty metres in front of him. He saw him run across the quay and down towards the boats. For a moment he'd lost sight of him but then he felt sure he caught sight of him again getting into the side door of the cabin of a small fishing boat.

He had grabbed his binoculars that he had borrowed from the

sergeant at the lieutenancy and he was rewarded almost immediately when he saw him come back out onto the deck. It was definitely his man, no doubt about it. He watched as he saw him come back up the ladder and run across the cobbles to the same front door before letting himself in with a key.

He'd got it him. But now he needed some troops.

He had made his way along the back of the house's to the Leuitenancy and met with Major Keller, the lead officer assigned to the port of Hornfleur.

He had soon assigned twelve troops to assist him in entering and searching the house. Klass had briefly mentioned the boat but said he would see to that,

'it was nothing to worry about, I'll deal with it'.

He wanted to 'deal with it' for his own ego and satisfaction. He wanted to find things that he was sure his man was hiding on it. He didn't want anybody else grabbing his glory, not now, not at the final act, the climax of a magnificent piece of detection on his behalf.

And so it was there that that would be his downfall.

Klass had been told many times by his superiors that his own self importance sometimes got in the way of his judgement and could cloud his vision on occasions. This was no acceptation.

His vision was shortly to become very cloudy indeed.

At 04:30 Connor saw some movement from the left hand side of the Leuitenancy. Six soldiers moving quickly, walking towards the street that led to the rear of the houses on the western side. It was quickly followed by six more walking on the front of the houses along the quay, walking parallel to their comrades towards the house. Behind them walked a Major and behind them was Klass, smoking his cigar.

He watched them walk silently towards their target and then stop outside the big oak front door.

All apart from Klass who carried on walking and then stood at the ladder above boat number one.

The Major turned to look at Klass who nodded his head as approval and then a whole world of noise exploded as the troops smashed their way through the front door and, thought Connor ', the same at the back door'.

He then noticed a gentle rocking of his boat. Something had disturbed the mill pond. 'Klass was on his way' thought Connor.

He stood up and slowly walked to the left of the right hand cabin door.

He felt Le Dauphin rock a little more now. Somebody had come aboard.

He watched the handle of the door slowly move downwards. It had been stiff, Connor had noticed that when he had opened it earlier. The door slowly opened and then Klass walked in. Connor span him around and head butted him on the bridge of the nose smashing the bone to pieces. Klass stumbled backwards but Connor was on him immediately forcing him down onto the floor and punching him as hard as he could, winding him badly. Connor grabbed his rope and tied his hands. He had found an old rag covered in engine oil under the seat and stuffed it in Klass's mouth causing him to gag. The struggle didn't stop but became a lot more subdued when Connor put the rusty Fishermans knife to his throat. Klass's eyes wide, and staring darted from left to right looking for help that wasn't there. It was never going to be there either, the mayhem in the house was still going on judging by the noise that was coming from that direction.

Connor rolled his man over and tied Klass's feet together and then wrapped the same rope through the loop around his hands and pulled, he pulled hard causing Klass to scream as his arms made their way towards the back of his own feet, a movement only a gymnast would have been proud of.

Connor pulled him by the back of his cream coat, now with a nice crimson red bib on the front, and dragged him out the left hand door towards the edge of the boat. He jumped onto the Rouge Gitan and pulled Klass over the edge and down onto the deck of the Gitan with a thump.

He quickly pulled him inside the cabin, dragging him all the way to the small cabin at the rear and then propped him up against the side of a bench that ran along the stern. He breathed hard, trying to get his breath back.

For the first time they looked at each other in the eye. Connor wished that he had had a hat on so he could have tipped it towards him, but he didn't.

"Evening Major, or should I say morning, time flies when your'e enjoying yourself" said Connor.

Klass just looked at him, his eyes still full of worry, still not quite believing what had happened. He couldn't speak anyway, his mouth was still full of a diesel covered rag.

And then the boat moved.

Klass's eyes, changed to smiling eyes almost immediately.

Help was coming.

Connor grabbed the knife.

The door opened and in walked a tall man wearing a cap.

From the darkness Connor spoke,

"Good morning Captain Distan",

"Ah, good morning Billy its good to see you again" said the Captain,

"And I cant tell you how good it is to see you too, but I'm afraid I'm not alone this time, we have another passenger",

" I see" said the Captain " and may I presume that you have something to do with the commotion thats still going on in the house out there",

"Yes",

" Then perhaps we ought to be making our way as soon as possible",

"That would be good".

In less than five minutes they were leaving the inner harbour and making their way out to sea, to meet with the loch ness monster.

Once they had left the estuary Connor removed the cloth from Klass's mouth. He could scream and shout all he wanted now, nobody was going to hear him.

Connor sat on the bench and now having untied Klass's feet he had sat him up leaning against the port side of the boat.

"Are you going to kill me" asked Klass.

"Major, or should I say Captain, Captain James Plowman, which would you prefer",

"Lets be grown ups shall we, you can call me Fredric if I may call you Billy, or should I say Connor, Connor Gillian, which would you prefer",

Connor looked down at him and smiled,

"Connor is fine",

"That is good, you see Connor, as we sit here, don't you feel that sometimes the most profound conversations between men are sometimes held before one of them is about to die" said Klass,

"Thats very deep Major, I've never really thought of it like that, but I don't usually have conversations with people that I kill",

Klass smiled back.

"Fredric, its Fredric, are you sure about that Connor, didn't you have any conversation with a Mr Cain Milburn before you shot him all those years ago, or is it that long a go that you cant remember"

Connor's smile had gone.

Klass continued.

"You see Connor, I know a lot about you, a hell of a lot",

"I'm sure you do Major, but you know nothing that is going to hurt me now",

"No not hurt you, no, I agree with that, you have won this little battle I'll admit, I'm in no position that I can hurt you, not in a physical way anyway",

"And what exactly does that mean"

"It means Connor, I can help you"

"Really, and how can you help me"

"I could give you what you want, or I could take it away forever"

Connor looked at him hard. What was Klass playing at with these mind games, where was all this going.

"Why would you give me what I want, I'm taking you back to England, if you think that I'm turning this boat around because you might tell me something that I want to know your badly mistaken, they will deal with you back there" said Connor.

Klass looked him back in the eye and said,

"But I know where he is".

Connor knew who he meant instantly.

"Turn the boat around and I will tell you where he is" said Klass.

Connor did exactly what Klass wanted him to do.

He reacted.

Connor jumped down onto him and grabbed him around the throat, starting to strangle him.

"Your bluffing, your just trying to squirm and wiggle your way out of this, your a spy and your facing death, you don't know where he is, your lying through your cigar stained teeth",

Klass could hardly breath but strained to answer him,

"Am I, if you kill me you will never know will you".

Connor tightened his grip and Klass's eyes started to roll into the back of his head and then Klass whispered the last words that he thought he would ever speak.

"Father Henry Edmond Milburn, I know where he is".

The cabin door opened and Captain Distan dived on Connor and pulled him away.

Klass fell sideways onto the floor gasping for his breath.

"Billy no, not now, not on my boat, we leave it to the people that do this", said the captain pushing Connor towards the cabin door.

"Its okay, I'm sorry, I'm really sorry Captain" said Connor,

"Its okay" said Distan "you lift will soon be here, we need to get you both outside".

And so, as the two of them sat side by side, outside in the swaying boat, they looked at each other for the final time, one winner one loser.

Neither of them knowing which one was which.

By the following day Connor had returned to Snettisham hall. He had breakfast with Sergeant Hunt and then went to see Colonel Southall in his office.

The Colonel had somebody he wanted Connor to meet.

"Connor, I cant say how good it is to see you again" said the Colonel,

"Its good to see you too Sir".

They smiled and shook hands and the Colonel briefly placed his left hand on Connor's shoulder at the same time, as a small show of respect for the man that stood in front of him, small, but huge in impact for Connor.

The respect was totally equal.

"I want you to meet Emma" said the Colonel introducing the attractive 30 year old brunette who stood at his side.

"Please to meet you" said Connor.

"Please to meet you too Captain" came the quiet but confident reply.

"Emma here is going to work with you" said the Colonel,

The look of shock of Connor's face must have said it all but the Colonel quickly explained himself.

"What I mean by that Connor is that Emma is going to be working here for us and when you return from one of your trips, shall we say, you will sit down with her and recount as much information as you can recall and she will record it. All that information will be disseminated and used by various departments for future deployments. It doesn't matter if you cant remember everything and likewise, don't worry about giving us too much. We can weedle out what we need and what we don't later".

"Okay" said Connor "when do we start",

"Right now", smiled the Colonel

Over the next two days Connor emptied his brain.

Pages and pages of information were typed by the dutiful Emma. At times she sat in amazement at the clarity and exactness of the information being given. He would describe the routes he had taken in such detail that it appeared he had been watching from above, bird like almost, flying and photographing the scene below him, in all their colour and gravity, showing where troops were deployed, where tanks were hidden, where ambushes were likely to be, where problems were likely to occur, where rivers could be crossed, the best routes in and out of towns, everything the allies would need. But that was what Connor did. He stored all of these things within his brain, 'the gift', Cain had called it, and it was just that, a wonderful, wonderful gift.

* * *

NO PLACE LIKE HOME

Over the next two years Emma would sit in anticipation for when he would return. His brain full, ready to be emptied. She would worry as the days turned into weeks without any contact. She and Connor had grown close, very close as far as she was concerned, not so for Connor, she thought. But he kept his feelings deep within him. She knew that he liked her, but she wanted him to love her. But you couldn't make somebody love you. She knew that.

And now she waited again in anticipation. He was on the way home, Colonel Southall had told her exactly that, they were expecting him anytime within the next two days. He had also told her that they had managed to pass a message to him telling him that he needed to return to Snettisham as a matter of urgency. But he didn't tell her why.

The following morning she woke to see the sign that he was back, a dead poppy head, outside of her door. Whenever he returned he would always bring back the same thing and she would sprinkle the seeds from it into the gardens outside. Come summer time the poppy population would seem to have trebled from the previous year.

She hurried down to breakfast hoping to see him but he wasn't there yet, 'he must have got back late' she thought to herself.

He hadn't.

He'd been called to the Colonel's office by Sergeant Hunt at 07:00hrs.

As Connor walked into his office he knew immediately that something was wrong, he could see it on the Colonel's face. No formalities, no welcome back.

"Sit down Connor" said the Colonel.

"Thank you Sir" said Connor "is there something wrong",

"Yes Connor I'm afraid there is and I'm so sorry that I have to bring you such bad news this morning",

Connor looked at him trying to think what it could possibly be.

"What is it Sir, is it that bad",

The Colonel looked at him and handed him a telegram.

"I'm so very sorry Connor but its your Mother……She passed away four days a go."

Connor sat as if in a trance, the words still trying to get into his head but he didn't want to let them. 'My Mother dead, she can't be, she's all I've got left'.

He took the telegram from the Colonel and slowly, he let his brain read it.

'FOR THE ATTENTION OF CONNOR GILLIAN---STOP

DEAR CONNOR--STOP

I'M SO VERY SORRY TO INFORM YOU THAT YOUR MOTHER SUDDENLY PASSED AWAY ON SATURDAY 16TH OCTOBER 1943--STOP

SHE DIED PEACEFULLY IN HER SLEEP----STOP

SHE HAD ASKED ME THAT IF ANYTHING SHOULD HAPPEN TO HER I SHOULD INFORM YOU---STOP

SHE IS TO BE BURIED IN ROSSBRIDGE, COUNTY KERRY, IRELAND, AT 1PM ON FRIDAY 22ND OCTOBER 1943---STOP

I HOPE THAT YOU ARE SAFE AND WELL AND THAT YOU WILL BE ABLE TO ATTEND---STOP

SHE WOULD HAVE LIKED THAT--STOP

HER EVER LOVING HUSBAND---STOP

GEORGE----STOP

Connor's eyes filled with tears as he looked at the message again, and then he read it again and again.

"Connor" said the Colonel, half waking him from his trance.

"As I have said, I'm so sorry to have to inform you of this but you must, and I will insist on this, take some time off. You need to go home".

Connor listened to what he was saying and tried to make sense of what was being said, but it was as if he had suddenly been bought to the realisation of one simple fact.

'Actually, he no longer had a home'.

Arrangements had been made for Connor to return to Ireland by plane on the following day Wednesday 20th. He was to stay for as long as he needed and when he wanted to return he was to get in touch with the Colonel by telegram.

"Go home Connor and rest, there's something brewing that we need you for and we need you to be fully rested and ready to go. I cant tell you what, obviously, but it's big. Our thoughts will be with you and if you need anything then you let me know immediately" said the Colonel.

Connor looked at him and nodded his appreciation.

"Thank you Sir, your'e a good man" said Connor.

The Colonel waved away the compliment,

" But you rest, understood" he said,

"Understood" said Connor.

The next day, having spent some time with Emma, he flew to Kerry aerodrome in south west Ireland, it was just 12 miles from Tralee, but he'd never been there before.

He was given the use of a car. They said that he had been designated a driver but he refused the offer and took the car himself.

'I always work alone'.

He headed for Tralee but found himself slowly but surely being drawn towards Rossbridge. The funeral wasn't for another two days but he felt that he needed to go and see the place he used to call his home.

As he came over the brow of the hill he slowed as he passed the burnt out ruins of Manor Farm. He felt nothing, no sadness, no anger, no remorse, nothing, until he saw another much smaller building further down the hill.

Rose Cottage.

For the first time in over eighteen years, he was back at the place he used to call 'home'.

He stopped the car outside and for the next thirty minutes he just sat and looked at it. The memories, so many of them coming flooding back in waves. Some bad, but mostly wonderful happy ones.

He remembered his grandad Riley, his wonderful stories and his loving way, he remembered his mother, some of it real and some of it from his dreams and nightmares. And then he remembered his Nana, her wonderful caring ways, her heart of a lion, his Nana, full of joy and happiness, her smiling eyes and cheeky grin. He realised then that he missed them all so much and he missed having a home. But now he was back home and it felt so good.

He could see from the outside that Rose Cottage was empty. The curtains he felt sure were still the same. The front door, still painted green, but had faded and some of the paint had peeled off.

He got out of the car and walked around the back and into the courtyard. The weeds and grass were waist high. The painted windows, like the front door, were in poor repair and the barns were only just standing. One of them had no roof at all. He walked into the barn with the roof. The feed store was still up there above him but the ladder had gone. He looked around for it and caught sight of a piece of wood buried beneath some dusty hay and straw. As he got to it he pulled it out. It was the ladder, minus a rung or three but it would do.

He placed it against the edge of the feed store and as he got to the top he pulled himself over the edge and made his way to his old hiding place. He reached around with his hand and found what he was looking for.

His mother's letter. Still there, dusty, but nobody had found it and nothing had started to eat it. He placed it in his pocket and went across to the right, and put his hand into his grandad's hiding place. It's contents were still there too. He pulled out the rolled up rag unrolled it and placed the gun in his waistband and slid back down the ladder.

He walked into the kitchen through the unlocked door and stood looking around.

Somebody had clearly lived there since he had left but nobody had been in there for years. He wondered if it had been Molly. He sat down at the kitchen table and didn't move for almost three hours, reading his mother's letter over and over again and then sitting deep in his thoughts and memories.

Some good, Some bad.

And then he went upstairs and went to sleep.

The next morning he was up early. He had things to do and people to go and see. Whether they would see him was another matter.

He headed for the square in the centre of Tralee, parked his car and decided to have a walk around the town. The pubs were still there, the Stonebridge and The Raindeer. Nothing else had changed much either, the market was busy, the smells of the various stalls were still the same, the aroma's of cooked meat mingled with that of the vegetables and flowers.

And then he saw the first one.

The first one of three.

Byrne.

Lanny Byrne, now an old man in his early seventies, but the red hair was still there. Connor watched as he went into the front door of number 27 Market Square.

He made his way around to the back of the house along the Clog Istigh. He knew where the back gate would be, he had worked that out in his brain already. He lifted the latch and stepped inside the rear yard. A small Jack Russell ran up to him barking out its warning to anybody that would listen. He stepped to the side, moving behind the outside toilet and the dog followed him. He knelt down on the floor and began to stroke the head of the dog, it stopped barking almost immediately.

He heard the back door open and then a man's voice shouted 'Eric'.

'Nice name' he thought.

Slow steps on the cobbles followed by another 'Eric'.

He let the red haired man walk by him and towards the gate.

"Eric's here with me, Mr Byrne".

Byrne stopped he didn't turn around he just stood with his back to him, deadly still.

"Did you hear me Mr Byrne" said Connor.

He watched the man, still with His back to him, slowly nod his head.

"Yes I heard you boy", said Byrne "Are you here to kill me",

"I don't know yet, it depends on what you have to tell me" said Connor,

"because if you are, I don't want to see it, just get it over and done with",

"Mr Byrne shall we go inside, I need to ask you a few questions",

Byrne slowly turned around and looked at the boy who he had

last seen nearly twenty years ago, and nodded his head.

They went into the kitchen and sat down at the table, Eric, now sat on Connor's lap, was enjoying his new friend gently stroking him.

"Would you like a cup of tea or something stronger" said the frail old man shuffling across the small kitchen.

"Tea is fine, I'm not one for drink" said Connor. Byrne filled the kettle and put it on the hot stove. He turned toward his visitor and said,

"We have been told you might be coming over, we have heard about the news of your Mother, I'm very sorry about your loss".

Connor looked at him.

"Are you. Why are you sorry Mr Byrne, she was nothing to you, you didn't know her",

"No son, your'e right, I didn't know her, but I knew what happened on that day when your father was killed. Why she had to run away. We all knew, Cain told the three of us".

Byrne then sat with Connor and told him the story that Cain had himself told him of exactly what had happened on that fateful day and why his mother had to flee for her life.

"Did you believe him" said Connor,

"Who Cain" he looked at Connor who nodded his response,

"Yes I believed him, why wouldn't I. Why would he tell us a lie about killing somebody. No, It definitely happened the way I just told you. If he hadn't been so trusting of that idiot 'Parrot' none of it would have happened, but it did. Parrot was a coward running away like that, he should have faced the music",

"Is that what he did, he ran away",

"Yes, never to be seen again. Cain hated him for that, leaving him to try and sort all the mess that he had created. Cain had just been giving the boy a warning shot nothing more, but like I just said, Parrot shot the lad in the back".

Connor stared at the wall, imagining his Father seemingly running for his life and then his Mother being stalked by Parrot before she smashed the rock into his face and killing him.

He was bought back to his senses by Byrne.

"And what of Henry, have you caught up with him yet, he knows you want to find him" said Byrne.

"Still looking, but I'll not stop, we have some catching up to do. Do you know where they are",

"I'm sure you have, and no I don't know where they are, but what I do know is they are not in Ireland. What will you do when you do find him",

"Well I wont be having a cup of tea with him thats for sure".

They smiled at each other as Connor stood up.

"And what of me then lad, ……are we done" said Byrne.

Connor paused a while before he held out his hand to shake that of Byrne's and then he said.

"Yes Mr Byrne we are done. Your'e lucky, I like Eric. I wouldn't want him to be on his own, it's not very nice being on your own".

Connor made his way towards the back door and Byrne said

"I wont tell Dermot or Niall you have been to see me",

"You tell them what you want Mr Byrne, it wont change anything. I will still kill them if I need to".

He stepped out the door and closed it behind him.

He wasn't going to go to their houses to find them. 'They knew he was coming', but he knew where they would be.

At a little after one o'clock he walked back to his car and placed the gun under the seat. He then walked across the square and climbed the steps and entered the bar of the Raindeer.

Brady and Ramsey sat right there in the Holy corner, Three pints of beer on the table in front of the two of them.

'They knew he was coming'.

Connor walked straight over to them and sat down.

"Good day Connor, you haven't changed at all, it's good to see you again" said Brady with a tinge of sarcasm, Ramsey just looked at him and nodded.

"Is it" said Connor, "whats good about it, why does everybody seem so pleased to see me all of a sudden",

"Come on Connor lad, have a pint with us" said Brady pushing the pint over towards him.

As Connor grasped the pint pot he sensed somebody behind him, not one but two people.

"Let me introduce you to Manny and Tommy", said Brady "they're my boys, they have come to luck after their Grandad, just to make sure no harm comes to me".

Connor stood up but was stopped from turning around by two sets of hands gripping his arms. Brady looked to the one on Connor's left and said,

"Check him Manny".

Manny then brushed his hand all over Connor but found nothing, 'a reasonable search but not a good one, not a professional' thought Connor.

Manny shook his head and Brady nodded as a sign that they could leave them alone. But they didn't go far, just back over to the other side of the bar, to where Connor had seen them when he entered.

"So Connor what do you want with us, are you here because you've missed us so much, or is it that you felt you needed to go down memory lane" said Brady.

Connor sat quiet for a moment before he answered.

"I'm here to bury my Mother Mr Brady",

"Ah yes your Mother, somebody told me that the bitch was coming back, but I actually didn't know, until yesterday, that the good news was that she was actually dead, it wasn't till yesterday either that we knew her Bastard son would be coming as well",

Connor showed no reaction but just stared at Brady for a moment……

"Mr Brady, I understand that you may not like me being here, but I ask for your respect whilst I lay my mother to rest. That is all",

Brady started to laugh, a laugh full of contempt for the man that sat opposite him.

"Your'e asking for my respect, …… are you fucking serious. Do you honestly think you can just wander back into Ireland as if nothing has happened. You are responsible for the death of a very good friend of mine and now you want my respect".

Connor looked him in the eye.

"This friend of yours that was killed, you know I was responsible do you, could I ask how you know that" said Connor,

"Don't you worry boy, I know, we all know, we haven't any proof, but you see Connor, we don't work on proof, were not the bloody police, we don't need any evidence, all we need is the belief that you killed him, and there lies your problem, because we, all of us that are still alive to remember, we believe that you killed Cain, and that my old friend, is enough, so no, I wont give you respect and I wont give that whore of a mother of yours any either, do I make myself clear".

Connor still showed no reaction and answered him calmly.

"Clear enough Mr Brady, but it's not you I'm here for. As I've said, I've come to bury my Mother, I've no interest in what you believe that I may have or have not done. So tomorrow, I will go to the church and see my Mother given up to god and then I will be gone, if you can't bring yourself to let me do that then please don't say that I didn't warn you."

It was Brady's turn to sit quietly for a moment before he answered.

"Your aren't threatening me are you Connor",

Connor leaned over the table closer to Brady, barely a foot away from him and almost in a whisper he said.

"Mr Brady, I have obviously not made myself clear, because yes, I am threatening you, because tomorrow, my mother shall be buried in peace and her resting place shall remain untouched for ever more, because if its not, for as long as I live and breath, I will hunt you down and I will kill you".

Connor leaned back onto his seat and looked around the bar as if taking taking in the surroundings.

"There's no plaque on the wall if thats what your looking for", said Brady

"I'm sorry" said Connor,

"The last time a Gillian sat here, it didn't go so well, but you knew that anyway didn't you" smiled Brady.

Connor looked at him, no reaction.

"They cleaned the place up real well didn't they, no sign of anything, no blood, no bits of bone, nothing" said Brady.

Still no reaction.

"Thats enough Dermo" said Ramsey,

"Is it fuck" said Brady,

"I said thats enough" said Ramsey again.

"Connor, Is there anything that we can help you with, because if not, your'e probably best to leave, you have my word, we won't bother you while you bury your Mother but after that I can't guarantee your safety, your not welcome here" said Ramsey.

Connor didn't look at Ramsey but remained staring at Brady as he spoke.

"And what about his, do I have his word or not",

Brady went to speak but Ramsey put his hand on his friends chest silencing him immediately.

"Yes, you have his word",

"Thank you, you have both been very helpful, there's nothing else I need, I'll see you again no doubt".

He took a small sip of his drink and nodded his goodbye.

As he watched him begin to turn and walk away Brady looked at him and said "Oh I'm sure we will" and then he spat on the floor.

Connor ignored it and walked towards the exit, passing the younger Brady's on the way out, subconsciously memorising their faces and everything else about them.

He spent the rest of the afternoon visiting his Nana's and Riley's grave in Rossbridge church. A whole in the ground gave away where his Mother was to be buried, just to the left of his Nana and Riley the soil at the side turning to mud as the rain coming in from the West turned the tiny picturesque graveyard into a windblown quagmire.

By early evening he had returned to Rose Cottage. He parked his car half of the grass edge half on the road by the front door and walked around the back. The rain still lashing down from the angry grey clouds above.

He went inside and then upstairs closing the curtains in the front bedroom and lit a candle, whilst taking the briefest of glimpses across the fields towards the small copse about 500 yards away to the East on the edge of the road that led southwards towards Farranfore. His watchers were 'probably getting very wet' he thought. He couldn't see them but thats where they would be, he was sure of it.

He was right on both counts. Manny and Tommy were on the very edge of the trees and yes .... They were very very wet.

'They would be back in home not much after midnight' thought Connor.

He lay on the bed and went to sleep.

At a little before midnight he woke and sat up in bed. He rolled out sideways and dropped onto the floor and crawled across to the front window and blew out the candle. The rain was still falling heavily and he opened the curtain just enough to see across to where he knew the road met the copse. He couldn't see it but he knew exactly where it was, he'd looked out towards that unchanging view that he had looked at thousands of times over the years. And then he waited.

Not five minutes later, the giveaway lights of a vehicle were switched on, and then they slowly started to move north along the road towards Tralee. Two minutes later they were gone. So he went back to sleep.

His night had been full of dreams, all of them about his mother. And he could see her face in every one of them. He woke up happy but wished that just one of them had been real.

He dressed in his suit, not a uniform, the Colonel had insisted that he shouldn't wear it, he wanted him back alive and well.

At just after midday he left by the kitchen door and made his way on foot towards the village and the church.

It was barely a ten minute walk but the rain had stopped so he ambled slowly down the hill. A car approached him from behind, he knew who it was going to be but it wasn't their fault, they were just following orders.

As it slowly went by he saw that Manny was the driver and Tommy was sat in the front passenger seat. They both nodded towards him and Connor nodded back. He watched as it passed the church 50 yards in front of him and then stopped just beyond.

'Don't get out boys, please, not today' thought Connor.

They didn't, they stayed inside.

He walked up towards the church door and slowly opened it. It was empty.

He walked to the front row and knelt down below the crucified christ and dipped his head. He'd never been one for religion, he could take it or leave it, but today, out of respect for his mother and Nana, he whispered a small prayer.

As he stood back up the church door opened and the Priest stepped inside. Connor had never seen him before but he knew who Connor was.

"Hello Connor, its good that you could make it" he said and held out his hand "I'm Father Mathew, I'm the Priest of this parish",

"Its good to meet you Father, are you expecting anybody else today or am I it", said Connor looking around the empty building.

"No, no, your'e not 'it', your mother's husband, George, is with her now and I believe there are a few more people that knew your mother from her theatre days are supposed to be coming, I never met your mother but by all accounts she was a well respected actress was she not".

Connor stood and for a moment, lost in his thoughts. His mind going back to the short but so wonderful time he spent with her in her new home of America. He'd been to see her in a play in somewhere called Broadway. She had said that she had a part in it and she would be thrilled to have him there to see her. It had been her dream for so long that he would attend along with his Nana but sadly that had never happened. He had gone alone to watch her and as the play went on he sat it utter amazement as his mother put on the show of her life, playing the leading lady in a play called Bachelor's Brides. At the end of it he had felt utterly overwhelmed and so proud of her that he just stood, and along with everybody else, clapping and cheering, but he, her son, was the only one that could shout, and he did, very, very, loudly, "that's my Mother, that's my Mother". People were slapping him on the back shouting 'bravo, bravo' it had been the proudest moment of his life and still was too this day.

"She was wonderful", Connor managed to say eventually "Truly wonderful",

"I'm sure she was Connor. Would you mind doing something for me" said the Priest.

Connor looked at the smiling Priest.

"Yes of course Father, anything I can do to help",

"Excellent, would you mind saying some words about your mother to the congregation".

Connor had never spoken in public and was a little taken aback by the request.

"I'm sure your Mother would have liked that you know" said the Priest sensing Connor's hesitation. "A few words thats all".

Connor looked at him and nodded.

"Have you a pen and paper" said Connor,

"I have" said a woman's voice from behind him.

He turned around to see who it was.

It was Molly.

She stood there smiling at him and then held out her arms to embrace him. They kissed each other on the cheek and then she introduced him to a young girl stood by her side.

"This is my daughter Emily, and Emily, this is my old friend who I have told you and your brother and sister about, this is Connor".

They smiled at each other and Connor gently shook her hand.

She placed her hand inside her handbag and handed him a piece of paper. Connor then sat down on the front row and asked Molly if she would like to join him, which she did.

As he began to sit and write Molly held out her hand and smiled at him.

"Give it to me, you tell me what to write",

He smiled back at her, "thank you Molly" he said.

As he and Molly slowly worked on what he was going to say, they were lost in concentration, totally oblivious as to what was actually going on behind them.

The church was slowly but surely filling up with people.

A short time later the Priest walked over to Connor and bent down a little to speak to him.

"Are you nearly ready Connor, your mother has arrived outside" said the Priest.

Connor, his mind thinking of other things, looked up at the Priest.

"Sorry Father, yes I'm ready" said Connor.

The Priest smiled at him and said softly.

"I told you that you wouldn't be alone" and at that he looked over Connor's shoulder and nodded towards the congregation behind him.

He stood and turned to look behind him and then looked in absolute amazement.

He couldn't believe what he was seeing, the church was completely full, people were having to stand down both sides, out the side doorway, all along the back beyond the pews. Theyr'e were hundreds and hundreds of people.

Molly looked at Connor, the shock on his face was saying it all.

"Your Mother was well and truly loved Connor",

Connor couldn't speak, for the first time in his life he was totally overwhelmed.

The service began and the Priest spoke his words, the hymns were sung, and the prayers were said, and then the Priest said.

"May I now ask Aibbi's son Connor to say a few words about his Mother".

As Connor stood a small whisper went around the seated and the standing, but then as he climbed the pulpit it suddenly stopped.

You could have heard a speck of dust drop let alone a pin.

As Connor raised his head, he realised he had never seen so many people in one place, and all of them looking straight at him. He was used to working in the shadows, not like his Mother, in the spotlight.

'She must have been absolutely petrified' he thought to himself.

He coughed slightly to clear his throat and then steadied himself before he spoke.

"Firstly, I would like to thank you all for coming today.

To see you all here really is something of a shock to me. I feared that I may be burying my mother alone. Clearly now, that is something that I shouldn't have been worried about.

I know now that many of you have come a very long way, so where ever you have all come from, whether that be a thousand miles or just one, I would like to thank you all from the bottom of my heart for helping me to give her a good send off. I think she would have liked that.

I would just like to take this opportunity to say a few words about her if you wouldn't mind.

My Mother.

My Mother grew up in this village of Rossbridge and until the age of sixteen she lived with her parents Diabbi and Riley in Rose cottage on the outskirts of the village. She had known my Father, Mally, for sometime and although they were very young, she told me that she had loved him very much.

I never knew my Father, I wish that I had but sadly it proved to be that my father had been killed, murdered in fact, before I had even been born.

Sadly, through my younger years, when I was growing up, I didn't see my mother, because I couldn't. Many of you sat here in this church, might not even have known that she indeed ever had a son, but she did, and here I am.

My mother then moved away to Dublin, not because she wanted to but because she had to.

When I was two years old she left me with my grandparents,

mainly for my own safety but also for hers. Her life was in danger, and that was something that sadly, never went away.

I do not hold that against her, I never have and I never will. I know now why my mother had to go away, I know because she told me, and please believe me when I say that she really did have to go away.

I have heard it said that she abandoned me.

She didn't.

In later life when we were reunited, I found her to be the most caring, wonderful person. Her heart was warm and loving and I knew that she truly loved me as I did her. We had been kept apart not because she or I wanted it but because circumstances had made it so.

For a few years I was fortunate to live with her and George in America and as I look around the faces in front of me I realise that I have met some of you before, please forgive me if I do not know your names, I may not have been told them, but all the same, whoever you are, I thank you all for coming here today.

I'm so very happy that she met and married George, and I thank you George for loving her and looking after her and making her so happy with life for she truly deserved some happiness.

Some of you, as I do, knew her as Aibrean, some of you knew her as Aibbi, but it's most likely, for most of you present, you knew her as Ellen, Ellen Gillian, star of the stage and theatre.

But it gives me so much happiness that I can say that I ..... I knew her as "Mother" and that is truly the most wonderful feeling someone could ever have.

So today I'm not here to say goodbye.

She will remain in my heart and in my memories for ever more.

I hope that she will be in yours too.

In my dreams she will never grow old. But will be young and full of life.

Sleep tight my darling Mother.

God bless you'.

The church was deathly silent, it as if the building itself was holding its breath, if Connor couldn't have seen the throng of people in front of him, he would have thought they had all left.

But then it began, at first a small ripple, but then it grew and grew, the sound of applause echoing around the church, people everywhere were beginning to stand, and then it was if he had been back at the theatre on Broadway as the shouts of "bravo, bravo, reverberated around the big stoned building.

His first and probably his one and only standing ovation, and all thanks to his Mother.

As the service grew to a close George, who had been sitting next to Molly and her Daughter leaned over and whispered to Connor.

"Would it be okay if some of her friends came to the burial, not all of them obviously, just a handful of close friends, thats all",

" George, of course it's okay, you have whoever you want at the graveside, myself, Molly here, and Emily, obviously will be there, but apart from that there's nobody else, not unless I get any more surprises" smiled Connor.

And so as they walked outside, the majority of the church drifted away and left Connor, Molly, Emily, George and the few select friends to gather around the graveside.

As they slowly lowered her into the ground Connor looked up and saw three men standing over by the edge of the graveyard about fifty yards away.

Two young men stood either side of one old man.

The two young ones had their heads bowed in respect.

The old man didn't.

The old man was smiling and laughing.

It was the last smile his face would ever have.

Connor would be making sure of it.

Connor spent the afternoon talking to many of his Mother's friends at the small town hall that George had hired out for the wake. Over 200 of them had sailed over to pay their respects to a woman from Ireland with beautiful thick strawberry blonde hair, who they had grown to love and admire in their homeland of North America.

He also spent time with Molly, she told him that indeed it was her that had stayed and lived in Rose Cottage. She had lived there for just over five years, quietly hoping that he would return one day but sadly that was not to be. She left when she had an offer of a new job in a school in Limerick, her mind was in turmoil for weeks before she decided that she couldn't wait for him any longer. She left for Limerick and after a year she met and then married her husband Tom, having two children with him both girls. She then saw an advert in her local newspaper advertising the headmistresses job at the school in Rossbridge. She jumped at the chance to return to the place that she called home.

"Nobody lived in Rose Cottage after I left Connor. It has been empty ever since" she said,

"What happened to Duke, do you know" said Connor.

"Yes I do, he was taken in by the Lord's, he died a contented retired milk float puller, I can assure you of that".

Connor smiled. He liked that.

Molly said her goodbye's apologising that she had to leave but she had to return to get her husbands and son's dinner ready "they would be home soon from work and they don't like to be hungry" she smiled.

As the darkness began to fall he himself said his farewell's and made his way back to Rose Cottage. He was going to get some rest. As he walked into the bedroom he took the candle, snapped it in half and lit it.

Tonight he was going back to Tralee. To work in all the shadows that he knew so well. He knew where each and every one of them was. Their denseness, their size, their angles, their heights, every single thing about them.

He was going back to his other home in the shadows.

At a little before 9:30pm he slipped out the back door and into the fields behind.

He hadn't blown out the candle.

It had at least another 3 hours of life left in it.

'That should be enough' he thought.

Within an hour he was in the centre of Tralee and in the darkness. He walked past the side of The Raindeer and took the briefest of glimpses through the bullnosed glass window. Sat in the holy corner was a big man and a not so big man.

He'd found who he was looking for.

Five minutes later they came out.

'Be a creature of habit Mr Brady, just for me and my Mother' thought Connor.

He did.

The two of them crossed the square, swaying a little and bumping into each other occasionally.

Connor ran down the cobbled street towards River walk.

Ten minutes later the two men walked into 11 River walk. They sat in the front room laughing and smoking and drinking some Irish malt whiskey that Ramsey had stolen from somewhere the day before.

At 00:15hrs his candle went out at Rose cottage.

Half an hour after that a double tap on the front door of number 11 alerted them that somebody was outside.

Ramsey walked to the front door and said quietly,

"Yes",

"It's Dan" came the reply.

Ramsey slowly opened the door and let the two brothers in.

"So" said Brady.

"So,....the lights went out at a quarter past midnight and so he's fucking asleep", said Manny "Its fucking freezing up there, waste of fucking time, thats what it is".

Brady got up and walked over to his eldest grandson and put his head right next to his.

"Now you just listen to me boy, I will tell you when it's a fucking waste of time, and this ain't a waste of time and I'll tell you why. That animal out there that you have been watching, is the most clever devious human being that you or I will ever have the displeasure to meet. What that bastard can do is not natural, it's as if he isn't human at all, he's a freak of nature. He can walk around as if he's invisible and so, he's a very dangerous man, very, very dangerous. So no, it's not been a waste of time at all. I need to know when he's back on that plane and going back across the water, until then you pair of fuckers are going to keep Niall here and me safe. Do you understand",

Manny stood and nodded his head, trying not to breath in the putrid breath of his Grandfather.

"Good" said Brady "now one of you stands at the river end of this street and one of you stands at the other. It's not hard any idiot can do it. I want you watching all the time. Don't bother hiding because he will see you anyway. Just front it out and stand on the street and if you see him, you fucking give him what for, but remember we don't kill him, we have to save that pleasure for the Boss. Now fuck off outside before it's too late".

The two young men stepped back out into the cold, one went right and one went left.

But It was already too late.

Connor had been in the loft of 11 River Walk not long after they had crossed the square.

2 hours later Connor dropped down from the loft, with a piece of 2x2 inch timber he had found in the rafters, in his hand. He opened the first bedroom door and looked inside. A small person was covered over with blankets. He could see it was an elderly woman. He closed the door gently behind him and moved to the second bedroom. Again he slowly opened the door. This time it was a very large framed man.

Ramsey.

Connor crept inside and hit him hard on the back of the head with his timber weapon, knocking him out cold. He hit him again across his left side and then once on his leg. Nothing too powerful, just enough to give him some bruising. He grabbed Ramsey's left hand and took off a gold signet ring, which he had seen him wearing the day before. He had noticed that he wore it the wrong way around, as in the face that held the diamond stone was on the inside of the finger, on the palm side of his hand. He placed it on his own left hand ring finger and made his way outside the door and quietly closed it behind him. He moved slowly down the stairs and into the front room.

Brady lay on the sofa in his drunken stooper snoring loudly. 'It seemed such a shame to wake him' he thought, but he was going to all the same. He wanted him to see who was about to send him to his maker.

Connor placed the timber gently across his throat then kneeled on it either side of his short stubby neck. He flicked the end of his nose and woke him up.

Brady's eyes stared wide eyed in shock but he quickly realised who it was.

"I asked you for your respect, but you couldn't give me or my mother any at all could you" said Connor quietly.

Brady couldn't answer, the plank of wood was pressing down

hard onto his adams apple. He tried to speak with his eyes, pleading with him to release the choking piece of wood from his throat.

"Where's your Boss" said Connor and then ever so slightly released a tiny bit of pressure with his knees.

Brady croaked his response of "who" which had the immediate effect of Connor putting the pressure back on.

"You know full well who I mean Mr Brady, but if you need me to spell it out to help you, where is Father Henry Edmond Milburn",

He let the pressure off again.

"He's over the water" whispered Brady,

"Well done Mr Brady" said Connor " and where exactly over the water would that be then",

"I don't know, I really don't know",

"That's a shame Mr Brady, I was hoping that you might want to help me",

"I do, but I don't know. All I know is that he may be going to France",

Connor looked at him in the eye. He believed him.

He took the piece of wood from his throat and replaced it with his left hand.

"All I wanted was respect for my Mother, that was all"

He tightened his grip now with both hands and strangled him.

Two minutes later he crept back up the stairs and walked into Ramsey's bedroom. He placed the piece of wood at the side of his bed.

Then he took off the signet ring and placed it back onto Ramsey's wedding finger, turning the ring so the stone was back on the inside, the palm side.

Forensic science had come along way.

He climbed back into the loft and went back the way he had

come. Hopping from loft to loft across the top of the rafters in the row of houses on River Walk. As he reached the end house he lowered himself down through the open hole and landed at the top of the stairs. The house was unoccupied and had been for some time. He'd spotted it on his walkabout on the day he had arrived. The house had looked like it had been empty for a long time. He stepped out the back door and into the yard and then pulled himself silently up onto the 6' wall. He looked to his left and saw the shape of a young man stood half asleep leaning his head against the wall about 10 foot away.

It was Tommy.

Connor dropped down silently onto the cobbled street and turned right, away from his watcher, and walked in the shadows and out onto the square.

As Connor walked away, he could see the headline now.

'A drink fuelled night turns to Murder'.

6 hours later he climbed into his bed at Snettisham. It had been a busy day.

* * *

DOGS OF WAR

December 1943

He'd had a bad feeling about his latest assignment. He didn't know why. Was it that he hadn't been to that specific area before. Not really, he'd been to new places before and it hadn't worried him at all.

It wasn't what he had been told what was required of him, he had done all what he had been asked to do, tens of times before.

It wasn't apprehension, it was something else.

He didn't want to go.

Was it because of the recent loss of his Mother, or was it because Emma didn't want him to go, he really was'nt sure. She hadn't told him so but he knew. He and Emma had become very close. She wanted more, he knew that and so did he, but something always held him back.

Being a friend of his was a very dangerous pastime.

Some scars would never heal.

And so....on a freezing cold winters evening Connor said his goodbyes and climbed in the car with Sergeant Hunt. He was off to Langham to get his flight.

He was going to Normandy.

They wanted him to look at some beaches.

For the next five months he stayed in the area of Normandy. Moving around constantly hiding in houses and his own man made hideaways, which he could return to when in their area. He had had a few close calls with the enemy but nothing that he couldn't handle. All the time he fed back the usual information with the help of his feathered friends and dead drops.

But then at the end of May 1944 they sent a message to one of his dead drops, it said that he needed to make his way to the area of Ouistreham.

He'd been there a few weeks earlier and he hadn't enjoyed the experience at all.

The place had been absolutely full of Germans.

Having been away now for over five months, he was beginning to feel it both physically and mentally. His body was starting to fight back against the constant adrenaline rushes and battering's that it was taking. He was taking longer to recover. He also knew that because of it, he was now at his most vulnerable. His concentration had occasionally started to lapse and he had found himself sleeping so heavily, that some days he wasn't waking up until nearly midday. But now, they wanted him to go back to Ouistreham, somewhere where he would need to be at the peak of concentration and alertness. But he knew that he wasn't, and he wasn't likely to be anytime soon.

He had made his way close to the village of Merville which was about a mile and a half to the East of Ouistreham. It was early evening so he decided that he should stop for the night in the small wood about 3/4 of a mile south of Merville.

As usual he dug his whole, not the best but it would do for one night. He settled down in his hide and started to eat the loaf of bread he had stolen earlier in the day.

Shortly after he heard them.

Dogs.

He could deal with a dog, he knew that. But more than one was a bit more of a problem.

And there was definitely more than one.

It sounded like there was at least three but possibly more.

The barking was coming from directly in front of him but he

couldn't see them. They sounded like they were at least a hundred metres away but in the darkening light he couldn't be sure. But the barking was definetly getting louder and louder.

They were coming his way.

He had to make a decision and make it quick.

Run or stay.

He ran.

He got up from his whole and climbed out the back and ran further into the wood. The further he went, the darker it got.

Normally, darkness was a good thing, but that was when you were hiding from humans.

Dogs hunted with their nose not their eyes.

They were closing on him and fast. He could hear the owners shouting their dogs.

And they were shouting in German.

He could hear them getting closer and closer, it felt as if they were running at his side.

As the first dog got to him it bit into his right arm, and it didn't let go.

As the second arrived it took a leg, making him fall to the ground. The third and fourth would no doubt be soon to arrive. Now he knew he was in desperate trouble.

Somebody had once told him that if a dog was to bite you then the way to get it to release its hold was to pick it up by the back legs. Fine in theory, not good in practice. Of all the dogs that Connor had come across, their teeth were at the front and no where near the back legs.

He rolled over and over, the dog that had his leg was forced to let him go but the one on his arm was having none of it. He punched it in the face as hard as he could causing the dog to yelp loudly and fall away. He climbed to his feet and ran again, blindly now through the pitch black darkness of the wood, trees smacking him in the face and lashing at his legs. And then out of the blackness he saw a brick building loom up in front of him. Decision time again. Take refuge in the building or carry on running.

He knew it was only a matter of time before the dogs caught him again, and when they did he doubted he would be so lucky the next time. He ran to the building and pulled on the wooden door. It opened, he jumped inside and pulled the door behind him. He stood panting for breath. His heart pounding and his head banging with the pain from the bites on his arms and legs.

And then he heard them again.

But they weren't barking this time.

They were sniffing at the door.

He stood deadly still. Nowhere to run and nowhere to hide.

It was almost a minute before he heard the voices.

There were at least three males, and all of them speaking in German.

"Komm raus oder ich schicke die Hunde rein" ("Come out or I send in the dogs").

Connor didn't answer.

"We know your in there, now come out or I send in the dogs",

Connor answered him in French.

"Okay, okay, I'm coming out",

He pushed on the door but it wouldn't open. Something at the bottom of the door was stopping it.

The German changed to broken French.

"I said come out",

"I'm trying too but the door is stuck" said Connor.

He pushed at the door again but it was still stuck.

And then he heard them laughing. He looked down and he could see the soldier had his foot against the door.

But then the door opened a little.

And then the soldier threw in the dogs.

Connor drifted in and out of consciousness. He knew he was in a bad way. He'd been savaged by the dogs and then beaten by the soldiers. Now all he knew was that he was on the back of a vehicle of some sort, but what it was and where he was, he had no idea, and then the world went black.

The next time he woke it was daylight. He was still travelling in the back of a truck, the sun was now streaming through a crack in the tarpaulin that covered the rear of whatever he was in. He slowly looked around him and saw that he was alone.

No dogs and no soldiers.

He knew that if he got to wherever they were taking him to, then he was more than likely a dead man. He needed to get off the truck, and soon. He tried to stand but he couldn't, the pain in his legs was immense. He slowly rolled himself over and over towards the rear. The shooting pains all over his body and head made him scream. He forced his hand over his mouth to deaden his painful yelps. As he got to the back he stopped against the foot high tailgate. A few minutes later he felt the truck begin to slow and then start to take a left hand bend. It was now or never. He rolled himself up onto the edge of the tailgate and held himself on the lip, one leg and one arm hanging outside. He could see they were in the countryside, there were fields to the left and woods to the right. He took a breath, closed his eyes and rolled himself out.

He hit the ground hard and rolled several times before he dropped off the edge of the track and into a ditch.

And then the world went black again.

※ ※ ※

THE VOICE OF THE DEVIL

Mid August 1944

Whether it was the medication or his injuries, or a combination of both, he wasn't sure. But the hallucinations were slowly starting to diminish. He hadn't a clue as to where he was but what he did know, he was in a hospital somewhere.

He had felt the drip wires coming from his arms and he had also felt the bandage that was wrapped tightly around his head to just above his mouth. He had also had some horrific nightmares for as long as he could remember before waking in a cold sweat and then drifting back into a state of unconciousness. As he woke he again tried to open his eyes, but still he couldn't, due to the bandages. He had again drifted in and out of consciousness when he heard somebody talking to someone else close by and they were speaking in English.

He thought he recognised the female voice. Was It the nurse that had been looking after him for however long he had been here, he wasn't sure.

But then he heard another voice and he recognised it immediately.

It was a voice that turned him to stone.

It was the voice of Father Henry Milburn.

He couldn't see him due to the bandages but the voice was unmistakable, even almost 20 years on since he had last heard it.

He felt himself drifting back into unconsciousness, he fought it trying to stay awake but he felt his eyes rolling back into his head. 'Stay awake, stay awake' he told himself.

He could hear them walking around close to him but the man was speaking so softly he couldn't be sure.

'Am I dreaming, is this real' he fought off the sleep.

Slowly he came to his senses again. He could tell that the two of them were closer now, over to his right, 12 foot away, no more.

He heard the man speak again. He was asking somebody a question.

"Where are you from my son",

He heard a muffled reply.

'It must be another patient'.

He heard him ask another question.

"And what regiment are you from",

Another muffled reply.

'It's another patient he's speaking to'.

He heard them move again. Now directly in front of him but on the other side of the room.

'They must be at the bottom of the bed opposite his'.

The man whispered his question again.

"And where is this young man from".

The nurse answered for him but Connor couldn't hear her.

'He must be unconscious' thought Connor. 'Has he been here before, does she know where I am from, have I told her, does she know my name'.

He needed to see who it was but the bandages were wrapped

around his head to just below his nose. But he needed to try. He slowly started to tip his head gently backwards. As he did so the bottom of the bed opposite slowly started to come into view. He could see the legs of the nurse to the left of the bed and to the right he could see the legs of a man. He forced his head further backwards but as hard as he tried he could only see up to just above the waist of him. He looked back towards the bed and could see that the man was holding the hand of whoever was in the bed opposite.

It was no good, he couldn't see the man's head. He slowly started to drop his head back down and then he saw it, his very own telltale sign that if it was seen by Father Henry, would most definitely give him away, it was staring him in the face.

ADR tattood on his right wrist.

Henry could have seen his grandad's own tattoo before, and if he saw his, it wouldn't take too much working out, he knew that if he saw it that was it, the Priest would know who he was.

Without trying to be seen to move, he slowly lifted his right hand towards his left hand and tried to slowly pull down the bandage on his right arm to cover the tattoo. The bandage was so tight it would hardly move. He knew his time was running out. He slowly pulled up the bandage managing to cover 3/4 of it but the bottom of all 3 letters was still visible.

'This isn't happening, I'm dreaming, I must be dreaming'

He heard the seat moving backwards as the man got up. The footsteps started walking towards him.

Suddenly a scream shrilled out from over to his left.

He heard the nurse run over towards the area from where it had come from followed by the steps of the man.

Connor seized the opportunity and placed his right hand under his covers and then moved his left hand on top of his sheet and onto his stomach.

He heard the nurse attend the patient trying to calm him, soothing him with her soft voice. But then she stopped and Connor held his breath as they made their way over towards his bed. He could hear his own heart pounding, it felt as if it was coming out of his chest. He wanted to leap up and rip his bandages off and see the man who was stood there before him and if it was him he would kill him with his bare hands. But he knew that he couldn't, he could hardly move let alone fight.

The man arrived at his bed side. It had worked, the man must have seen that he couldn't hold Connor's right hand so he approached Connor's left side and then sat on the chair beside his bed. He then reached out and held his left hand. Connor didn't move or react.

"And who Is this unfortunate soldier".

Connor froze.

It was him, Henry Milburn, he now had no doubt at all.

'Please god, please don't tell him who I am' thought Connor.

And then time seemed to go into slow motion, it seemed forever before the nurse answered him but then she did.

"We don't know who he is Father, all we know is that he has come from behind enemy lines, and from his injuries we think that he has been very badly tortured and beaten but thats it, I'm sure we will know more when he gets a little better and can speak ".

Connor felt the Priest gently squeeze his hand and the urge to pull away was immense, but then the nurse carried on.

"I think he may be Irish though, because the few words he has uttered sound very similar to your tongue father",

"oh" said the priest "then let us hope he recovers very soon then".

Connor then felt the Priest lean over him and then he softly whispered into his ear.

"I will return to see you soon soldier, perhaps then we can talk then about our mother land".

He heard the Priest and the nurse move on down the ward and then he heard the door open and then close again.

Connor drifted back into unconsciousness.

Sometime later he started to wake again. As he slowly came around he sensed somebody at his side. Immediately he recalled the visit from the Priest. 'Had he been dreaming, was it real', he didn't know, he couldn't think straight, he slowly looked down and could see the nurses hand from under his bandaged head. She was holding a chart and was writing something on it.

The nurse sensed him waking and in barely a whisper she asked.

"Good afternoon, you've had a very long sleep, do you feel a little better".

Connor knew that this wasn't the nurse that he had heard that was with the Priest, this was another nurse that was tending to him now, She's was new, new to him anyway.

Not really wanting to draw too much attention to the question he needed to ask, he said.

"Have you seen the Priest today".

"No I haven't seen him, I've not met him yet I only arrived today, but I'm sure he will come to see you all later. Would you like me to get him to see you",

"No, no, it's fine. I will see him whenever, please don't trouble him".

Connor drifted back into a deep unconsciousness.

It was much later that night when Connor woke again.

He didn't know what it had been that had roused him but now he could hear that somebody was moving around the ward. He could hear their soft footsteps, they seemed to be at the bottom of his bed. They were a man's footsteps.

His brain was telling him so.

They stopped somewhere near the bed opposite his own. He very slowly, and as far as he dare, tilted his head back.

He recognised who he was immediately.

It was the Priest, only this time he was alone.

He watched as the Priest took hold of the prone soldiers hand, but then his other hand moved up the soldiers body.

To his neck.

He watched in total shock as the Priest then placed both his hands around the man's neck. The soldier started to rouse, but then the Priest stood up and started to use the weight of his own body to press down. He removed his left hand from around the man's neck and then pulled the sheet over his head. He then grabbed the sheet and wrapped it around and around the face of the man.

The soldier, who up to now hadn't moved, seemed to sense what was happening to him and started to thrash out with his arms and legs, trying to punch and kick whoever it was that was trying to suffocate him. But Connor could see that the soldier was too weak, he was never going to win this battle the Priest was too strong.

He so desperately wanted to get up and pull the Priest off him but he knew that it was helpless. Eventually the inevitable happened, he watched as the man went limp, he had taken his last breath.

Connor could hear the Priest breathing hard now as he recovered from the struggle, the tears of anger and sadness were streaming down Connor's face but he couldn't do anything, he knew he couldn't do a single thing. He felt useless and pathetic just laying there watching a poor man who couldn't defend himself die in such an awful way. But it was what he heard next though that chilled him to the core as the Priest whispered into the soldiers ear.

"God loves us all in different ways my son, you are still serving the cause even in death, may you now be in peace".

Connor very slowly lowered his head. He heard the Priest get up and move away from the dead soldier and listened as the Priest's footsteps hurried him out of the room.

The next morning Connor woke to somebody quietly asking.

"Are you awake". It was the old nurse, she was back.

"it must be morning" whispered Connor,

"it is and you must be feeling a little better" she replied in her wonderfully soft French accent.

" Now then, let's see how your head is looking".

She very gently started to remove the bandages from around his head and for the first time they looked into each others eyes.

Connor looked to see a very attractive woman, around her late twenties to early thirties with beautiful deep brown eyes, kind eyes, he thought.

"what's your name" asked Connor,

"my name is Elsa and I've been looking after you for the past four weeks on and off, and hopefully I won't have to call you D21 anymore, can I ask what is your name is",

"It's Billy" said Connor.

"Well ……..Billy, its very nice to meet you, you've been very badly injured you know, but the doctors are still hoping that you can make a full recovery but that will take some time".

She paused and looked at him with those kind eyes and then Connor sensed what the next question was going to be.

"Do you know what happened to you and how you came to get your injuries".

Connor looked at her and pondered on his answer for a while before he said,

"No, I cant remember anything at all, do you know how I got here",

" Well, I know that you were in a terrible state when you first arrived. The doctors didn't give you much of a chance at first, your head had been split wide open and",

she paused again,

"you had obviously taken a very bad beating. I know that a farmer found you in a field, he thought you were dead but he felt that he couldn't just leave you there so he took you back to his farm. When he got you back he noticed that you were still breathing. He and his wife then looked after you for over two weeks before they handed you over to a British medic and then you eventually ended up here. He told the medic that while they tended to you, you had mentioned several times, the words British and Southall. I hate to ask this, but the doctor said that when you wake your boss needs to be informed immediately and wants to know if you had been tortured in someway, but I suppose you can tell him that when he arrives, he's coming to see you on Saturday".

"Saturday", Said Connor shaking his head trying to look confused but also trying to keep his calm,

"When's that, I haven't a clue what day it is"

"Its Tuesday and that gives you three more days of rest and to try and remember what actually happened to you".

Connor nodded his response.

"Tuesday when, Elsa, what's the date today",

"It's Tuesday the 15th of August".

Connor couldn't believe it, he'd been "asleep' for over two months.

Connor nodded gently and already felt that he needed to go back to sleep but he had one more question that he desperately needed the answer to,

"Elsa, I'm not sure if I was dreaming, but I'm sure I heard a Priest talking to me yesterday, at least I think it was yesterday, does he come every day",

"No no, he tries to get here at least twice a week if not more, but he's very busy as you can probably guess, he will be back Friday evening but if you really need to see him I can try and get a message to him if you like",

"No, no thats fine I can wait, its nothing urgent and I think I need to rest anyway",

" Yes you do, most definitely Billy, you need all the rest you can get, now let me put you some fresh bandages back on your head and it is very nice to see you feeling a little better".

Connor lay back on the bed as Elsa gently tended to his wounds. Friday he thought, thats three days, he had three days to get the strength to walk out of the hospital and disappear before the Priest returned. He knew that he desperately needed to see Southall, but he couldn't risk another visit from the Priest. Seeing his boss would have to wait.

Three days later and three more days of wonderful care from Elsa, Connor was feeling much better and was getting more and more movement in his legs. The bad news was, it was Friday, and his head was healing, which meant that Elsa had removed the bandages to let the air get to his wounds. Connor knew that this was now a very dangerous time for him and if the Priest came back early, which was highly likely due to the high number casualties that they were receiving, he would recognise Connor immediately. Connor knew that it was now time to move. His legs, which could barely carry his weight were the problem. He had stocked up his food supply over the last three days by saving food under his bed but he knew that it was going to be extremely hard trying to get out of the hospital let alone achieving his prime objective, which was to follow the Priest.

If he did get out, he also knew it was going to take some time, but he had time, he had waited this long to find him and however long it took he wasn't going to waste this massive stroke of good fortune and give it up now. This was it, this was his one and only last chance of finally getting revenge for all the hurt done to his family and to all the others who had suffered at the hands of this evil man.

He had confirmed with Elsa what time the Priest was due and she had told him that he would be visiting after evening meal which was usually around 6:30 pm.

In the short time he had spent with Elsa he had enjoyed her company and thought that she in turn had enjoyed his too judging by the amount of time she spent with him compared to the other injured soldiers.

It was now 16:30 and he knew that he needed to make his move but he also knew he couldn't move until Elsa left. She usually left around 17:00 and the late nurse wouldn't get to his ward until around 18:00. This was his window when he had to leave.

At 16:45 Elsa appeared on her final round as she approached his bed she had her usual lovely smiling face "are you leaving me again Elsa" said Connor smiling back.

"Only for a while Billy, I'll be back to boss you about tomorrow, don't you worry",

"Oh no, I thought I might get a day off as it is Saturday" said Connor jokingly,

"no chance, I've been told to keep my eye on you and thats exactly what I intend to do".

Connor laughed but inside he felt sad that this was probably the last time he would see Elsa and those beautiful brown eyes. But he needed the answers to some very important questions. Because for the first time in years, Connor hadn't a clue to where in the world he was.

"I've been meaning to ask you", he said, "exactly where am I, as in what hospital am I in, because I haven't got a clue what country I'm in let alone whereabouts, I just presumed I am in France as you are obviously French, but why am I here, are the British here, is the war over ",

"Well Billy your powers of observation are very good" she smiled at him half mockingly,

"Yes indeed, you are in France and you are in a hospital on the edge of a small town of Charmes on the river Moselle, about 25 kilometres south of Nancy, and yes the British are here, along with the American's, but sadly no, the war goes on but the Allie's are slowly pushing the German's back to where they belong",

"When did it start, when did the invasion happen",

"It was the 6th of June when they landed in Normandy",

Connor smiled at her, 'Normandy' he thought, 'at least it hadn't been a waste of time'.

"Oh I see, and where do you live Elsa" said Connor.

she paused and looked at him slightly quizzically.

"You have a lot of questions Billy and why do you ask that, are you going to pay me a visit",

"No, no, it's just that I've been asleep for such a long time, I cant really comprehend what has happened to me" said Connor rather embarrassed by the way she had looked at him.

Elsa laughed at him and he realised that she was teasing him.

"Don't you worry Billy, lets blame it on your hallucinations, you have been having plenty of those, you don't like dogs do you" she smiled at him.

"If ever you pass by a little village further down the river to the south called Portieux you are very welcome to stop by for tea",

"Thank you Elsa thats very kind, I'm sorry if I offended you, I didn't mean to pry, I just wondered", she interrupted him with a wave of her hand, "Don't be silly, it would be nice but first we must get you better".

she held his hand and then felt his pulse with her other hand. Was it in his head or did she hold his hand for longer than she needed to.

"Ok Billy, I think you're on the mend at last although your pulse seems to be a little faster I think", again Connor looked at her rather embarrassingly, Elsa tipped her head back and laughed happily at him and he laughed back.

"Elsa, thank you for looking after and caring for me, I really mean that and it has been lovely to meet you and one day I might just pay that little village a visit, that is if you wouldn't mind of course",

Elsa now looked at him and looked deep into his eyes.

"Are you telling me something Billy".

Connor knew that he had already said too much, he wished he could tell her the truth, but he knew he couldn't. He couldn't tell her a thing, it was far too dangerous to get her involved in something like this.

"No, no, Elsa, nothing, I'm just saying I have really enjoyed your company",

"well I have enjoyed yours too, now, I must be on my way and I will see you tomorrow", she held his hand and very gently squeezed it. As she turned and walked towards the door Connor said "Goodbye Elsa and thank you".

She didn't turn around she just held her hand up in a silent wave and slowly walked out the door. As she walked outside a lonely tear trickled down her cheek as she knew that was probably the last time she would see him.

✣ ✣ ✣

SNAKES AND LADDERS

Fifteen minutes after Elsa had left, Connor slowly got out of his bed. His legs felt like they were made of warm wax. Every bone in his body hurt, he looked around the ward, all his fellow patients must have been either asleep or in a coma as nobody stirred as he slowly moved around.

Under one bed he found some boots and under another a jumper and some trousers. He dressed as quickly as he could and then placed his food, that he had taken from under his pillow, into a pillowcase. He walked quickly towards the door and quietly slipped outside the ward. he slowly closed the door behind him and noticed that it had the number 7 painted on it in black.

He was now in a long narrow corridor which must have been 50 to 60 yards long, the walls were painted a pale turquoise, faded by the sun that came through the windows from the East. He could see that there were further doors like the one he had just exited all along the righthand side of the corridor and he could also see that the next door had a black number 6 painted on it, 'ward 6' he thought. Along the lefthand side were tall sash windows dotted indiscriminately along the outside wall. His intuition and the decreasing numbers told him, that he was towards the rear the of the building but he didn't know for sure. He was definitely on the ground floor as he could see the gardens outside the windows.

He decided to make his way along the corridor towards what must be the front of the building. He knew he was now at his most vulnerable. If he met a doctor or nurse he could say he needed to stretch his legs, but if he met the Priest it was game over.

The Priest had in fact, finished his rounds in ward 4 and was now making for the exit door to move on to ward 5. Connor was now passing Ward 5 trying to walk as quickly as he could but it was more like a shuffle. As he approached Ward 4 and got level with the door he noticed the handle turning. He carried on, slowly passing the door.

On the other side of the door the Priest began to exit, just as the soldier shuffled by, and carried on down the corridor, the Priest turned, his attention drawn by something, "what was it" the Priest thought "The hair, the build, something familiar, but what was it".

Connor sensed the door opening just behind him, he then heard movement, "don't look back, never look back" thought Connor.

Instinctively, the Priest's eyes followed the soldier, he frowned trying to figure it out what it was that bothered him, but then as the night nurse exited the door behind him and as the Priest watched him walk away, he shook his head still not knowing what it was that stirred within his brain, he turned and walked with her towards ward 5.

Connor continued along the corridor and could sense that the person or persons behind him were going in the other direction. He could now see a large wooden glass door just ahead on the left hand side which was wide open and he could feel a cooling breeze coming from its direction. He walked through the door and he was straight outside into a courtyard. The fresh air was beautiful but the noise was horrendous, his head was throbbing but he had to keep on the move. As he took in his new surroundings he saw that the courtyard to the hospital was a hive of activity as ambulances were arriving and dropping off injured soldiers and then driving out of the grounds again, it was constant. He walked towards the exit of the hospital, he didn't plan on going far once outside, he needed to see the Priest arrive, or even better, see him leave.

The road outside was quiet. The hospital was situated on a small country road on the edge of the town of Charmes. His plan was to wait and see what the Priest arrived in and then to follow him to where he was staying. This was a very broad plan but one that would take a lot of time. He had no means of transport and there was only him going to be following him so he had to be very careful.

His method he was going to use was what he called snakes and ladders.

He would follow, which basically meant he would walk in the same direction that the Priest went, until the first point of deviation of which the Priest could take. If on arriving at that point and there was more than one likely route the Priest could take, he would hold at that point, observe it and wait for the Priest to come back another day and so on. If at the junction it had only one major route he would carry on past it until the next junction and so on and so on.

Up the ladder.

If the Priest didn't go to the next major junction then he had to return to the last junction.

Back down the snake.

Snakes and ladders.

It was a very time consuming method but it worked, he knew it worked, he had used it countless times before.

The only problem he did have was transport.

He didn't have any.

It worked much better with a car or motorbike. But anyway that was something he could work on.

Outside the hospital gate, he briefly looked up and down the tree lined country lane and across towards the small wood opposite the entrance. As he looked to the right, a 7 foot high wall signified the boundary of the hospital grounds. It ran for about 60 to 70 yards along the road in both directions. As he looked to the right, he could see it turned right again and ran down the side of the Hospital and away from view towards the rear. He looked to his left and could see the same wall re-appearing at the left hand side of the hospital and then turning right running along the country lane back towards the gated entrance.

The gates were open and were at least 10 foot high and made of wrought iron with a stunning crest in the centre of both, they looked very very heavy which was probably why they hadn't been closed for some considerable time. On looking back towards the hospital he could see that it was a magnificent country Chataeu. The front of which faced to the west and was still bathed in the evening sunshine. It could have been at least 150 years old probably older, with 10 shuttered windows on each of the three floors which were all shut to keep out the sun, or more probably, shut due to the blackouts which still continued, a large stone staircase of about 10 steps led you up towards the main entrance. As you looked to the right of the building there was a single story annex which had several army ambulances parked outside. This was where he had exited. The building seemed fairly well intact apart from some damage to the wall just in front and to the right of the annex probably caused by a stray bomb or shell. It had obviously exploded on the outside of the wall as most of the stone had been blown into the hospital grounds. It was another way out should he need it when he returned into the grounds later.

He then looked up and down the lane. He couldn't see another building in either direction. it looked as if the Chateaux was the only building for a mile or so which was good because he wouldn't be seen leaving, but not good because he was probably going to have to walk some distance before he could get any sort of transport. He stood and briefly pondered, left or right he thought, he decided right and to the north, he crossed the road and walked up the lane ready to duck in behind the trees should a vehicle approach.

Although he hurt from head to toe, it was wonderful to be outside again and the heat from the early evening sun felt nice on his back. The smell of the pine trees opposite smelled absolutely wonderful compared to the antiseptic and sweat and death from inside the hospital. He walked about 80 yards away from the entrance to the hospital and then waited. He found himself a nice hedgerow to crawl into on the opposite side of the road. He could now see the entire wall which ran along the hospitals right hand side to the north. it was at least 8 foot high all the way along and had several wall high buttresses coming down at an angle to support it. The wall ran for about 150 yards towards the rear. He could see only one small gate which was made of solid wood but was very old and looked to be rotten. What was on the other side of it he couldn't tell but it may be an option. The land then dropped gently away behind the hospital's rear wall, 'probably towards the river' he thought.

He got himself as comfortable as he could, and then waited for his prey to arrive.

He had already arrived.

The Priest was already on his rounds around the ward's, he had arrived early.

There was a reason.

He needed a new victim.

He had a good idea who the poor unfortunate soldier was and

was now to be next on his list.

He knew he was from Ireland, the nurse had told him that, and he also knew that if he was found dead it wouldn't be that much of a surprise as the last time he had seen him he was in a very bad way.

It was the fact that he was from Ireland which was to be the soldiers downfall. The Priest needed him for the cause. He would help the cause even in death, and he would tell him so as he strangled him to death in his hospital bed.

The Priest had entered ward 7 with the night nurse and they walked slowly over to Connor's empty bed.

"Oh dear" said the Priest "It appears that the poor soul is no longer with us".

He knew this wasn't a major problem as he knew full well where the body's of the dead were taken. He could catch up with the dead soldier later. It had probably saved him a job.

The Priest moved on to the next bed. The nurse, looking a little puzzled, had stopped at the end of the bed, trying to read the notes, but she knew that the Priest was always in a hurry. She could check on the soldiers fate later.

The evening was now getting late, Connor sat and waited but he knew he would need to move soon, he needed to find somewhere to sleep. He couldn't risk moving about much in daylight as the area was still busy with military vehicles and soldiers, but moving at night was probably even more dangerous as he would be likely to be shot at first sight and asked questions later. The British who were re-taking the surrounding area were jumpy and suspicious about everybody. He had no identification and an Irishman found wandering about at night could be on anybody's side.

His head told him it was about 21:00, the light was slowly beginning to fade and he was frustrated the Priest hadn't arrived. It probably meant that he would have to wait until next

Monday or Tuesday for his next visit. He could wait, time was on his side, the longer it took the fitter he would get, providing of course he could find food and water.

And then……

There he was.

That mass of black hair.

No mistake, as the open top jeep pulled out of the hospital entrance, the Priest was sat smiling and chatting to the driver. It turned right and headed straight towards Connor.

It passed him within 3 feet.

He could have touched him.

The Priest was looking straight at him as he passed. Connor knew he hadn't been seen, he was confident of that. He had had german soldiers virtually standing on his head behind enemy lines on several occasions. Stay still. Don't move. Trust your'e training trust your'e skill and most of all trust yourself. Because If you move your dead for sure.

The jeep sped off into the distance.

Now his work began.

❋ ❋ ❋

DO WHAT YOU DO.

It felt so good to be out again. His body, not only his mind, knew it too. The energy was returning, slowly, but he was definitely feeling better.

He needed a map, just a look would do. He would memorise it within seconds. The problem was that he knew that it meant his best chance was going back into the hospital grounds to look around the vehicles.

He lay there going through the options in his head. Do I go now and risk detection and get put back on the ward, or, do I wait until dark and risk being detected and shot at. He decided on the latter.

So he waited.

It was now around Midnight he thought. He didn't know the exact time but his head was telling him so. The flow of traffic into the hospital had almost stopped. There hadn't been a vehicle of any description for at least 45 minutes. The only foot traffic he had seen were a very flirtatious french nurse and a British soldier who was hoping it was his lucky night, walk out of the gates. They had smoked a couple of cigarettes each before returning into the hospital grounds giggling as they went.

Connors thought's turned to Elsa. What would she think when she returned to work tomorrow and to find his bed empty. Would she be sad, would she be mad, or worried. Should he have told her what he was doing. He couldn't have, it went against all that he had ever done before.

Secrecy had saved his life countless times he knew that, but this time, this time he knew that he had come so close to confiding in Elsa and telling her exactly what he was going to do. He'd fought against it, 'don't do it, do not do it' he'd told himself and he hadn't but it didn't sit well. For some reason his heart was telling him he should tell her but his brain had won. It always did. Never let your heart rule your brain, "Your brain wont hurt you, but your heart, your heart has the power to kill you whenever it wants to my boy", his Nana had said it to him so many times.

His mind now drifted to his wonderful Nana, the nicest person he had ever known. Riley used to remind him of the time when he was about 5 years old, he had said to his Nana, "Nana, I love you so much" "do you" his Nana had replied "Yes Nana, you are the nicest person in my family". His Nana had shed a little tear at that one.

'Oh Nana' he thought 'What would you think of me now, wanting to kill another human being', he hoped she would find forgiveness, this man had bought so much pain and heartbreak to his family and to that of so many others too.

It was time to move.

He slowly stood, stretching his still aching limbs. He waited for at least a couple of minutes before he stepped out onto the little country road. He slowly started to walk towards the hospital entrance.

He walked along the hedgerow, prepared to dive into it at any time, should he have to. On reaching the gate he slowed and backed into the hedge and looked into the courtyard. It was quiet and very, very, dark. The moonless night was perfect. He waited for his two minutes to pass through his head. He moved slowly onto the gravelled courtyard. He moved quicker now, his feet, heel to toe, heel to toe to lesson the noise. Great in theory but not when your legs felt like they belonged to somebody else. The hospital was mainly in darkness to the front anyway mostly due to the shutters. A couple of rooms were lowly lit on the second floor but that was it. He moved to the righthand side and towards the ambulances. Maps, they would be full of maps, well thats what he hoped.

And then he heard somebody giggling.

The nurse and soldier hadn't gone back inside at all, the noise was coming from the back of an ambulance. He stood with his back to the hospital wall hiding in the dark shadow of one of the wall buttresses, he was only about 10 yards from the rear of the ambulance. The giggling had now stopped and he could hear the soft voice of the nurse. He knew who it was. It was the night nurse, no mistake, it was her. He froze. If she saw him he would have a lot of explaining to do. He had to move, he backed around the buttress moving nearer to the ambulance in order to move onto the next one which was parked further to the rear of the hospital.

"No", Connor heard her say, followed by another "no" and then a soft low groan. He knew he was ok now, she was going to be otherwise engaged, for a short while anyway.

He drifted past the gently rocking ambulance and walked in the shadows towards the second. He moved around to the drivers door, the furthest away from the new lovers. He peered very slowly inside. It looked like a grenade had been thrown in to it, either that or the crew were not tidy people. Probably too busy for tidiness. He gently opened the door. Good no squeak, and straight away he saw it even in the darkness he could make out the folded up creamy brown weathered map. He slowly pulled it from between the two seats and slipped it inside his waistband.

On the floor was a dark coloured jacket, he slowly lifted it and searched the pockets, a pen, useful, a torch, again useful, tissues, no, money, very useful, not much but it would do, cigarettes, he didn't smoke, never had, but he'd take them to trade. A further rummage around the floor and he found his best find yet, a compass, it wasn't made of gold but it was worth more than anything he'd ever seen made of gold. He placed all the belonging's in his pockets.

He moved further to the rear of the hospital away from the ambulances, one of which, was rocking quite excessively now and much faster. "Not long before they are done best get as far away as possible" he thought.

He continued walking close to the wall and eventually got to the rear of the hospital. He turned left and now walked along the rear of the building along a neatly cut lawn. More windows but all shuttered and no lights from within. He continued to walk circling the hospital anti clockwise, and then again he heard voices.

This time it was in French and it was two males.

He stopped still against a small shed and waited. He couldn't see where it was coming from but he could smell them. Well not them specifically but what they were actually cooking. The unmistakable smell of freshly baked bread. He was near to the kitchen no doubt about it.

He could now hear the clanking of pots and pans and noticed further on towards the end of the rear of the building, an open window. He crept very gently to the window and could see three freshly baked loafs of bread cooling in the window. He grabbed all three and silently moved away, no point in just taking one, they would notice one missing so he might as well take all three he thought. He scurried around the corner and was now walking back towards the front of the hospital along the North wall. He skirted the wall hoping to find the rotten wooden gate.

A path.

'A path always led to somewhere, and more than likely to a gate' he thought. He walked to the side of the gravel path along the grass. Sure enough there it was, the small wooden gate. He slowly and very gently pulled on the gate and to his amazement it opened. He quickly moved through the gate to outside the wall and then shut it behind him.

Within 5 minutes he was back in his hedgerow with his treasure. He was very pleased with his little journey back into the hospital. He thought he'd been out for about an hour and a half which meant it was around 01:30 hrs. He would eat for energy and then move north in the same direction the Priest had taken and travel as far as he could or to the first point of a major deviation.

God he ached, every bone in his lower limbs seemed to pound back double at his heart with every step. He thought that he'd been walking for at least 2 hours which meant on average at 4 miles an hour he should have walked about 8 miles. But he wasn't walking, he was hobbling, and badly at that. He guessed he had walked barely half what he should have, 3 to 4 miles if he was lucky. He also knew that if he was walking properly he took 52 steps on his right foot per 100 yards, so, if he put 17 stones in his pocket and passed one to his other pocket every 52 steps he would have walked just short of a mile when he ran out of stones. Again useless as his right leg was taking about half a step at a time.

He had passed two small lanes to the right which were really dirt tracks and a cross roads where he went straight on, just because it felt right but he knew that, that, was the point where he had to return to if the Priest didn't show up but he'd carried on, part out of stubbornness and part out of their being absolutely nobody about. It was totally and strangely quiet. He hadn't seen or heard anything or anybody since he'd left his hedgerow.

Move while you can, hide when you can't.

He decided his cut off point would be time or shelter whichever came first. 0530hrs and no more.

He'd walked for about another two and a half hours along a country lane through no villages or towns, passing a large wood to his left, but as he walked on further north he slowly but surely began to make out buildings over to the North West on his left hand side, they were about 200 yards away. A small farm perhaps, nothing more, as he got closer he could see in fact there was only one small single story building and then something attached to it on the right. It had taken a beating and had obviously been the centre of some small battle at some point not so long ago.

Worth a look.

He stepped over the 4 foot deep ditch at the side of the road and slowly walked across the furrowed field, watching and listening for any movement. As he got about 50 yards away, the smell hit him.

It was the smell of death.

You couldn't mistake it for anything else.

Somebody or something nearby was dead and it was in that building no doubt about it. He began to relax a little, simply because if anybody was thinking of hiding in there they wouldn't have been in there long. The smell was horrendous. It was a small cow shed with a small lean too at the side.

But the smell wasn't a dead cow.

The rotting corpse of a dead German soldier lay half sitting on his left side, halfway out the shed door. He had sensed that he couldn't be far from the front line but 'the line' was an invisible one. There was no painted white line running and zigzagging across the land. At any time he could be on the right side and then move a mile down the road and be on the wrong side, the only way you found out which you were on was if you were shot at or you weren't.

He looked down at the dead soldier. Half of his head was missing and he looked as though he'd been there for sometime, a week or so at least. Connor looked at him, his hands looked young, he thought, and his body looked lean and fit, definitely not an old soldier. Probably more like the Hitler youth. Time for the pockets thought Connor, whatever he'd got on him was no good to him now.

He slowly rolled him onto his back looking for any booby trap wires or grenades ready to go off underneath him but there was nothing. He started on his jacket.

Nothing in his pockets.

He unbuttoned his tunic, nothing inside.

A small gold chain around his neck.

He gently pulled the chain out of his shirt and there at the end of the chain was a small crucifix.

Connor held it in his hand for a few seconds looking at the tiny intricate form of Christ suspended on the cross.

It was made of gold and was quite simply, beautiful.

Whoever had made it had made it well.

It was no more than an inch long and at its widest point, the arms stretched out wide upon the cross, half an inch at most. And then the tiny intricacies, the bones in the feet, the muscles in his legs, the loin cloth around his midriff, the wavy long hair which looked thick but well kept, the chiseled slighted bearded chin and then finally the eyes. Although closed, they seemed so full of sorrow and sadness.

Jesus Christ had never himself struck a single blow and he hadn't asked of, or wanted anyone of his followers to do such a thing either, but in these eyes Connor could see, it had been a battle lost.

As he sat looking at it he couldn't help but think, what a waste, a waste of time, a waste of life, a waste of a world in which we all try to live in. Where would it all end he thought.

He gently placed the Christ back inside the soldiers shirt.

On his right wrist was a watch, unusual as in it is normally on the left wrist. I could do with one of those he thought. He didn't recognise the make but it said it was 04:45 hrs so it must be about right. He slipped it off his wrist and on doing so and to his surprise, he saw his holster on his left hip. And It wasn't empty.

He was a leftie.

If anybody had already searched him they hadn't bothered to turn him over as nearly everybody carried their gun on their right hand side.

He slipped the gun out, it was an Astra 900, not a bad weapon but odd that this boy should have it. He'd probably found it as well. As Connor examined it, he found that it had 8 rounds. Enough for now.

It was time to sleep. He would be as safe here as anywhere. He felt tired but happy with his nights work. He'd move again in the evening if he needed to.

He didn't sleep for long.

It wasn't midday yet but he was woken by the distinctive noise of tank tracks squeaking and screaming across rough ground and they were getting louder.

He came to his senses somewhat abruptly, startled almost as if he was still in a dreamlike state. The drugs he had been on in the hospital had clearly not gone out of his system.

He scrambled for his gun and ducked down behind the walled remains of the farm building trying to work out from which direction the tank was approaching from.

Then he saw it.

At speed, coming from the right, about the same direction as where he had crossed the ditch a few hours earlier.

He recognised it immediately. It was a German Panther IV. It was a big tank, and more worryingly, it was usually supported by infantry.

Not today though.

This tank was on the run and it wasn't interested in what he was doing whether they had seen him or not.

As it sped past his make shift hide, no more than 30 yards in front of him, he caught a glimpse of the driver through the peephole. A blood spattered face and eyes like that of a startled rabbit.

'Boom' an ear shattering blast from further over to his right followed by a cloud of smoke from within the small wood he had passed the night before.

A split second later a huge explosion just to the far side of the 'on the run' tank and thankfully further away from him, Connor saw the tank lift upward on its right hand side as a result of the shell blast but it hadn't hit it and it raced on. It swerved heavily to its right, a good manoeuvre 'thought Connor' he had turned into the line of the oncoming fire but invariably, it would be the right reaction as generally the attacking force would alter their angle of fire.

But .....'Boom', ... they'd been second guessed. The attacking force, whoever they had been, had gone for the less likely option of staying on the same trajectory. It had caught the fleeing tank on the rear of its turret, smashing it to smithereens, plumes of thick black smoke billowed from the innards of its remaining belly as it swerved uncontrollably from left to right and then back again until it came to a slow moving halt.

And then, as if it had been a living thing, its intestines began to spill out on to the ground below, but of course, it wasn't its intestines, it was its crew, screaming and crying, burning and dying, helpless to their fate as they fell to the floor below, none of them, apart from one managing to half get up, but he, even then, only managed a somewhat pathetic crawl for a couple of yards before he too, for the last time, placed his head towards mother earth.

Connor sat totally still, and watched.

He watched for more than two hours.

Nothing happened. No more tanks. No more blasts. No more smoke from the woods. But he knew they would be watching.

They'd been watching when the leftie soldier had been sat exactly where he had been sat right now. But he knew he'd been lucky, unlike leftie, he had arrived in the blackness. The night was his friend, it always had been. But now he had a problem.

If he moved they would fire, no doubt about it. They wouldn't know that he was a British soldier hiding close to enemy lines, hiding in order to kill one of his own. As soon as he moved the likelihood of him being shot at was extremely high. But if he saw the Priest, then that was exactly what he needed to do, move. The decision this time might not be his to make.

He ate, then drifted back to sleep, partly due to tiredness, partly due to the drugs, but mainly due to the smell. You didn't smell things when you were asleep.

It was late afternoon before he woke again. No noise of tanks, just the burning sun having come around to start burning on his eyelids. And of course the smell.

The tank, some 60 yards away in front of him, was still smouldering and smoking. The body's from it hadn't moved but were now just burnt out shells of human forms contorted in pain, stiff and lifeless, just some more sad shapes of war.

Shortly after half past four in the afternoon Connor heard the distinct sound of a British jeep coming towards him from the North. As he looked to his left waiting for it to come into view he watched as the heat ripples reflected off the road. It was a very hot day, and a very smelly one. The flies had come out in force to visit his dead companion. And he needed water. His plan was to wait until dark and visit the remains of the tank to see what he could salvage.

The jeep came into view. It raced by him left to right, some one hundred yards away. But he could see him. It was definitely him. The Priest sat in the front with the same driver as the night before. They looked like they were talking and he was sure that the Priest was laughing.

Connor sat back happy for now. He was on the right road. It was more than likely that the Priest would head back the same way in a few hours time.

The downside to that was when he did return it was still going to be light. The sun might have set but it would still be too light for him to move closer to the road. He could try a pot-shot from where he was but no matter how good a shot Connor was, and he was a good one, the chances of hitting him or the driver were virtually nil. To add to his problem, if he did shoot then the boys it the trees would hear it, no doubt about it.

He didn't want to upset the boys in the trees.

He would have to be patient. He had learnt well from his grandad Riley.

'If you really really want something, then wait, then wait some more and it will come' he used to say.

It was 8:40pm and the sun had just descended below the horizon over his right shoulder when he saw the dust cloud over to the right giving away the arrival of something on the road. There had been no traffic whatsoever since the Priest, heading for the hospital, had passed over four hours earlier, Connor was therefor pretty confidant this was his prey.

Half a minute later the jeep came speeding into view, but then, it began to slow.

And now it was stopping.

It stopped on the roadside directly inline of sight with the burnt out tank but another thirty yards beyond it.

90 or so yards away, 'still too far for a shot, oh for a rifle' thought Connor.

The remnants of the tank was slightly obscuring his view but he stayed where he was. He watched. ' what were they doing' he thought.

He was sure they hadn't seen him. Not a chance.

The Priest got out first followed by the driver.

They were looking towards the tank, and, which was more of a concern, towards him.

He watched as they jumped over the ditch and slowly began to walk towards the stricken vehicle, and, towards him.

The urge to take a shot was immense. He had never wanted to pull the trigger of a gun so much in all his life. He very slowly raised it to his eye as he crouched behind the barn wall peering through the whole where a shell had no doubt passed through a few days earlier.

Connor to a brief look towards the boys in the trees but there was no reaction.

' Keep walking you murdering bastard' whispered Connor to himself,

'Keep walking, keep walking and you will be a dead man'.

He didn't keep walking.

He stopped at the tank.

They walked around it and as they came around into Connor's view again they stopped with their backs to him.

They were 50 yards away.

Connor pressed on the trigger. He didn't pull it, he just put pressure on it but if they came any nearer they were getting the good news.

He watched. He could hear them talking. He could make out the odd word. He heard the words 'dead' and 'useful'.

Then the driver turned around and looked over to where Connor lay.

Connor knew who it was immediately.

It was Glendon.

No doubt about it.

The youngest Milburn, brother of Father Henry and the dead Cain.

Connor smiled to himself.

He knew now what it was they were doing.

He watched as the Priest bent down and searched the dead body of the German soldier he had watched die some hours before. He found a pistol.

He waved it at Glendon, smiling he did so. He placed inside his coat pocket.

He moved onto the next dead soldier. Same result. And the next, and the next.

Four dead soldiers, four pistols.

'We all know where they will be going' whispered Connor to himself.

He slowing lowered the gun and released the pressure on the trigger.

He watched as the Priest and Glendon made their way back to the jeep. As they got to about half way he saw the Priest wave a thank you towards the 'invisible' boys in the trees.

He now knew what they were doing and it was now more important that he should know how they were doing it.

'Wait some more and it will come'.

He watched the jeep carry on its route northwards until he couldn't hear it anymore then settled down to wait for nightfall.

At half past midnight Connor said goodbye to his dead leftie companion and slowly made his way over to the still smoking tank.

The heat from it was still fairly hot and as he got closer he knew there was no way he could take a look inside it. It was pointless searching the dead as they had probably already been fleeced of anything useful but he had a quick look.

He had a result.

The lover of mother earth had a knife, still sheathed in its leather holder, tucked down the rear of his waistband. He quickly removed it, it was time to move on.

He walked silently on Northward, parallel to the road, always keeping it 50 yards to his right. Only Occasionally having to go back onto the road when small woods and high hedgerows prevented his direct route.

He had now been walking at least 2 hours and had made good progress along the fairly flat terrain with only very small country tracks going off left and right from the road and as he turned a left hand corner around the edge of a small copse he saw the very slight rise in the road. It was a bridge. Too small for a railway. Please be a stream he thought.

It was.

He unsteadily slipped down the bank to the left of the bridge. He stopped and listened. Not a sound.

He lowered his head into the running stream and cupped his hands filling his mouth with water. The back of his throat seemed to burn and sting with the shock of the cold liquid hitting it but god it felt good. He ducked his head completely under the water and washed his hair and face. He drank some more and then sat back on the bank.

He sat for five minutes more and was about to move on when he heard something.

An engine of some sort but it was still too far away and it seemed to be coming from the North.

He listened, it was definitely getting nearer. It was a motorbike and it sounded like a NSU601, he had ridden one once shortly before being caught in Normandy. He crossed the stream to the North side and watched and waited, crouched behind the small brick wall.

He listened as it slowed, probably due to a bend in the road he thought. He heard the revs increase, it didn't sound far away now. It slowed again. It was slowing for the bend and the bridge, the rider knows the road 'he thought'.

It rounded the bend only 40 yards in front of him, he saw the blacked out headlight with just the small slit of light splicing through the taped glass front.

He was a German soldier, he could tell by the shape of his helmet.

That in itself was a brave statement. He still felt that he was close to the enemy line. The tank on the previous day had shown him that. The rider was indeed wearing a German helmet, and had on a German uniform, and was riding a German motorcycle, but around this part of France, Germans were sometimes dressed as the British and likewise the British dressed as the Germans, and then, thrown into the mix, were the French resistance who could be dressed as anybody.

But Connor wanted the bike. He watched the bike go by, he wasn't ready to take it yet, and so he listened to it carry on its journey to who knew where. But then as quick as he had first heard it, it stopped and then he heard the engine turn off. He guessed It was no more than a mile away. He knew he was a German now. He was a spotter, and a very brave one at that.

He walked back down the track, the same direction the bike had gone. Looking at the hedgerow. After about fifty yards, he found what he was looking for.

It was a four inch thick branch of a Hawthorne bush that lined the roadside facing south, protruding about two foot into the road and about four foot in the air. Connor then searched in the tree's for a branch the split off in two at the top, in the shape of the letter Y. He found one, snapped off the branches that left about a foot for each end of the 'Y', then walked ten feet back up the road and dropped it on the floor. He walked back to his overhanging branch and took hold of it and then slowly pulled it backwards until it ran virtually inline with the hedgerow and road, only now it was facing in the opposite direction, to the North. He then wedged it back with his Y shaped branch.

And then he waited.

It was over an hour before he heard the bike start up again. But then it didn't hang around. It was coming back towards him at a rate of knots.

Connor sat on the floor and steadied himself, his feet on the Y shaped stick, ready to kick it away at just the right moment.

The bike got closer and closer and as it rounded the bend and came hurtling towards him he let the rider get to within 20 feet away and then kicked the stick away and the branch whizzed over the top of his head. He had timed it to perfection. The Hawthorne branch swung back out into the road heading straight back to where it had come from but was stopped halfway there as it smashed into the riders chest and pushed him straight off the back of his bike, and onto the rough track. As the bike carried on down the track, Connor hobbled over to him and put both his knees onto his chest.

He needn't have worried. The landing, or the branch, had knocked the riders helmet clean off and as a consequence, the hard landing onto the track, had knocked him out cold.

Connor got to his now, very unsteady feet, and dragged the unconscious soldier down to the bank at the side of the stream. He rolled him onto his left side and quickly looked him over for anything of use. He found a Luger pistol strapped into his holster. He pulled it out and placed it in his pocket. Under his jacket he found an ammunition belt with three full pouches of 9mm bullets, 'enough to start his own little war'. He took just one pouch which would be more than enough for what he needed.

He scrambled back up the bank, found the helmet and then hobbled to the bike which had crashed into the wood about 30 yards further up the track.

And then he listened.

He listened because the biker had been in a hurry.

Then he heard them. At least one bike and possibly a lorry, both coming his way and fast.

He pushed the bike further into the tree's. The smell of spilt petrol took his breath away.

30 or 40 seconds later the bike came past him fast. He watched it as it flew over the bridge and taking off into mid air. 20 seconds later the troop carrier came by. It didn't quite make it into the air but it wasn't far off. He listened to them both disappear into the distance, heading North.

The same way he was going.

He needed to find the mortuary.

❋ ❋ ❋

A MEMORY OF ONE, A DREAM OF ANOTHER.

The next ten days were spent going up the ladder's and down the snake's.

It was pain staking work, especially when he had to take into account a fleeing German army. But the motorbike had been a godsend, without it would have taken him not days but months. But he had now had to abandon it, he had crashed and split the petrol tank after being shot at by an advancing American unit.

But he had now followed his prey to a small village called Thelod in the North Eastern corner of France, a few miles south of Nancy, where he had come to another set of cross roads and had now lost them again and had no idea which way they had taken which inevitably meant that he needed to wait for them to return. As he lay hidden watching the world go by, of which there wasn't many, something from the depths of his brain had stirred a memory, he felt sure that he had heard somebody speak of Thelod but it must have been only briefly for he couldn't remember why. If something of significance had occurred there, then he would have stored it away deep within his brain for a reason, but there was nothing else forthcoming.

He had now been waiting in another of his man made holes for over three days and every day, he had heard the gun battles raging on to the north of him within Nancy itself. Only in the last week had it come under the control of the Allie's. But In some eastern parts of the city the battle's continued to rage on through the streets but they seemed to be lessoning by the day now.

Over the next three rain sodden days he had lay watching the passing lorries. He had noticed that most of them had been American with the odd British one every now and then. He had also noticed that all of the American vehicles had headed North East, towards Nancy, where as, all but two of the British, had turned West, away from the battle.

There were only two reasons why you wouldn't be going towards where all the noise was coming from.

You were either injured.

Or you were already dead.

As darkness fell he decided it was time to get out of his whole and start to walk.

It was time to take a gamble.

He headed towards the West, away from the Americans, away from noise, and hopefully, towards the injured and the dead.

As he walked along the road, It wasn't long before he found himself in the middle of a thick forest. The overhanging branches from the tall conifers kept a lot of the rain off him but the moonless night meant you couldn't see more than twenty yards in front of you, and it was deathly quiet. His legs were now feeling much better, they had been getting better day after day and he had also felt his strength beginning to return all over his battered body, but he still needed his whits about him, now so more than ever. The Allies were on the offensive and were beginning to make ground very quickly. So he didn't need to be caught out, walking towards them, in the middle of a forest, and in the middle of the night. But the rain would help, even in war nobody really liked getting wet.

The road had now turned into more of a gravel track. It was covered in broken branches which made him concentrate more on where his feet were, rather than on what danger lay ahead.

He fought against looking down, but every now and then he found himself looking down at his feet instead of straight ahead. In this environment though, his ears were more important than his eyes. If a vehicle was to come towards him, from either direction, he would hear them from at least a mile away and probably more. At a spur in the track, the further track turned towards the North West, Where as the original track seemed to carry on directly towards the West. He hesitated, it was something which he very rarely did, he was generally very quick to make a decision but this time he wasn't sure. For some reason his gut instinct was telling him to take the right hand spur, his brain was telling him to take the left, possibly due to the ruts in the ground heading that way from the heavy lorries that were obviously using it. He looked again at the right hand track and could see that it also had had some traffic but nowhere near as much as the other one.

He stepped right and headed North West. He could always turn around and come back.

By 4:30am and after a somewhat uneventful journey, he had reached the far edge of the forest.

As he quietly stepped out of the tree's he peered into the darkness and could see that now, ten yards directly In front of him, and running from left to right, was a very high metal fence with barbed wire along the top and also, the track that he had walked along, had now come to a T junction, one track heading south and one heading north. A hand painted sign was fixed to the fence, it had an arrow pointing left which read 'Allain' and underneath it had another arrow pointing right 'Gimeys'. He turned and walked back into the forest.

He knew now why he had heard of Thelod.

As dawn arrived he could see that the fence and the track, ran away from him in both directions for as far has he could see and now In front of him he could see why the fence was there.

He was at an airbase, and a very busy one at that.

He looked at the ground on the other side of the wire and could see that there had been some very heavy foot traffic on the muddy grassy ground. Probably due to the newly erected 8' high fence. He imagined the soldiers standing in the rain dutifully erecting the fence and the barbed wire, cursing the weather, and cursing the fact that they were here instead of shooting Germans that was presuming of course that it was occupied by the Allies, he felt sure that it should be, but nothing could be taken for granted at this moment in history.

He decided that he couldn't stay there to watch the base, he needed to get to the high ground so he turned right towards 'Gimeys' and began to walk along the north track up the hill.

He knew that somewhere up there, there would be a great view to sit and watch from.

He'd been told about it before.

He also knew that It was something that he probably shouldn't be doing, it wasn't really necessary, but he needed to do it, he wanted to do it, it was a place that he had to go and see.

As he walked just inside the cover of the tree's, still with the airbase fence to his left, he could see that about a mile and a half in front of him the forest rose rapidly, higher and higher, the tops of the tree's still covered in the early morning mist.

He carried on.

He was looking for a small waterfall that would be just inside the tree line.

He heard it before he saw it.

Now having been walking for nearly 3/4 of an hour, he could hear the soft trickle of water coming from his right. He turned towards it and walked further into the tree's and just fifty yards in, he stepped into a clearing and then he saw it.

The beautiful waterfall was just as it had been described and exactly as he had always imagined it. The water flowing down over the different coloured rocks underneath. Blues, greens, reds, a full kaleidoscope of colours stretching up in front of him, climbing almost 200 feet high into the hillside and the mist. He stepped into the shallow stream and walked to the base of the waterfall and then stepped up onto the first stone and then to the next and he began to climb up 'the invisible staircase' beneath the flowing water.

He needed to get to just below the top.

'About 30 feet from the top there was a deep red stone, it was about three feet wide and it looked just like a mushroom' he had been told many years ago.

Thirty minutes of climbing later, there it was, just as it was described. A deep.... red.... stone... mushroom.

He placed his hand on it and felt the stoney texture on his fingertips. The damp and coldness of it surprised him a little considering how warm the day was now becoming. He stepped over it and now walked left along a very thin ledge which had an almost vertical drop to his left hand side straight down to the stream nearly 200 feet below him. He carried on slowly, all the time counting his steps as he went. 61 steps on his left foot was 100 metres. What he was looking for was 50 metres from the mushroom.

He needed to stop after 31 steps of his left foot.

31 steps.

He stopped.

'I knelt down and pulled back the ivy and there it was' he had said.

Connor knelt down and pulled back the Ivy, now mixed in amongst other foliage.

He peered into the dark whole behind it and waited for his eyes to get accustomed to the darkness and then he saw it, just as it had been described. A small cave carved into the limestone cliff face, it had probably been there for thousands of years but around 26 years ago, it had been made a little bigger.

Inside, on a small metal hook, screwed into the root of a tree, hung a pair of binoculars, but it was the carved letters and numbers on the wall that confirmed it was the place.

RG 1917.

For the next hour Connor sat in the cave, as he slowly traced the RG with his finger, he imagined his Grandfather Riley sat there with his pal Corporal Hayworth, watching the scene down below. He remembered now how his grandad had described the beautiful waterfall with an invisible staircase behind it that led up to a cave with the most amazing view towards a town called 'Gimleys', and how they had watched the weird and wonderful flying machines 'the likes of which I had never seen before in my life' and the soldiers running around getting the planes ready to send back out again to reek their havoc and devastation on the poor enemy below.

Connor had only been able to imagine this beautiful place before and had dreamt about it many times, and it was remarkable how accurate his dreams had been, but then his grandfather Riley had described them so vividly to him it shouldn't really have been to much of a surprise.

Not much had really changed in the last 27 years.

The planes were just bigger that was all. It was the same actions leading to the same result only this time it was the Germans who would be on the receiving end of the havoc and devastation.

As Connor sat, he watched for the next three hours as Wellington's and American Skytrains descended on to the base in their droves. Each time one approached a loud siren would start to warn anybody close to the runway to move away, and then as it landed, tens of troops spilled out of their doors and then they ran into the huge hangers that were over 500 yards away over on the far side of the airfield from him and stretched the whole length of the airfield for what must have been close to a mile long. It was endless, the planes came one after another, then another and another. The only time it stopped was when something needed to take off, whether that was a fighter heading out for the front line or one of the troop carriers heading back to wherever they had just come from. It also stopped when, not the siren, but a klaxon started, this was obviously to warn of a possible attack. He watched as the large guns swung around searching for their foe and sending up some small amounts of flack. This was a very busy place.

Connor was happy.

Because a busy place was a much easier place to hide in.

But 'the getting in' was always going to be hardest part.

By late afternoon he had seen enough, but then, as he was about to leave, he saw a small vehicle racing from the gate at the far end of the airbase 'the Allain end' and then it began heading towards the buildings nearer to him at the "Gimeys end'. He watched it through the old binoculars as it got nearer and nearer.

It was a Jeep.

As it pulled over to the last but one building to the northern end, still 500 yards away, he watched as the driver got out and then the front seat passenger climbed out also. His thick black hair swept back from the high speed journey.

One Priest, one Brother.

He watched as they walked towards the building and then enter a green metal door. He smiled to himself, looked up to the sky and whispered "Thank you Riley". He had gambled right.

He slowly placed the binoculars back on the hook, ran his fingers one last time over the letters, climbed out of the cave and lowered the ivy back to where it had been.

It looked exactly the same as when he had found it, that was apart from a small change that had been made to the cave wall.

'RG 1917'

'CG 1944'

He wondered when it would be when somebody would find it again.

He hoped that it would be a very long time.

For mankind's sake if nothing else.

As usual he had a plan, and a very simple one really. It revolved around getting one of the lorries to stop and getting them to stop was going to be very easy within a forest full of fallen trees. It was 'where' it stopped which was important. He needed it to be on a reasonably sharp bend, not a 90 degree one but more like 130, because a 130 degree bends should have a blind spot directly behind any vehicle going around it, which meant that anybody approaching it from behind wouldn't be seen, of course, this was providing that nobody was sat in the rear.

As night time fell he walked back where he had come from earlier in the day and as he got to the T-junction he turned left and walked back into the forest to look for a suitable bend but he didn't get far.

He heard a vehicle from behind him and coming towards him, from the direction of the airbase.

It was a jeep.

The sound of a jeep was very distinctive. It had a bity kind of sound all of its own.

He backed into the forest and knelt down with a view of the track just ten yards in front of him. He heard the jeep slow for the T-junction and then start to increase its speed again, just 30 seconds later it passed him heading towards Thelod.

One Passenger one Driver.

One Priest, one Brother.

'No doubt they were off to get another poor dead soul or worse, to make one' thought Connor.

He listened to the jeep carry on into the distance until he could hear it no more and then he started to continue his walk back into the forest looking for his bend.

An hour or so later he found it. It was a 130 degree left hand bend if you were travelling towards the Airbase. 'Perfect' thought Connor, now all he needed was a substantial fallen tree or to be more precise, fallen tree's, of which there were hundreds.

The only slight problem to his plan succeeding was the possibility that the first vehicle to come along the track was from the direction of the airbase and then as a consequence, this would lead to the moving of his tree's.

But a fifty fifty chance was better than no chance at all.

For the next hour he dragged and pulled and lifted and dropped. At the end of it he had two tree's laying across the track, both strategically placed so that anybody needing to move them, it would be easier to move them over to the right hand side of the track rather than to the left. Because for the plan to work, he didn't need anybody at all on the left hand side of the vehicle.

He walked back down the track away from the airbase and to the start of the bend. He found himself a nice spot on the right hand side of the track looking back to where he could just see the very far end of the 'fallen tree's' on the right hand side of the track about 50 to 60 yards away, and then he waited. By now the forest was completely black, the moonless night gave no light for him to see. He decided to get some sleep.

When he woke early the next morning it was a beautiful sunny day but by midday there had been nothing apart from a motorcyclist coming from the airbase. He had heard him slow for the tree's and felt for a moment that the biker was a conciencous man and had stopped to move the tree's for any vehicle that was heading that way but he needn't have worried. The bike slowed and then he heard it rev and slow again as the biker swerved through a small gap between them. Within seconds he was off on his journey again oblivious to Connor as he watched him speed by. It was early evening before he heard anything else but then from his left he heard the clunking gear change of a truck far off in the distance over from the area of Thelod.

It got louder and nearer and by how slow it was going he was sure it was a lorry of some description. He sat watching over to his left until it eventually, five minutes later, it finally came into view.

It was a British Bedford carrier. The 3 ton 4 x 4 was the work horse of the British army. Its huge square radiator grill on the front looked like a whale's wide open mouth ready to swallow whole anything that got in its way. As it passed him, he was very pleased to see that the back of it was covered in its green tarpaulin, the side sheets fully pulled down and tied at the sides.

This was almost as much as he could hope for, providing of course that it was empty.

As it carried on trundling by him he watched as the vehicle came to an abrupt stop just in front of the carefully placed fallen tree's.

Nobody got out the back.

Connor didn't hesitate. He was up and walking on a course that if you had placed a drawn line from the front right headlight diagonally across the roof to the rear left hand tail light and then carried it on towards his position. He was completely in the blind spot of anybody in the front of the lorry. He carried on walking along the invisible line straight towards the rear left corner of the truck, some 60 to 70 yards in front of him. As he got closer he could hear that the engine was still idling. As he got to 20 yards from it, he heard a male voice coming from in front of it, cursing and grunting as he struggled to move the tree's.

He got to the rear and slowly peered into the back and could see that apart from four large wooden boxes, the lorry was completely empty. He climbed quickly and silently in and moved right up to the rear of the bulkhead and hid behind two of the boxes.

Out towards the front he could hear the driver still grunting as he struggled to move the second tree.

A few moments later he felt the lorry sightly tip to the right as the driver climbed back aboard and then they were off.

Good news.

There was only the driver to worry about.

Shortly after he felt the lorry begin to slow as it approached the T-junction from where he had walked from earlier in the day. He felt it swing sharply to the left and accelerate again and continue on its journey, the airbase now on his right hand side. A short time later a further swing around a bend, this time to the right. Connor knew that they had met the left hand end of the airbase. Now he wanted another right hand turn, a right hand turn would mean they would be entering the airbase.

He wasn't to be disappointed.

After no more than a minute he felt the lorry slow again and turn sharply to the right and then slow to a stop.

He heard the driver shout.

"Jonno, gate, I'm bloody starving man",

"Patience Woody, patience, I have the security of the British Empire to worry about you know",

"Security my arse" came the reply " just open the bloody gate man before my clutch slips and I drive right through it" said the now laughing driver.

He felt the lorry lurch forward and move through past the invisible gate and then accelerate once more. It continued on a straight line for what seemed like forever but he knew that it would take sometime for it to get to the other end and that was what he was hoping for, he wanted to get to as near as he could to the last but one building at the 'Gimeys' end.

A short time later he felt the truck begin to slow and then abruptly come to a stop before he felt the lorry back up again. His next move needed to be timed just right. As the driver got out Connor dropped out the back and straight onto the floor on the rear left corner of the truck. He needed to see which way the driver was heading.

Connor had seen that they had backed up to a building, four from the northern 'Gimeys end'. Not the one he had wanted but it could have been a whole lot worse.

As he lay on the floor he heard the driver light up a cigarette and then cough loudly. If the driver went left then Connor needed to move around the rear of the vehicle in the opposite direction.

The driver went right. Towards the southern end buildings. Connor stayed where he was and watched him as he walked away. When he was happy he climbed back into the lorry and grabbed a box. From how light it was he presumed It was empty.

He peered out the back and dropped over the edge he then leaned back in and grabbed the box.

Though evening light was now fading, it wasn't quite full dark but he couldn't hang around outside for much longer. He walked back towards the huge building behind him and tried the small green door, identical to the one that he had seen the Priest enter on the building two away to the north from him.

It opened.

He stepped inside, taking the box with him.

Inside it was huge. He had never seen such a vast open space of nothing.

There was the odd pallet of wooden boxes much like the one he was holding but apart from that, the place was completely empty. 'The Germans must have taken everything with them' he thought 'and judging by the amount of planes that he had seen landing, we will soon be filling them up again'.

He carried his box over towards the other boxes and placed it on the floor. He lifted the lid of one of the other boxes and looked inside.

It was full of ammunition. The other boxes were the same.

He walked over to the door from which he had entered and stepped outside.

It was time to look busy.

'Look busy and you will always look like you belong there' he had been told.

He climbed back into the truck and started to remove the rest of the boxes.

On his last box he saw the driver returning to the truck but now he wasn't alone, he had two other soldiers with him. They walked towards him, all three of them smoking their cigarettes.

Connor looked over at them and smiled.

"Is that the lot" said Connor.

"Bloody hell boys" said the driver "we've got another one of them 'Fighting Mick's', what the hell are you doing here I thought you lot were over at Arnhem"

Connor laughed,

"We're everywhere us lot mate, we always turn up when we're not expected" said Connor.

The man who was stood next to the driver said.

"You can give me and Jack here a hand with our boxes if you like"

They all walked over to two other trucks parked in a line next to the one he had just stole a journey on.

Four the next hour they emptied identical empty boxes off the lorries as the conversation continued between the four of them, introducing themselves to each other amid the laughter and banter that ensued. By the time they had finished, it was if they had known 'Billy' for months, they were happy in his company and as they walked off back in the direction to which they had come from, Connor went with them, all of them still laughing and joking as they went.

As they got to the last but one building Connor could smell the fantastic aroma of hot food. He hadn't eaten properly for days and now he could smell it, he needed it.

"I've a mouth on me boys, anybody coming in for some Bia" Connor laughed,

"That's food to you lot",

Woody, 'the driver' made his excuses and walked on but Connor's two knew friends, Jack and Terry were up for it.

Connor instinctively held the door open for them and followed them in, he didn't know where he was going, but they did.

This building may have looked the same from the outside but inside it was totally different. They walked along a narrow corridor which had doors going off to the left and right, but he knew they were going the right way, the aroma was getting stronger.

After walking about fifty yards down the corridor Terry stopped and opened the door to his left. This time Connor had to go in first. They were in the Naafi, It wasn't a problem, Connor took the opportunity to wave at an invisible friend who was invisibly sitting over to the left hand side. He walked up to where the chef was spooning hot stew into the bowls of grateful soldiers and waited inline.

Once served the three of them went over to a table where three other men sat eating their meals. They nodded as Connor sat down with his two new friends.

They ate rather than talked but Connor tried to take his time not wanting to appear to be starving, which he most definitely was.

When they had finished it was Jack who spoke first.

"Your with the Irish Guards then Billy" said Jack looking at Connors badge.

"I am",

"How come your here then, its a long way from Arnhem is it not",

"It is, your right" said Connor "but I got injured and ended up in hospital".

He saw Jack and Terry look at the scars on his head.

"But I had enough of laying in a hospital bed so I left and somehow I have ended up here" said Connor smiling.

"There nasty scars mate, how did you get those if you don't mind me asking" said Jack.

"Bloody hell Jack, what's this, you sound like its a fucking interrogation, leave the man alone" said Terry,

"Its okay" said Connor, "It was dogs, I got caught by three dogs"

"Bastard things them dogs" said Jack,

"Yes they are" said Connor "But it was my own fault, I got sloppy",

Jack stood up "right who wants cup of cha, that's tea to you lot" he said laughing.

Both Terry and Connor said "yes" and laughed.

As Jack walked away Terry looked at Connor and said quietly.

"You any friend of that Father Henry, being as your both from over the water".

Connor felt a shiver run down his back, he hadn't been expecting that question at all.

He sat for a moment before he answered him.

"Yes I know Father Henry but not that well, we're not close if that's what you mean",

"He's a strange bloke he his" said Terry "he treats that bloke who drives him around like shit, Glendon, I think it is. 'Do this do that, not like that like this' I'd tell him to do one, he's a bloody control freak".

"I take it you don't like him then" smiled Connor.

"Cant stand the Irish Bastard" said Terry before realising what he had said "Sorry Billy, didn't mean to offend you",

"No offence taken" said Connor smiling.

"How long has he been here, Father Henry I mean" said Connor.

"Well, I've been here for a month and he's been coming here all that time, but before that we were at a place near Riems and he was there as well. I heard a rumour that he was always travelling back to Ireland to repatriate the Irish dead but I suppose that would be about right because sometimes we don't see him for days",

"I see, do the dead come here then",

"No, no not all of them, it seems that the Irish do though, they go to the morgue",

"thats the building last but one to the north",

"Yes that's the one, but you don't want to go in there mate, its not a pleasant place, the smell is horrendous" said Terry.

Jack came back and placed the three cups of tea on the table.

"I was just telling Billy here not to go into the Morgue" said Terry,

"Bugger that mate, why would you want to go in there, the only time I'm going in there, I won't know anything about it, because I'll be brown bread" said Jack,

"Thats dead, to you and me" said Terry.

They all laughed and touched their cups in a 'cheers'.

Connor knew he would be paying a visit to the morgue very soon.

* * *

THE FINAL DELIVERY.

As nightfall fell, the busyness of the place subsided a little, not a lot but enough for him to be able to have a look around.

At a little after midnight he made his way through the shadows towards the building that held the morgue.

As he arrived at the door he pulled the handle. Nobody generally wanted to get in and certainly not many were coming out, so not surprisingly it was open.

He stepped inside.

It was cold and very quiet.

He was in another corridor which was more or less the same layout as the one where he had just eaten. There were two doors on the left, he tried the first but it was locked. He walked on to the next, the door opened, he quietly stepped inside. In the low light he could make out that it was some sort of workshop. It was about 16' square with benches running along the opposite wall. The Bench had a vice fitted to it and an electrical grinding wheel. There were wood saws and rasp files and some small needle files, all untidily laying on top of the bench and the lovely smell of timber filled the air. He looked around the other walls but apart from a blackboard with some scrambled numbers on it, there was nothing more of significance. He placed one of the needle files into his pocket and came back out of the room.

He moved further on down the corridor. As he walked along it he had the same sensation as he had had in the building containing the Naafi as the smell got stronger and stronger, he knew he was going the right way, only this time it wasn't food he could smell, it was the unmistakable smell of death.

The corridor had low lighting which was a very pale orange colour but at the far end, fifty or so yards away, he could see much brighter lighting shining out from a glass pain above a door.

'The Morgue' he thought to himself.

As he got to the door he stopped outside and as he placed his ear against it, he moved his left hand to the rear of his waistband and gripped the top of his pistol.

There was nothing.

Total silence.

He tried the handle and it opened.

Nobody wanted to be going inside.

Nobody inside would be going out.

He stepped inside.

He was in a small room, no more than ten foot square. It had a table in the far left hand corner and a door on the opposite wall to the door he had just entered. There were two chairs close to the table, one pushed under the nearest end to him and one pushed under the right hand side.

He saw a wooden cross standing in the centre of the table. It had the body of Christ on it. As he walked over to it he saw that it had been beautifully carved, it reminded him of the cross that he had seen on the young German soldier some days before. It had always amazed him that all the statues and all the jewellery that he had seen, Christ was almost identical, not only his looks but also his stature. It was if all the artist's, all the jewellers, and all the sculptures of the world had all been to the same school at the same time. He knew that they hadn't of course, but he often wondered how everybody on the planet that had painted him, sculptured him or made wonderful pieces of gold of him, seemed to be able to mirror somebody else's piece that was on the other side of the world.

In front of it was a bible. It was a medium sized bible about 8" wide and 12" in length. Its cover was of black leather with gold letters on the front.

It looked very old.

It also looked exactly the same as the bible that he had seen next to the fire in Manor farm. It could have been the same one but he doubted it, that should have perished in the fire, he also remembered seeing one very similar to the one he had seen as a young boy when he had looked through the letterbox at the house in Sheep Street, he didn't know if it was one of the same, but it wouldn't have surprised him. Along side the bible was another book, also black in colour but it had the words ' In Remembrance' written in gold on the front and beside it lay a black fountain pen.

He turned to his right and tried the other door. Same result. It opened. But it was a much heavier door. The door seemed to hiss as it opened it, like it was some sort of air lock.

He stepped inside.

A bigger room this time. It was twice as wide and probably three times as long. Cupboards ran along both outside walls. Their doors were 3' by 3' all the way along, four high.

His was in the Morgue that was for sure.

He walked over to the second row and looked on the small piece of paper that was folded into the metal strip on the front.

It read;

Private John Mulligan 18071 Irish Guards.

He pulled on the handle and slid the stretcher out towards him. It was heavy but it rolled freely enough.

There lay the body of Private Mulligan. At his feet were his personal belongings and his folded uniform, all carefully placed inside a see-through plastic bag.

He rolled the stretcher back inside the cupboard and looked at the other doors. At least 2/3 of them had names on. All had one thing in common. They were all from the Irish Guards.

Over to the righthand side of the room were thirty to forty coffins all stacked on top of each other, to the right of them were more boxes but they were all covered by white linen sheets and he knew why they were.

He pulled back one of the sheets.

The coffins were of a simple wooden design of no expense. They had been mass produced in their thousands and sadly, quite a lot of them were now being used.

He tried the lid of the first coffin and saw that although it had been screwed down, they hadn't been fully tightened and the lid could be moved just slightly.

He tried the first of the four screws to see if it moved. It did.

He removed all four of them and then slowly slid the lid to the side.

Inside lay the body of another soldier, the lid said his name was Private L Thomas Irish Guards 14033.

Private Thomas wasn't alone within his coffin.

Inside it, Connor wasn't surprised to see that It also held, 6 hand grenades, 5 pistols and 2 rifles, along with a large box of ammunition.

'They were fighting for the cause, even in death'.

He placed the lid back and screwed down the top.

He repeated his discovery on the remaining 5 coffins. All with the same results, only varying on the number of each of the items within.

He pulled the sheets back into place and made his way over to a desk near to the door. He tried the small drawer that was just under the desk top. It was locked. He pulled the small needle file from his pocket and placed it in the lock whilst turning the other file around and putting the tiny handle in the lock also. He turned one of the files, putting pressure on the lock, while moving the other file gently backwards and forwards.

It opened.

He pulled the drawer back. Inside was a browning pistol. He picked it up and saw that it was loaded, he pulled back the hammer and looked at it. He knew what he had to do.

He stepped outside the room and walked back to the workshop turned on the grinding wheel and placed the inside of the hammer against the wheel. The sparks flew from the wheel as he very gently ground away the striking pin. Once he was happy that the pin was now gone he rubbed his finger along the greasy top and rubbed the dirt over the now shiny metal where once the firing pin had been. He walked back to the desk in the second room, placed the gun inside the drawer and locked it again with his needle files.

Happy with his work he walked back into the first room and walked to the table, opened the book of remembrance, tore out the last page, and then picked up the pen.

He wrote his message and folded it, and then placed it on top of the bible.

He left the building and walked back to one of the lorries climbed inside the cab and as he lay down to go to sleep he felt a calmness come over him that he hadn't felt for a long time, not since those magical years that he had spent with his mother in America. They had been so special and something that he would never forget, but now he knew that this was the moment. The moment that he had dreamed of since the day that he had killed Cain. It wasn't that he was looking forward to doing what he had to do, nobody liked or enjoyed killing people, not really. But it was something that he needed to do and had promised himself he would do from that day and now he knew that it was almost in his grasp.

As he lay on his back he suddenly thought of his Nana and knew then what it was that he needed to do.

He climbed back out of the truck and walked back inside of the building. He reentered the building and walked to the first door and stepped inside the room. He walked over to the table and knelt down in front of the cross, lowered his head and for the first time since he was a boy, he said a few words of prayer.

"My darling Nana,

To kill a fellow man, I know is a sin, but sometimes those that have sinned bring vengeance upon themselves.

It is not something that I should, or ever will be proud of, but kill him I will.

This is something that needs to be done and now after all these years, the time has come, it is time to right the wrongs that have been bought upon us by this evil man and those that have chosen to work and kill with him.

And so Nana, I seek your forgiveness and should I ever see you again, I hope you will understand why it had to be done, for I promise you it will be done, if not now, then another day, for I will never rest until it is.

I love you Nana and always will,

God bless you".

As he finished his prayer the tears rolled down his cheeks.

He quietly stood and walked back outside to the truck, lay down again and slept a very peaceful sleep.

At just after 06:30hrs in the morning his sleep was broken by the siren signifying that a plane was approaching. It sounded ten times louder than it had from his vantage point the day before. It was absolutely deafening. He looked out of the window of the truck and saw that each of the buildings had two huge speakers in the apex of their roofs, 'one siren and one klaxon, noisy but very useful' thought Connor.

He climbed out the truck, stretched his aching limbs and made his way towards the Naafi. It was time to eat.

For the next two days he worked, he ate and he slept, but there was no sight of The Milburn's. Had they seen him and he hadn't seen them, he doubted it but it could have happened, it was a busy place. Had one of the driver's bumped into him and spoke about the 'Fighting Mick', plausible, but again he doubted it.

'Wait and then wait some more and it will come'.

So he waited.

It was Wednesday 22nd September 1944. He'd been at the Airbase for nearly a week and was now seriously beginning to think that the trail had gone cold again. As he finished his dinner, he walked back to the lorries to carry on loading again when he saw Jack walking towards him. Connor had an idea.

" Hello Billy Boy, how's things" said Jack,

"All good here mate, but I'm getting a bit bored with this loading and unloading crap. I was wondering, is there any chance that you could take me out with you, just to break the monotony if you know what I mean, I'm going crazy in here",

" I don't see why not mate, let me can some grub down me while you start loading my wagon back up and we'll go back out, I've got to do a night run tonight and it'll be good to have some company to be honest" said Jack,

" That's great" said Connor "I'll see you in a bit then".

Connor carried on walking to the other lorries at the far end close to the Morgue. It was then that he saw it.

A jeep was parked outside the Morgue building. It must have arrived whilst he was eating his dinner.

The jeep had actually arrived around thirty minutes before.

Father Henry and Glendon had gone inside the building containing the Morgue and had gone straight into the second room where the bodies were. They were in a hurry, they needed to hide some weaponry, they had had a good few days and had accumulated several pistols and rifles along with a few hand grenades. They went to the furthest empty coffin away from the door and lifted the lid off. It hadn't been screwed down as the coffin was currently empty but that wouldn't be for long.

They placed their 'stolen' arsenal at the side of the the plain wooden box and walked back over to the cupboards that held the bodies of the dead.

"Who's n..n..n..next to go home Henry" stammered Glendon to his older brother.

Henry spat out his vile whispered response "I don't really give a fuck who's next Boy, but we need to get those guns inside with him whoever it is, I don't like it when there out in the open, just go and look in the book and pick one that's been here the longest and hurry up about it".

Glendon made his way back into the first room, walked towards the table, and then stopped dead in his tracks.

"Brother, you b...b...b...better come in here" shouted Glendon

"For fucks sake Glendon just get the bloody book would you" rasped Henry.

"Henry, you n.....n...n...need to come here, and I m...m...m.. mean right now" shouted a clearly concerned Glendon.

"Jesus is there nothing you can't do on your fucking own".

Henry made his way through the door and into the first room. As he walked towards the table Glendon didn't turn round but was stood deadly still apparently staring at the table two feet in front of him.

As Henry got along side of him he spat more fury in the direction of his bullied youngest brother "for gods sake, what's the problem now".

He stood at the side of him and saw him looking at the table and then saw what he was actually looking at was the bible on the desk.

The bible had a piece of paper that had been placed on top of it.

It had been folded in the shape of a diamond.

It was a Diamond note, written on the front of it were two words.

'FATHER HENRY'

They both stood for a moment as if transfixed by what was in front of them, and then both instinctively turned around to see if anybody was behind them, which they're wasn't.

Eventually Henry looked at his brother and then stepped towards the table and then very slowly, he picked up the note.

It had been almost a quarter of a century since he had seen one of these notes, but now somebody had now delivered him another. He slowly opened it and then he saw the message that had been written within. It read.

'GOD LOVES US ALL IN DIFFERENT WAYS'

'C'

Henry looked at Glendon and then whispered.

"Go and get one of those pistol's from in there and then go outside and look around, but be careful Boy, we both know what this Bastard is capable of."

Glendon didn't say a word but just nodded his response.

They both went back into the room with the 'dead', Glendon picked a pistol and checked that it was loaded. Henry walked over to the desk, took a small key from his pocket and unlocked the drawer and took out his loaded gun.

Glendon walked quickly out of the room and having walked through the first room he stepped out into the corridor.

He made his way as quickly as his left leg would allow him towards the front of the building checking on the workshop first but it was empty. He moved onto the next door but that was locked. He then made his way to the door that led to the outside and slowly opened it.

It was getting dark now, still not completely dark but it would be in about thirty minutes. He needed to check the area as quickly as possible, he didn't want to be wandering about in the dark, the dark was Connor's friend, everybody that knew of him was completely aware of that.

He looked to his left, there was nothing apart from a mechanic laying under the engine of one of the trucks. He turned to his right, he could see three men standing about 50 yards away but in the diminishing light he couldn't be sure any of them was Connor. The other problem that he had was that he hadn't seen him for what was probably twenty years or more. Some people change a lot in that time. He decided to walk closer to the three men just to make sure. He placed his hand in to his right pocket and took hold of his gun just incase.

When he was within twenty yards he knew none of the three were his man. He looked on past them and could see nobody else.

He decided to walk back towards the morgue before it was completely dark. As he got to the door he could see the legs of the mechanic still sticking out from beneath one of the trucks. He slowly walked over to him, he could ask him if he knew anybody by the name of Connor if nothing else.

He got to the feet of the man and then somewhat more nervously than he normally was, stammered his question.

" S..s...s sorry to bother you, m..m..m..mate but I don't s..s... suppose you have seen anybody by the n..n..name of Connor have you"

The mechanic didn't move but just shouted his reply of

"Eh"

Glendon struggled to squat down and as he began to start to ask his question again, the right leg of the mechanic swung back and smashed straight into his mangled left knee. Glendon crashed onto the floor screaming in agony, his knee now temporarily bending in an angle that it shouldn't be.

Connor crashed out from beneath the truck and with lightning speed jumped to his feet and smashed his right elbow into the side of his head knocking him out cold. He quickly grabbed him by his tunic collar and pulled him back towards the building, quietly opened the door and pulled him inside.

He closed the door behind him and looked down the corridor. It was empty but the light was still shining out from the room on the right at the far end. He quickly dragged Glendon into the workshop, found the gun in his pocket and left him in the room.

He walked slowly down the corridor, he felt as if the ghostly figures of all the suffering people he had known were standing on both sides giving him a guard of honour as he walked closer to the door, as if they were all urging him to do what needed to be done. It was all in his head, he knew that, but he wondered, 'Is this what they mean by your life flashing by before you, just before you die. Was he about to die, was this it, was he close to his final moments'.

He stopped at the door, the door that led to the first room, the room of remembrance. He slowly opened the door and stepped inside.

It was empty.

He looked at the bible. The note had gone. They knew he was coming, he already knew that, Glendon had asked about him.

He walked towards the door that led to the second room, the morgue. It was about to have another one of the dead to add to its numbers, was it to be Henry or was it to be him, it would be one of them that was for sure.

He opened the door, stepped inside and there he was. The man who he had searched for over half his life, facing him, sat in a chair just twenty yards in front of him.

They looked at each other the first time in over twenty years, but both had no doubt who each of them, were looking at. He signalled for Connor to sit a second chair just inside the room, 15 or so yards from his own.

Neither spoke for a minute or too, both just sat taking in what was before them, and then it was Henry who spoke first.

"So Connor, at last we meet again, I hear that you have been looking for me",

" You could say that" said Connor "I've actually been looking for you for the past twenty years or so",

"Indeed, and so, what may I ask is it that you want of me".

Connor looked at him. The man had hardly changed at all. A little older around then eyes, a little thicker around the waist but nothing more. The horrible evil smirk was still there, it smirked back at him right there and then. Connor looked him straight in the eye.

"I want you dead" he said.

"I thank you for your honesty, honesty is a fine attribute of any a decent man",

"I'm no decent man Father, I can assure you of that",

"That all depends on which way you look at it, as you wrote on your note, God does indeed love us all in different ways. Whatever we do in our lives, he manages to find the good in all of us don't you think",

"Father Henry, I struggle to believe that even he could find any good in a man with such evilness as yourself. Look at you, sitting there with your dog collar and cross around your neck, a man of god. Your'e not a man of god, you never have been and never will be, you're a fraud and if there is a god then he should strike you down".

Henry looked at him and smiled.

"But he hasn't has he, I'm still here. You say that all I have done has been evil and wrong, but I'm still here, still doing what I do. My brother and I are doing our work with the total belief that we are doing what god would want us to do. We carry on with the fight, we won't give in to the British who want our Ireland. Unlike you Connor, for it is you who has sold his soul to the devil, not I. But I respect your feelings, everyman should be allowed to express himself and believe in whatever he wants",

"You didn't respect my Grandfather",

"Firstly Connor let's get one thing straight, Riley wasn't your Grandfather was he. He was married to your Grandmother but that bitch of a Mother of yours wasn't his Daughter was she, unless that whore of a Grandmother of yours had her way with him out of wedlock. But then, she would be a Bastard child much like yourself Connor, ironic, but I think, most probably not true.

We killed that stupid thick Idiot Riley because he listened to something he shouldn't have, that is all. If he hadn't been so stupid, then he would probably still be a general dogs body for us even now, but then again the cripple probably wouldn't be able to walk by now would he, but again, that serves him right for fighting for the British, much liker yourself Connor, but you will reap what you sow. Talking of cripples, what have you done with my Brother Glendon, is he still alive or have you killed him too, just like how you killed my brother Cain",

"Do you care" said Connor.

Henry was now turning into his mother again, the vileness now fast building up inside him.

He spat on the floor and then carried on building himself up into a frenzy.

"I don't really give a fuck about anybody Connor least of all a cripple who can't even speak right, but then I remember that god does really love us all in different ways, he really does. If we have done something wrong in our lives then he will punish us for it" he began laugh to himself then carried on "Glendon has obviously seriously pissed our Lord off at some point in his life".

Connor was calm on the outside but inside his blood was coming to the boil but now it was his turn to turn the screw. He knew exactly what was going to light the blue touch paper.

"Have you never cared for anybody, anybody at all or are you just so wrapped up with your beloved god and yourself" said Connor,

"I care for god, of course I do, I truly believe, that is why I was put upon this earth",

"But apart from god, have you never felt love for somebody, not anybody, didn't you love your Father or your Mother".

He saw the change immediately in his face. He'd got him, Connor was now enjoying himself.

He saw the happiness in his eyes as he said.

"I loved my Mother dearly, she was my rock. I felt cheated

when she was taken from me so young."

And then Connor watched him as his face changed from a smiling happy face back to the face of his mother, the vile creature that hated everything that had ever walked in front of her.

"But I hated my Father, I never had any love for that evil man, he hated me and I hated him back, twice over".

Now It was Connor's turn to strike.

"Why was that Henry, was it because of anything you had done, or did he just hate you for no reason".

He watched as Henry seemed to go back in time, remembering happy times and sad and angry times, his face ringing through every emotion in just a few split seconds.

But then Henry seemed to come to his senses and stared Connor.

Henry now looked at Connor pitifully.

"Did you kill him too" said Henry,

Connor played with him.

"Your Father, no, you know I didn't kill ,

"Not my Father, you know I didn't mean him".

Connor smiled at him.

"What would you like me say, would you prefer that I had killed him or would you rather him have walked away with another man".

"Please tell me that you killed him",

"You would rather me have killed the man you loved than him live a life with another man. That's very sad Father, I thought our god loved life not death. There is one thing that has always played on my mind and seeing as we are here together at last, I can ask you.

I've always wondered why he beat you, did you enjoy it, why did you let him do it if you didn't, you didn't have to stay with him not if he treated you like that, no one, not even you Henry should stay and take that".

Henry stared at him, anger written all over his face.

"Tell me that you killed him, just tell me right now that you killed him".

For the first time he watched as Henry raised the gun from beyond waist height.

"No Henry, I didn't kill your lover, the dutiful Mr Dower. The last time I saw him he was with a much younger man than yourself. They both seemed so very happy". He watched as the anger boiled up within him and now it was time to make him explode.

" And do you know, I never saw him beat him once, not once, they seemed so loving towards each other, a match made in your heaven I would say".

He watched as Henry tipped over the edge as he stood and pointed the gun at him.

"You fucking evil bastard, you think you are so clever sitting there but you look at me, I'm the one with the gun, you stupid thick son of a Prodi bastard. You think your immortal, sneaking around in the shadows like some invisible freak, but I tell you, nobody is to live forever, especially not you, not anymore. You of all people should have known that I wasn't just going to let you walk in here and kill me, I'm the man that has had half your family killed so why should I stop now. But your'e not as clever and wise as you think you are, but then like I say, your half Prodi so it shouldn't be really a surprise now should it. Now get on your knees because I want you to grovel for your life".

"I won't grovel for anybody, least of all you" said Connor.

Henry raised the gun higher as he said "I said get on your knees".

Connor sat and stared at him and then he started to smile, a smile that then turned into a laugh.

He saw Henry start to walk towards him and then he stopped just a few feet in front of him.

Connor looked into his eyes.

"Have you ever actually killed a man Henry or is this to be your first time. You see, I think you are like all the other coward's that sit at the top of the tree. Barking his orders to all the servants and slaves down below you, making them do your dirty work, it's because deep down, you know that you can't actually do it yourself".

"Oh I can do it don't you worry yourself, now get ready to meet your maker, and you will ask for his forgiveness" said Henry,

"Well you can ask him yourself because I'm not going anywhere" said Connor as he lowered his sight from his eyes to the finger on the trigger. He watched the trembling hand tighten its grip and then saw the index finger tighten and put the on tension.

He pulled the trigger.

Nothing.

He pulled it again, then again and again. Still the gun didn't fire.

The shock on Henry's face staring at Connor said it all.

"I needed to see if you could really do it" said Connor "I needed to see if you were to die still the coward that I think you are".

Henry dropped the gun and turned and started to run towards the coffin's behind him but Connor was up an out of his chair and was on his prey within a couple of strides. He smashed his own gun into the back of his head knocking him out and making him crash to the ground.

It was the next morning before Henry came around. When he opened his eyes he saw that he was still within the morgue but he was now tied to a chair, as was his brother next to him. He looked over towards the door and then saw Connor sat on the chair close to the desk.

Connor had seen him starting to stir, and so had Glendon. The look of fear in the youngest brother's eyes was plain to see.

"Why haven't you killed me" said Henry.

Connor looked at him deep in thought.

"And why haven't you killed him" he said looking at Glendon.

Connor looked at them both. 'Do I kill them both, do I let Glendon go, do I let them both go' his mind was in turmoil. He had worked and lived for this moment for over half his life and he had always thought that come the day he wouldn't hesitate with what he had, and what he had always wanted to do.

"Do you hear that Glendon, your brother here thinks I should have killed you already, but then he might be right, my grandfather has saved your life once already, so why should I bother to do it again".

Connor saw Henry look back again towards the door.

"It's locked if that's what you're wondering Henry, we won't be getting any visitors" said Connor.

Henry looked at Connor his face pleading for forgiveness.

"Connor, you know as well as I do, you've won, you have what you want, me and the 'boy' here, just hand us over to the authorities, let them deal with us, and then you can go back the hero",

"I'm sorry but I can't do that, I made a promise to myself and my family many years ago that I would make you pay for all that you have done, so here we are and now we wait".

"But what are we waiting for, you can see that I'm a beaten man" said Henry.

" No Henry, your wrong, only a dead man is a beaten man" said Connor.

Glendon looked at Connor and could see that he looked troubled. He was right. Connor was struggling within himself with what he had to do, but he would do it, he had to do it.

And then he heard what he was waiting for. The first plane of the morning circling the airbase getting ready to come in to land.

He heard the siren's start to wind themselves up. They got louder and louder and then when they were at their deafening full power, he walked over to the Priest, placed the gun to front of his head and pulled the trigger.

"Now your'e beaten".

Connor walked slowly back into the first room and knelt before the cross on the table.

The tears ran down his face as he said a small prayer and then he asked again his Nana for forgiveness.

At last it was all over.

His vengeance complete or so he dearly hoped.

He walked back into the room and walked over to Glendon.

He looked at the old frail man in front of him, his eyes looked different somehow, he seemed almost at peace within himself, resigned to the fact that he was about to die next.

"Glendon, I have no bone to pick with you. If I let you go what will you do, will you run or will you inform those that need to be told, and I talk about both sides of the water, not just the British".

Glendon looked at him for a moment and then he spoke with hardly a hint of his stammer.

"Connor what you have just done, your'e not the only one to have been released by it, you have released me also. I have hated my life for so long.

When your Grandfather saved me I was indebted to him for the rest of my life, all the other boys would have just left me to drown but your Grandfather, he didn't. He was a good man, a decent, honest man.

But I tell you this, what has happened here today must stay

between the two of us, as has been said in the past, never tell anybody your secrets for it won't be a secret for very much longer".

Connor bent over and released his ties. Glendon then slowly got up and they stood facing each other. Connor held out his hand and Glendon reached forward with his own and shook Connor's hand.

Two minutes later, Connor heard the jeep start up and drive away.

He stood in silence for a moment, he really did hope and pray that this was the end of all the killing, but he doubted it.

❋ ❋ ❋

TIME TO GO HOME

The Priest smiled at the pretty nurse accompanying one of the badly injured soldiers that was being loaded onto the plane. She smiled back then turned to check on her patient. He watched as she gently covered the soldier with a blanket and briefly held his hand. As he sat in the plane's hold waiting for the cargo to be loaded aboard, the nurse, satisfied that her patient was settled, walked over and sat down on the wooden slatted bench opposite the Priest.

" Your new" she said, smiling again "where's father Henry this morning",

The Priest smiled back "he won't be coming today, something came up".

She nodded her response and looked at him with her smiling eyes. She placed her hands under her as if she didn't know what to do with them.

"Very uncomfortable these benches aren't they" said he Priest

"Yes very" she said,

"Here have this" the Priest passed her a discarded blanket that had been left on the bench next to him.

She reached over and took it from him and then held out her hand in order to introduce herself.

"Thank you Father, I'm Alice, its nice to meet you",

The Priest slowly stood and reached out and gently shook Alice's hand, noting what a delicate touch she had.

"I'm very pleased to meet you too, I'm father William, but most people call me Billy".

As they patiently waited, along with the badly injured, 15 coffins holding the dead bodies of fifteen brave Irish soldiers were slowly loaded onto the plane. But the bodies weren't alone in they're slim wooden homes. Hidden inside each coffin were the 6 hand grenades, 5 pistols and 3 rifles. Along with one large box of ammunition.

They were helping the cause even in they're death.

As the plane roared along the runway it rattled and weaved slightly before leaving Mother Earth once more.

Ireland was 2 to 3 hours away. The Priest was going to enjoy this trip.

The newly adorned Father Connor had a thing about nurses.

What would he do when he returned, he would do what he had always done, he would fight for who he felt was right against those he felt were wrong.

Who that would be he didn't know, only fate or God would decide that, it was not, and never was, his decision to make.

But the news of the cold blooded murder of Colonel Southall would mean that the killing wouldn't be stopping anytime soon.

Oh, it is hard to work for God,
To rise and take his part
Upon the battlefield of Earth,
And sometimes not lose heart.

He hides himself so wondrously
As though there were no God
He is at least seen when all the power's
Of ill are most abroad.

Ah, God is other than we think,
His ways are far above,
Far beyond reasons height, and
Only by childlike love.

Workmen of love, O lose not heart
But learn what God is like.
And in the darkest battlefield
Thou shalt know where to strike.

Then learn to scorn the praise of men
And learn to lose with God,
For Jesus won the world through shame

    And beckons thee his road.

    For right is right, as God is God,
    And right the day must win.
    To doubt would be disloyalty,
    To falter were to sin.

10th December 2006

The snow was slowly falling as the horse drawn milk cart travelled through the square of Tralee.

On the back of it was a solid oak coffin. The flowers along the side of the coffin read, Father, Grandad and Billy.

It stopped at a break between two tall old buildings. At the side of the passageway between the buildings was a brass plaque on the wall, it simply said 'The Point'.

The driver of the hearse looked over towards 'the Point' to see a man stood just inside the alley. The man was dressed in a black suit and black hat.

The driver watched as the man took off his hat and tipped it in respect towards the man encased within the coffin.

A few moments later, the cart moved on and the man disappeared as quickly as he had appeared.

Connor 'Billy' Gillian, had died aged 100 years old. He was a man of many secrets, a few of them told, many of them not.

Not yet anyway.

Printed in Poland
by Amazon Fulfillment
Poland Sp. z o.o., Wrocław